WHAT A GHOUL WANTS

A GHOST HUNTER MYSTERY

Victoria Laurie

D0047618

AN OBSIDIAN MYSTERY

OBSIDIAN
Published by New American Library, a division of
Penguin Group (USA) Inc., 375 Hudson Street,
New York, New York 10014, USA
Penguin Group (Canada), 90 Eglinton Avenue East, Suite 700, Toronto,
Ontario M4P 2Y3, Canada (a division of Pearson Penguin Canada Inc.)
Penguin Books Ltd., 80 Strand, London WC2R 0RL, England
Penguin Ireland, 25 St. Stephen's Green, Dublin 2,
Ireland (a division of Penguin Books Ltd.)
Penguin Group (Australia), 250 Camberwell Road, Camberwell, Victoria 3124,
Australia (a division of Pearson Australia Group Pty. Ltd.)
Penguin Books India Pvt. Ltd., 11 Community Centre, Panchsheel Park,
New Delhi - 110 017, India
Penguin Group (NZ), 67 Apollo Drive, Rosedale, Auckland 0632,
New Zealand (a division of Pearson New Zealand Ltd.)
Penguin Books (South Africa) (Pty.) Ltd., 24 Sturdee Avenue,
Rosebank, Johannesburg 2196, South Africa

Penguin Books Ltd., Registered Offices:
80 Strand, London WC2R 0RL, England

First published by Obsidian, an imprint of New American Library,
a division of Penguin Group (USA) Inc.

First Printing, January 2013
10 9 8 7 6 5 4 3 2 1

PUBLISHER'S NOTE
This is a work of fiction. Names, characters, places, and incidents either are the
product of the author's imagination or are used fictitiously, and any resemblance
to actual persons, living or dead, business establishments, events, or locales is
entirely coincidental.
    The publisher does not have any control over and does not assume any respon-
sibility for author or third-party Web sites or their content.

continued . . .

"Victoria Laurie continues to excite and entertain with her ideas and characters and also inform John Q. Public in matters metaphysical. Cannot wait for the next from Ms. Laurie!" —AuthorsDen.com

"Perhaps what makes this story and this series so good is that Victoria Laurie is actually a professional medium. She knows what she's talking about, and she sure can write a good story." —A Bibliophile's Bookshelf

"A great, fast-paced, addicting read." —Enchanting Reviews

"A great story." —MyShelf.com

"Entertaining.... With witty dialogue, adventurous mystery, and laugh-out-loud humor, this is a novel that you can curl up with [and] get lost in."—Nocturne Romance Reads

"This highly entertaining book has humor and wit to spare." —*Romantic Times*

Praise for the
Abby Cooper, Psychic Eye Mysteries

"Victoria Laurie has crafted a fantastic tale in this latest Psychic Eye Mystery. There are few things in life that upset Abby Cooper, but ghosts and her parents feature high on her list ... giving the reader a few real frights and a lot of laughs." —Fresh Fiction

"Fabulous.... Fans will highly praise this fine ghostly murder mystery." —The Best Reviews

"A great new series ... plenty of action." —*Midwest Book Review*

"An invigorating entry into the cozy mystery realm ... I cannot wait for the next book." —Roundtable Reviews

"A fresh, exciting addition to the amateur sleuth genre." —J. A. Konrath, author of *Cherry Bomb*

"Worth reading over and over again." —BookReview.com

ALSO BY VICTORIA LAURIE

The Ghost Hunter Mystery Series

What's a Ghoul to Do?
Demons Are a Ghoul's Best Friend
Ghouls Just Haunt to Have Fun
Ghouls Gone Wild
Ghouls, Ghouls, Ghouls
Ghoul Interrupted

The Psychic Eye Mystery Series

Abby Cooper, Psychic Eye
Better Read Than Dead
A Vision of Murder
Killer Insight
Crime Seen
Death Perception
Doom with a View
A Glimpse of Evil
Vision Impossible
Lethal Outlook

For Katie Coppedge

Who keeps me sweetly ensconced in a pink bubble of kindness and care and showers me with friendship and love. A better BFF a girl never had.

Acknowledgments

Most people don't know this about me, but I'm an introvert. For reals. I may appear to be an outgoing, high-energy, let's-go-party-like-it's-1999 kind of gal, but the *real* truth is that I like my world small and peaceful, with just a few close friends, not a lot of drama, quiet mornings, quiet afternoons, quiet evenings. . . . You get the picture. Too much social interaction tends to exhaust me, and it took me a long time (forty-five years to be exact) to figure this out and explain it to others so that they could understand why I sometimes just "vant to be alone." Along the way I've sadly lost a few friends who didn't understand that in those long stretches of silence, I wasn't withholding from them—I was simply regenerating all the energy I'd just given away to other people—but I've actually come out ahead because all the people still left in my inner circle are the *most* wonderful group of family and friends any lucky schmuck like me could ever hope to have.

Coincidentally (or perhaps not), this list of wonderful people includes those amazingly talented folks who assist me professionally too. I'm crazy blessed, I tell you!

So, without further ado, I'd like to share a few words of thanks to them for all they do and let them know that I am deeply grateful they remain faithfully devoted to me and the cause.

First, my editor, Mrs. Sandra Harding-Hull. Few people in this world surprise me, but Sandy does it on a regular basis with her keen insight, kind words, amazing advice, and all-around *goodness*! I would go to the ends of the earth for this woman, and what a lucky, lucky thing to have her editing my series. In short . . . she's da bomb!

My agent, Mr. Jim McCarthy, whom I truly think of as my brother. The benefit is that we don't have all that sibling rivalry, mom-likes-you-better baggage between us. He's simply my bro, and I adore him, and with every new book I delight in the opportunity to let him know how grateful I am to have him as my agent, muse, friend, and an honorary part of my family. Love you, sweetie.

Also, HUGE thanks go to my Obsidian team, Elizabeth Bistrow, Sharon Gamboa, Michele Alpern, and Claire Zion. I wish every book lover could understand how selfless and dedicated you publishing folks are. I wish more people could know your names and sing your praises, because, to a person, you are *remarkable*, and I'm very, very grateful for all you do for me and the books.

Katie Coppedge, to whom this book is dedicated, gets a giant shout-out for being just the most wonderfully kind, caring, amazing, and awesome BFF a girl could ever, ever have! Honey, there just aren't words to describe all you mean to me, or how grateful I am for all you do to support victorialaurie.com. What kismet to have met you and ultimately realize what a very special lady you are!

Sandy Upham—my sistah! Love you so much, honey. Thank you for being there and for sharing my past, present, and future with me. I couldn't have asked for a better person to go from cradle to grave with.

Team Lo also gets a special mention here too, because if not for the miles and the races they've been making me run lately, I would've succumbed to the overbearing weight brought on by the bags and bags of potato chips that each book requires. Also, they're a pretty spectacular group of ladies as ladies go—each of them a personal hero of mine. K-Lo (Karen Ditmars), Lee-Lo (Leanne Tierney), and Kat-Lo (Katie Coppedge), I lurves ya, and here's to that next half marathon! ☺

One more very special shout-out goes to my writing/conference buddies who've taken me into their group and delighted me with their loveliness, wit, sincerity, and charm! Juliet Blackwell, Sophie Littlefield, and Nicole Peeler, whenever I'm around you three, I feel like we could (should!) rule the world!

Finally, the rest of that inner circle must be mentioned! Jackie Barrett, Will Barrett, and Jo Angelli—my family away from family. No words to express how much you three mean to me, so I'ma just say thank you from my whole heart for all your love and support and send you three some GIGANTIC mental hugs and loves here, m'kay? ☺

More of those mental hugs and loves should go to the Brosseaus! Nora, Bob, Liz, Kate, Mike, and Nick. You guys rule! And while I'm sending hugs, loves, and thank-yous, more should go to my supersmart, supercool nephews, Matt and Mike Morrill (so proud of you two!); Steve McGrory (McGlorious!); Shannon and John Anderson (waving at you!); my beeeeautiful cousin Hilary Laurie (more waving and blowing kisses!); Thomas Robinson; Silas Hudson; Suzanne Parsons; Drue Rowean; Betty and Pippa Stocking; John Kwiatkowski and Matt McDougall (heart you both HUGE!); Juan Tamayo and Rick Michael; Nicole Grey; Molly Boyle; and Martha Bushko.

I love each and every one of you. Forevs. ☺

Chapter 1

My best friend, Gilley, has this list. It's not necessarily a long list, but it's definitely growing. The list is best described as:

Things That Give Gilley the Weirds.

Once an item gets listed, it's never removed. If you make it onto the list, you're there for life.

It's probably good, then, that there's only one actual named person on Gilley's list—Dakota Fanning. Why her? Well, in Gilley's words, "No one that young should be that talented and that smart. It's just weird."

Other notable items include mice—but not rats or bugs; lady parts—for obvious reasons (Gil is as gay as they come); baby corn ("It's not corn, but it *looks* like corn, and that *can't* be okay!"); leggings worn as pants; people who give an uncommon spelling to an otherwise common name, like Jyan, Mykel, or Dyafdd; and Cirque du Soleil acrobats ("*No* one should be able to bend like that!").

Animated talking animals are near the top of the list, and if you combine these with Dakota Fanning—say, in the movie *Charlotte's Web*, for example—you're liable to send Gil right over the edge.

Last on Gilley's list, but certainly not least, are ghosts.

Yes, you read that right. Ghosts give Gilley the weirds. Which can be super inconvenient given that Gil is also the technical adviser on our ghost-hunting cable TV show, *Ghoul Getters*.

In fact, the ghost thing was proving more than a little problematic on this particular evening—or midafternoon according to my watch, now set to Greenwich Mean Time— as I squatted next to Gil in the middle of the aisle of the British Airways jet that had brought us back to England.

"Gil," I said for the eleventieth time. "Please. For the love of God. Let go of the armrest and come off the plane."

"Sir, ma'am, I really must insist," interrupted the most unhelpful flight attendant ever. "You *must* deplane immediately."

Gil ignored him and focused his fearful gaze on me. "Please don't make me, M. J.," he begged. "I can't do it."

I rubbed his arm. "Sweetie," I said, fighting to keep my lids open. I was so exhausted I felt punch-drunk. "Come off the plane and we'll talk about it, okay?"

"Talking about it means you'll make me do it," he countered. He knew me too well.

My eyes flickered nervously to the front of the plane where Gopher, our TV producer, stood watching us with an impatient and irritated look on his face. "Gil," I said (eleventy times plus one if you're counting), "I swear to you, I'm not going to try and talk you into anything other than coming off the plane and heading to bed. I know you must be exhausted, right?"

Gil bit his lip. "I want to go back," he whispered.

"Ma'am," said the flight attendant, "if he doesn't deplane, I'll have no choice but to alert security."

I turned my head and glared so hard at the attendant that he frowned and took two steps back. I then refocused on Gilley. "Honey," I said gently, "this plane is parked for the rest of the day right here. It's not going anywhere for the next thirteen hours. You don't want to sit here for thirteen straight hours, do you?"

"If it means going someplace other than the next ghostbust, I'll stay put," Gil said stubbornly.

"But you won't be able to sleep," I told him.

"I can sleep okay," he replied, and I knew he was right. Gil could sleep standing up.

"There'll be no food," I tried next.

I heard a tiny gurgle from Gil's stomach. Still, he pressed his lips together and gripped the armrests even tighter. "I'll be fine."

I sighed and thought for a second. Then I had it. "Well," I said, "you won't be able to use the restroom, Gil. And I saw you gulp down at least two bottled waters and a couple of Cokes on the way here. That's gonna be hard to hold until tomorrow morning."

Gil shifted in his seat.

"I mean, don't you have to go even right now?" I asked, standing up like I didn't care anymore if he refused to get off the plane.

Gil squirmed again and crossed his legs.

"I know *I* really have to use the restroom," I lied. I'd hit the head right before our final approach. "Yep. Has to be a pretty uncomfortable feeling, knowing you'll have to hold it for the next thirteen hours."

Gil set his jaw with determination. "I can do it."

I nodded like I totally believed him. "Sure you can, honey. While you're holding it, I'm gonna hit the ladies' room. Then I'm gonna head to the hotel and drink a nice big glass of water. Then I'm gonna take a nice long shower. You know the kind where you just turn the water on and stand under it forever? It's like standing in the rain. Water just streaming down and down . . ."

With an irritated grunt Gil unfastened his seat belt and bolted to his feet. Tearing down the aisle, he nearly took out Gopher as he pushed past him on his way off the plane.

I bent down and grabbed Gilley's gear before hurrying after him, making sure to send the flight attendant one final glare before the exit.

By the time I made it to the top of the Jetway, Gil wasn't in sight. Instead my boyfriend and fellow ghostbuster, Heath, was there waiting for me. "He ran into the men's room," he told me when I looked all around for Gil.

"Thank God," I said. "I thought I'd never get him off that plane."

"What's gotten into him?" Heath asked me.

I rolled my eyes and made a face at Gopher, who'd also just appeared at the top of the Jetway. "Gopher just *had* to tell Gilley all about the ghost that haunts Kidwellah Castle."

"I told you not to let them sit next to each other," Heath reminded me.

I shook my head and sighed. "It's not like I could've done anything to stop Gil from sitting next to Gopher once our oh-so-helpful producer announced he had a twopound bag of M&M's for the flight."

Heath smirked. "How many of those two pounds do you think went into Gil?"

"At least one and a half, which of course gave Gil a really good sugar high and he soaked up everything Gopher had to tell him about Kidwellah and the haunted moors."

The castle and the surrounding moors I was referring to were located in northern Wales, in a lovely-sounding place called Penbigh, and by the looks of our research, it appeared to be one of the most interesting haunted places in all of Britain. I'd seen a picture of the castle complete with drawbridge and its huge adjoining moat. I'd gotten excited about the prospect of exploring it the minute I'd seen the photo.

Truth be told, Kidwellah was exactly the type of location we needed after shooting our last episode in Dunkirk, which had been a complete bust (no pun intended). We'd investigated a crumbling ruin that lacked a lot in the way of panache, and the most we'd managed to record were some faint disembodied footsteps and the sound of a horse whinnying in an abandoned stable. Otherwise, it'd been a whole lotta footage of Heath and me searching for spooks and finding nothing interesting.

But the moors in northern Wales held such promise, which was why we'd all agreed to it . . . well, except Gilley. We hadn't told him. And the reason we hadn't told him was that for the past few weeks, he'd been acting crazy. I'm talking more crazy than normal, which for Gil meant—*CRAZY!*

He's always been afraid of spooks, but as long as we give him a nice safe place to work from, like a van parked somewhere outside the haunted zone, he's usually more than willing to provide his considerable technical expertise to our shoots.

But in Dunkirk something had happened, and I still didn't quite know what. Gil stopped showing up for our daily pre-shoot meetings, and every time he thought he saw something creepy on one of his monitors, he flipped out. I'd been called off the location a couple of times to try and talk some sense into him, and my calm, rational reasoning had worked well enough to finish the shoot and load him onto the plane, but I hadn't counted on Gopher going on about how creepy Kidwellah was. Supposedly, its moat was haunted by the ghost of a woman who could pull in any careless soul who ventured too close to the water. Gopher had even suggested that there'd been one or two drownings credited to her, but I doubted those stories were true. Still, the surrounding moors had at least a long list of ghostly sightings, so if we couldn't find enough spooks within the haunted halls of Kidwellah for a good show, at least we had a fighting chance to capture something spooky out on the moors.

But now that Gopher had stupidly triggered Gilley's breaking point, I hoped I'd be able to get him straightened out before it came time to investigate the castle. The last thing I needed right now was to deal with Gilley's meltdown. Before bolting to the men's room, Gilley had tried to tell me that he knew the ghost in the moat was going to come for him, because they *always* came looking for him.

The sad thing is . . . he's mostly right. Gil makes a nice target for a spook. It must be something about the electromagnetic frequency he puts out, because ghosties just love him. Or, more to the point, they love to terrorize him. I've never actually told him this, but I've been in enough haunted locales to understand that Gilley is a magnet for spectral activity. It's like he's wearing Hai Karate for spooks.

After ten minutes of waiting near the men's room door with no sign of Gil, I sent Heath to check on him. He was back in a minute to tell me that our little buddy had locked himself in one of the stalls and wasn't coming out until morning.

In turn, I rounded angrily on Gopher. *"Why?"*

"I didn't know he didn't know!" our producer exclaimed. "You guys gotta tell me what's safe to tell Gil and what isn't!"

"Nothing," I growled. *"Nothing* is safe to tell him, Goph! You got that?"

Gopher shifted the strap of his duffel to his other shoulder. "I do now. . . ."

I turned away angrily and looked about for the rest of our production crew, spotting John, our sound guy; Meg, our production assistant; and Kim, our assistant producer. I waved them over, noting how worn out they looked. Our crew is a decent-looking bunch: John's tall and broad shouldered with dishwater blond hair and a long face that suits him. Meg is a pretty little thing, with curly strawberry blond hair and a heart-shaped mouth, and Kim is thin and carries herself with a grace that you'd see on a ballet dancer. She has long black spiral curls that bounce when she walks and an olive skin tone. "I'm sure you can tell we have a situation," I began when they'd joined us.

"Gilley *again*?" John asked with all the irritation that my BFF having yet another meltdown could inspire.

I sighed heavily. I was exhausted, and I knew they were too. Gil's timing couldn't have been worse. "Yes, John, unfortunately it's Gilley again. He's locked himself in the men's room, and he's refusing to come out until morning."

"What do you need?" he asked. I liked John. He was a good guy and he was always ready to do what I asked.

"I need for you three," I said, pointing to him, Heath, and Gopher, "to go in there and get him out of that stall. Then we've somehow got to get him through customs without causing an international incident, and take him to the hotel. He just needs a nice long rest. If we let him sleep, feed him, and don't talk about the shoot, he'll be back to his old self by morning." I sounded far more confident uttering these words than I actually felt about the situation.

Heath, John, and Gopher all exchanged uncomfortable looks. They knew how big a challenge it was going to be to get Gilley to go anywhere he didn't want to.

Still, without a word they marched into the men's room, and Kim, Meg, and I all stood outside, where we heard a pretty good commotion erupt.

At last the four of them appeared, Gilley's torso slung between Heath and John while Gopher carried his legs, and all the while Gil was putting up a really good fight, kicking and struggling for all he was worth. I looked around at the alarmed passengers, and sure enough, two security guards began to trot over. "I guess avoiding an international incident was a little much to hope for," I grumbled, moving to intercept the guards.

Two hours later we were still being detained by those same guards at Manchester Airport. By this time, Gilley was asleep next to me, his head on my shoulder. Having thrown his temper tantrum, he'd exhausted himself, but managed to get us into deep doo-doo in the process. He was lucky I loved him and had known him most of my life—otherwise, I would've killed him and hidden the body without a pang of guilt.

I looked down at my best friend and softened just a little. He'd had the same big head with black unruly hair and a nose that was a bit too big for his face since he was eleven. He'd been the smallest person in our class—next to me, of course. Neither Gilley nor I had ever had much of a growth spurt, and although I was still slightly taller than average at five-feet-four, he remained on the short side at just a hair over five-feet-seven. His big head was starting to hurt against my shoulder, though, so I shifted in my seat and his chin lolled forward. He snorted himself awake, looked about blearily, and asked, "What's happening?"

"Nothing," I told him icily. "We're still being detained."

Gil yawned and took in all the angry faces of the crew glaring back at him. "You guys shoulda just let me get back on a plane and go home," he groused.

"Trust me," I told him, "we're all currently in favor of voting you off the island."

Gil looked down at his hands and sighed. "I can't help it," he said. "I'm really scared this time, M. J."

"What's so different about this time?" I asked. "Seriously, Gil. We've faced some supercrazy stuff before and you've come out of it okay. What's so bad about this time?"

Gil leaned his head back against the wall, and I could see that his eyes had gotten moist and he was trying to hold back the tears. That took me by surprise. I had no

idea he was so upset about coming here. "It's just . . . ,"
he began, without adding anything more.

"Just what, honey? Come on, Gil. Tell me. What's got
you so freaked-out?"

Gil wiped his eyes and cleared his throat. He wouldn't
look at me, which troubled me greatly. "At some point,"
he finally said, "I think my luck's gonna run out. Someday, on one of these busts, either you or me or Heath or
one of our crew is gonna end up dead, M. J."

"Oh, Gil," I whispered, laying a hand on his arm.

I wanted to throw my arms around him and hug him
until he wasn't afraid anymore, but then Gilley looked
up at me with big liquid eyes and said, "And this time, I
really, really feel that something *really* bad is gonna happen. And when really bad stuff happens, it usually happens to me first."

Gilley then dissolved into tears and I hardly knew
what to do. I'd never seen him so undone before, so I
threw my arms around him and hugged him as tight as
I could. When Heath met my eyes across the room, I
shook my head. I found I couldn't talk. And deep in my
heart I noticed for the first time my own sense of foreboding. It was like a small dark hole had suddenly opened
up in the center of my chest, and try as I might, I couldn't
ignore the feeling that maybe, this time, Gilley might
be right.

It took another twenty minutes for airport security to
confirm we weren't a bunch of terrorists or hoodlums,
and by the time they shook all of us awake, we were so
groggy and punch-drunk that it made for some comical
stumbling out of the airport.

Because we were so bushed, we took a vote and instead of renting a couple of vans, we sprang for a couple
of taxis to take us to our destination. For once, Gopher
agreed with me that we could always rent a van later if
we needed it.

The taxis took us to Kidwellah Castle, an incredibly majestic structure moated on three sides and the fourth backing up to Lake Byrn y Bach.

The castle itself was truly glorious, complete with turrets, parapets, towers, and a huge drawbridge. It was like something right out of Camelot. Even Gilley, who'd been slumped and pouty in the seat next to me, perked up when we rolled down a hill and the view of the castle opened up. As we drove closer to the structure, I could see the beautiful moat, gleaming dark blue as the setting sun's rays danced across it. It didn't look scary at all and I could almost see the gears in Gilley's brain turning with that very thought, because the stiff set of his shoulders relaxed a little as he took in the lovely setting.

As we got closer, however, I happened to take in the row of signs lining the road on both sides of the drawbridge, warning pedestrians to walk in the center of the drawbridge, and to keep off the surrounding rocks leading to the moat. SWIFT CURRENT! read one sign. NO SWIMMING! read another, and all of them warned of DANGER!

But as we crossed onto the drawbridge—a massively wide affair without railings and set low to the water—I didn't see anything stirring in the calm waters to either side. Gil turned to me as if to silently ask me if I thought the moat was as dangerous as the signs posted about warned. I merely shrugged, because I truly didn't know.

Across the main bridge we rolled into the castle's bailey—or the large enclosed courtyard leading to the main building and the keep—which were actually separate structures, but connected by a parapet about two stories up.

It's hard to give a scale to what we were looking at, but suffice it to say that the castle was *huge* and—according to the goose bumps forming on my arms—chock-full of ghosties.

The two taxis parked in front of a massive iron door,

propped open by a block of wood. As we exited and stretched our limbs, a slight-looking man in his late twenties or early thirties, dressed in an army green wool sweater and matching trousers, approached with his hands clasped together in front of him and his frame slightly bent. "Good evening," he said formally. "I'm Merrick Brown, the hotel clerk. Welcome to Kidwellah Castle."

I shook his hand and received a ready smile from the man. He was an extremely interesting-looking character, with bright carrot-red hair, a round face, bushy brows, a wonderfully hooked nose, and twinkling blue eyes. I warmed to him immediately. "Thank you, Merrick," I said. "I'm M. J. Holliday."

"Oh, yes, Miss Holliday, I've looked you up on the Internet and I have to say, I'm rather impressed! By what I've read, you and Mr. Whitefeather seem to be quite the pair of amateur investigators! I'm dead chuffed you and your crew will be visitin' our little patch of Wales for a wee bit of ghost hunting! I should think that you'll find Kidwellah up to standard for that sort of thing. The countess herself is very excited that her castle will be on the telly. She's hoping your show will bring in the tourists and such."

"Wonderful," I said, attempting to muster up some enthusiasm, but I was too tired to give the word any oomph. "Sorry we're so late, but we were unexpectedly detained at the airport."

"Bloomin' security, I imagine," Merrick said with a knowing wink. "It's why I never goes anywhere."

"I'm tired," Gil whined, dragging his backpack on the ground as he shuffled forward like a five-year-old.

I frowned at him before turning back to the charming clerk. "I'm afraid we're all exhausted. I know it's still early for you, but I think we're ready to drop where we stand unless we get to bed very soon."

"Of course, of course," Merrick said, waving our group forward toward the main door. "We'll just get you lot your assigned rooms, and then you can be off to catch your rest."

"Thank you, baby Jesus," Gil mumbled, quickening his step to be first in line at check-in.

Gopher sidled up next to me. "This is gonna put us behind schedule."

"Do you know that you say that at the start of every single bust we do, Goph?" I was sick of everybody complaining. Actually, I was sick of everybody, and I just wanted a real bed to crash into for a good night's sleep—which, by my estimation, I hadn't had in over forty-two hours.

"Well, it's true," Gopher replied irritably. Then he quickened his step too.

I inhaled a deep breath and let it out slowly, trying to put a damper on my short fuse. "How you holding up?" Heath asked me as we walked through the door behind everyone else and into a gigantic main hall.

I didn't even answer him, because I was too busy gawking at the gorgeous digs.

The interior of the castle was sparsely decorated, but truthfully, it didn't need much because the architecture was so stunning. A huge stone staircase led up to a catwalk that completely encircled the large square room. Off the catwalk were four hallways positioned in the center of each section of the square, and I guessed that our rooms were down at least one of those hallways.

On the main floor there were several full suits of armor positioned at random sections around the square, a seating area, and a grand piano. A narrow window let in very little light, but the main hall was well illuminated by a massive iron chandelier that had to weigh several hundred pounds.

The air inside the castle was damp and chilly, probably a result of the cold stone bricks, which held in very little warmth and allowed moisture to collect where it would.

It was the perfect ambience for a haunting and I only hoped that the ghosties would hold off visiting Heath and me until morning.

Just as I had that thought, however, I saw a shadow dart down one of the hallways upstairs. I elbowed Heath and pointed up. "You saw it too?" he asked.

I nodded. "This should be interesting."

Heath and I were the last to check in and receive our rooms. Merrick looked to his logbook as he searched for our names and corresponding keys. "I've selected a suite of two rooms in the VIP section of the castle," he said merrily, his expression slightly starstruck.

Heath bounced his eyebrows at me and mouthed, "VIP?"

I had a feeling that Merrick might believe we were far more well-known than we actually were. "It's a lovely set of rooms, removed from the regular guests, and as we have a large and rather boisterous party in residence at present, I believe you'll appreciate the peace and quiet of the VIP wing. And you'll even have your own key to access that section of the castle."

"Our own key to that section of the castle?" Heath repeated, and I could sense that he was a little uncomfortable being mislabeled a VIP.

Merrick slid the rather large antique-looking key at us. "Yes, Mr. Whitefeather," he said. "We reserve that wing for our most important guests and locking it ensures that none of the riffraff get in."

If I'd had the energy, I would have set Merrick straight about the fact that Heath and I were just as riffraff as the next person and we didn't need our own private section of the castle, but the truth was, I was secretly pleased about being treated like a celebrity. So when Heath eyed me to see what I thought, I nodded. Plus, I was pretty sure that once Gopher found out we'd been located in the VIP section, he'd blow a gasket at the added expense something like that was bound to come with, so why not enjoy it for one night before he forced us to move?

After handing us our room keys and drawing Heath a map to the VIP wing, Merrick turned from congenial to downright sheepish when he added, "I'm so sorry we've no one to take your bags for you, but I'm afraid I'm needed in the kitchen to help Mrs. Farnsworth prepare for supper."

"No sweat," Heath assured him, swinging his duffel over his shoulder, and taking the handle of my suitcase up while he was at it. "We pack light."

As we thanked Merrick and turned toward the stairs, Heath leaned in to kiss me sweetly on the cheek. "How you holding up?"

I put my hand on his shoulder and moved close to him. "I think I'm asleep on my feet."

"I hear you," he agreed, before pointing across the huge front hall to a sign. "There's a dining room here," he said. "Should we get some food to take up to our rooms?"

I sighed and closed my eyes. "If you're hungry, go for it, but I'm passing. All I want to do is fall into bed for the next twelve hours."

On the way up the stairs, Heath stopped to reach over and steady me, because I was swaying so badly that I was in danger of falling back down the stairs. At the top he offered me the handle of my bag and said, "Sweetheart, you've gotta pull it for a little ways while I look at the map, okay?"

I nodded dully and shuffled along clumsily behind him. I never lifted my gaze from the backs of his shoes and I couldn't tell you how long it took or how many corners we turned, but eventually we ended up at a locked door and Heath inserted his key, turning it with some effort to gain us entry. The door gave way with a loud creak, and if I'd had the strength, I would have commented on how appropriate the setting was for two ghost hunters like us.

The corridor beyond was dim and dreary. It was also quite damp and a chill went through me, raising goose bumps along my arms. Heath and I both hesitated in the doorway, and with effort I focused on the atmosphere. "The VIP wing is haunted," I said.

Heath eyed the corridor warily. "It's thick in here, Em. Do you want to go back and have Merrick assign us another room with the riffraff?"

I smiled wearily. "Wait till Gilley hears he was labeled part of that crowd and we were given VIP status."

"He'll demand to stay in this section too, even with the additional spook factor."

I knew Heath was still waiting for me to decide what to do, but I was so numb with fatigue that I was having a really hard time thinking. I didn't like the feel of the place, but it was such a long way back, and Merrick had suggested he was going to help out somebody in the kitchen, so even if we went back down and asked to be reassigned, in all likelihood we weren't going to have anyone to assist us for some time. "Let's just stay here the one night and ask for another room in the morning," I said at last.

Still, Heath seemed to hesitate, and he looked around worriedly. I could see the goose pimples on his arms too. "Unless you think we really should go back?" I added with a sigh.

Heath's eyes flickered to me, and he softened. "I think it'll be okay," he said. "After all, the worst spooks at this place are supposed to be haunting the moat and the moors. One night won't kill us."

I trudged through the opening, blinking heavily. "Exactly. Even the dead won't wake me tonight."

Heath grabbed for the handle of my luggage again, and I stumbled along clumsily, fighting to keep my eyes open and my legs moving. Heath then passed me and led the way to our room, which by now felt like it was located on the other side of the moon. At last he stopped at one of our assigned rooms and inserted another key. Pushing the door open, he motioned with his arm for me to move ahead, and when I did, I nearly came up short. The room was quite small, as in barely enough room for the queen-sized mattress. It was also dark and musty smelling, like it hadn't been aired out in a very long time. "*This* is the VIP suite of rooms?" I said.

Heath eyed the numbered keys in his hand, then backed out and looked down the hall. "He also gave us the room next door."

"Is it any bigger?" I asked. Truly if I had known the rooms were this small and this musty, I would've insisted we take a regular room.

Heath moved out of sight for a minute and I heard him turning the other key in the door. He then reappeared and said, "It is a little bigger. Come on, babe, let's get you to bed."

I shuffled out of the room and over to the one next door, which still smelled pretty musty, but at least was slightly bigger. Once inside I shrugged out from under the strap of my messenger bag, letting it fall to the floor, then wiggled out of my coat, letting it plop on top of the bag, and crawled onto the bed, finally falling face-first into the pillow. The most effort I exhibited after that was to curl around into a fetal position and exhale a relieved sigh. I'd sleep in my clothes and be happy for it. And that was one of my last clearly conscious thoughts, but even as it entered my head, I could feel Heath tugging off my boots, jeans, and sweater before covering me with the comforter. I also think he kissed my cheek and told me he loved me, but that part I honestly could have dreamed.

I slept like the dead (no pun intended) for several hours until something roused me from a lovely slumber. I remember opening one eye with a slight whimper. I was still heavy with fatigue. What had it been that'd woken me up?

I listened for a minute, and could hear only the rhythmic sounds of Heath's steady breathing next to me. I closed my eye with a little sigh, ready to tuck back into la-la land, when something from the other side of our door made me snap the lid open again.

I listened, and this time I could hear a sound like a woman crying from the hallway. At first I just listened, wondering if perhaps she'd simply had a spat with her boyfriend or her spouse, but I hadn't heard any arguing, and didn't Merrick say that he'd put us in an unoccupied part of the castle? Then I immediately wondered if Heath had locked the riffraff door behind us. Knowing him, he hadn't; he wasn't someone who looked down his nose at anybody. If some guest of the castle wanted into this section, Heath would hold the door for him.

The crying just beyond our door continued, and I waited for the woman to move back to her room, but the sound of her pitiful weeping went on and on. Finally and with a grunt of irritation I pushed up off the pillow and shivered in the damp night air.

Hugging my sides, I moved to the door and tried to feel for the peephole, as there was no light coming through from out in the hallway.

It took me a second or two to understand that there was no peephole—the Welsh maybe aren't as paranoid about strangers at their door as we Americans. I stood there for about five more seconds, wondering what to do, and after listening to the woman continue to sob in distress, I decided what the hell, it wouldn't hurt to check on her. Hiding my nearly naked bottom half behind the door, I turned the knob and pulled.

The door opened with a considerable squeak, and as I leaned out, I could see someone huddled in the hallway startle at the noise. Even though the corridor was dimly lit, I could make out the figure of a woman dressed in a long white nightgown and a black knit shawl, cowering against the wall. She got up when I leaned out to take a look, and she began to limp along down the hallway while trying to cover her face with her hand and the shawl. I stared at her for a moment, and one thing became quite clear: Judging by her disheveled appearance and the purple bruises I saw on her wrists and forearms, the poor thing had been in some sort of awful scuffle.

"Are you all right?" I whispered. Her demeanor was so timid and frightened that I was afraid I'd scare her even more if I spoke at full volume.

She simply shook her head and tried to limp away, pulling her shawl even more closely about her. But then she happened to glance back at me over her shoulder and through her tangle of hair I could see a black eye and a puffy lip. Someone had roughed her up pretty good.

"Ma'am?" I said. "Do you need some help?"

She ducked her chin again and limped with a bit more effort to put some distance between us.

I hovered indecisively in the doorway for a few anxious moments. Should I go after her and try to help or console her? What the heck happened to her, anyway? Had she been attacked by someone she knew? Or was there a predator on the loose in the castle? Whichever, the woman needed medical attention—that much was clear.

Finally I backed into the room and hunted around in the dark for my jeans. At last I found them on the floor by the bed and shuffled into them as quickly as possible. My sweater was harder to locate, as it had ended up partially kicked under the bed. Heath stirred a little when I muttered in irritation, but otherwise he didn't wake up.

After hastily getting into the sweater, I darted to the door, opened it as quietly as that awful squeak would allow, and ran out into the hall ... which was empty.

There was no sign of the woman. Undaunted, I moved

down the corridor, listening as I went for the sound of her whimpering, but nothing came to my ears. At the end of the hallway I looked first right, then left, but couldn't see anyone about. "Dammit!" I muttered. Which way had she gone? Had she come to this wing to hide from her assailant? Had she perhaps moved back through the riffraff door to her side of the castle? And where the heck was that door, anyway? I realized I hadn't paid any attention to where the door was located in this maze of corridors.

I moved to my right first and went quietly along the hallway, listening for any sign of the distraught woman. I thought about calling out to her, but she seemed so spooked by my appearance that I didn't want to send her any deeper into hiding.

Still, as I traveled up and down both the right hallway and then the left, I could find no sign of her, or the main corridor leading out of this wing of the castle.

"Well, that sucks," I muttered when I turned a corner and saw that it was a dead end. Only an open window greeted me. The wind was pulling the two halves of the shuttered casements back and forth, and I was a bit scared that the glass would break if the wind was strong enough, so I moved to close the two panes. As I reached for the separate halves, I heard a loud splash from below. It was still very dark out, but I could just make out the gleam of the water in the moonlight. I peered into the dim waters of the moat, but saw nothing that would have been responsible for creating such a loud splash. "Weird," I whispered, closing the window and throwing the lock.

A shiver went up my spine and I felt more than a little creeped out all of a sudden. I had a fleeting thought that the woman I'd seen might have gone through the window and into the moat, but wouldn't I have seen her jump?

I shivered anew and turned back toward the way I'd come. I'd taken only about five steps away from the hidden corner with the window when the bulb right over my head suddenly went out, plunging me into an even murkier gloom. The hairs on the back of my neck stood up on end, and I looked around uneasily. A cold chill also seemed to fill the hallway, and suddenly I *really* didn't want to be in that hallway. I wanted only to get back to my room—stat.

I started trotting in that direction when all of a sudden I heard a sort of low, guttural growl, but not quite like a dog might make. It was a rumbling of sorts, like the sound a cat makes right before it hisses, only this particular rumble was much deeper and had more timbre.

It came from behind me and reflexively I paused to look over my shoulder. There was nothing in the hallway, but I could identify where the low rumble was coming from—it was from the last door on the left where I'd been standing only seconds before.

The rumble grew louder, more carnal and vicious, and for a moment I stood frozen, my brain trying to make sense of what was happening even as the internal warning bell we all carry sounded, demanding that I turn tail and run.

Just as I was about to take off, however, there was a screech from behind the door, followed immediately by a tremendous crash against it. I jumped and let out a frightened squeal, staring hard at the door, which sounded as if it was rattling on its hinges.

It was as if someone . . . or some*thing* had just launched itself right into the door at full force. The low rumble picked up again, and I didn't wait around for that door to break down and whatever was behind it to come out and get me. I bolted.

Just as I reached the intersection to my hallway, I heard another tremendous crash and the sound of splintering wood. Whatever had been in that room was now breaking out of it.

I rounded the corner and ran like my life depended

on it—which, let's face it, it probably did. I dashed down the hallway listening for the sound of that door giving way, but all I heard was that terrible low growl, until one last crash and a tremendous boom let me know the door had given way.

As I ran, the lights above me went out one at a time the moment I passed underneath them, and I could feel that I was on the verge of being plunged into total darkness.

Ahead I could see our door; it was still slightly ajar and one light was still lit in the hallway, drawing me like a beacon. I was just a few yards away when I heard that terrible rumble again, followed by the sound of something *very* big giving chase.

I could hear the pounding of its feet charging toward me. It sounded as big as a tiger, but I dared not look back. I kept my focus on making it to the door of our room and used my arms to pump faster and faster. Even as I tore down the corridor, I could feel a bone-chilling cold engulf me and its appearance was so startling that it almost caused me to stumble.

Somehow I managed to keep my footing and ran as if my feet had wings. *"Heath!"* I cried as the bitter cold wrapped itself around me and threatened to freeze me from the inside out. *"Heeeeeeeeeath!"*

The pounding footfalls of the thing giving chase drew nearer and nearer. Whatever it was, it was faster than I was. Abject terror seeped into my bones like that frigid cold, and as I opened my mouth to scream, the last bulb went out overhead, enveloping me into total darkness.

Behind me the footfalls sounded like they were right on top of me now, and just as I was about to be tackled, a light inside our room came on and the door pushed open, flooding the hallway with light, and Heath stood in the doorway looking at me as if he could hardly believe his eyes.

I barreled into him, throwing us both into the room,

and somehow reached back to slam the door behind us.
"What the . . . ?" he gasped as my momentum shoved
him right onto the bed.

"Shhhh!" I whispered, shivering while I whipped
around to throw the dead bolt. A second later whatever
was giving chase slammed right into the door with such
force that I was knocked back off my feet.

Chapter 2

I fell right into Heath, who grabbed me around the waist, twisted on the mattress, and pulled me to the floor. He then tugged me around the far side of the bed, positioning me as close to the far corner as possible, before putting himself and the bed between me and the door. I wrapped trembling arms around him, and from over his shoulder I watched the door with thundering heart and heaving lungs, waiting for whatever had slammed against the door to strike again.

I could see the wood had splintered from the force of whatever had hit it, and the screws in one hinge appeared to have been compromised. Another solid slam and the whole thing would give way.

But the seconds ticked by and nothing else happened. Still, we huddled in that half-crouched position for many minutes, waiting and watching, but only silence filled the room and the hallway beyond.

At last Heath turned to me with big wide eyes. "What the *hell* was that?"

I could only shake my head. I had no earthly idea.

Slowly he helped me to my feet and sat me down on the bed, where he ran a hand over my cheek and studied me with grave concern as if he was looking for any sign of injury. Finally he said, "Tell me everything."

At first I didn't quite know where to start. I must've started and stopped my story six different times, and I could see the confusion in Heath's eyes, but I wasn't able to make sense of all that'd happened since I'd been awakened either.

"You say this woman was hurt?" he asked when I'd finally gotten most of the story out.

I nodded.

Heath eyed the door warily. "Could she still be out there?"

"I looked for her and I didn't see any sign of her. I'm not sure what happened—she could've gone back to her side of the castle or maybe she headed to the front desk for help."

Heath squeezed my hand before moving to the door. He put his ear to it first and listened closely; then he turned the dead bolt very slowly so as not to make a sound. He placed his hand on the knob, then seemed to think better of it.

Turning back to face me, he took in the room, and I could tell what he was thinking—he wanted to have handy anything he could use as a weapon. The room was so spartan there wasn't much to utilize, but finally he grabbed the small metal trash bin and edged back to the door. He looked at me over his shoulder and I nodded. Opening the door a tiny crack still caused the door to squeak. I braced myself, not knowing what to expect, and Heath put his eye to the crack. I could already see that the overhead lamps had come back on in the hallway, as the slight opening allowed in a thin ray of light.

For several seconds I watched Heath just stare out into the hall, but then he backed up a bit and opened the door a little farther. I crossed the room and stood behind him, trying myself to get a peek. What I could see was an empty corridor, still dimly lit but clear of anyone or anything that might cause us alarm.

Heath then stood back and I followed suit. As he did so, he pulled the door open all the way and considered it. "What?" I asked.

"Whatever hit the door should've left a mark," he said, but I couldn't see any outward sign of damage from the force of the impact of whatever had slammed against the door. Only the splintering of the wood and the compromised hinges on our side showed any sign of damage.

Absent too was the bone-chilling cold that had so enveloped me as I raced down the corridor. And I couldn't exactly remember if the cold had left the area before I'd reached the room, or some time after—I'd been far too scared in the seconds following my escape into the room to pay much attention. While the air in the hallway was still chilly, it wasn't anything like the freezing cold that had crawled under my skin and taken root in my insides. I shivered even thinking about it.

"You okay?" Heath whispered, eyeing me with concern again.

"Fine. What do we do now?"

Heath closed the door and took my hand. Leading me back to the bed, he clicked on the bedside lamp and stared hard at the small night table. "Where's the phone?"

"What phone?"

"Shouldn't there be a phone for us to call down to the desk?"

I blinked. He was right. "What is it with these VIP digs, anyway? Small musty rooms, no phone to speak of, and no clock either, did you notice?"

Heath grumbled with irritation as he shuffled around the bed looking for his own jeans and sweater. I watched him until I thought to check my phone for the time, but when I tapped my screen, it wouldn't come on. "Huh," I said, attempting a second and third time to get it to work.

"What?" Heath asked, pulling his sweater over his head.

"My phone's dead."

"Didn't you charge it at the airport?"

I nodded. I had charged it there, so it should still have substantial power now, because I hadn't used it since. Getting up, I went over to my messenger bag and rooted around for the charger, and then the challenge became finding an outlet. Finally I pulled out the plug from the lamp and got the phone some juice. "It's three a.m.," I said once the display came to life.

"At least we got a few good hours of sleep," Heath remarked, coming over to slip his arms around my middle. "I'm headed down to the front desk. I think we should let someone know there may be an injured woman somewhere in the castle."

I turned in his arms to look up at him, suddenly afraid for him. "But what about that . . . that . . . *thing*?"

Heath eyed the door. "I'll have to risk it."

I didn't know what it was that I'd encountered in that corridor beyond our door, but one thing I did know—it wasn't human . . . and it almost certainly wasn't alive. "I'm going with you," I said firmly.

Heath shook his head, but I wasn't having it. Pushing out of his arms, I moved over to my messenger bag again and rifled through it.

The magnetic spikes we use to combat the worst of the poltergeists we encounter on our ghost hunts were packed away in a large canvas bag that John was in charge of, and therefore were probably safely tucked away in his room. I hadn't even thought to carry any spikes into the castle, as all I'd wanted to do was get a little shut-eye.

The best I could do was to come up with a few refrigerator magnets that I had on hand just in case one or two of the magnets glued to the protective sweatshirt Gilley wore came loose.

In other words, if Heath and I did encounter that thing again in the hallway, we wouldn't have much in the way of defenses. Still, I also managed to come up with an electrostatic meter, which would measure the electrostatic energy around us as we made our way to the front desk and hopefully give us at least a running start. "Em," Heath said when I handed him two of the magnets and moved toward the door, "you should stay here."

I didn't even bother with a reply. Heath is one of the sweetest, most chivalrous guys on the planet, but sometimes he forgets that I can be pretty tough too. I opened the door and prepared to step into the hallway when I felt his firm grip on my shoulder. "Me first," he whispered.

The old me would have rolled my eyes and defiantly pulled out of his grasp and stepped into the hallway. New me—the me that had been through a lot of rough stuff in recent months—allowed him to go first.

As we entered the hallway, I turned on the meter. The needle surged a little as the power came on, but then it settled into that comfortable normal range and I breathed a teensy bit easier.

Heath led the way, slowly and cautiously, and neither of us spoke a word. We moved in the opposite direction from where I'd gone looking for the poor woman I'd encountered in the hallway, and I was grateful that Heath seemed to know where he was headed, because I was very quickly lost.

At last we came to the riffraff door, and beyond that, the large staircase I remembered climbing wearily several hours earlier. We went down the stairs side by side with Heath still holding tightly to my hand. "Did the meter register anything on the way here?" he asked quietly.

"Not even a small surge," I said. Sometimes the needle on one of our gadgets will bounce if the location we're in has quite a bit of electrical current running through it—like a modern building made to house a lot of computer equipment or wiring, but these old buildings usually have fairly low voltage capacity, and that keeps the meters pretty flat.

It's a good thing too, because then we know to trust them—when those needles begin to bounce, it's because some spook is on the move. But our whole way to the front hall not much had registered, which in its own way was a little odd, because these castles usually come with a whole host of spiritual activity, and I knew we'd seen something spectral when we'd first entered the main hall upon our arrival.

Still, I didn't dwell on it overlong; I was just grateful to reach the front desk, but that relief faded the moment we stood in front of it and discovered that no one was manning it.

I rang the bell and Heath and I both looked around, but no one was there to help us.

Heath pulled out his phone from his back pocket and tapped the screen, but his phone didn't light up or come on. "My phone's out of juice too," he said with a puzzled expression.

"That confirms it," I said. "Whatever that thing was that chased me down that hallway was definitely spectral. It drained both our phones and all the lights in the hallway."

Heath nodded. "We'll have to get the scoop on what else might haunt this castle ASAP," he said, looking around the desk as if he was trying to find something. Leaning over the high counter, he finally came up with what he'd been searching for. "Got it," he said, holding up the phone triumphantly, then digging around until he'd located a phone book.

"Who you gonna call?" I asked, then followed that quickly with "Do *not* say you're calling Bill Murray or I will have to hurt you."

Heath chuckled as he thumbed through the first few pages of the directory before lifting the receiver. The phone was one of those old-fashioned contraptions with a rotary dial. "I'm calling the police."

My jaw dropped. "For reals?"

Heath nodded and held up a finger, indicating someone on the other end had answered. "Good morning, sorry to call so early, but I'm a guest at Kidwellah Castle, and I think a female guest at the hotel has been hurt."

Heath proceeded to tell the person on the other end of the line as much as he knew before he began to ask me questions. What did she look like? Where exactly had I seen her? What seemed to be the extent of her injuries? Did I know her name? Where was she now?

It went on like that for a bit until I took the phone and answered all the questions myself. It turned out that I was talking to the secretary of the Penbigh police. She seemed a very thorough woman, intent on discovering if in fact she had sufficient cause to wake the poor fool who would have to come out and search for the injured lady I'd seen.

Finally she asked, "Will you be there to greet the constable on duty, miss?"

My gaze landed on the desk clock tucked to the side of the check-in counter. It read three thirty a.m. "Yes," I said, holding in a sigh. "We'll be here."

After hanging up with her, Heath and I settled in for the wait, finding the two thrones set up near one of the the armored knights to be kind of comfortable. "Still tired?" Heath asked once we'd taken our seats.

"Very. You?"

Heath yawned. "Yeah. All this travel wears on you, doesn't it?"

The sigh I'd been holding in escaped me. "How many more shoots do we have until we get a break?"

Heath rubbed his eyes. "Three, maybe four more after this one, I think."

I was quiet for a while after that. Mostly I was so homesick I could barely stand it. We'd had a chance to head back to the States about three weeks earlier, but our visit to New Mexico—Heath's home state—hadn't been even remotely pleasant. It'd been as much work as one of our shoots, in fact.

And although I'd been in the States, I hadn't been home. I missed Boston. I missed my condo. But mostly I missed my sweet bird, Doc—the African gray I'd had since I was eleven—and of course my Boston friends something fierce. And while I'd spent a few quality days with Doc while we were in New Mexico, the short visit with him had only emphasized how much I'd missed his little feathered self, and it was a thousand times harder to leave him when we boarded the plane back to Europe.

"Maybe they won't renew us for another season," I said quietly.

Heath laid a gentle hand across my neck and began to massage the tense muscles there. "You miss your bird."

"I miss him like crazy. But I also miss home, you know?"

Heath's expression became clouded with guilt. "My family and their troubles took up all the time you could have spent in Boston, Em. I'm really sorry."

I waved a hand dismissively, even though my eyes were starting to mist a bit. "None of that was your fault, Heath. Gil and I volunteered to go with you to your uncle's funeral, and we also insisted on staying when things got dicey."

Heath leaned back and closed his eyes. "Maybe this shoot will go by quick," he said wistfully.

"Well, it can't go too quickly. If it unrolls like Dunkirk, we'll be in trouble with the network again."

"That place was a total bust," Heath agreed.

I leaned back too and closed my tired eyes, wishing the constable would get here already. Within a few moments I had inadvertently dozed off.

Only a short time later the sound of someone yelling startled me awake. *"Arthur?"* a male voice shouted. "Arthur Crunn, are you here?"

Heath and I both shot out of our chairs like bullets. I was so out of sorts that it took me a minute to figure out where I was, and that was further complicated by the tall lanky fellow with a thick mustache standing in the front hall holding a flashlight and giving us a quizzical look.

"I say," he said, "but you lot look a bit worse for wear."

I attempted to smooth out my hair and collect myself. "Who're you?" Heath asked brazenly, and by the look of his sleepy face I knew he'd nodded off too.

"Who am I? Well, young man, I am Inspector Lumley," the lanky fellow with dark brown hair, pale skin, and a long thin nose said. For emphasis he pulled out a small leather case from his coat pocket to flip it open and reveal his identification. "Is the manager of the hotel, Arthur Crunn, about?"

"Inspector?" I repeated. "I thought a constable was coming to meet us."

"Yes, well, he was, but he was waylaid by the dead body floating in the moat, you see. Called me immediately to come have a look."

My jaw dropped. "Dead body?"

"Yes," the inspector said, wrinkling up his nose. "Terrible sight that. And the reason I stand before you now. So, allow me to repeat myself: Is the hotel manager, Arthur Crunn, about?"

Inspector Lumley had more of an English accent than Welsh. His enunciation was most crisp and clear, and I wondered if he'd moved here from someplace closer to London. "No," Heath told him. "When we came down here, nobody was around."

The inspector pivoted on his heel to turn his attention to the front desk and took three purposeful strides to it in order to peer around it and see for himself.

"Was the person in the moat a woman?" I asked, afraid that the battered woman I'd seen outside my room had come to a bad end after all.

"No," the inspector said, raising his hand to shine his light into the small hallway behind the front desk. He then turned his attention to me, his brown eyes shining with intelligence. I had a feeling not much got by him. "Why do you ask if it was a woman?"

I took a small step back, uncomfortable under the inspector's intense gaze. "We called the police about a woman in distress."

"Woman in distress?" Lumley repeated, his eyes squinting as they assessed me head to toe. "I wasn't told of any woman in distress. I heard only that there was some sort of disturbance here at Kidwellah."

Heath wrapped his arm across my shoulders. "We're guests here at the hotel," he said. "About an hour and a half ago my girlfriend woke up to the sound of someone crying in the hallway outside our door. When she opened the door, she found a woman huddled there who appeared to have been beaten, and she also seemed too afraid to accept M. J.'s offer of help. When M. J. woke me to let me know what she'd seen, we did a quick search for the woman but couldn't find her. We then came down here to find some assistance, saw that the front desk was unmanned, and called the police."

It didn't faze me that Heath had left out the part about some paranormal creature almost beating our door down; I would've left that part out too. And I couldn't be sure, but I suspected that Inspector Lumley had stopped listening to Heath's explanation halfway through the story. The moment he mentioned the battered woman, the inspector seemed to frown and look elsewhere. "I shall have to have a talk with my secretary," he muttered distractedly. "She should know better than to discharge a constable for calls of that sort from here. Still, I suppose that sending Niles over to take the report did lead us to the body in the moat. . . ."

Heath and I exchanged looks of confusion. What the heck did he mean by that? "Sir," I said, catching the inspector's attention again. "I can assure you that our call to your station was very serious. The woman I saw in the hallway outside my door had been beaten, and she was so distraught and obviously traumatized that I still fear for her safety."

Lumley's expression was almost bored. "Yes, well, I can't very well do anything for that poor woman *now*, can I?" he said.

"*Excuse* me?" I said. Was he serious?

Lumley pulled out his cell and began to tap the screen with his thumb. "Ma'am," he said to me. "The woman you saw is deceased."

I gasped. Next to me I heard Heath gasp too. "You found her body too?" he said.

Lumley placed the phone to his ear. "No," he said, a slight smirk tugging the ends of his mustache up. "But if you travel across the moat and out to the graveyard on the highest hill next to the keep, you'll find her headstone."

I turned to Heath and mouthed, "What the hell does that mean?"

We couldn't ask Lumley, because he was already talking into the phone. From the sound of it, he was trying to reach the hotel manager, Arthur Crunn, and had gotten his voice mail. "Arthur, it's Inspector Lumley. You must call me back immediately. We've found a body in your moat, and I must speak with you at once."

Lumley hung up the phone and placed it back inside his pocket. He seemed to catch our expressions, because he said, "Don't tell me you've come all the way to Kidwellah without hearing of the ghosts in residence? I thought that was why all you Americans come here."

Heath and I both shook our heads. "We know very few specifics about who haunts this castle," I said without offering up any details about our TV show or our psychic abilities.

Lumley checked his watch and sighed. "Well, I've no time to explain the late Lady Catherine's appearance outside your room tonight, miss, but suffice it to say that there is nothing anyone can do to help her now. And if you'll excuse me, I must get back outside. If you happen to see Mr. Crunn, please send him immediately to the north side of the moat, all right?"

I nodded numbly and watched as the inspector strode away.

Heath and I stood there for a few beats trying to make sense of it all. At last he said, "I think we need to find Gopher. He should know more about this late Lady Catherine."

"Good plan," I said, truly shocked that I, of all people, hadn't figured out that the woman in the hallway was a ghost in the first place. Then again, I was operating on very little sleep and a major case of jet lag. "Do you know which room Gopher's in?" I asked Heath.

My sweetheart frowned. "No." Pulling out his cell phone again, he tried in vain to get it to turn on before asking me, "You don't happen to know Gopher's number by heart, do you?"

I shook my head. Heath looked around before he seemed to think of something and then he moved to the other side of the clerk's desk and opened up the logbook — apparently the hotel staff still did things the old-fashioned way, without computers.

"Should you be looking through that?" I asked nervously.

"Probably not, but it's the only way we'll know what room Gopher's in. Ah, here it is, room two-oh-two." Heath then picked up the phone receiver and dialed the number. I could hear the ring from the receiver Heath held to his ear, and then Gopher's raspy voice barked, "Yeah?"

"It's Heath. We've got a situation. You need to meet us in the lobby right now."

It took a little convincing to get our producer to cooperate, but finally he promised to meet us in the front hall in ten minutes. I thought we had a ten percent chance of seeing him, as I was sure Gopher would likely fall back asleep.

Heath made his way again over to the set of throne chairs, but I forced myself to stand. If I sat down, I knew I'd be out like a light.

About the time I was going to urge Heath to call Gopher again, a disheveled elderly man, probably in his mid-seventies, appeared at the top of the stairs wearing a blue silk robe, striped pajamas, and leather slippers. Gripping the railing, he made his way steadily down the steps and when at last he took his eyes off the stairs and spotted us, he appeared truly surprised that the front hall had two people in it, and he swiped a shaky hand through his unkempt hair. "Terribly sorry," he said when he arrived at the landing, and looked around as if expecting to see someone else in attendance. "Have you been waiting here long?"

"A little while," I said, thinking he must believe we were waiting for the desk clerk. "I'm M. J. Holliday and this is Heath Whitefeather. We're guests at the hotel too."

The elder man's brow rose. "Too? Oh, no, miss, you misunderstand. I'm Arthur Crunn, the hotel manager. I'm afraid I assumed you had just arrived and were looking for my clerk, Mr. Brown."

"No, sir," I said. "Mr. Brown checked us in several hours ago. We're the ones who called the police."

Mr. Crunn's eyes bulged a little and he appeared quite rattled. "Yes, I received a most distressing message from Inspector Lumley."

"He's outside, waiting for you, sir," I said.

Crunn ran another shaky hand through his hair and pulled at his robe. He appeared to be in no hurry to go out and meet the inspector. "Are you all right, sir?" Heath asked gently.

The older gentleman nodded but put two fingers to his lips. It was a moment before he could speak. "The inspector said something about a drowning in the moat...."

"Yes, I'm afraid so," I said. "He told us that his constable discovered the body and called in the inspector. Lumley told us that if we saw you to tell you to go out to meet him on the north side of the moat, where they discovered the poor man."

Crunn's face had now become quite pale and I was afraid he might faint. Moving subtly to his side, I placed my arm under his to steady him and said, "Would you like us to go with you to meet the inspector?"

At first the older gentleman shook his head, but it wasn't a very convincing headshake. "That's very kind of you," he said hoarsely, "but I believe I'll manage."

Heath put a hand on my back. "I'll go with him, Em," he whispered.

But I didn't want to be left alone. The old castle was suddenly giving me the creeps. Also, it occurred to me a little belatedly that if the dead man in the moat had drowned, it was quite possible that he hadn't been able to cross over. If I could locate his spirit nearby, I might be able to quietly assist his journey to the other side. "We'll all go," I said, looping my arm through Arthur's. "Come on, Mr. Crunn. We'll keep you company. And if it gets to be too much, you just give us the word and we'll bring you back inside the castle, all right?"

Crunn gave a pat to my hand. He seemed a kindly elderly man, and I had a soft spot for kindly elderly men. "Thank you, Miss Holliday. You and Mr. Whitefeather are most considerate."

We escorted the hotel manager outside into the damp morning and I realized there was a fair amount of fog settling in. Although I hadn't looked at a clock since being awakened by the inspector, I still estimated that it was somewhere around four thirty or five o'clock in the morning.

We moved through the mist, making our way nearly soundlessly across the cobblestones. Crunn led us across the inner courtyard to a small wood door set to the left side of the main keep that was cleverly obscured by the surrounding ivy and architecture. If Crunn hadn't stopped in front of it, I'd never have known it was there. "We can take this across to the north side of the moat," he said, fishing around in his robe for a set of keys, which he used to unlock the door.

Once he had the creaky door open and reached for a light switch on the inside wall, Heath and I moved through to enter a low-hanging tunnel. I felt goose bumps immediately line my arms as the cold dampness of the stone walls seeped through my clothing. The tunnel was very poorly lit by only three dim bulbs and I could see that both Heath and Crunn had to bend at the waist so as not to bump their heads on the ceiling.

After moving a few feet forward, I could see that the floor was actually a bridge with a very low stone wall only about two feet high, and below the bridge the slight gurgling of the moat echoed against the walls. It wasn't far across, but I was anxious to get over the bridge and back out into the open. The tunnel seriously gave me the creeps and I didn't like it. By the looks of Heath's face when I turned back to catch his eye, he didn't like it one bit either.

Finally we came to another door; this Crunn unlocked from the inside, and we stepped through it to head up a series of stairs. At the top of the stairs was yet one more door, which Crunn also unlocked, and we were at last back out into the open. The early-morning mist obscured most of the surrounding area, but I guessed that we were at the far end of the castle, very near Lake Byrn y Bach.

From here Crunn led us over a larger bridge that extended over the rest of the moat, then down a narrow path, which curled to the left to follow the round exterior wall of the castle and the curve of the moat. At last we spotted an array of lights, which led us to a small cluster of people at the edge of the moat.

As we approached, I could see several cars parked nearby. One looked to be an ambulance, and another was a marked police car. Two more were small compact vehicles that I assumed belonged to the inspector and perhaps to the coroner.

When we were within about ten yards of the lights, the mist swirled and I was able to pick out the inspector from the other people gathered there. He saw us and waved impatiently to Arthur, who quickened his step, and we did too.

As we came abreast of the inspector, I kept my focus on Crunn. He was trembling outright now and he'd gone so pale that I was starting to really worry about the possibility of him collapsing. I reached out and took his hand to help steady him, and he cast me a grateful glance before focusing on Lumley. "Jasper," he said, "is it really true? Has someone fallen into our moat?"

The inspector waved a hand to an area just behind him, and reflexively I leaned out around Crunn to take a look.

There on a black tarp looking bloated and blue was the figure of a young man with bright red hair, pouty lips, and eyes wide open. I put a hand to my mouth and had to steel myself. The sight was horrible.

There was a gasp to my left and I realized that Mr. Crunn was vigorously shaking his head back and forth, as if he was willing the sight away. "It can't be!" he said in a voice barely audible.

I felt a nudge on my elbow and looked away from

Arthur to see Heath tugging at me. "Merrick!" he mouthed. "The clerk!"

My eyes widened and I looked back again to the figure on the tarp. We were close enough not to be hampered by the mist, and the body was well lit by the portable lights set up for the police and the coroner. When I took a second look, I realized Heath was right. Disguised by the blue of his skin and the bloating to his body, he was hard at first to identify, but that shock of red hair and the set to his chin were enough to convince me. Well, that and the reaction of poor Mr. Crunn. "That's my clerk," Arthur said, pointing feebly at the body. "Merrick Brown. He was supposed to be on duty overnight."

"What time did his shift begin?" the inspector asked him, scribbling furiously into his notebook.

"He was on a twelve-hour shift," Crunn said. "Six p.m. to six a.m."

"That's quite a long stretch to be on duty," the inspector said, and I noted the hint of disapproval in his tone.

"He's allowed a cot in the hallway behind the clerk station. He can sleep the whole night through if none of the guests require his services. It's often a very quiet shift, and Merrick prefers it. Er . . . preferred it." Arthur seemed unable to tear his eyes away from the tarp, and as the inspector was opening his mouth to ask him another question, the poor old man swayed on his feet, and his hand fell out of mine. In an instant Heath had him under the armpits, holding him up when Crunn's knees gave out from under him.

Inspector Lumley stepped in front of me to help Heath ease Arthur to the ground. "Arthur? Are you all right?" Lumley asked as Crunn's head wobbled on his neck.

I wanted to yell at him. Of course he wasn't! I looked around and saw that one of the men standing nearby wore a paramedic's uniform. "Hey!" I called to him. He looked up from the body and noticed Arthur sitting dully on the ground. He was in motion in an instant.

I stepped out of the way and so did Heath, and we watched while the paramedic tended to Crunn, who was now hyperventilating and complaining that he felt dizzy.

Lumley appeared rattled by the fact that Arthur had gotten so upset, and I could see a bit of guilt cross his countenance as he helped the medic tend to the older man.

After taking Crunn's vitals, the paramedic said, "He's having a panic attack, Inspector."

Lumley's frown deepened. "Arthur," he said as the medic placed an oxygen mask over the old man's nose and mouth. "I'm sorry for all this distress. Is your sister at the castle?"

Crunn was taking heaving breaths and holding tight to the oxygen mask. He lifted one hand and it shook violently as he attempted to point to the keep. The inspector seemed to take that for a yes and stood up to call to a round man with droopy eyes and a series of double chins, wearing a constable's uniform, standing nearby. "Niles," he said. "Go inside and see if you can rouse Mrs. Farnsworth, Mr. Crunn's sister."

"What room is she in?" Niles said.

Arthur reached up and grabbed my hand. I bent down and he managed to gasp, "Kit . . . chen."

I placed a hand on his shoulder. "Do you want me to go with the constable to help find your sister?"

Arthur gave one slow nod.

I stood and motioned for the constable to come with me. Heath tucked in behind us as we backtracked along the same route we'd come by, moving up the hill again at a faster pace this time. I was terribly worried about that poor old man. I wondered if the sight of his deceased clerk had perhaps been too much of a strain on his heart, and I was also a little furious at the inspector for exposing a fragile elderly gentleman to such a grim and distressing thing.

We crossed the bridge without a word and I was the first to reach the door. Arthur had left it unlocked, but the moisture was making it stick a little and I struggled with it until Heath's strong arms wrapped around mine and he helped me. The door gave a tremendous squeak and I looked back at him gratefully.

I went through first, followed by the constable and then Heath. We descended the stairs and went through the next doorway without incident, then out onto the low bridge that spanned the moat. The bridge was quite narrow and we could travel across it only one at a time. As I took my first several steps onto the stone structure, I could feel my breath quicken.

It took me a moment to realize that the farther into the tunnel I went, the more distressed I was becoming. I felt as if the low-hanging ceiling was starting to close in on me. At first I tried to tamp the feeling down. Traveling through tunnellike enclosures has never been a pleasant experience for me. I'd nearly met my maker in one or two of them in fact.

So it was no wonder that I was having this reaction. But the more I tried to calm my nerves, the more apparent it was that the anxiety mounting inside of me may not have been exclusively due to the architecture.

About five yards onto the bridge, I came to an abrupt halt, which caused the constable to bump into me. "Sorry," he muttered, and I could feel him waiting impatiently for me to continue.

"M. J.?" Heath said a bit farther back. "You okay?"

I nodded out of habit, but the truth was that I wasn't okay at all. Goose pimples were lining my arms and the air in the tunnel had suddenly become so cold that I could clearly see my breath in the dim light. "Something's wrong," I whispered.

"Eh?" asked the constable. "What's that?"

"Em?" Heath called again.

I backed up, or tried to, but the policeman was still

right behind me and we bumped together again. "You all right, miss?" he asked.

My heart was pounding in my chest and my sixth sense was going haywire. Something was in the tunnel with us. Something bad.

Behind me I heard Heath's sharp intake of air. He'd sensed it too. "We need to find another route," he said softly.

"What's the matter with you lot?" the impatient constable snapped. "It's straight through here to the main keep. Just carry on, miss, and we'll be there in a moment."

"No," I said, pushing back against him. "We're not going across this bridge." All I wanted to do was get out of that damn enclosed space.

I could feel the constable's impatience as he resisted my attempts to push him back the way we'd come. "Listen 'ere," he said, but the moment the words were out of his mouth, there was a sound . . . like a hiss at the other end of the bridge, and I could feel a rippling sensation all along my skin. The atmosphere had just gone from really bad to way worse.

The sound affected all of us the same way; no one moved or said another word for several seconds. Finally I risked an anxious "Heath?"

"I'm right here, but we need to get out of here. Now."

Behind me I could feel the constable's weight shift slightly away from me, so either he was inching back or Heath was physically pulling him. And for the briefest moment I actually felt like we were gonna get out of there without the evil spirit noticing, but that was quickly quashed when another rather unearthly sound reached our ears. I'd call it laughter, but it was hardly that. It was the cackling sound of a lunatic and it filled the tunnel from floor to ceiling, echoing and bouncing off the walls and our bodies.

It grew louder too, and soon it was at such an awful volume that I reached up to cover my ears. *"Stop!"* I shouted when even that became unbearable, and the most unusual thing happened: The cackling ceased and once again we were plunged into eerie silence save for the quiet lapping of the water beneath the bridge.

"What the bloody hell was *that*?" the constable squeaked.

"Nothing good," I replied, once again pushing against him as I tried to back up away from the source, which I knew remained ominously in front of us. "Move!" I growled when the constable stood rooted to the spot by his own fear.

He had taken one step back when all of a sudden a figure appeared just fifteen feet or so from us. I let out a startled squeak, as did the man behind me.

Out of the corner of my eye I saw the constable raise his flashlight and illuminate a set of tattered rags, which hung loosely about the gaunt figure of a woman with pale white skin, marred by several long scars, and when the beam of the light shone on the woman's face, we all gasped anew.

Wide wild eyes stared at us with an intensity that chilled me to the bone. Her long hair was so matted, tangled, and dirty that it was hard to tell what color it was, and as I stared at her in shock, a wicked smile spread across her evil face, revealing a rotted row of brown teeth and cracked, bleeding lips.

I backed up into the constable again, but he wouldn't budge—likely so terrified by the horrible figure in front of us that he'd gone temporarily immobile.

The hag's eyes narrowed and she trained her evil stare at me before she strode purposely forward to stop just a few feet from us. I could smell the fetid odor of her breath and I nearly gagged on it. She spoke then, her voice raspy and thick, but I couldn't understand a single word she said. When I didn't respond, she lifted a thick black chain that I hadn't noticed she'd been holding. I stared at it for a few beats before inching my own hand up to move the beam of the constable's light along the black metal as it trailed to the floor and away about six or seven feet to attach to a metal collar secured about the neck of a Merrick Brown who looked as frightened as I felt. Maybe even more so.

I was so stunned to see him standing there that for several seconds my brain couldn't quite make sense of it. He seemed to be struggling with the circumstance of being there too, because in a desperate tone he asked, "What's happened to me?"

At this the haggard woman in front of us whirled around and flew at him; crossing back across the bridge, she charged Merrick, who cowered at her approach but did little else to defend himself as she raised her hand and smacked him with far more force than I could've imagined she was able to wield. She then uttered something guttural and spat at him and he shuffled back a few paces. Behind me Heath yelled out, "Hey! Leave him alone!" and the crazed woman merely looked over her shoulder and smiled wickedly before smacking Merrick hard again.

I wanted to do something to stop the assault, but my brain was finally putting the mystery of Merrick's appearance into place. "Heath!" I yelled. "Grab the constable and run!"

I then turned and shoved the constable so hard that he nearly fell backward. Heath reached out at just the right moment to catch him by the shoulder and pull him along, and we moved swiftly toward the stairs. *"Go, go, go, go, go!"* I shouted, feeling the presence of the hag bearing down on me, and just as Heath made it through the doorway, I felt her grab hold of the collar of my sweater and yank me back so hard that I lost my footing.

I fell to the stone floor, landing flat on my back, and the impact knocked the wind right out of me. I reached out blindly and tried to call out to Heath, but I had no air. A freezing cold hand latched on to my upper arm and gave a tremendous pull and then the hag's face filled my vision, her eyes wicked and cruel. I tried to swat at her, but she ducked my hands, squeezing my arm even harder and giving me a swift kick in the ribs to boot.

"Heath!" I managed, and in an instant he was there. I felt his strong arms grab hold of my legs, giving me a good tug out of the clutches of the spook before he lifted me into his arms, hugging me tightly to pivot around and push me forward toward the door. Somehow I got my feet underneath me and limped quickly to the steps, but just as I'd made it up the first two stairs, I felt Heath's presence at my back suddenly vanish.

Whirling around, I saw him being dragged away by the hag, back onto the bridge. The scene seemed impossible — the hag was barely as tall as I was, and yet she was overpowering Heath like he was a small child. He struggled mightily, but her grip on him was too firm and he couldn't keep her from pulling him backward onto the bridge.

I made to jump back down the stairs, my arms outstretched to help, but the door slammed shut in my face. Frantically, I grabbed for the handle, yanking hard on it, but it was stuck fast. *"Heath!"* I screamed, pounding on the door. I could hear his strangled voice from the other side as he struggled with the ghostly hag. "Heath! Heath! *Heath!"* I cried, banging on the door and pulling at the handle, but it was no use. The door was locked tight and I couldn't get through.

And then, above my cries and pounding I heard a loud splash, like someone being plunged into the water. I gasped and stopped pounding on the door to press my ear against it. Through the wood I could hear the sounds of more splashing, as if someone was flailing around in the water, and intuitively I knew that Heath had been pulled or had fallen over the side of the low stone wall. In a state of panic I flew up the stairs, nearly knocking the constable over in my haste, and I moved to the railing of the bridge, searching the black water for any sign of Heath. But there was no sign of him.

"Heath!" I shouted. I heard faint splashing sounds, which were coming from inside the outer wall of the castle. From up here I could see a low overhang where the moat flowed freely underneath the outer wall. My chest tightened. Heath was athletic and strong and a solid swimmer to boot, but that splashing was taking on a frantic rhythm and I had the most horrible feeling that he was right then in the fight of his life.

The constable suddenly appeared next to me and shone his flashlight at the dark water along the wall. "Where is he?" he demanded.

I didn't answer. Instead I kicked off my boots, tore off my sweater, and grabbed for his light (praying that the thing was waterproof). I then pulled myself up onto the lip of the bridge wall, and dived in.

Chapter 3

The water was freezing. I came to the surface gasping for air and trying to clear my head from the shock of its icy feel. "What do you think you're *doing*?" the constable shouted.

I ignored him.

With effort I raised the hand holding his torch and found that it was in fact waterproof. Gripping it tightly so as not to lose it, I pointed it straight ahead toward the wall and began to take several breaststrokes forward. "Heh ... Heh ... Heh ... *Heath!*" I cried, my stuttering voice echoing loudly back and forth over the stones and the water.

"*Em!*" I heard to my left, but the call was weak and garbled, like Heath was calling to me with a mouth full of water.

I changed direction and headed straight for where I thought he was, which was somewhere under the bridge. I came to a pylon and raised the flashlight toward it. It seemed to mark a narrow arch just big enough for a small boat to get through. I swam as fast as I could through the arch and aimed the beam of my flashlight into the dark interior. "Heath!" I cried again when I saw nothing but walls and water all around me.

There was no answer. My teeth began to click together and the frigid water seemed to seep through my skin and into my bones. I was so cold I could barely take in a full breath. "*Heeeeath!*" I shouted desperately, spinning in a circle searching for him.

And then I felt something brush against my foot. Reflexively, I kicked out and pushed away from the spot where I was treading water, but then I aimed the flashlight down and I saw something moving through the murky water. I was so scared that I stopped paddling and began to sink, but then the murky object took on a more defined shape and I realized what was moving around in the water. It was Heath and the hag.

Taking as big a breath as I could manage, I dived under the surface and swam as fast as I could toward the object. As I drew closer, the two of them became even more defined, and my heart raced with panic as I noticed how blue Heath's face was. His eyes were open and his hands were at his throat, pulling at the bony arm wrapped tightly about him.

I shoved the flashlight into the neck of my undershirt and the sports bra I had on before reaching out for Heath, managing to grab on to his foot. I clawed forward with my other hand and grabbed on to his pant leg and reached one last time to grab the waist of his jeans; then I reversed direction and kicked for all I was worth.

My efforts were met with considerable resistance and I didn't know if I had the strength or the breath to fight against it. My lungs were protesting mightily and I had to fight the urge to inhale. I kicked and kicked and kicked again, straining with all my might toward the air above, which I prayed was only a few feet away.

Heath suddenly jerked in a most unnatural way, and

in the back of my mind I had a thought that his body might be seizing. I kicked again and again, fighting for every inch as stars began to pop and sparkle around the edges of my vision. My lungs begged again and again to inhale, and I clenched my stomach muscles to keep myself from sucking in a mouthful of water.

Heath's body seized again and I almost lost my grip, but at last with one final kick my head broke the surface and I took in a huge breath of air. Panting and nearly faint with exhaustion, I treaded water while I pulled up on Heath's body to wrap my arm across his chest and lift him onto my torso, rolling onto my back to give him air. The flashlight was partially buried by his form , but it still gave off enough glow for me to dimly see the side of Heath's face as it too broke the surface. His eyes were open, staring sightlessly out into space, while his complexion was a frightful blue, and worst of all, he wasn't breathing.

I was shivering now so violently that I didn't know if I could hold on to him, and my hands had gone almost completely numb, so I wrapped my free hand across his torso too and scissor kicked my way over to the wall, searching for the archway.

At first I couldn't find it, but then I realized I could hear shouting from somewhere above and I followed the noise along the wall to the arch.

With nearly the last of my strength I moved through to the open air and out from under the bridge just as someone yelled, "There! She's there!"

A moment later there was a loud splash right next to me, but I was so numb with cold and fatigue that I could scarcely pay attention to it until I felt a hand on my shoulder. I turned slightly and saw the strained expression of the constable attempting to wrap a rope about me. "Take ... Heath ... ," I gasped, feeling myself starting to slip away. I just wanted to close my eyes and rest for a minute.

"Stay with me, miss!" the constable yelled. "Stay with me!"

I pushed my lids open but they slid closed again. My grip on Heath loosened. I felt the water come up over my chin and mouth, but I no longer cared. I was slipping into the darkness. *"Miss!"* the constable shouted again, but I was already gone.

I woke up in an ambulance. It was the sound of the siren that pulled me out of unconsciousness. Those European sirens will do that to you. "Make it stop," I whispered, struggling to open my eyes.

"There, there," said an unfamiliar voice. "Just lie still, miss, and we'll take right good care of you."

Feebly I managed to open one eye. A very kind-looking black man with gleaming white teeth dressed in a blue jacket with a red patch on the arm smiled down at me. "Nice to have you back in the land of the living," he said jovially.

I nearly smiled in return, but then the memory of what'd happened barreled into my thoughts. "Heath!"

My voice sounded muffled and it was a moment before I realized my mouth and nose were covered by an oxygen mask.

The paramedic looked quizzically at me as he laid a calming hand on my shoulder. "Lie still, please."

I ignored him, struggling to sit up, but I was covered in several blankets and was frankly too weak to get very far. "My boyfriend!" I said to him, pleading for him to tell me that Heath was okay. But then I remembered Heath's blue face as it emerged from the water, and the fact that he hadn't been breathing, and then . . . that I had let go of him at the end.

"He's in the other ambulance," the paramedic said. "We sent him ahead of you. He should beat us to hospital by several minutes, I believe."

I blinked back the tears that had suddenly clouded my vision. It took me a moment to take in what the paramedic said. Heath was in an ambulance. He'd gone ahead of me to the hospital. They wouldn't have taken him there if there hadn't been a chance that he could be revived, right?

"He wasn't breathing," I whispered while the kindly paramedic jotted down some notes onto a clipboard he'd just picked up.

He looked at me then, and I saw sympathy in his eyes. "I think they got him back right after we pulled up," he told me.

My lower lip quivered and for a minute I couldn't speak. A few years earlier I'd pulled another boyfriend out of the water after he'd almost drowned too, and I didn't know if I could be that lucky to have two lovers survive such similar near-death experiences.

The paramedic set aside his clipboard and took my hand in his, squeezing it to let me know he cared. "There, there, miss. Not to worry. We've got one of the best hospitals in all of Wales just a few kilometers from Kidwellah. They'll take such good care of you, you'll feel like you're on holiday."

I swallowed hard and shivered under the blankets. I wasn't going to panic until I got some sort of official word that there was a need to worry. Heath was young, strong, and in amazingly good physical shape. He'd come back. I knew it.

As my fears subsided, I seemed to sink into the cold, however, and my thoughts became foggy. It was almost as if once the adrenaline had worn off, I stopped being able to think clearly. I shivered and shivered, and the man attending to me put on another blanket. "I know you're probably freezing," he said. "Just a few more minutes and we'll be able to warm you back up."

I nodded dully but I could feel my lids blink heavily. I wanted to drift back off to sleep.

"Stay awake, miss," the paramedic commanded. My eyes snapped open again, but it was hard to fight the crushing fatigue. To help me stay awake the paramedic began to ask me questions. What was my name? Where was I from? How old was I? What was my birthday?

My answers were difficult to form, both in my brain and as I spoke them. Nothing wanted to cooperate, not my mind and not my body.

At last the ambulance slowed and made a tight left turn. As we straightened out, the siren cut off. A moment later we stopped and the doors were flung open.

My personal information and my vitals were rattled off and I had a thought that the paramedic had said I was from New York, which was wrong, I knew, but my brain was even more fuzzy now and I was even less able to form coherent thought.

The stretcher I was lying on was quickly wheeled through the brightly lit corridors. I watched the fluorescent lights scroll by, too weary to pick my head up and far too cold to do more than just lie there and shiver violently.

At last we came to a row of curtains and one was pulled aside while I was swiveled 180 degrees and backed against a wall. A woman in pink scrubs who'd walked alongside the stretcher as it was wheeled through the halls placed a thermometer into my ear. It beeped and she said, "Thirty-two-point-three." I think she must have seen my fear and confusion because she added, "That's ninety-point-three for you Americans. Far too cold for your own good, lass. But we'll warm you up in a jiff, not to worry."

No wonder I was freezing. My temperature was crazy low. Or was it? What was it supposed to be again? I couldn't remember.

The three blankets covering me were lifted and several nurses and aides got to work pulling me out of my wet clothes. I clenched my teeth together to try to stop them from chattering, because even though my clothes had been wet, they were still something against my bare skin to help keep in what little heat I had left.

At last I was naked and an odd sort of thin, aluminum-looking blanket with wires attached was placed over me. The blanket was very warm and I closed my eyes with relief. I ignored all the chatter going on around me, and allowed the doctors and nurses to do what they needed to do to warm me up without protest.

An IV was placed into both of my arms and I felt the odd sensation of warm saline dripping into my veins. My body and sides were then lined with full bags of heated saline and slowly the violent shivers subsided. That foggy confused feeling I'd had in the ambulance also lessened and at last I could focus on the doctor hovering above me as he asked me my name.

"M. J.," I told him weakly. "Holliday."

"And what day is today?" he asked, reaching out to gently probe my head for bumps or abrasions.

I sighed. "No idea."

He squinted down at me. "Did you knock your head when you went into the water?"

"No," I said, working hard to form the words because physically it was difficult to talk or even move. "Travel. Lots. Tuesday?"

He smiled. "You're either a very good guesser, Miss Holliday, or you've managed to work it out. Today is in fact Tuesday."

I nodded but the truth was that I didn't give a damn what day of the week it was. "My boyfriend. Here?"

"And where were you born?" the doctor said next, ignoring me.

I wormed one arm out from under the blankets and warm saline to take hold of his wrist so that he could focus fully on what I was going to say, and the effort gave my mouth a little extra to form the words. "Will answer questions, but first . . . need to know . . . my boyfriend?"

The good doctor's gaze settled on the hand latched to his wrist. "That's a strong grip you've got there, Miss Holliday."

I didn't let go. "His name . . . is Heath. Whitefeather. Please?"

The doctor leaned away from me to glance around the curtain before focusing on me again. "He's being attended to by my colleague, Dr. Patel. But I believe Mr. Whitefeather is stable."

I let go of his wrist and closed my eyes. It was a moment before I could speak. "Valdosta, Georgia," I said when I'd gotten hold of my emotions again.

"I'm sorry?"

"Where I was born. Sweet, beautiful Valdosta, Georgia. U.S.A."

An hour later the curtain to my little area was pulled back and in came my producer carrying a large paper sack. He took one stunned look at me and said, "Shit, M. J.! What the hell happened?"

"Well, good morning, Gopher. Nice to see you too, but please, don't worry yourself. I'm fine. Just a touch of hypothermia. Nothing too serious other than nearly dying and ending up here."

Gopher's expression turned to one I'd never seen him wear before—contrite. "Sorry," he apologized, setting down the sack on the end of my bed before stepping all the way forward to me. He then did something else that was most unusual; he took my hand and squeezed it. "Hospitals make me nervous."

"What's in the sack?"

"Your sweater and your boots," he said. "Thought you might need them when they let you out of here."

I thanked him and then asked, "Have you seen Heath yet?" Even though my doctor had assured me that Heath's condition was stable, I wasn't going to believe it until I actually laid eyes on him.

"Not yet. They wouldn't let me into his room."

I bit my lip. "We can't see him?"

Gopher shook his head. "No, *I* can't see him. You're his emergency contact, so whenever they let you up out of bed, you can go see him."

That took me by surprise. Heath and I were getting pretty serious, but I hadn't thought that he'd made me his emergency contact. The revelation caused me to smile. "How'd you get in to see me?" I asked, wondering at it because Gilley was my emergency contact.

"I lied," he said. "I told them I was Gilley Gillespie. Your cousin."

That made me chuckle. "Where is Gil, anyway?"

"Still asleep, I think." Gopher let go of my hand to pull up a chair. "I knocked on his door a couple of times and called him on his phone, but you know how hard he sleeps."

That I did know. Gilley was nearly impossible to wake up once he'd gone into a deep slumber. His mother used to keep a set of cymbals handy for those occasions when he wouldn't wake up for school. To this day Gil can't listen to the sound of a marching band without flinching. "Did they give you any information on Heath's condition?"

"They only say that he's stable."

I frowned. That's all they'd tell me too. "Maybe I should call the nurse and have her take these IVs out." I was still pretty cold, but I figured I could warm up on my own.

But Gopher was shaking his head. "Your temp is still too low, M. J. I already asked the nurse about you and she said you had at least another hour or two to go before they'd check your temp again. You have to be above thirty-five degrees Celsius, or ninety-five degrees Fahrenheit, before they'll unhook you."

"What's my temp right now?" I asked.

Gopher squinted at one of the machines above my right shoulder and took out his phone to tap at the screen. "You're at thirty-four degrees Celsius, so that's . . . about ninety-three degrees Fahrenheit."

I glared at Gopher. I knew it wasn't his fault, but the situation was still frustrating. He smiled as if he knew exactly what I was thinking. "Tell me what happened."

I rubbed my eyes wearily. The jet lag and all the events of that morning were really taking their toll on me. "It was all a crazy chain of events, buddy."

"So start from the beginning."

By the time I'd finished telling Gopher exactly what'd happened from when I'd awakened that morning to the sounds of a woman crying outside my door all the way to how I'd ended up here, the nurse had come back in to check the thermometer and pronounced me warm enough to be released. As soon as I ate a bit of breakfast, that is.

I looked pleadingly at my producer to say something to the nurse so that I could go see Heath, but he seemed to be absorbed in thought, processing what I'd told him. It wasn't that Gopher didn't believe me; it's that he'd witnessed enough freaky stuff to really know the danger we'd just landed ourselves in. Trouble is, when it comes to facing down murderous spooks for a good bit of footage, Gopher is the first to volunteer us for duty.

"So you're saying this ghost actually tried to drown Heath?" Gopher asked the minute the nurse was out of hearing range again.

I hugged the large bag of hot saline she'd left me with and wondered if I'd ever feel really warm again. "Yes," I said. "She pulled him into the water and by the time I got to them, she'd already dragged him about ten feet under the surface."

Gopher turned a bit pale. "She's *that* strong?"

I knew what he meant. Heath was six feet of solid lean muscle. He was young and powerful in his own right, and a great swimmer, as we'd both watched him do lap after lap to get some exercise in the pool at the hotel we'd stayed in during our recent trip to Dunkirk. "She is," I told him. And then something else quite troubling came to mind.

"What?" Gopher asked, reading my expression.

I bit my lip. "I don't think Heath was her first victim of the morning."

Gopher cocked his head. "Meaning?"

"You heard about the clerk who'd checked us in, right? Merrick Brown was found drowned this morning, his body floating in the moat."

"Yeah ... that was tough to hear. I mean, he seemed like such a nice guy."

"Well, I saw him."

"You saw him ... where?"

"I saw him chained to that hag on the bridge inside the castle wall overhanging the moat. Merrick had this metal collar around his neck, and he was attached to that awful spook that tried to drown Heath."

Gopher squinted his eyes at me. "Come again?"

I sighed and was about to explain when the curtain was pulled aside again and a hospital worker entered the area with a tray of food. "Here we are," she said merrily, setting the tray down on one of those sliding bedside tables that scoot over the gurney and allow you to eat.

Gopher got out of her way as she slid the table into place near my waist. "You'll want to eat all that up, miss. Your body burned a few extra calories this morning and this will help set you back to rights."

With that, she gave us both a bright smile and exited. I lifted the plastic dome covering the dish and discovered a steaming bowl of oatmeal with a side of toast. Next to that was a dish of fruit and rounding out the meal was a fresh cup of tea.

Quite suddenly, I was famished. Diving in, I explained to Gopher what I thought I'd seen. "I think she drowned

Merrick," I said after taking a large bite of the oatmeal, which was slightly overcooked, but laced with enough cinnamon to make up for it.

"After she let go of Heath?"

I shook my head. "No, buddy. Before. I'm positive it was his ghost on the bridge with her."

Gopher's mouth fell open. "No way," he said, and I could see the gears working as he thought that through. "We've got to get some film of him!"

I leveled my gaze at my producer. "We're *not* doing that."

Gopher looked affronted. "Why not?"

"Because it's unseemly, Gopher! I mean, the man *just* died and you want to go shoot his ghost like it's some sort of circus act? Jesus, what the hell is wrong with you?!"

"M. J.," Gopher said, in that way that suggested I was about to get a lecture, "getting footage of ghosts is what we *do*, remember? And if we don't get something really good to show the network brass soon, then neither you nor I will be *doing* much of anything for a while."

"What about his family?" I protested. God, could Gopher really be *that* insensitive?

"No one said they had to watch the show, M. J."

I shook my head in disgust. Apparently he could. "You're a piece of work, you know that?"

"Oh, well, *excuse me* for trying to keep us all employed," he shot back testily. He then got up from his chair and moved to the curtain. I'd struck a nerve. "I'll be in the waiting room," he said tersely. "Have the nurse call me when you're ready to head back to the castle."

He left in short order and I let out a sigh. I knew that Gopher received a daily phone call from one of the network execs wanting to know how our shoots were coming along. Gopher had fought like hell to get our first two episodes released from the original network that'd hired us, but so far, they were holding on to the rights pretty tightly, which meant that we'd been filming for a few months now and had only a precious few good episodes under our belts, certainly not enough to keep our ratings above the cancellation bar for the whole season.

Without him saying as much, I could tell that Gopher thought this could be our last ghostbust if we didn't shoot something pretty spectacular here in Wales.

I also knew even without asking that there'd be no way that the network brass would let us come off this location and go find another. In fact, if they learned what'd happened to Heath that morning, they might pull the plug anyway for insurance purposes.

No, it was either continue with our plans to investigate the ghosts of Kidwellah Castle or go home and file for unemployment. I could always return to doing readings for clients and trying to eke out a little extra cash conducting local ghostbusts from my home base in Boston, but that would mean saying good-bye to Heath, who'd most certainly head back to his home in New Mexico.

"Dammit," I swore as I swirled the rest of my oatmeal. I hated being caught between a murderous ghost and a hard place. I lifted my chin and eyed the curtain moodily. I didn't want to make this decision alone, and quite possibly it wasn't even mine to make.

After slurping down the rest of my breakfast as fast as I could, I rang for the nurse. She came and pronounced me fit to discharge. She then helped me get dressed, and I was gratefully surprised to discover that my clothes had been thoughtfully dried by the hospital staff, and even though my jeans and undershirt smelled a little musty, I was glad to put on something warm.

Once dressed I felt close to normal, but still chilled through, and the nurse advised me that was likely to persist for another few hours. "Find a nice cozy fire and sit near it for the rest of the day, Miss Holliday. You'll be back to feeling yourself by morning."

"Thank you. You've been really kind and I appreciate

it," I told her, pulling on my boots. "Can you please tell me where I might find the other patient from Kidwellah? The young man with the name Heath Whitefeather."

"Come with me," she said with a wink. "I'll show you the way."

I followed behind her anxiously. Until I saw my sweetheart with my own two eyes, I wasn't going to be satisfied that he was okay.

We made our way out of the curtained area and down a long corridor before we turned left and stopped at an elevator. "He's been moved up to the second floor," she said, pressing the button.

As we went in and the door shut, I asked, "How long will he have to stay here?"

"Oh, that I don't know, miss. You'll have to ask his nurse on two."

I tapped my foot until the doors opened again and we headed down the corridor, where my nurse stopped at room 221 and knocked gently on the door. "Em?" I heard from inside.

That brought me up short. Somehow he knew it was me. Were we a good match or what?

The nurse opened the door and I poked my head in. Heath lay there covered with the same bags of warm saline and extra blankets that had covered me downstairs.

"How'd you know it was me?" I asked.

He looked at me dully and blinked in a slow sluggish way. "Gramps," he said, pointing to a corner of the room. My eyes flickered there and I saw a small circle of what looked like vapor expanding and contracting. "He told me you were on your way up."

The nurse giggled and laid a gentle hand on my shoulder. "He was a few degrees colder than you when he came to hospital, Miss Holliday. He's still a wee bit daffy, I'm afraid, but as he warms up, he'll come round, so not to worry."

I smiled. If only she knew that Heath wasn't nearly as out of it as he seemed. I thanked the nurse for all her kindness again before stepping into the room to close the door behind me. "Hi, sweetie," I said shyly, feeling my eyes mist. I wasn't normally this sentimental, but seeing him alive and well and breathing was such a relief that I was overcome.

In return Heath offered me a weak smile and with effort he lifted his arms and said, "Get over here, woman."

I moved swiftly to his bed and threw my arms around him. For a moment we just held each other. "You gave me a hell of a scare," I told him.

"Look at it from my side."

I squeezed tighter. "You remember what happened?"

"Yeah." For a minute he was quiet and then he added, "They don't tell you how much it hurts."

I lifted my chin to look at him. I hadn't known he was in pain. "You're hurting? Tell me where, honey, and I'll ring for the nurse."

He shook his head, and I knew that I'd misunderstood. "Drowning. It hurts like a mother."

I swallowed hard. Jesus. Heath had *actually* drowned.

Behind me I could feel the presence of his grandfather come closer and then his voice filled my mind. *Thank you*, he said.

Don't mention it.

"Hey, Gramps," Heath said weakly.

I turned my attention back to him, and he seemed to be looking at something right over my shoulder. "You can see him?"

He nodded. "He's been hanging out with me ever since he pushed me back down."

I let go of Heath and moved to sit on the bed next to him. Taking his hand, which was ice-cold, I said, "He pushed you down?"

Heath nodded. "Yeah. I crossed over, Em. It was so cool."

I felt a terrible chill run down my spine. "You . . . crossed over?"

"Gramps was there," Heath continued, as if I hadn't spoken. His eyes were far away and there was the most peaceful smile on his face. "And my uncle Milt and aunt Bev. Oh, and my stepdad, Frank, and my real dad! I saw both of them."

I squeezed Heath's hand tightly. He was far too excited about having nearly died for my taste.

My sweetie closed his eyes and sighed contentedly. "I know we hear from spirits about how beautiful it is over there, but you know what? They don't tell you the half of it. It's like . . . amazing, Em."

I glanced nervously over my shoulder and saw the small circle of vapor hovering right next to us. *I don't like this,* I said in my mind.

He almost wouldn't go back, Sam Whitefeather replied. *It took both me and his two dads to get him back into his body.*

I had to swallow again. That meant that Heath had come really, *really* close to a true death, and that frightened me to the core.

Thank you, I told him, realizing I should have been the grateful one from the start.

It was a team effort, Sam replied, and I could hear his gentle chuckle along with it.

I eyed the temperature gauge next to Heath's bed. It read 30.8 degrees. They hadn't let me out of bed until my temp had been 35, and according to Gopher that was about 95 degrees Fahrenheit, which meant that Heath had been *cold* when they'd brought him in.

He shivered slightly while I sat next to him, and I let go of his hand and tucked it back under the blankets, pulling them up to his chin. He gave me a grateful smile and closed his eyes. "Man, I'm tired," he mumbled, and a moment later he was asleep.

I sat there for a long time, just watching him and letting a few tears fall too.

Sam Whitefeather hovered just behind me the whole time, and I knew that he understood what had me so undone. I was in love with his grandson and I'd nearly lost him to that bitch in the moat.

The longer I sat there, the more my emotions turned from fear and worry to anger and determination. At last I leaned down and kissed Heath's cheek, then headed out to get some answers.

Chapter 4

The first place I went looking was at the nurses' station. I found Heath's nurse, identified myself as his emergency contact, and she let me know that they were going to keep Heath there overnight. "There is the rare chance of an infection to the lungs," she explained. "He did take in quite a bit of water, Miss Holliday, and we want to make sure he doesn't develop a fever or pneumonia."

"Please keep him as long as you need to make sure he's okay," I told her, taking up a nearby pen and scrap of paper to jot down my phone number. "That's my cell number. Please call me with any new developments, and I'll be back later to check on Heath."

I then headed back downstairs and found my own nurse ready with my release papers. Gopher was watching a soccer match in the waiting room when I tapped him on the shoulder and motioned that we should go.

We didn't speak on the way outside and he waved down a taxi for us. For the first few miles in the back of the cab we ignored each other, but then I finally turned to him and said, "Okay."

"Okay what?"

"Okay, we'll shoot this bust on one condition."

Gopher raised a skeptical eyebrow. "Which is?"

"If you capture any footage of the poor clerk who drowned, you'll have to promise to scrap it." Gopher opened his mouth to protest, but I held up a finger and added, "I mean it. We are *not* shooting any footage of the ghost of any recently drowned victim. And I don't care if his family won't see the show or not. We've got to have *some* standard of decency!"

Gopher's eyes dropped to his lap. "M. J.," he said, "you just don't understand what kind of pressure—"

"Oh, I get it," I interrupted. "Trust me. I know the brass has been all over you about getting something scary on film, but you have to remember how dangerous this work is, buddy. We've all had our lives on the line a time or two, and this bust doesn't look like it's going to be any different. Which is why I'm putting my foot down. If you're going to ask me to risk my ass again, then we need to come to an understanding about what footage gets passed on to the network."

Gopher slouched in his seat and stared sullenly out the window. He didn't talk to me for several minutes and I had to work very hard to wait him out, but finally he turned to me and said, "Yeah. Okay."

"Okay what?" I wasn't trying to be difficult; I just wanted him to understand I wasn't going to sacrifice my ethics for ratings. Ever.

He glared at me. "I won't put anything you don't agree with on film."

My brow rose. "Really?"

Gopher rolled his eyes. "Yeah, really. But you guys better help me get something good to send to the network, M. J., or we can kiss this whole gig good-bye."

"Trust me," I assured him, "if I know this hag—

which, by now, I kinda think I do—she won't be camera shy."

The taxi stopped in front of the drawbridge and the driver said he didn't want to go across it. He was a local and had probably heard the stories of the ghost haunting the moat. We didn't argue with him, but I couldn't suppress a shiver or two about the thought of crossing on foot.

Gopher paid the cabbie and we got out of the car. He stuck close to me and we walked in the center of the wooden planks. My eyes darted about as I searched for any sign of the ghostly hag, but the day was bright and sunny and there was no sign of her anywhere. Not even my sixth sense picked her up, and I was relieved about that at least.

Gopher and I entered the large front door and found Arthur Crunn sweeping the main hall. He was so engaged in his work that he must not have heard us, because he jumped when I called to him. "Miss Holliday!" he said, setting aside the broom to hurry to my side. "Are you quite all right?"

"I'm fine," I assured him. "Thank you, Arthur. And how are you?"

He waved his hand dismissively. "As you know, I had a terrible fright this morning, but the doctor has seen me fit for duty." The kindly old man then looked past me as if searching for someone else. "How is Mr. White-feather?"

"He's still in the hospital, but he's recovering nicely."

Arthur shook his head from side to side. "I'm so sorry you've had such a run of awful luck on your first night with us. I've already spoken to the owner, and she has granted me permission to take care of any charges to your room for the duration of your stay."

"Thank you, sir. That's very nice of you," I said.

"Least we can do," he said with a cluck of his tongue. After I thanked him again, he said, "May I have the kitchen prepare you something to eat? I expect you'll want to retire to your room and I can have a tray sent up straightaway, if you'd like."

"Oh, no thank you, Arthur. I ate only a little while ago. But, about my room . . ."

"Yes?"

"Is it possible to move to another part of the castle?"

Arthur's eyes widened. "Your room, ma'am? Was there something wrong with it?"

I didn't want to blurt out that the hallway outside our door was haunted by a weeping ghost and something else that seemed even nastier, so I settled for another grudge I had with it. "Well, it's just that our room is really a hike from here. Do you have anything closer to the main hall?"

Arthur scratched his head. "But your room is right up those stairs and to the left, miss."

It was my turn to appear confused. "No, Mr. Crunn. Our room is way on the other side of the castle."

The hotel manager had the oddest reaction; he actually gasped and moved quickly away from us to the other side of the clerk station, where he turned the page in the ledger. "No," he said. "I assigned you room number two-oh-six, Miss Holliday."

I shook my head. "Merrick put us in the VIP section, on the other side of the castle, in room seventeen."

Crunn's face paled and I swear, he looked completely taken aback. "That's impossible. We have no VIP section."

I wanted to offer him proof, but I had nothing but my word, so I walked over to the desk and said, "I promise that's where he put us, sir. To get there from here, we had to go up those stairs, down that long hall to the end, through a locked door, then wind our way through the corridors to room seventeen."

"You went *through* the locked door?" the old man gasped.

Truthfully I was having a hard time figuring out his

reaction, so I just kept to my story and nodded my head. "Yes. Merrick gave us a key for it. He said it was to keep out the regular guests so that the VIP guests could enjoy their privacy."

Arthur's eyes widened even more. "But, as I said, Miss Holliday, the castle has only one section for guests, and no one is sent to that side of the castle . . . ever."

We both stared at each other in confusion for a few seconds when Crunn added, "Why in heaven's name would Merrick make up a VIP section and send you to an abandoned part of the castle that is strictly off-limits?"

I could only shrug. "I have no idea, sir."

"You say that section is off-limits?" Gopher asked. "Is there something wrong with that part of the castle?"

"Yes, indeed," Crunn said. "It's quite unsafe for guests of this establishment."

Crunn appeared quite rattled again, and I wondered what the heck was going on. But then I noticed that Crunn seemed to be holding something else back, and I guessed what. "Is it unsafe because it's haunted, Mr. Crunn?"

The elderly gentleman gulped. "Quite."

"And that's why the door is locked," I said.

Crunn nodded. "I can't imagine what Merrick was thinking putting you up there."

And then something occurred to me. "Does the hag haunt that section along with the moat?" I asked.

"The hag?" Crunn repeated. "You saw her?"

I let out a mirthless laugh. "You could say that. She pulled Heath into the water from that little shortcut you led us through this morning."

Crunn's hand flew to his mouth. "She *did*?"

"She nearly drowned both of us," I told him. "Surely you heard about it from the constable?"

Both Arthur and Gopher shook their heads, and I remembered that I'd had to tell Gopher the whole story about Heath being dragged into the moat by the hag.

Arthur said, "Miss Holliday, Constable Bancroft was far too cold when he was fished out of the moat to say much. It was only related to me by Inspector Lumley after he'd sent his good constable home to warm up that there had been some sort of accident in the tunnel and Mr. Whitefeather had fallen into the moat and that you had gone in after him."

"It was no accident, Mr. Crunn, I can assure you. That tunnel is haunted by the most beastly hag, and she attacked me, then went after Heath and pulled him into the water where she then attempted to drown him."

The old man shuffled over to a cane chair behind the desk and sat down hard. He seemed terribly undone by what I was telling him, and I worried that he might have another panic attack. "I had no idea she could do that," he insisted. "I've used that route for years to get to the lake side of the castle without incident. I promise that's the truth, miss, or I never would have led you through."

I walked around the desk and over to him. "I believe you, Mr. Crunn, but right now I need to know more about this old hag. Who she is, and why she's been so active lately."

"Well, to be quite correct, she's not a hag, Miss Holliday. The evil spirit you encountered was the former Lady Mortimer. She ruled Kidwellah from 1552 to 1589, and never a more vile woman disgraced these halls."

I wondered suddenly about something the inspector had said to me, about a Lady Catherine, whose ghost I'd seen weeping outside my door much earlier that morning. "Is Lady Mortimer connected to Lady Catherine?"

Crunn's furry brow rose in surprise again. "How did you hear of Lady Catherine?"

"I saw her very early this morning and Inspector Lumley gave a name to the figure. Her ghost woke me with her weeping, and when I tried to help her, she ran away. That's what prompted us to come downstairs looking for some help in the first place. We thought she was a guest at the castle and had been in some sort of domestic dispute."

Crunn made a *pffft* sound. "Yes, you could say that Lady Catherine had quite a few domestic disputes during her married life here at Kidwellah. She ruled here from 1546 to 1550. She was also Lady Jane Mortimer's older sister. Lady Catherine was forced to marry Sir John Mortimer, who quickly grew to despise her. Many speculate that—as John had been marred by smallpox in his youth and had a rather brutish way about him—Lady Catherine found him most unappealing as a husband. He beat her quite regularly, and most historians speculate she died as a result of one such beating."

I winced. "The poor thing," I said.

"Indeed," Crunn agreed. "The Duke of Lennox—Sir Mortimer—and Lady Catherine's father, the Duke of Hereford, nearly went to war over it, as Kidwellah had been part of the Lady Catherine's dowry, but a resolution was worked out between the two when Sir Mortimer agreed to pay a sizable fine and consented to marry Catherine's youngest sister, Lady Jane, who even as a youth was a terribly unruly creature. Most believe she was quite mad from the cradle, and her childhood exploits lend credence to the theory that she was indeed a psychopath.

"She caused so much havoc at her father's home that the Duke of Hereford was likely desperate to find someone to take her off his hands, and the murder of her sister presented him with a golden opportunity. The terms of the restitution agreement between the two dukes stipulated that if it could be proven that Lady Jane died at the hands of her husband, Kidwellah and all its holdings would immediately revert back to the Duke of Hereford and a cause for war would be brought. Sir Mortimer's family had fallen on hard times, and by the time he came into dukedom, most of his family's fortunes had been squandered. His own forces were pathetically ill equipped to fend off the Duke of Hereford's forces. He readily agreed to the restitution.

"So it was that a terrible union was forged. The mad Lady Jane and the bitterly angry Sir Mortimer. They despised each other from the beginning, and at the wedding Lady Jane had to be bound and gagged while the priest performed the ceremony. On their wedding night Lady Jane attempted to stab her husband and things only worsened from there.

"Sir Mortimer soon resorted to beating her too, but he always stopped short of killing her. It made no difference; she would recover from her beatings and set out to drive him mad. She gave away his favorite horse, set his dogs loose on the moors, filled his bed with snakes and leeches, and attacked him with any object she could get her hands on. He resorted to locking her away in the south section of this castle, walling up most of the doors and windows, and leaving her in near total isolation. But that didn't seem to stop her. Somehow she managed to find a way out and torture him relentlessly. Her goal, they say, was to drive Sir Mortimer mad.

"By all accounts she succeeded. The Duke of Lennox went quite insane, insisting his residence at the south end of the castle was haunted by evil spirits that also inhabited the moat. During the years he ruled here, some of his closest friends and advisers were found drowned in the moat. Even his own aunt fell victim."

"It was Lady Jane, wasn't it?" I asked. "She drowned them all."

"Most likely," Arthur replied. "There are documented accounts of Lady Jane being seen swimming in the moat on warm summer days, taunting her husband, who would have her hauled out and sealed up in the south wing again. She was obviously a strong swimmer, something quite unheard of for a noble in those days."

"So what happened to him? The duke, I mean. Did she kill her husband too?"

Arthur shrugged. "His fate is unknown. One morning he could not be found anywhere within the castle or on the surrounding grounds. Some say he was drowned by his wife, and his body was never recovered. Others say that he finally went mad, wandered out onto the moors during the wet season, and succumbed to the cold. The moors would have swallowed his body quite quickly if that were the case. There is even a local legend that says that the duke's spirit haunts the moors near the lake. They call him the Desperate Duke, and it's said that anyone he appears to will be the next victim of the Grim Widow."

"The Grim Widow?" I repeated. "Is that what they call Lady Jane's ghost?"

"It is," Mr. Crunn confirmed. "After her husband's death, the castle reverted to the duke's cousin, Sir William Mortimer, who preferred the south of France over cold, drizzly Penbigh. He wanted nothing to do with Kidwellah or his cousin's mad wife, so she was left to terrorize the castle staff until they all but abandoned it. She died in 1589, and in all probability she died of starvation as the remaining staff eventually stopped feeding her after two members of their ranks were also found floating in the moat."

"If Lady Jane was suspected of killing people, especially the duke's friends and family, why didn't any of the other nobles step in?" Gopher asked.

"Lady Jane had powerful friends," Arthur told us. "She was a first cousin to Queen Elizabeth, and they had played together as children. Elizabeth was the only person able to keep Lady Jane calm and somewhat stable until Jane's madness completely overtook her.

"Before Jane was married to Sir Mortimer, Elizabeth spent some time in the Tower of London, a courtesy granted to her by her sister, Queen Mary. It was Jane who convinced her powerful father to support the effort to free Elizabeth, and Elizabeth never forgot the kindness. Once she became queen, she all but looked the other way as Jane drowned some of the lesser Welsh nobles. It helped that the Duke of Hereford lived to be a very old man and suppressed any rumblings from the Welsh courts."

I shivered again, remembering the sight of that awful-looking woman on the bridge with that chain slinking its way from her to Merrick Brown. "Mr. Crunn," I said, wondering if he might know anything about why she would be keeping Merrick's spirit captive, "this morning when we took the constable back through that tunnel on our way to find your sister and we first encountered the Grim Widow, she wasn't alone." He cocked his head quizzically and I had second thoughts about telling him about Merrick. I didn't want to upset him all over again. "She had another person bound by a chain. Do you know anything about that?"

Crunn opened his mouth to reply, but at that moment a whole troop of people came rushing into the main hall, filling it with their giggles, catcalls, and loud voices. I turned to watch them file in, taking note that there wasn't an ugly person in the bunch. Or a short one.

In all I counted at least a dozen model-looking types, both male and female. At the back of the group was a stately-looking couple who appeared to be dripping with money. They wore luxurious fabrics and walked with a distinct air of importance. Just in front of them was a man who was so striking that for a moment my breath caught.

He was dark-haired with a goatee and thin mustache. His hair was jet-black with a hint of gray around the temples, and his features were almost elfin. He was tall like everyone else, but too old to be a model; at least that's what I thought. And then my suspicions were confirmed when I noticed the expensive digital camera around his neck and another one in his hand.

I must have caught his eye, because his gaze fell on me, then casually away, but came back again and this time it came with a smile. He then stopped midstride, raised his camera, and took my picture. I was so startled by the move that for a moment I didn't know what to think.

"Ah, Arthur, there you are!" said the gray-haired man who was part of the couple that seemed to be dripping with money. "Are you ready to give up your magnificent hall?"

Arthur moved away from us to go speak with the elegant man and his wife. Meanwhile, next to me Gopher nudged my arm and motioned to the photographer. "That guy just took your picture."

"Yes, I know," I said, still watching the man as he scrutinized the shot he'd just taken in his viewfinder. He seemed to nod to himself and raised the camera again and pointed at us, his finger clicking several more times before he lowered the lens to study the images again.

"Now he's taking *our* picture," Gopher said.

"Nothing gets by you, does it?"

Gopher eyed me crossly. "Well, he is!"

"He's a photographer, Goph. That's what they do."

"Yeah? Well, two can play at that game." Before I knew it, Gopher had his smartphone out and had started snapping photos of the photographer.

Seeing this, the gorgeous man laughed and walked over to us. "You must excuse me," he said with a distinct Scottish brogue. Extending his hand out to shake Gopher's hand, he added, "My name is Michel Keegan and I meant you no harm."

Gopher lowered his camera so that he could shake Michel's hand, but he appeared a little flustered by the encounter.

I stifled a laugh and extended my own hand. "No harm done, Michel. I'm M. J. Holliday, and this is Peter Gophner."

The photographer gripped my palm and immediately

placed his other hand over it. "Oh, my, but you're freezing, lass!"

"She fell into the moat," Gopher told him.

We both looked oddly at him, and Gopher cleared his throat. "Well, she did. And so did her boyfriend. Remember your *boyfriend*, M. J.?"

I felt my cheeks flush. Stupid Gopher. But Michel only smiled kindly at me and said, "You fell into the moat? Are you all right?"

"I'm fine, thank you."

Michel let go of my hand and stepped back. He raised his camera for a third time and snapped again. "You have the most beautiful skin," he said, lowering the camera to show me the shot through the viewfinder.

"Thank you," I said, feeling my cheeks heat even more. I gave a cursory glance at the image and my breath caught. My hair was an awful mess. I tugged at it self-consciously, and Michel took notice. "Don't worry about that," he said. "The wild look is all the rage these days."

"Michel!" someone called, and we all glanced up to see one of the male models pouting at the photographer. "André says that we can go to lunch before the afternoon shoot. Take me to lunch, okay?"

I barely caught the small sigh from Michel before he pushed a smile onto his handsome features. "Of course, love. Be right with you."

Inwardly I was surprised. My gaydar was almost as good as Gilley's and I hadn't caught a hint of that from Michel. But after he excused himself and the other younger man came to take up his hand, it was quite obvious the model was sweet on the photographer.

I glanced at some of the other young men chatting away in the hall. Not a straight one in the bunch. Gilley was going to be in heaven. And that thought made me wonder where he was. "You said Gil was still asleep when you came to the hospital?" I asked Gopher.

"Yeah. I couldn't get him to answer his phone or the door."

I reached for Gopher's wrist and turned it so that I could read the time on his watch. "God, is it only noon?"

Gopher yawned. "I know, it feels more like midnight."

The one thing about filming in all these foreign locations was that we were constantly fighting jet lag. I saw Arthur scoot behind the counter and overheard him politely refer to the elegant gentleman as Mr. Lefebvre. The name sounded familiar to me, and then it hit me who he was: none other than the fabulous fashion designer André Lefebvre. I even owned a pricey cocktail dress designed by him, but Gilley was the real fashion horse. He loved the Lefebvre label.

It was clear that Lefebvre and Crunn were discussing the main hall as a setting, because the designer kept holding his hands in a square, as if looking through a camera lens. At last he seemed satisfied and Lefebvre motioned to his wife to follow him toward the dining room, probably on their way to lunch, leaving his models to continue their loud chitchat and gossip in the main hall.

I approached the desk, still needing to arrange a better room, when I heard a very loud cry of alarm from somewhere up the stairs. The chatter in the main hall came to an abrupt halt and we all turned our attention to the top of the stairs as another high-pitched cry sounded.

I recognized that shriek and, in a panic, was about to bolt for the stairs when Gilley suddenly burst into view and came dashing down the steps. "Taxi!" he cried. "I need a taxi to take me to the hospital!"

Just behind him came John, and it was clear that John was trying hard to catch up to Gil and calm him down.

All eyes in the main hall were still pinned on Gilley as he tripped and nearly tumbled down the rest of the steps, but he caught himself in the nick of time by clutching the railing and then he used his momentum to pull himself up and over the railing to drop gracefully onto the stone like something out of a Jackie Chan movie. Gil was wicked agile when he wasn't busy stuffing his piehole . . . or complaining.

His acrobatics elicited a few gasps from the people in the hallway, but he hardly noticed. Instead he set off like Usain Bolt, passing right by me. I even waved to him, but he didn't seem to recognize me. Instead, as he whizzed by, I saw him nod slightly, but he didn't stop or slow down.

So I waited as he sped across the wide hall and through the main door. I then smirked sideways at Gopher—who was watching slack-jawed—and I held up three fingers, beginning to count them down. "Three . . . two . . . one . . ."

"M. J.!" Gil shouted, appearing again in the doorway. *"You're alive!"*

I opened my arms wide and Gilley sprinted straight at me, crashing into me with such force that we both nearly went down. "John said you nearly drowned in the moat!"

I couldn't help it—I laughed. Gil's enthusiastic display of affection did a lot to set me back to rights. "Well, Gil, I—"

"Who're these people?" Gil suddenly asked, picking his head up to look around. I could see his gaze home in on the cluster of beautiful men standing nearby, now eyeing him with keen interest.

Gil let go of me in a snap and stepped toward them. "Why, hello there," he said casually.

In short order Gilley was surrounded and I knew I'd lost him for at least the rest of the afternoon. John, who'd made it down the stairs and over to us, stepped up to Gopher and me and apologized. "Gopher called me from the hospital and it took me until just a few minutes ago to wake Gil up. The minute I started to explain where you were and what'd happened, he flew out of his room like a crazy person and I didn't have the chance to tell him you guys were okay."

I put a hand on his shoulder. "It's okay, John," I assured him. "Gil wouldn't have listened anyway. He's the type to panic first, think second."

"Miss Holliday?" said a voice behind us. I turned to see Arthur hold a key out for me. "I've given you another room assignment. Your previously assigned room was apparently given to Mr. Gillespie, and we only have one of the smaller rooms available for you and Mr. Whitefeather on the second floor. As soon as there is a vacancy in one of the suites, I'll offer it to you at no additional charge."

I took the key gratefully and was about to thank him when someone came up behind me, pushing slightly at my back to get me to move, and said, "Crunn! What's this about a death here at Kidwellah this morning?"

I turned to see a bloated man with a bright red face and bushy mustache pushing his way next to me to demand information from Mr. Crunn. I gave him a dark look, as I have little patience for rude people, which he completely ignored. Beside him, however, a mousy-looking woman met my eyes shyly, and she blushed. I could tell her husband's brutish behavior was an embarrassment to her.

For his part Mr. Crunn looked terribly caught off guard as the entire crowd of people fell silent a second time and focused on him. I felt bad for him as he stammered out apologies for the fact that his own clerk had drowned in the moat. The overbearing man acted as if it were somehow Crunn's fault, and in any other circumstance I would have gotten in middle of the discussion and told the man to piss off, but I wasn't up to verbally sparring with anyone else that afternoon.

I did, however, insert myself between Mr. Crunn and the ass causing a scene and glared hard at him until he backed off a little. Then I motioned to Gopher and John to come away from the counter. Just as we all walked away, Gopher's phone rang. He looked at the display and frowned. "It's Chris," he said. Chris Weller was Gopher's boss (which technically made him our boss too). He was part of the network brass who were constantly hounding us for better footage. Gopher turned away as he answered the phone. I knew he'd be stuck talking to Chris for a while.

"Is Heath still at the hospital?" John asked.

"He is," I told him, moving wearily to the stairs. I really wanted to take another nap, but I was anxious about retrieving my stuff and Heath's belongings from our old room. If my phone, passport, and other identification weren't all still there, I would've left my clothes and bought new ones, but replacing that stuff was beyond a pain in the neck. I'd have to brave going back to that room. Still, venturing through those hallways to retrieve our personal items wasn't something I wanted to do alone.

"Can I do anything for you, M. J.?" John asked while I considered my options.

I smiled at him. "Actually, you can. I have to get my stuff and Heath's from our old room. It's in the south wing of the castle and I don't want to go back there by myself. Would you come with me?"

John eyed me curiously. "If I didn't know better, I'd think that you were scared or something, M. J."

"Oh, trust me, buddy, I'm terrified. That wing is wicked haunted."

John stopped in his tracks. "Do we need spikes?"

"Most definitely."

We went to John's room to gather up some magnetic spikes and I also stopped by the room that Arthur had assigned to me. I found it much cozier, and even though he had suggested the room would be small, it was still bigger than the old one. Plus, it had its own bathroom, so I wasn't about to complain.

Discovering its charm and spaciousness gave me pause, however. *Why* had Merrick put Heath and me in such danger by sending us to the south wing of the castle? He had to know there was a rather dangerous poltergeist lurking about there. He'd seemed like such a nice man, who'd genuinely been impressed by Heath and me. So what was his true agenda, and why had he gone out to the moat in the middle of the night when he should have known that was dangerous territory too?

I also wondered if the Grim Widow truly had drowned Merrick. Even though I'd seen her nearly drown Heath, I had to allow for the possibility that Merrick had simply slipped on the drawbridge, hit his head, and fallen into the water, where he'd drowned. And once the Widow became aware of his grounded spirit, maybe she'd pounced and had somehow taken it captive?

I made a mental note to ask Gilley to research one ghost's holding another ghost captive, because it was something I'd never heard of and had no idea how to deal with.

John and I left the comfort of our rooms and headed toward the south wing. Along the way, I filled him in on all the harried events of that morning.

He'd heard about the castle employee's accidental drowning, and I was quick to suggest that I wasn't convinced it was an accident. "Hold on," he said as we passed the stairs and saw that Gil was still chatting it up with the male models. "You're telling me a *ghost* drowned that guy?"

"I think so. At least I know she's capable of it."

John caught my shoulder, pulling me to a stop. "But . . . *how*?"

"She's unbelievably strong, John. And evil. Or crazy. Maybe a little of both. Either way we're gonna have to be really careful on this bust."

John stared at me hard for several seconds without letting go of my shoulder. "Maybe we should quit this castle and head to the next location, M. J."

I offered him a mirthless laugh. "If you can talk Gopher into that, then I'm all for it. For now, let's just focus on getting my stuff and Heath's things out of that room."

John continued to look at me doubtfully. "Is there anything in your old room that you and Heath can't live without?"

I sighed. "My passport, ID, credit cards, money, and phone. Ditto that for Heath. Granted, all of them are replaceable, but it's the middle of the day, the humidity is as low as it's gonna get today, and this is the best chance we'll have of getting in there and out before anything spectral notices."

I could see John consider all of that and he finally let go of my shoulder, but for a few seconds I didn't know if he was going to follow me or make a run for it. I took a few tentative steps away, hoping he'd come along. Even though I believed everything I'd just said to convince him, I *really* didn't want to venture down those dark hallways alone, and at last he seemed to make a decision and fell into step beside me.

We crept along stealthily, neither of us speaking. John had been on enough ghostbusts to know how to wield a magnetic spike—which acts like pepper spray should any spook want to get too close. John was also a big guy like Heath, but he wasn't my boyfriend. He had neither the experience nor the same connection to the spirit world that Heath had, and as we rounded the corner into the south wing, I was acutely aware that if anything jumped out at us, I'd have to be the one to take charge and get us out of there.

Remembering the force of the blow against my door that morning, and how strong the Widow had been to wrestle Heath over the stone wall and into the water, I was feeling a little less confident than when I'd given

John the speech, but my mind was made up. I wanted my damn stuff back.

We passed through the door leading to the south wing, which was still unlocked from when Heath and I had gone through it that morning, and I paused in the doorway, waiting to feel out the ether.

John stood right behind me and I could feel him taking stock of the dimly lit corridors and the nervousness of his energy.

I sent out my intuitive feelers and found the energy in the south wing to be ... well ... icky. Goose pimples lined my arms and the hair on the back of my neck stood on end. The atmosphere was alight with dark forces, and it was amazing to me that the night before I'd gone through that very door with barely a pause. It was likely a testament to how exhausted both Heath and I were that we didn't halt and refuse to go beyond the doorway.

Still, nothing super creepy jumped out at me, and I figured we could get into my room, grab the stuff, and get out before anything too terrible happened.

After another few seconds of checking the ether, I motioned silently to John and we continued on.

We moved along the hallways, and I was relieved to see that somehow I remembered the way. At last John and I entered the hallway leading to my room, which was drafty and cold—much colder than the hallway feeding into it.

I held up my hand and we both halted so that I could assess the situation. There was a foreboding feeling that snaked its way through this corridor in particular.

John leaned in and whispered in my ear. "You guys actually *stayed* here last night?"

Obviously he could feel it too. "Get your spikes out and stay close to me," I whispered back.

I took out four spikes from the containers strapped to the loops of my utility belt and took a big breath before making my way down to the door of our room. The feeling of something nasty in the air was getting thicker, settling in both in front of us and from behind. In fact, I seemed to be feeling it from all directions. By the look on John's face I knew he felt it too. His eyes darted all around the hallway and he held his spikes up like he was ready to charge at anything that might jump out and go boo.

Then again, the more I looked at him, the more I thought he might chuck the spikes and make a run for it. He was as scared as I've ever seen him, and John doesn't scare easily.

"You okay?" I whispered.

His eyes cut to me and he leaned forward to speak softly. "Let's get your stuff and get the hell out of here!"

I wanted to tell him to stand guard at the door while I packed, but with my stuff and Heath's I already knew it'd be too much for me to carry. "Okay, let's get in, throw anything you find that belongs to me or Heath in a bag, and get out fast."

John's eyes were still scanning the hallway, but at least he nodded.

I was about to turn the handle on the door when an involuntary shudder went through me. The awful energy permeating the hallway seemed to ratchet up a notch. I looked all around again, but I couldn't sense its direction. It seemed to be coming at us from all directions. I shivered again, recalling the terrible presence of that evil energy that'd chased me through the hallways and slammed against our door. In a near panic, I turned the handle, but it was locked. With my own fear mounting I tucked my spikes into the waistband of my jeans and searched my pockets, finally coming up with the old key, which—miraculously—hadn't fallen out of my back pocket when I'd gone into the moat. After inserting the key with shaking fingers, I turned the handle, but the door was stuck. All the while I felt the malevolent energy grow thicker and more pervasive, and I just wanted to get the hell out of that hallway, because I couldn't pinpoint the source or the direction, but I knew that danger was very close.

"It's stuck!" I told John. He pressed his weight into me and shoved on the door. I could feel him trembling too, and knew he was just as affected by the surge of evil all around us as I was. I put my hip against the door and gave it a good hard bump, and the door opened abruptly, as if it hadn't been stuck at all.

Stumbling forward with an involuntary squeak, I let go of the handle to catch myself on the wall. Behind me I heard John cry out with fright and I straightened up and looked back at him, but he was staring past me, into the room toward the bed.

My eyes darted to the bed, and there, floating just above it, was the figure of the Grim Widow, pale white, dressed in rags with her wild eyes and even wilder hair. She sneered at me in the most malevolent way before hissing like an angry cat and flying toward me as if she meant to grab me up.

I screamed and put my arms up defensively, but John got between us first, and thrust two of those spikes right into her. She shrieked so loud my ears rang and she whirled away from the two of us, hissing again as she went.

John looped his arm around my shoulders, pulling me back into him protectively while keeping his spikes pointed toward the Widow. For a minute we both stood there frozen in terror. "Do something!" he finally yelled.

I reached for my own spikes, but what I could do against this wretched ghost was anybody's guess.

Meanwhile the Widow spat at us and began climbing up the far wall on all fours like something right out of a horror movie. I'd never seen a ghost do that before and I felt a new level of fear turn my cold blood even colder.

Behind me, John was trembling so hard that I was convinced he was on the verge of passing out. "Ma . . .

ma . . . *move!*" I yelled at him, hauling up my spikes when the Widow reached the ceiling and began to climb upside down along it toward us.

But John didn't budge, so I pushed him hard with my back. *"Move, move, move!"*

That seemed to do the trick, and John let go of me and took off out the door. I followed right on his heels, not brave enough to even look back. We raced through the corridor and at every step that awful sinister presence dogged us. I ducked low as I ran, the image of the Widow crawling along the ceiling replaying over and over in my mind, and I felt close to panic when I thought about her at my back or, worse, overhead.

At the end of the hallway John turned left instead of right and I cried out to him, but he was too panicked to hear me. A cackling laugh filled the atmosphere—it surrounded me and seemed to vibrate right through my body.

I stopped at the juncture and shouted out to him again, but he continued down that hallway as if he hadn't heard me at all. For a few seconds I watched him anxiously, trying to decide what to do. He was running so fast I didn't think I could catch him. But as I wavered, I saw a dark shadow emerge from the doorway of one of the rooms between me and John.

It was large and catlike and simply radiated evil. As it came out from the door, it crouched low before giving chase to my friend.

"John!" I screamed at the top of my lungs, and took off after him. The black shadow loped along, gaining ground on John. As I ran, I brought up one fist to eye level, and saw that I still clutched two spikes. With grim determination I put on a burst of speed, gained a little ground, then threw my spike right at that black shadow.

It struck the thing dead center and the effect was immediate. It was as if my spike had blown it into a dozen smaller pieces. It broke apart in front of my eyes and there was also this terrible sound accompanying the dissipation. The best I can describe it was that it was like a shriek from something definitely otherworldly.

The black pieces of the shadow flung against the wall, and for a minute I thought that I'd vanquished it, but then the most terrible thing happened.... Those individual black little blobs began to scurry along the walls and floor and even the ceiling, moving like inky spiders after John.

"Oh, sweet Jesus!" I cried, hardly believing my eyes. "What the hell *are* you?"

I'd never seen or heard of anything like it, but one thing was for certain, and that was that John was in very real danger. Putting on another burst of speed, I charged forward, raising my remaining spikes high as I shouted out a primal war cry.

At last, John heard me, and I saw him glance over his shoulder. His eyes took me in first, then the little globs of black evil chasing after him. He shrieked in fear and lost his footing. I watched him reach out instinctively and grasp at the wall. His hand connected with a small sconce and for a moment he was able to prevent himself from hitting the floor, but then the sconce gave way and there was a grating sound. The next thing I knew, John's upper body had disappeared from sight!

Chapter 5

I shouted out to John for a fourth time as his feet lifted up off the ground and followed his torso into the wall. I heard him cry out as well, and watched in horror as all those black little globs dived after him. *"John!"* I screamed, running as fast as I could to close the distance between us. As I came abreast of him, I could see that he hadn't actually disappeared directly into the wall; he'd fallen into a narrow gap that had opened when he'd pulled on the sconce—a secret passageway, no doubt—and as I came to a stop, I could see that the newly opened gap led to a circular staircase. John's feet were at the top of the stairs and he was sort of sprawled out on the next few steps leading down. There was no sign of the little black demons, but that might have been because the staircase was barely visible by the dim lighting in the hallways and I couldn't see much in the darkness.

I bent to grab hold of his wrist, but my palms were sweating and I was shaking with fright. He slipped out of my grip and I had to reach for his waistband and give a tug on it. "Get up!" I commanded. "John, get up!"

He groaned and I knew he had probably hurt himself, but his limbs were moving, so I didn't think he'd been hurt too badly. "What the hell ha—"

A sad low moan cut him off and that was followed by another, then another, until there were too many moans to pick out individually. They echoed up from somewhere down the stairs, out of sight, and filled the hallway beyond us. Among the moans were whispers and cries of pain and pleas for help. It sounded as if a dozen tortured souls had suddenly become aware of us in their vicinity, and they were crying out to us, but we were in no position to help them.

John reached out and clutched my arm and with a determined pull I hauled him up so that he could get his feet under him. Still, he was wobbly on those feet and I threw his arm over my shoulders, gripping his wrist to keep him upright. I then wrapped my other arm around his waist to move him out of the hidden doorway and back into the hallway.

Once we'd cleared the door, I reached with my free hand and pushed up on the sconce. The hidden panel closed, shutting off the noise, and we were alone in the hall.

For several seconds we both stood with our backs to the wall, taking in great lungfuls of air. I kept my eyes peeled for any sign of the Widow or the black shadows, but as if some switch had been thrown, all sense of the malice that had haunted us from the moment we stepped into the corridor leading to my room disappeared.

"We gotta get out of here!" John whispered.

"Totally," I agreed, and indicated the hallway to my left. "You took the wrong turn back there."

John nodded at the barely visible outline of the hidden doorway next to us. "And another one right there."

"Are you hurt?" I asked him, hoping he could walk, because I was now so drained I knew I wouldn't get far if I had to support him.

He shook his head. "No, I'm okay. You?"

"I'm fine. Let's get out of this wing before we're attacked again."

John and I made it back to the safe side of the castle without further incident, and when we went through the door, I had him help me move a medium-sized bureau in front of the door. Heath was the last person with the key, and I didn't want some wayward guest of the hotel taking a wrong turn into that wing.

After the bureau was in place, we headed in the direction of our rooms. Just as we turned the corner to our section, Gopher came running down the hall toward us. He didn't look happy. In fact, he looked quite pale.

"What's happened?" I asked straightaway. I knew it was bad by his expression, and I wondered if the Grim Widow had ventured past the south wing and perhaps gone on the attack again.

"We have until one a.m. to get some usable footage or the network brass says we're all fired," Gopher said bluntly.

My mind had been going in a completely different direction.

John and I looked at each other blankly for a minute, and then John said, "I'll be in my room, updating my résumé."

Gopher reached out and grabbed him by the arm. "Hey, hold on there, pal! The fat lady hasn't sung yet. We've still got until one a.m., and who knows, maybe we'll get lucky and something creepy will happen."

I had half a mind to tell Gopher to take his handheld camera and go pull on a certain sconce in the south wing, but I held back. Instead I said, "Dude, we're done here. I quit." I'd start doing readings for clients again. Hell, I'd even take some sort of day job in corporate America before I'd go back for one minute of playtime with Kidwellah's ghostly freak show.

"What?" Gopher cried as I began to walk away. "M. J.! You can't be serious! You *can't* quit!"

"Watch me," I told him over my shoulder, and motioned for John to fill him in.

Gopher called after me a couple of times, but I ignored him. All I wanted was a few hours' sleep and then I'd go visit Heath in the hospital and deliver the bad news that the show was over and we were headed home. I hated to think what that would mean for our relationship, but I had faith in us, and that somehow we'd make it work.

It wasn't until I was through the door to my new room that I realized all my personal belongings and identification were still back in the old room. Heath's stuff was also still there and we'd need our passports at the very least to get back to the States.

I could call the U.S. embassy, I knew, but my credit cards were also still back in the south wing, and I had only about a hundred quid on me. Not enough to carry me through until we got replacement passports. "Dammit," I swore. "How the hell am I gonna get our stuff out of there?"

I looked down. I was still carrying three of the four magnetic spikes I'd taken into the south wing. Then I thought of something; there was another secret weapon we had at our disposal—Gilley's sweatshirt.

A while back we'd come up with the brilliant idea to glue thin refrigerator magnets to the inside of an extra-large sweatshirt so that Gilley could be protected from the various poltergeists that found him so oddly irresistible.

Over the past several months we'd made a few of those sweatshirts, because they kept getting ripped or worn out from overuse. We hadn't thought to make more than one at a time, and right about then I was wondering why we hadn't made a whole wardrobe of them.

Well, one thing was for sure; if I had any thoughts of retrieving our stuff from my old room, I wasn't going to do it unless I was covered in magnets head to toe, which meant I'd have to convince Gilley to part with his sweatshirt without telling him the full story behind why I needed to borrow it. If he knew any of the details, he'd put it on and refuse to take it off again until we were out of Wales.

With an exhausted sigh I entered my new room and lay down on the bed. I'd worry about all of that later. For now I just wanted to rest.

Just as I was beginning to set the alarm on the small clock by the bed, I heard yelling through the walls. It was muffled, but it was loud enough for me to glean that some man was angry at a woman named Fiona for booking him into such a miserable old place like Kidwellah. I listened for a minute and could hear a woman's voice feebly trying to defend herself, but she was cut off by the overbearing man.

With another sigh I got up from the bed and trudged over to the wall, pounding on it as the yelling got louder. The man fell silent immediately, which gave me a tiny measure of satisfaction, but then a few seconds later I heard the door of the room next to mine slam hard. "Bastard," I muttered, and shuffled back to the bed to fiddle with the clock again. I set the alarm for late that afternoon. I planned on going back to the hospital after I'd had some rest. Hopefully, Heath would be almost back to normal by then and we could talk about what to do next. I then turned onto my side and fell immediately to sleep.

About four and a half hours later, I awoke to the *beep, beep* of the alarm, and as I sat up, I was famished but better rested. With a big yawn I pushed myself up from the bed and looked around blearily. Even though

I'd had a great nap, I was still a bit sluggish and muddle-brained.

It took me a couple of minutes in the bathroom to freshen up, and once that was taken care of, I went in search of someone from the crew. Leaving my room, I nearly bumped right into the woman staying next door, and I recognized her as the mousy woman from downstairs with that bloated bastard of a husband who'd yelled at Mr. Crunn.

The woman backed up quickly, apologized, her face flushing crimson, and because she'd jumped back so quickly, her head struck the wall with a little thump.

"Oh, ma'am!" I said, stepping forward. "That sounded like it hurt, are you okay?"

The poor woman appeared very rattled and her hand flew to her head to rub the spot where she'd bumped the wall. "I'm fine!" she insisted, her face flushing a shade deeper. "I'm a silly woman and I should be more careful."

I wanted to say something to put her at ease, but my attention was drawn to the inside of her wrist still raised to her head. There was a terrible black bruise in the form of a handprint clearly marked there. I stared at that bruise in alarm, and she seemed to catch on, because she quickly lowered her hand and dropped her eyes. I studied her face, and to my disgust, I could see that her nose looked as if it had been broken at least once, and her lower lip appeared to be a bit puffy on one side. Also, there was a very faint bruise on the side of her cheek hidden carefully by makeup, but the shadow of it was still there. Her face flushed even more and she said, "Please excuse me," before shuffling past me to her door.

I watched her with a feeling that I should say something to her, like tell her to get away from that horrible bastard of a husband, but even as the thought formed, I knew it would be useless. I was pretty sure lots of people had begged her to get away from him over the years.

My shoulders sagged when her door closed. I felt like I'd just missed the opportunity to help her. And then I had an idea and vowed to myself to offer her a free reading. If she wouldn't let me do one impromptu, then I'd give her my cell number—assuming I got my cell back—and assure her that she could call me anytime. Sometimes the power of hearing from our deceased loved ones is more than enough to help us find the courage to move forward with our lives. It was the only thing I could offer her that I thought might help. Well, other than introducing her husband to a certain Grim Widow.

I snickered to myself at that thought while heading down the stairs. From that vantage point, I had a good view of the front hall, which was filled with models, bright flashes of light, and light screens. Michel was at the center of all the action, clicking away on his camera while the beautiful people struck poses. Well, most of the beautiful people. There was a short guy in the middle, wearing tons of makeup and a fedora and a rooster tail pinned to his butt. The short guy was striking the most awkward poses—Madonna-vogue-type poses—while all the other models kept spinning around him like a top.

As I descended the stairs, I couldn't help but duck my chin to hide a smirk—clearly the short guy didn't realize he was the foil in the photo shoot, and I wondered what modeling agency had thought to send him over. Still, there was something a bit familiar about him. I looked up at him again as he pranced to the side and stuck his bum out—wiggling that rooster tail and playing up the flamboyant gay for all he was worth.... I stopped in my tracks, realizing why he looked familiar.

"Gilley?"

The name escaped my lips before I could stop myself. Michel and the others paused to look up at me, but Gil ignored me and struck another couture-looking pose—all elbows and rooster tail. "I'm a little busy, M. J.," Gil called, like he was all that and a big box of Froot Loops.

I shook my head and continued down the stairs. Obviously Gil wouldn't be able to tell me where the rest of the crew was, as he looked like he'd been at the modeling gig for at least the last few hours.

With a sigh I reached the landing and moved over to the counter, but Mr. Crunn wasn't around.

I rang the bell, but no one came into view. Eyeing the clock, I could see that it was now nearly five thirty, and I wanted to get to the hospital before visiting hours were over, so, taking one of the bus schedules displayed on a nearby table, I set off out of the hall. As I stepped outside, however, I happened to catch a glimpse of two figures embracing under the cover of a low-hanging tree. I didn't think they knew they weren't truly concealed, because as I moved onto the cobblestones, I could clearly see who they were, and my brow rose in surprise.

Having a really good snog fest was the fashion designer André Lefebvre and the model I'd seen attach himself to Michel. I quickly averted my eyes to give them some privacy and continued on my way, but as I walked across the large open area, I happened to spy Mrs. Lefebvre sitting on a stone bench, her eyes narrowed and the most angry look on her face as she watched her husband make out with the model.

I winced when I saw her, not able to imagine how upset I'd be if I caught Heath making out with another guy. Cheating is cheating. It's a betrayal of the worst kind.

I averted my gaze from her too and tried to appear like I hadn't seen a thing, but when I snuck a glance in her direction again, it was clear that she had eyes only for her cheating husband and the model. Or she was patently ignoring me, because she never once looked in my direction. I moved on quickly and made for the bus stop.

The sun was waning as I made my way across the drawbridge. When I got to the hospital, I'd call the castle and leave word with Mr. Crunn about where I was so that he could pass that on to Gopher and the others. I didn't think they'd worry about me, but in light of the serious creepy events of the past twenty-four hours, I thought it a good idea to let everyone know where I was just in case.

It took me over an hour to reach the hospital by bus, and I was lucky that I'd had a small stash of twenty-pound notes stuffed into my back jeans pocket to pay for the ride. Gilley's mom—who'd practically raised me as her own after my mom died—had instilled in me the need to always keep at least a hundred bucks hidden on my person. "A lady should never be without the means to get herself from here to there," she'd said. "Always carry five twenties with you, Mary Jane. That'll be enough to see you home without needing to depend on some man for assistance."

Gil's dad had walked out on the family when Gilley was only five years old, clearing out the family's bank account as he went. Luckily for Mrs. Gillespie, her father had been a man of significant means, and while he was alive, he'd paid all her bills; then he'd made sure that his daughter was taken care of for the rest of her days by leaving everything to her in his will. Mrs. Gillespie now lived in a grand manor-style home and she owned a ton of real estate in and around Valdosta. It made me feel good to know that someday, after that dear sweet woman passed on herself, Gil wouldn't want for anything either.

After exiting the bus at the stop near the hospital, I zipped into a Wimpy and wolfed down a grilled ham and cheese sandwich with chips—or fries, as I mistakenly referred to them when I ordered. Then I hustled to the hospital and up to the second floor.

I found Heath alert and looking very nearly like his old self. Just the sight of him did a lot to set me at ease. "Hey, there," he said with a warm smile the minute he laid eyes on me. "Have I been missing you the past couple of hours. Get your cute butt over here, woman."

I practically ran to his bed and threw my arms around him. He still felt a little cold, but nothing compared with how cool he'd been that morning. "God, it's good to see you," I told him.

He lifted me off my feet and pulled me into bed with him, and for a long time all we did was lie there in each other's arms. Heath hugged me very tightly and whispered, "You saved my life again. That's one point for you."

I chuckled. Heath and I had been in some really harrowing situations nearly from the moment we'd met, and somewhere along the way we'd realized that we kept saving each other's lives. That had prompted a little lighthearted banter. "What's the score?"

"You're up by two."

I lifted my head to smirk at him. "Winning!"

Heath laughed and it was a sweet, sweet sound, believe me. "What'd you do all day, Em? Did you get some rest?"

That brought my mood crashing back down. In short order I told him what'd happened when John and I had ventured back into the south wing. Heath held my hand and looked grim. "Wish I'd been there."

"She's already had one crack at you."

Heath rubbed his neck where I could see a faint bruise beginning to form. "Don't I know it."

I smoothed away from his face the streak of bright white hair he'd gotten as a souvenir from the last evil spirit we'd encountered, and told him about the show. "The network is insisting we get some good-quality ghost footage by one a.m. tomorrow or they're pulling the plug, and since there's *no way* I'm doing *any* kind of a ghost-bust at that castle, effectively we're done."

Heath gazed at me with a lopsided grin. "You already quit, didn't you?"

"I'm that obvious, huh?"

He shrugged. "It's what I would've done."

Still, I felt oddly guilty. "Sorry," I told him.

"Why're you sorry?"

"I feel like I cost both of us our jobs."

"Em," he said soberly, "if it'd been you here and me there, I wouldn't have agreed to do another shoot. That spook is *crazy* powerful. No way do we want to tangle with the likes of her ever again. And if that means we both catch the first plane home tomorrow and start doing readings for private clients in Santa Fe, well, then that's what we'll do."

I sat up straight and stared at him. "Wait . . . Santa Fe? You think we're both going to live in Santa Fe?"

Heath took my hand and kissed it. "I know we haven't known each other very long," he said with a shy smile, "but I want you to move in with me."

My jaw dropped. "Heath . . . ," I began, but couldn't really figure out what to say next. "I . . . my . . . it's . . ."

His face clouded and I could see the hurt already forming in his eyes. "You don't want us to be together?"

I shook my head. "No! I mean, yes, I want us to be together, but I can't move in with you!"

"Why not?"

I tried to laugh, but it rang hollow. "Because you don't even have a house anymore! Yours burned down, remember?"

Heath frowned. "They have apartments in Santa Fe, you know, Em."

I sighed, a little exasperated. Why had he just assumed I'd be happy to leave my home in Boston? "I don't want to live in an apartment," I said maybe a *tiny* bit testily. "I have my own condo in Boston."

Heath let go of my hand and sat back against the pillows. "Ah. I get it," he said in that way that suggested he really didn't.

I sighed heavily. "And what about Gilley? He'll never want to move to Santa Fe."

"I wasn't asking him," Heath said levelly.

That took me aback. "Wait . . . what? You want me to just . . . *leave* my best friend in Boston?"

"I thought it was better than leaving your boyfriend in Santa Fe."

I looked down at my hands. How had this conversation suddenly taken us in such a nasty direction? I took a breath (or three) and said, "Heath, I really, *really* appreciate your offer to move in together, but for the past fourteen years my home has been Boston. And I don't know how you can expect me to just drop everything and move with you to Santa Fe. I mean, if you think about it, doesn't it make more sense for you to come to New England and move in with me?"

"You own real estate in Boston," Heath said. "My *family* lives in Santa Fe, M. J. Family trumps real estate any day of the week."

I bit back what I wanted to say, which was something like "Unless we're talking about real estate trumping *your* family," because I really didn't care for most of Heath's relatives. Instead I said, "Well, Gilley is *my* family, Heath. And so is Teeko, and Mama Dell. They all live in Boston. It would be just as hard for me to leave them there as it would for you to leave your family and your home."

"So . . . what?" he asked me. "You want to break up?"

"No!" I said quickly. "It's just . . ." My voice trailed off. This was an impossible conversation.

"There are no easy solutions here, are there?"

I stared again at my hands. "I guess not."

Heath took my wrist and lifted it to kiss my palm. "Something tells me we're gonna be racking up the frequent-flier miles."

I felt a small smile tug at my lips. "I'm so, so sorry."

Heath took hold of my head with both hands and pulled me forward to kiss me sweetly. "Don't sweat it," he said next. "If we're both in this for the long haul, we'll survive the geography."

I looked into his beautiful brown eyes hopefully. "You're in this for the long haul?"

He grinned. "I have been from the start, pretty lady. Or didn't you know?"

Visiting hours ended at nine and I left the hospital only after I'd had a nice long chat with Heath's nurse about his condition. She assured me that he would need to stay only the night, and that as soon as the doctor got to Heath on his rounds the next day, he'd be released with a clean bill of health. "Come round anytime after ten in the morning," she said merrily. "He should be ready to go by then."

I walked to the bus stop and realized I'd just missed the nine twenty. It would be another twenty minutes before the next bus, and I had a lot of time then to think about the fact that I hadn't called the hotel to leave word with Gopher about where I was.

I looked around for a phone booth, but they were as scarce in Wales as they were in the States now that everyone and their brother had a cell phone. Everyone but me, that is. I grumbled some more while I waited on the hard cold bench and thought about the bad luck of having my phone stuck in a haunted castle probably for good. Had I backed up my contacts to Gilley's computer? He'd been bugging me to do that, but I didn't think I'd gotten around to it yet. I sorely wanted my phone, but Heath and I had talked about it, and he'd convinced me that going back into the south wing, even covered head to toe in magnets, was suicide.

That meant that the both of us would have to figure out how to get our stuff replaced, and then of course there was the added problem of getting a new passport without any form of ID. I'd probably have to go to the U.S. embassy very soon, which was no doubt in London, and I'd somehow have to get there on only the eighty pounds left in my pocket. Unless Gilley loaned me some dough, which he probably would, but then he'd never, ever, ever let me forget about it.

With a sigh I wondered if anyone would be worried about me back at the castle. I checked my watch. By now they'd have noticed that I wasn't in my room, and someone from the crew was bound to raise a red flag when they couldn't find me. "Smart, M. J.," I muttered. Gilley was likely freaking out. If he'd managed to pry himself loose from the photo shoot, that is. Oh, who was I kidding? With a horde of beautiful flamboyant men in ready abundance, I'd be lucky to ever catch Gilley's attention again.

The bus was late and chock-full of passengers, so it had to let people off at nearly every stop, which got me back to Kidwellah at close to midnight. I trudged up the road wearily; all I wanted was a solid night's sleep. As I pushed through the door into the main hall, however, I knew that sleep was likely the last thing I'd get that night.

Gathered in the front hall and huddling close like frightened children were John and Gilley, along with Arthur Crunn, who appeared so tired he looked haggard.

"M. J.!" John called anxiously as he came hurrying toward me. "Where've you been?"

"I'm really sorry, guy. I was at the hospital visiting Heath and I forgot to leave a note and my phone is still stuck in my old—"

"Never mind about that! We've got bigger issues!" Gilley snapped, adjusting the collar of his magnetic sweatshirt, which I'd noticed he'd traded the fashionable outfit, fedora, and heavy makeup for.

"Boy, do we ever," John said, his eyes pinched with worry.

"What's going on, fellas?" I asked, hoping that if I adopted a reasonable tone, it would help to calm them down.

"I told them not to go," John said to me, his face racked with guilt. "M. J., I swear I told them not to go!"

"Told who?" I asked. I didn't know what'd happened

while I was away, but the hair rising on the back of my neck told me it was something bad.

"There's no sign of them," someone up the stairs called down. I looked up and recognized Michel. "And the chest has been moved aside from the door."

"No sign of whom?" I asked, sensing the mounting panic in the room, and when no one immediately answered me, I grabbed Gilley by the fabric of his sweatshirt and pulled him close. "Tell me what the hell is going on!"

Gilley's eyes were wild and frightened and he looked like he wanted to be anywhere but there. "It was Gopher's idea," he whimpered. "I overheard John trying to talk him out of it, but you know how stubborn Gopher can be! I didn't know he'd recruited Meg and Kim until John came to tell me! I swear I didn't, right, John? I didn't know he'd taken—"

I tugged again on Gilley's sweatshirt to get his attention because my heart was now racing. Gopher had done something. Something bad, I was sure of it. "Land that plane, Gilley, and just tell me!"

It was John who answered me. "Gopher talked Meg, Kim, and one of the male models from Michel's shoot into going on a ghost hunt. He wanted to send the networks some footage and, like an idiot, I told him all about our encounter with the Grim Widow. I think he and the girls went into the south wing to try and get her on film."

The shock of what he'd just said made me feel light-headed. "Oh, God!" I whispered. "How long ago?"

Gilley gulped. "It's been nearly two hours, M. J."

I bit my lip as I thought about the spikes still in my room. Even if John had lent Gopher the six he'd been carrying when he'd come with me, that was hardly enough spikes for four people to fend off the Widow and whatever demon had chased after me and John. "Did they have *any* kind of protection?"

John cast his eyes to the floor. "I thought that by not

giving Gopher any spikes he'd think twice about going on the stupid hunt. I had no idea he'd talk Meg and Kim into going with him!"

Meg was our production assistant and Kim was our assistant producer. They were really sweet young girls who tended to jump at Gopher's every command.

"So, to protect them from *the* most dangerous spook we've probably ever encountered, they have *nothing*?" I shouted at him, losing my cool big-time. "How the hell could you be so stupid?!" John flinched like I'd just slapped him and I immediately put a hand on his arm. "Oh, John, I'm so sorry! I didn't mean it like that!"

"No, you're right," he said contritely. "That *was* stupid. Kim and I broke up in Germany, so we haven't exactly been talking. I should've known Gopher would order them to go with him. I wasn't thinking straight."

I turned away from him and focused on Gilley. Pointing to his sweatshirt, I issued an order. "Gimme that."

Gilley's eyes widened in alarm and he quickly crossed his arms over his torso and hugged himself. "No way!"

I grabbed hold of his collar again and pulled his face to within two inches of mine. I had no time for his stupid theatrics and I wasn't about to go searching for my friends without some serious armor. "Gil," I said levelly, "I am *not* kidding around here. Give up that sweatshirt before I rip it off of you!"

"No!" he shouted. "You know what happens to me when I'm not wearing this!"

Now, I love Gilley. He is my best friend, my brother, and more my family than my own family, but at that moment I desperately wanted to throttle him. I let go of his collar and reached down for the hem of the sweatshirt, giving several hard pulls up on it. "Give . . . it . . . to . . . me!"

"No!" Gil shouted, swatting at my hands. "Let go! Quit it, M. J.! I need it!"

Gil and I struggled for several seconds before John

intervened. "Guys, guys!" he yelled, pulling us apart. "This isn't helping!"

I glared hard at Gil while I focused my argument on the sound tech. "You saw what we were up against today! If I'm gonna go look for Gopher and the others, I'll need some body armor—enough magnets to keep any spook at bay."

"But what about me?" Gil protested, still hugging himself lest John be swayed to help me rip the garment off him. "M. J., if I give this sweatshirt to you, then *I'll* be a sitting duck! You know how the ghoulies like to torture me!"

I crossed my own arms. "Fine, Gil, then *you* head to the south wing and bring back the crew!"

Gilley paled. "Maybe they'll come back on their own," he said weakly. Out of the corner of my eye I could see Michel watching us intently. I'm pretty sure he thought we were nuts.

Focusing again on Gilley, I rolled my eyes to show him how much of a drama queen I thought he was, but then I had an idea. For the most part, spooks are territorial, and if Gil wasn't here, then he couldn't be a target, now, could he? I pulled out my stash of twenty-pound notes and dangled two in front of him. "Here," I said. "There's a bus stop over the drawbridge and down at the end of the drive. If you hurry, you'll make the last bus headed to town. Take it and find yourself a nice unhaunted pub to hang out in until later. Then hail a cab back here. In the meantime, let me borrow your sweatshirt. I promise to return it to you just as soon as I find Gopher and the others."

"Oh, please," he scowled, waving his hand at the cash. "How cheap do you think I am?"

I cocked an eyebrow.

He stuck his tongue out at me but made to grab the pound notes, and I pulled them away. "Ah, ah, ah . . . ," I said. "Not until you hand over the sweatshirt."

Gil's scowl deepened. "Michel?"

"Yes?"

"Can I buy you a drink?"

I was sure Michel would say no—especially after this display—but to my surprise the good-looking photographer stepped forward with an amused look on his face. "Are you sure there's nothing I can do to help?" he asked me.

I smiled gratefully at him. He seemed like a nice guy. "Accompanying Gilley into town so that I can use his sweatshirt is all the help I need, Michel."

The raven-haired man nodded and moved toward the door. Gil shimmied out of his sweatshirt and tossed it in my direction without looking, his eyes intent on Michel's rear. The sweatshirt hit me in the face, and the magnets hurt. I made a move to whump Gil on the back of his head as he passed (snatching the pound notes out of my hand as he went), but John caught my arm. "Let's just focus on the job in front of us, okay?" he whispered.

With a (gigantic) sigh I pulled the heavy sweatshirt on over my head and looked for Arthur. He was over by the telephone, depressing the switch hook again and again. "What's the matter?" I asked, almost wearily because this was really turning out to be the most miserable twenty-four hours ever.

"The phone is dead," he said.

I walked to him, holding out my hand, and he placed the receiver in it. After I put it to my ear and depressed the switch hook a few times myself, it was obvious he was right. "Great," I said. "Were you trying to reach my producer?"

"No, Miss Holliday, I was actually attempting to alert the police."

"I'm not sure how much help they'll be," I muttered, but turned to John and added, "Can you lend him your cell?"

John shook his head. "It got smashed today when I fell into that passageway. Even Gil says it's toast. That's why I was so late hearing that Gopher had gone ahead with the shoot. I had to wait to hear it straight from Gilley."

"Will nothing go our way?" I snapped, thoroughly irritated with the constant obstacles we were being thrown. "Well, my phone is still back in the south wing. Arthur? Do you have a cell phone we can use?"

"No, Miss Holliday, I'm afraid I've no use for a mobile phone. That's a contraption for your generation."

Putting my hands on my hips in frustration, I looked to the door and shouted for Gilley, but he didn't reply. "Wait here," I told them. "I'll see if I can catch him. He's bound to have his cell on him."

I dashed from the hall and out into the cool air. Making my way across the cobblestones, I kept my eyes peeled for Gilley, and that's when I saw something very odd.

It was dark out, but the courtyard was well lit, and I could see all the way across it to the arch of the drawbridge, which appeared unusually dark, and what's more, I couldn't see the light from the lamppost that marked the bus stop. I ran faster until I was just under the archway, where I found Gilley and Michel standing in front of the massive wooden door of the bridge, which was closed. Gil must've heard me come up behind him, because he jumped and gave a little shriek, but when he saw that it was me, he put a hand over his heart and said, "Oh, M. J., thank God! We can't get out and I'll need my sweatshirt back."

I made no move to shrug out of the sweatshirt. Possession was nine-tenths of the law as far as I was concerned; plus, I'd paid him for it, so in my mind, the sweatshirt was rightfully mine. "What do you mean, you can't get out?" I asked (to distract him from the sweatshirt).

Gilley pointed to the massive door and looked at me like I was slow. "The drawbridge is up."

I let it go because I was much more concerned with the exit being blocked. "But . . . *how* could it be up?" I asked. I'd walked over it not ten minutes earlier.

Michel pointed to something that looked a little like a fuse box to the right of the bridge. "I've already inspected the lever," he said. "It's mechanized and it looks like someone pushed the button to pull up the bridge, then sabotaged the system by cutting all the wires so that it can't be lowered until we send for an electrician."

A cold shudder ran along my spine. The phones were dead. The drawbridge was up and the mechanism had been tampered with. I didn't know the castle that well, but I had a feeling that the only escape route we had at our disposal was through the same door that led to the tunnel-covered bridge where Heath had been hauled over the side by the Grim Widow. And now, even if we were able to get the police here, they couldn't come inside to help us look for our crew, because the bridge was up. Still, I knew I needed to alert them and get an electrician out here stat.

"We should go back inside," I said softly. I looked all around and up along the turrets. I had the most unsettling feeling that we were being watched. "And, Gilley, give me your cell phone."

"Where's yours?"

"In the south wing with the rest of my stuff."

Gil felt his pockets. "I don't have mine on me either," he said.

"Well, where is it?"

"I loaned it to Franco."

"Who's Franco?"

"One of the models."

I blinked. Gilley had loaned his cell phone to a relative stranger? Pigs must be flying. Or Franco must have been *very* cute. "What room is Franco in?" I pressed impatiently. I didn't have time for all this. Gopher and the girls were quite possibly in serious danger and I had to brave the south wing either alone or with the police. I preferred it be with the police.

"He's not in his room," Michel said.

"Then where is he?"

"He was the one that Gopher talked into going on the ghost hunt."

I shook my head. "Of course he was. Fine. Michel, can we borrow your cell phone, please? The landline inside is dead and we'll need to call the police and an electrician for emergency service to the drawbridge."

"I don't own a mobile," Michel replied.

Gil and I both stared at him as if he'd just spoken Martian. "Say what, now?"

"I find them distracting."

I was so tired and fed up with being stymied at every turn that I lost my temper. "You know what else is distracting? Needing to make an emergency call when your landline is dead!"

"M. J.," Gil said, "ease up, okay?"

I took a steadying breath and apologized to Michel. "It's fine," he assured me. "Usually I'm in the company of people who have their mobiles with them at all times, so it's not been an issue until tonight."

"Okay," I said, trying to think this through. "Is there someone we can wake up in the castle to borrow their cell phone? Like one of the other models, maybe?"

Gil and Michel shook their heads at the same time. "Everyone went into town for dinner and drinks," Gil said. "There's no one here besides us fools. Or maybe one of the other guests."

I knew of only two other guests at the castle: that horrible man and his frightened mousy wife in the room next to mine. I hated to think of waking them up, because I was positive the jerk would only take the disturbance out on his wife. "So we're stuck," I said miserably.

"It would seem so," Michel replied. "Unless Mr. Crunn knows of another way out of the castle, and there's sure to be one. Places like this always have a hidden door leading to the outside."

I pointed across the courtyard. "There's one right there," I said. "But I wouldn't go through it for all the tea in China."

Gil eyed me oddly. "What are you, a hundred?"

"It's a common expression!"

"Yes. For people born during the Roosevelt years ... the first Roosevelt."

I glowered at Gilley. "Bite me."

"Now, *that's* more contemporary."

I muttered something else a bit more contemporary and not so much to Gilley's liking before turning on my heel and marching away to head back inside to ask Arthur if there was another way out of the castle, but then I realized that being out of the castle wasn't likely to do anyone any good. The town was several miles away and I didn't particularly want to venture off across the moors in the dark. No, we'd be stuck here, so I should probably quit stalling and get busy trying to find Gopher and the others.

Gil caught up to me and tugged on my sweatshirt. (Like how I've already claimed it as mine?) "Hold on, M. J. Give this back."

"Nope," I said, tugging free of his grip and picking up my pace to a trot.

Gil wasn't about to give up that easily; he picked his pace up too. "You promised to give it to me when we got back."

"But you didn't go anywhere. When you go somewhere and come back, I'll hand it over."

He tugged on my sleeve again. "Be serious!"

"I am being serious, Gil. I need this sweatshirt to go after Gopher and the others in the south wing. Now stop pulling on it, would you?"

"M. J.!" Gil screeched. "I can't be here without my sweatshirt!"

"Of course you can. Between John and me, we've got at least eight spikes. That should be more than enough to keep you safe while I go look for the crew."

"If it's enough to keep me safe, then it's enough to keep *you* safe."

I didn't answer him because the fact of the matter was that even ten spikes hadn't been enough the last time. Of course, we hadn't had all of them exposed at the time the Widow and that big black shadow had come chasing after us, but still, I knew I'd have a much better chance of surviving another visit to the south wing only if I wore the sweatshirt. At the very least I had a decent shot at making it to my phone to call for help.

Gil continued to tug on my arm the whole rest of the way back into the castle. John and Arthur were still standing where I'd left them, and by the looks on their faces I could tell they'd been discussing something grave. "Did he call the police?" John asked me when we entered.

I shook my head. "Gil loaned his cell out to the model who went along on the ghost hunt, and Michel doesn't own a cell."

"What are they doing back here, then?" John asked.

"The drawbridge is up."

Arthur's jaw fell open. "What? But that's not right! It should be down!"

"Well, someone put it up and messed with the wires on the mechanism that raises and lowers it. We're stuck here unless you know of another way out of the castle so that one of us can go for help."

Arthur stared at me blankly as if he was having trouble taking in my words. At last he said, "Well, there is the door to the side of the keep that hides the tunnel that goes across the moat."

I shook my head vigorously. "No way. That's where the Widow ambushed us this morning."

Arthur's lips pressed together. "There is another exit," he said. "But it's on the far side of the castle. In the south wing."

My shoulders sagged. "Of course it is."

"How far is the police station from here?" John asked.

"Several kilometers," Arthur said. "At least two hours' walk."

"In the dark and across the moors, right?"

Arthur nodded. "I'm afraid so."

"Is there anyone who lives close by who might be of help?"

Arthur wrung his hands together. "The dowager owns most of the surrounding land. I'm afraid there's no one nearby for at least three kilometers or so, and even they would be difficult to locate in the dark."

I sighed. "Okay, then that does it. We stay put until the modeling troupe comes back and hopefully someone in their party will be bright enough to alert the authorities once they realize they can't get inside."

"André or Jaqui will certainly attempt to call," Michel said.

My mind was going in a thousand directions and for a moment I blanked on the names. "Who?"

"André and Jaqui Lefebvre," he replied.

"Ah, yeah," I said, remembering that even if André didn't think of it, his wife was certainly a shrewd customer. No woman spies on her husband like she'd done earlier without having at least a few solid brain cells.

"But what about Kim and the others?" John said, pulling us back to the urgent matter at hand.

I eyed him knowingly. I'd been certain that even though he and Kim had split up, John still carried a flame for her. "I'll go look for them now," I said before reaching into my pocket to pull out my room key. Handing it to John, I said, "Grab the spikes in my room and the ones from your tool belt and stay close to Gilley, Michel, and

Arthur until I get back. Protect them just in case the Widow comes into this section of the castle."

John looked like he wanted to argue with me about the plan, so I turned away and faced Crunn. "Arthur, has the Grim Widow ever come into this section of the castle?"

He shook his head vigorously. "I'd never work here if she did."

"So she sticks to the south wing exclusively?"

"Yes, that and . . ." Arthur seemed to catch himself.

"And? And what?"

"The moat. She's often seen at night swimming in the moat."

I had firsthand experience with that particular fact. "Okay, then, while I'm gone, see if you can think of another way to alert the authorities and get an electrician to make an emergency castle visit. Even if you have to wake up another one of the guests, do it. If a fire broke out, we'd all be in serious trouble."

Crunn blanched. "I hadn't considered that. Let me check the registry." And off he went to do that.

When I turned back to Gil, Michel, and John, they all wore identical expressions of doubt on their faces. "I should go with you," John said.

"No." I knew John meant well, and I was pretty touched that after his major scare earlier he'd still volunteer to come with me, but in dicey situations, he was unpredictable, and if he went running off in a panic again, I didn't know whether I could save him—especially if I managed to find Gopher and the girls and had them to worry about too.

"I'd like to volunteer," Michel said next.

"Thank you, Michel, but the answer is also no. The only person I'd be willing to take along on this hunt is currently lying in a hospital bed."

"M. J.," Gil said, but I cut him off.

"I'll be fine, Gilley. Stick with John and Michel and I'll be back as soon as I can." With that, I turned to the stairs, but thought of something as I was on my way up. Turning back, I said, "John, can you let me into your room? I want to grab a couple of flashlights and maybe one of the night-vision cameras."

"Gopher took all the cameras with him, M. J."

"Crap," I muttered. "I have a feeling I'm really gonna need one of those."

"He didn't take all of them," Gilley said. "One needed some repairs and I've got it in my room. I'll trade you it for my sweatshirt."

"Gil," I said wearily.

"I read up on this Grim Widow," Gil protested. "She really likes to go after hot young guys! I'm a prime target!"

I leveled my eyes at Gilley with barely concealed skepticism.

Gil glared right back at me, as if daring me to contradict him.

"I'll give you most of the spikes," John said to Gilley, coming to join me on the stairs. "And don't you have some spare magnets in your gear, Gil? I mean, I could've sworn I saw you pick up at least a dozen packs when we were in Germany from that tourist shop."

Gilley had a dozen packs of spare magnets? This was news to me. And when I saw his face flush with guilt, I knew it was true. I returned Gilley's glare, and then some. "While I'm gone, you can make yourself a spare sweatshirt or a pair of magnetic pj's for all I care. But for the time being, Gilley Gillespie, I'm keeping this sweatshirt and you *are* giving me that night-vision camera!"

Gil scowled but followed after us without protest as we headed up the stairs. When we got to John's room, he doled out two flashlights and the least reliable electrostatic meter we had (likely why Gopher had left it behind), and put fresh batteries in the night-vision camera that Gilley retrieved from his room. I noticed that Gil also brought along several packs of flat magnets, one of his sweatshirts, and a glue gun. He'd be busy while I was looking for the crew.

John took six spikes and stuffed them into a tool belt, giving the rest to Gilley. "I'll walk you as far as the door to the south wing," he explained.

When Gilley protested that that would leave him with only four, John pointed to Gil's stash of extra magnets and walked out without another word. I followed right behind him before Gil could start whining again.

"You nervous?" John asked when we'd walked for a bit.

"Terrified."

"Seriously, M. J., I think I should go with you. I mean, I could stick really close to you so that the sweatshirt might be enough to shield both of us."

Again the image of John flying down the hallway away from the black shadow demon played through my mind. "Sorry, buddy," I told him. "But I'm gonna need you to stay close to Gilley and make sure he doesn't lose it tonight."

Briefly, relief flashed across John's face, and I didn't blame him. Then he seemed to think of something. "Hey, wait here!" he said before dashing back the way we'd come. I had waited for him for all of three or four minutes when he came running back with a smug look on his face. After he handed me one of two headsets, I knew why.

"I almost forgot we still had these," he said, a little out of breath.

I put the headset on. "Do they work?" I seemed to recall the last time we used these had been in Ireland, and they'd been pretty beaten up on the bust we'd used them for.

John put his on too and clicked the power button. "Can you hear me now?"

I smiled. "Loud and clear, buddy. Okay, this is good."

"Gil also said he should be able to get a view through your camera feed, M. J. He's pulling up the link on his computer right now, so you can switch that on anytime and we'll know where you are and how to find you when . . . I mean *if* you get into trouble."

I placed a hand on his shoulder. "Thanks for the vote of confidence."

John's eyes dropped to the floor. "Sorry."

"It's cool. But if I *do* get into trouble, the last thing I need is for you guys to come running to my rescue and be picked off one at a time by the Widow. You gotta promise me that the three of you will sit tight. I'll figure out how to keep myself safe, okay?"

"What if she pulls you into the moat like she did Heath?" John asked.

I barely held back a shudder. "She won't," I promised, not quite believing I could stop her, but determined to try. "As long as I stick to the south wing, she won't have a chance to get me into the moat."

"Just don't pull down any of those sconces," John warned, stopping as we reached the door to the south wing.

"Noted." I took a big breath and stood in front of the door for a minute, gathering my courage. I reached for the handle and hesitated. "John, you'd better get back to the main hall. Arthur only said he'd never seen her come past the south wing—he didn't say that she couldn't."

John gulped. "Good point. Be careful, M. J., okay?"

"I'll do my best."

John turned then and jogged away. I waited until he was out of sight, then counted to ten and turned back to face the music.

"M. J.? This is Gilley. You copy? Over."

I think I jumped about a foot as Gil's voice echoed loudly into my ear. Once I'd calmed myself down, I whispered, "I'm here, guy."

"You forgot to say 'over,' over."

I ground my teeth together. "I'm over your overs, Gil. Now shut it for a minute, would you?"

"But I can't see anything! Did you switch on the camera?"

I looked down at my right hand. The little red button was unlit. After flipping on the camera's power, I raised it and turned the lens to my face. "Can you see me?"

"Yeah. Good. It's working. Okay, continue with the hunt!" he said, like he was my director or something.

I resisted the urge to turn off the headset and reached for the door handle. Very slowly I pulled it open a crack and peeked through. The hallway was ominously dark and none of the overhead lights were on. How'd I know this wouldn't be easy?

Lifting the camera, I turned the lens toward the opening and looked at the screen. The hallway appeared to be empty.

"What're you waiting for?" Gil asked me, his voice slightly bored.

"Will you shut up?" I snapped quietly. He was throwing off my concentration and irritating me no end.

"I just asked you a simple question," he said. "Over."

I closed the door and stepped away several feet from it. Putting my hand over my mouth to muffle the sound of my voice, I said, "Gilley Morehouse Gillespie, you hand this headset over to John *right now*!"

"God, M. J., are you PMSing tonight or what? Over."

"*Now*, Gil, or I'm gonna quit the hunt and come back there to throttle you!"

I heard the sound of plastic squeaking and then I heard John's voice. "Hey, M. J., you okay?"

I let out a little of the hot air welling inside of me. "Do me a favor and stay on with me, okay, John? Don't let Gilley have the headset back."

"You got it."

Taking another deep breath, I turned and trotted back to the door and reached for the handle. Pausing to grip it tightly, I counted to ten, lifted the camera, and opened the door wide.

The most hideous face met the lens of the camera as the Grim Widow jumped out right at me and hissed like a snake.

In my ear I could hear the sound of Gilley screaming and even John shouted out fearfully, but no one screamed as loudly as I did.

I jumped back and slammed the door, then turned tail and ran for all I was worth. I didn't stop until I'd reached the stairs leading down to the main hall. Below me in the center of the room were Gilley, John, Michel, and Arthur, all huddled close together and staring around with big frightened eyes. I knew my own expression likely mirrored theirs. *"You're alive!"* Gil exclaimed when he saw me.

I was breathing hard as I descended the stairs, looking over my shoulder as I went. When I reached the group, Gilley flung himself at me. "Oh, thank God!"

"I'm fine," I told him. "Severely freaked-out, but otherwise unharmed."

Gil continued to hug me. In fact, he even tightened his grip. "Gil," I said. "Let go."

But he wouldn't, and I suddenly realized he was less concerned about me and more interested in sharing the energy of the magnets surrounding me. It took me nearly a minute to pry him off me. "Did she hurt you?" Arthur asked once I'd managed to shove Gil away.

I shook my head. "No. She just hissed and I bolted."

"Did she come after you?" John asked, staring nervously toward the stairs.

"No," I repeated. "At least I don't think so. Arthur appears to be right. She sticks to the south wing."

"This section of the castle was exorcised by a priest in

the early 1700s," Arthur told us. "That seemed to keep her confined to the south side of the castle."

"Why didn't the priest take care of the whole castle while he was at it?" I asked. It seemed stupid to leave any part of the castle to that horrible spook.

"It took him a whole day to conduct the ritual on this side of the castle," Arthur explained. "He planned to finish exorcising the south wing the next day, but the following morning he was found dead . . . floating in the moat."

Gilley made a squeaking sound and moved over next to Michel, who also looked quite frightened, but seemed to be handling this better than Gil. "What do we do now?" Michel asked when the rest of us fell silent.

I stared down at the floor. After that encounter, I knew I couldn't leave Gopher and the girls to face the Widow alone. God only knew what'd happened to them, as no one had heard a peep (or cascade of screams) since they'd left on their hunt. "Let me see the footage," I said to Gil, motioning to his computer.

Gil paled. "Why?"

"I only saw her for a second through the viewfinder. I want to see how close she came before I got out of there."

"I repeat, why?"

"To see if this sweatshirt had any effect at all," I told him with a weary sigh. Why was everything an argument with him these days?

Gil bit his lip but sat down and picked up his computer. "Okay, but I'm not going to look at it again." As he lifted the lid, his computer dinged with an incoming e-mail. For a brief second, Gil's attention was diverted. "It's from Chris Weller. He wants to know if we've got any footage for him."

I made a face. Chris Weller was the last person on earth I wanted to distract me. "You know what? Send him the footage we just took and tell him to stuff it!" I was sooooo over the network brass and their constant harassment.

Gil began typing and belatedly I realized he'd taken me seriously. I almost told him to stop, but then thought, what the hell? Let Chris be scared out of his boxers. After Gil sent off the clip, he turned the computer around so I could see, and I squinted at the green and black image showing the door being pulled open and that incredibly frightful face bursting out of utter blackness to hiss into my camera. What I hadn't realized was that I seemed to have hesitated before turning on my heel and running away. For a second the camera had continued to film the Grim Widow as she came at me, but then she actually recoiled, her hands coming away as if she'd just touched something very hot.

"So the sweatshirt does work," I said. And I couldn't be sure if I was relieved or even more scared by the revelation.

"M. J., she came right at you!" John protested.

I shook my head and rewound the clip a few frames. "She backs off the moment she's about to grab me. See?"

John peered squeamishly at the screen. "She still comes way too close to you for comfort," he said.

I sighed. "Agreed. But I've still gotta get into that wing and try to find Gopher, Kim, and Meg."

"There is another entrance," Arthur said. "It's on this level through the kitchen. It's a very small and narrow entrance that the servants used to push Lady Jane's meals through."

"Why didn't you tell us that before?" John asked.

"Years ago we pushed a heavy set of shelves in front of it," he explained. "I know that it likely wouldn't stop a ghost, but putting up the barricade helped ease the fears of those of us who are frightened by openings leading to the south wing."

"Can a person fit through this opening?" I asked.

"Someone of your size should have no trouble, Miss Holliday."

"Will we be able to push the shelves aside and get through?" I asked next.

"Yes, I should think so," Arthur said.

I motioned to him with my hand. "Lead the way, Mr. Crunn."

Arthur walked with all of us close on his heels. Gilley stuck to me like white on rice, his arms and pockets literally brimming with magnets and spikes.

We followed Arthur through the hall leading to the dining room, across that large space, and into the kitchen, where Arthur flipped the light switch and the castle's kitchen was illuminated.

I was surprised by how modern it was but didn't linger on it, as we had work to do. Arthur then pointed to a large wooden set of shelves backed up against a wall. The shelving was at least six feet high and loaded with pantry items, but it seemed movable given the several hands we had available for the task.

After unloading the shelves of most of the breakable objects, Michel and John pushed against one side and got the unit far enough away from the wall to reveal the small door, which wasn't much bigger than three feet by two. I stepped into the angled space and pulled up on the levered handle to test the door. It gave a little pop and I knew it would open easily, but I'd have to crawl through on hands and knees.

"Okay," I said to the men, hovering around me, "I'm going through. You four should go back to the main hall and wait for me."

Gilley took off out of the kitchen in a manner that suggested I didn't have to tell him twice. Michel gave me a two-finger salute and wished me luck before leaving, and Arthur laid a hand on my shoulder and said, "You're an incredibly brave woman, Miss Holliday. Please, do take care, all right?"

"I'll do my best," I assured him, already feeling a little shaky with fear.

John was the last to go, and he tapped his headset and said, "I don't care what you think. If you get in trouble, you call me. I'll come running with every spike we've got."

"Thanks, buddy." I motioned for him to go and he left me alone to face my destiny.

Chapter 6

Turning back to the door, I squared my shoulders, lifted the camera, and pulled up on the handle very slowly. "Okay, M. J., we're all back in the main hall," I heard John whisper into my ear.

I didn't answer him, as I was convinced the Widow had detected my argument with Gilley and had come running to meet me at the entrance upstairs. Instead I got down on all fours, opened the door very carefully, and pointed the camera to the interior of the hall beyond the door.

It was a short corridor, and apparently unoccupied. With great care I crept forward a few feet, until only my torso was through the opening. I lifted the camera again and pointed it all around. I was trembling with fear, probably still rattled from the shock of the Widow's attack upstairs. I listened for any sound that might alert me to her presence, but nothing moved on the viewfinder and no disturbing sound came to my ears. Finally, after assessing the hallway for more than a minute, I spoke to the boys. "It looks clear."

"Tell her to be careful!" I overheard Gilley say to John. "And tell her if she gets into trouble to get her ass back through that door!" Most of the irritation I'd had earlier with him melted away. He genuinely cared about me and that mattered.

"Gilley says—"

"I heard him, John. Tell him I will, on both counts." I waited another thirty seconds or so before I felt brave enough to move forward all the way through the doorway. I wished for all the world that Heath was with me. It took every ounce of courage I had to creep forward far enough so that I could stand up again. Looking behind me at the small opening, I had even greater reservations. Getting through it quickly would be a challenge. What if the Widow managed to close it on me before I had a chance to escape?

"You okay?" John asked me, and I realized I hadn't moved or spoken in several moments.

"Yeah," I whispered, making an effort to steel my nerves. I'd learned a few things on these types of busts during the last few years, and one of the most valuable was that fear can act as a beacon to the spirit world— especially the more nefarious spooks. I had to admit to myself that as much as the Widow may have been alerted to my argument with Gilley, she may have also been summoned by my own fear. With effort I inhaled several calming breaths. *You're okay,* I said to myself.

Be careful, Mary Jane, another voice inside my head warned.

Sam?

I'm here, he assured me, and his presence did more to reassure me than I can even say. Sam Whitefeather is my spirit guide. In life, he was also Heath's beloved grandfather.

Do you see her? I asked him.

She's up, he said, and I knew he meant she was on the second story. *Her energy is the most evil human spirit I've ever seen. As long as you're here, you're in very grave danger, my spirit daughter.*

I have to find Gopher, Kim, and Meg, I told him. *Do you see them?*

Sam didn't speak for a moment and I wondered if he'd gone away. But then he said, *I cannot sense them, but that may be because these walls have absorbed the evil of the woman who haunts it and it radiates so loudly that I'm unable to detect much else.*

I knew what he meant. It's hard to describe what was bouncing off the walls of that hallway, but the best I can do is to say that they were practically pulsing with malice. *How should I proceed?* I asked him next. I still hadn't moved from that initial few feet I'd taken to get inside the door.

Very carefully, Sam said, and I knew he wasn't kidding around. *I'll warn you if I think she's headed your way.*

Sam's offer to play lookout did a lot to bolster my courage. Still, moving down that hallway was one of the hardest things I've ever done. I crept along as quietly as I could, all my senses on high alert, and every few feet I checked in with Sam to make sure I hadn't lost him.

It took me a while to make it down that hallway, and thankfully, John kept his trap shut and didn't push me to hurry. I knew he was anxious about Kim, and I was worried about her, Meg, Gopher, and that model too, but I had to go slow and careful with a dangerous ghost like the Grim Widow around.

At last I made it to the end of the hallway and there were two choices in front of me—left or right. Belatedly I wished that I'd had the sense to ask Arthur to draw me a map of the south wing, and for a brief second I considered going back, but we'd already lost too much time, so I quickly discarded that option. Instead, I relied on Sam and my own intuition. I took the right corridor and worked to tamp down the mounting fear that kept bubbling higher the farther away from the exit I got.

John had given me two stakes and I held one of them in my left hand while I navigated the dark interior with the viewfinder on the night-vision camera. I will admit that being smothered by darkness except for the green glow given off by the viewfinder left me feeling somewhat claustrophobic on top of also being scared out of my socks.

Still, I managed to make it step by step through the hallway, my ears pricked for even the smallest sounds. As I came to a door on my right or my left, I would tuck the spike into my holster and try the knob. Most of the doors were locked, but a few opened up to reveal empty rooms filled with cobwebs and dust.

Each time I found a room empty, I had dueling emotions—both the relief of not having something jump out and attack me and the frustration of not finding my friends.

Eventually I figured out the layout of the first floor. It housed many large and stately rooms along with several much smaller ones. I could only guess at their purpose from five hundred years ago, but now they were nothing but empty, cold, cobweb-infested shells.

After about an hour of searching I knew that I'd covered the entire first floor. The battery on the camera indicated that I had only about an hour or less left, and if I encountered the Widow and she sucked out the rest of the juice in the battery, I'd be up spook creek without a paddle.

With great trepidation I approached the central south-wing staircase. It was off a hall that mirrored the great hall at the front of the castle, but smaller. I stared up the stairs nervously. *I've got to go up there, don't I?* I asked Sam.

Afraid so, he said. *I'll keep an eye on the Widow. You focus on finding your friends.*

"Be careful, M. J.," John whispered in my ear.

I gathered a little more courage and was about to take

the first step when a loud bang caused me to jump and nearly lose hold of the camera and my spike. Whirling around, I found the source quickly. A door had banged shut. *Sam?* I asked.

I'm not sensing a spirit did that, he said.

I approached the door cautiously and put my hand up to it. A cold draft whistled through the crack between the door and the frame. Taking a deep breath, I pulled on the door and saw that it opened to the outdoors, but there was no landing, just a drop of about ten feet to the rocky terrain below.

If there had been a landing or a series of stairs here, they'd long since rotted away or been removed. Still, it was good to know that I had another possible escape route should the Widow find me skulking about.

I studied the ground below, and figured I could simply ease myself over the edge, hang by my hands from the opening, and drop the few extra feet to the ground without causing myself injury. Squinting a little more at the surrounding terrain directly below, I could see that a sort of skirt of land surrounded this section of the castle. I grabbed on to the doorframe and hung out of the opening to get an even better look, and saw that there was a pretty rickety-looking bridge to my left, which extended from the skirt across the moat to the other side. No way would I be going across that puppy in the dark, but still, it was good to know that at least someone could get across the water from here.

Leaving the door propped open by a loose board I found nearby, I moved back to the staircase and took the first step up. I'd be more vulnerable on the steps. Many malevolent ghosts had pushed or shoved their living victims down the stairs. It was a favorite trick of their ilk.

I hugged the railing on the right side as I went up, and with each step I could feel the malicious presence of the Widow grow stronger. My breathing started to pick up again and Sam reminded me to remain as calm as possible. *You're okay,* he said in my mind. *She hasn't sensed your presence yet.*

It was the "yet" that bothered me.

At the top of the stairs I hesitated, listening and turning the viewfinder all around, looking for any sign of the Widow. Nothing moved. I took a step and the floorboards creaked. My heartbeat quickened. *Stay calm, M. J.,* Sam warned.

That was easier said than done. I took another step and the floorboards creaked again. To my ears the noise was so loud I couldn't fathom it not calling attention to me, and I hesitated again, thinking Sam was going to tell me to run for it, but he kept quiet and I knew I needed to go on.

There was only one hallway off the stairs and I followed it cautiously to the first intersection. *Right or left?* I asked Sam, but before he could answer, I heard a sound from outside. It was coming from a window right in front of me whose pane had been broken.

I peeked through the pane and saw a man rowing a small boat in the water. I held the viewfinder up and tapped the zoom button, and just as the man was coming into focus, he and the boat completely disappeared.

I sucked in a breath, pulled back, and flattened myself against the wall. I wasn't scared so much as shocked by the sudden revelation that there was another ghost haunting the moat.

"Who was that and where the hell did he *go*?" John whispered.

I didn't answer him. Instead, I stood there motionless for several seconds while I worked to steady my nerves. Finally I pushed away from the wall again and had the urge to take another look out of the window. Raising the viewfinder, I looked first below, then across the moat to the other side, and that's when I saw the figure of someone walking along the moors. He or she appeared quite comfortable with the terrain, and looked to be steadily wending down to the water's edge. The way the body moved, I had the feeling it was male, but I couldn't be sure from that distance. I thought about calling out to the figure, but just as I was considering that, it too disappeared. "Whoa!" I heard both John and Gilley exclaim. They were obviously watching the footage through the camera feed. "Another ghost?" John asked me.

"Maybe," I whispered, staring down at the moors and trying to catch another glimpse of the figure. "Or the same one going through a series of sequences." Sometimes a spook will randomly choose to go through several sequences of the final moments of his life, and often these may appear out of order—almost like watching small sections of a movie that's slightly out of sync.

"I wonder if the spooks outside are any nicer than the ones inside," John said.

"Nothing could be worse than what's in here," I said softly, finally turning away from the window and heading to the intersection of the hallways again.

Right or left, Sam? I asked.

I'd go right.

I began to turn in that direction when another sound came to my ears. This one was utterly unexpected, if not unfamiliar. Immediately I turned away from the right-hand corridor and veered left, walking with purpose to the third door on the right. The sound of guitar strums echoed through the wood from inside. Quickly, I fumbled through the pocket of my jeans, at last coming up with my old room key, and managed to turn the lock just as the guitar strums stopped.

Closing the door quietly, I hurried to the bedside table and picked up my phone. The screen said that I'd missed seven new calls and I had as many voice mails.

I swiped my finger across the screen to unlock it, and the first thing I saw was that I'd just missed a call from Gopher. "No way . . . ," I whispered.

"What?" John said immediately. "Are you in trouble, M. J.? Do you need help?"

"What's happening?" I heard Gilley's panicked voice ask in the background. "Is it the Widow?! Does she have M. J.?! Is she coming for me?! *I'm too young to die!*"

Instead of answering, I held up the display of the phone to the camera so that everybody could see. "Gopher called?" John said, and I could imagine him pointing to the computer screen so that Gil wouldn't have a full-scale meltdown.

"I thought she didn't have her phone?" Gil said much more calmly. "Ask her where she got the phone!"

"John," I whispered. "Tell Gil to shut up for a minute." I couldn't think with all his yammering in the background.

"M. J. says to shut it, dude."

"Tell M. J. to shut it!" Gil replied.

I sighed and pulled the headset off. In my mind I said, *Sam? Is the Widow close by?*

No. She's still some distance away.

I have to make a phone call. Would you continue to play lookout for me?

Of course. Make your call. If she moves, I'll alert you. I thanked him, then pressed the callback feature on my phone and put it to my ear. "Where have you been?" Gopher demanded. "I've been calling you and calling you! And nobody's answering their damn phones! Not you, not John, not even Heath!"

I felt relief wash over me. Gopher was alive. Nervously I eyed the door, and even though Sam was playing lookout for me, I still moved over to the corner, hunched down, and spoke to Gopher very softly. "None of us had our phones on us," I reminded him. "I just found mine, in fact. But more important, are you okay, Goph?"

"No, I'm not okay!" he nearly shouted. "Some *idiot* put up the drawbridge and now we can't get back inside!

We're all freezing and we didn't get a frickin' minute of usable footage!"

I closed my eyes and let out a long breath. Thank God he and the others were okay. Still, I wanted to make sure everyone was with him. "The drawbridge had a mechanical failure. It's stuck."

"Great," Gopher grumbled. "Just great!"

"Are you with Meg and Kim?" I asked him next.

"Yeah."

"Where are you guys?" The wind whipping through his microphone and his knowledge about the drawbridge meant he likely wasn't inside the castle. Also the fact that he was still alive may have been a clue.

"We went out on the moors to try and find this duke character."

"John said you guys went into the south wing."

"Oh, we peeked through that door upstairs, but we decided against it. You weren't kidding about how creepy it is, and we figured the moors were safer for a ghost hunt."

"You could've told John where you were heading, you know," I said crossly. If Gopher had simply told our sound tech where he was heading, I wouldn't currently be risking my ass to save his.

"I left him a message," Gopher replied testily. "If John had answered his damn phone, he would've known where we were!" I was pretty sure John had told Gopher that his phone was toast, but our producer didn't listen very well. "And speaking of John," Gopher added, "did he tell you he's fired?"

The corner of my mouth quirked. "He did. He also said that I was fired."

"We're *all* fired, M. J.!" Gopher shouted. "I had a one a.m. deadline with Chris and that blew by over an hour ago!"

"Actually . . . ," I said, "we sent Chris an up-close and

personal encounter with the Grim Widow just after midnight. I'm pretty sure he won't pull the plug just yet. And I've captured some additional footage of a couple of ghosts out on the moors. I think that'll be enough to hold him over for now."

"You went out on your own?" Gopher asked, and I could hear the surprise in his voice. "Wait a second, where the hell are you, M. J.?"

"Looking for you fools."

"I repeat," Gopher said, his voice now nervous, "*where* are you?"

"The south wing of the castle."

I heard Gopher's breath catch. "Who's with you?"

"Nobody."

"You're alone?"

"Yep. Heath's still at the hospital and I didn't want to put anybody else in jeopardy by dragging them in here."

"Well, get the hell out of there! It's not safe!"

"You're telling me," I said. "Listen, I've gotta click off with you before the Widow discovers me. I'll have Arthur use my phone to call a mechanic for the drawbridge, but you should use yours to call a cab and take that into town. Find a room somewhere until the morning, then come back. We should have the bridge down by then."

"Okay, but send that additional footage to Chris, okay?"

I pulled the phone away from my ear and stuck my tongue out at it. Here I was risking my neck, and all he cared about was some stupid footage for his stupid boss. Putting the phone back to my ear, I whispered, "But I thought I was fired?"

Gopher chuckled. "You're rehired, okay? Now go. Get out of there and don't get caught."

I clicked off the line and put the headset back on. Gilley was shouting hysterically into the microphone. "I thought I heard her moan!" he cried. "M. J.! M. J.! Are you hurt? Did the Widow kill you?"

"I'm fine, Gil."

"She's aliiiiiiiiiiive!"

I winced and tugged on the earphone. God, he could be shrill. "I'm coming back through the kitchen," I told him, hoping he was done with the theatrics.

"Hey, M. J.," John said.

I blinked. "I thought Gil was wearing the headgear?"

"He was. I had just handed it to him because you wouldn't answer and I thought something bad had gone down. I was on my way to come find you when Gil shouted that you were okay."

"Yeah, well, I'm not okay yet. I still have to get outta here." I lifted the camera then and noticed that the stupid battery was running low. "Dammit. I'm almost out of charge. Listen, I'm going to go radio silent until I get off this floor. You guys just watch the camera to track my progress, okay?"

"Got it."

I moved the mouthpiece down under my chin and checked in with Sam, who hadn't entered my mind since I'd asked him to play lookout. He indicated that the Widow was still some distance away, so I felt it was safe to click on my flashlight and grab as many of my and Heath's belongings as I could. Our gear was exactly where we'd left it, and I moved around the room quickly stuffing as many things as I could into my messenger bag. I managed to get two pairs of my jeans and two pairs of Heath's jeans into the bag along with some clean underthings, and I figured we could buy some extra sweaters and toiletries in town.

I also looked around for Heath's phone, but realized it'd probably ended up in the moat, as I knew he'd had it with him when we first went down to report the battered woman in the hall. He'd have to replace it, but it wouldn't be the first phone we'd replaced since we joined the cast of *Ghoul Getters*.

After I'd done a quick but through search of the room

and made sure to pick up our passports, our wallets, and
the keys to my condo, I turned off my flashlight and
waited for my eyes to adjust to the dark again.

Once I was sure I could make out a few shapes, I
moved to the door and pressed my ear to the crack to
listen for any hint of the Widow.

Sam? I asked.

It's clear, but you should go now, M. J., Sam said.

I raised the viewfinder and pointed the lens at the
door, turning the knob as silently as I could. The warning
light for the low battery was starting to flash. I figured I
had maybe five minutes of battery life left; then I'd be
forced to use my flashlight—a scenario I didn't much
care for.

The door opened a crack and I pushed the lens
through the opening, angling it first to the right, then to
the left to look out into the hallway. No ghostly haggard
face appeared in my viewfinder, so I stepped forward
and squeezed through to the hallway.

I didn't even bother to close the door. I just crept
away on tiptoe as fast as I could.

Uh-oh, Sam said suddenly.

I stopped. *What's uh-oh?*

There's been a shift.

I put a hand over my heart, which had started to beat
a whole lot faster. *Shift? What kind of shift?*

The kind that means you'd better run!

I held back a terrified shriek and bolted, running
clumsily with the camera out in front of me and my messenger bag bouncing hard against my hip.

Stupidly, I'd put the extra two spikes I carried in the
bag, and before I left the room, I'd forgotten to pull them
back out again, and I couldn't very well stop to dig them
out, not with Sam's ominous warning.

M. J.! Sam said.

What?

Run faster!

"Shit, shit, shit!" I hissed, turning on the speed. It was hard, because I had to thrust the arm holding the camera out in front of me so I could see, which forced me to use my other arm to pump my stride, and all the while my messenger bag flapped hard against my hip.

I reached the stairs and could see them dimly without the aid of the viewfinder, so I lowered the camera and shot down them, nearly losing my footing—I was so scared. Behind me I could feel the malevolent presence of the Widow approaching. She came on like a bad storm—fast and furious.

I was breathing so hard that I was starting to get a little light-headed by the time I reached the ground floor, and because of that, for a horrible moment I lost my bearings. For the life of me I couldn't remember which of the four hallways surrounding the main hall I'd come from.

That brought me up short and I stared at them one at a time without really seeing them. "Which way?" I whispered. "Dammit! Which way?"

She's coming! Sam shouted. An instant later I was hit hard from behind and I went hurtling forward, barely managing to keep on my feet. Spinning around once I'd regained my balance, I could see the Widow about fifteen feet in front of me, spitting her vile ectoplasm and dribbling green drool out of the corner of her mouth. *Hissssss!* she spat. She held her hands up like they'd been burned, and I had no doubt that when she'd rammed me from behind, she'd felt the blow even more than I had.

I backed up and became aware that John was shouting furiously at me. My headset had been knocked slightly askew, and no doubt he'd been alerted that something was wrong by the jostling of the camera. "Stay back!" I shouted at the Widow, pulling up the viewfinder so that I could see her more clearly.

But she only grinned evilly and lowered her chin.

"Oh, *shit*!" I cried, turning to run, but the Widow

came at me with lightning speed and crashed into me again. This time I went tumbling forward and lost my balance; instinctively trying to save the camera from smashing into the ground, I took the fall on my left side. It hurt like a mother.

Still, I knew that if I gave in to the pain, the Widow would be on top of me in a hot second, and in the back of my mind I wondered where that big black shadow was. It couldn't be far behind.

I curled onto my knees, then pushed myself to my feet. My headset was dangling off one ear, but the camera was intact. I pointed the lens toward the Widow again. She spat at me and waved her hands as if they were very hot.

I figured she was going to crash into me over and over again until one of us was so banged up she couldn't move anymore. And I didn't think it'd be her.

The door! Sam shouted so loud in my head that I winced anew. Had he also been yelling in my ear since the Widow attacked me the first time?

The door! Sam repeated, and I felt the most insistent tug on my right side. Barely able to tear my eyes away from the Widow, I glanced quickly to my right and saw the door I'd propped open. It was maybe ten feet away.

I looked back to the Widow. She'd seen me eye the door too. Her lips curled back into a snarl and she let out a ferocious cry right before she came at me.

Not waiting to get sucker punched again, I bolted and ran those ten feet so fast my feet barely touched the ground. I didn't even stop when I got to the open door. I knew what was beyond. I'd take my chances with the drop and the thin stretch of land between the castle wall and the moat.

Leaping the last two feet through the door, I raised my chest high and waved my arms wildly, hoping I wouldn't break a leg when I landed.

I hit the ground *hard* and dropped to my knees, rolling to my side and crying out in pain. I didn't know if I'd just broken both my shins, but it sort of felt that way.

Hugging my legs, I lay there motionless for a minute as tears leaked out of my eyes. My breathing was still a little ragged, but eventually the pain in my shins subsided enough for me to become more aware of my surroundings. About then, I realized there was a pair of boots about six feet away from me. Instantly I felt a chill run up my spine, and for a moment I forgot my own pain and very slowly turned my head to follow those boots up, past a set of legs, a torso, and finally to a face. A man dressed in period attire was standing fairly close by, but he wasn't looking at me. With hands on hips he was glaring up at the open doorway, where the Widow was just barely visible. She spat at him, then disappeared, slamming the door hard in her wake.

The minute the door slammed, the man lowered his chin and looked straight at me. My breath caught. He was a frightful-looking person, and his stare was dark and cold. For several seconds all we did was look at each other, and then, quite unexpectedly, he vanished right before my eyes.

I gulped and pushed myself to a half-sitting position, my legs still curled up underneath me. From somewhere close, I could hear a squeaking noise, and after a minute I realized that my headset had finally come completely off my head and had landed just to my left. With a groan I clawed my way over to it and picked it up. "Hello?" I said, but there was way too much yelling for anybody to hear me. I closed my eyes, gathering my voice, then shouted as loud as I could into the microphone.

There was an immediate pause; then all I heard was *"She's aliiiiiiiiiiiiiiiiiive!"*

Gil seriously needed to drop the Dr. Frankenstein act.

"M. J.!" John said urgently. "Are you hurt? We saw the camera move toward the door, then fly up into the air a second before the feed cut out."

I lifted the camera, still strapped to my hand. The battery had died at last, but the component seemed to be intact. Which was better than I could say for myself.

"I think I broke my legs," I groaned, leaning back against the hard stone of the castle wall.

"Oh, man!" John replied, and I could tell he was pretty close to doing something stupid like charging through the south wing to my rescue. "Are you serious?"

I swallowed hard and ran my hands along my shins. "Hang on," I told him, and very, *very* gingerly I stretched out first one leg, then the other. They still hurt something fierce, but they seemed to be working. I then sat up straighter and planted my feet carefully, placing a little weight on each foot. "So far so good," I muttered.

"What does that mean?" John asked. "Are you hurt? Can you walk? Do you need me to come help you?"

"Hang on!" I repeated impatiently. Using my hands, I pushed up and managed a sort of pitiful crouch. I could support myself, which was at least half the battle. Taking one very careful small step, I let out a sigh of relief. I could walk. Just barely, but I could walk. "I'm okay," I said at last.

John started to speak, but I cut him off. "Just a sec," I said, taking a moment to really get a good long look at my surroundings. I was at the outside wall of the castle, trapped between a moat and a hard place. "Just my luck," I grumbled.

I glanced up at the door I'd practically flown out of, and saw that it was still shut tight. No sign of the Widow could be seen. "At least that's a good thing."

"Can I talk now?" John asked.

I sighed wearily. "Yes, John, sorry. Please go ahead."

"Where are you exactly?"

"I'm on this thin piece of land between the moat and the castle," I said, fishing through my messenger bag to pull out my flashlight. Clicking it on, I pointed it to the bridge just down from me. "There's an old rickety bridge about fifteen yards away, but there's no way I'm crossing that thing in the dark. Who knows if it's safe or not?"

"But you have your phone now, right?"

"I do."

"How's the battery?" John asked me.

I pushed away from the wall and gimped over to a nearby boulder at the edge of the moat to sit down before pulling out my cell from my bag. "I've still got a full charge."

"Great. Arthur says he's got a friend in town who can probably come out tonight and work on the drawbridge. He's got his own boat, so he can rescue you too."

I swiveled on the boulder to point the flashlight out over the moat. The thought of going across it in a boat gave me the willies. As the beam of the flashlight swung out over the still waters, I noticed something unnatural floating on the other side near the bank and my chest tightened.

"Hold on, M. J.," John was saying. "Arthur is getting the number now."

"Uh . . . John?"

"Yeah?"

"Tell Arthur to hold off on that number for a minute."

"Why?"

"Because my first call is going to be to the police. There's another body floating in this moat."

Chapter 7

By the time Inspector Lumley arrived, I was chilled to the bone. He came around in a small boat being rowed by the same constable who'd jumped in after me nearly twenty-four hours earlier. Neither of them looked very happy to have been called out here again in the middle of the night, nor to find me at the scene of another drowning victim.

I'd kept a wary eye on the floating corpse. Oddly, although I'm quite comfortable communicating with the deceased, dead bodies give me the serious willies. Who the victim was I couldn't tell, because the body was bloated and the face was submerged. But the silver hair on the back of the poor soul's head sent a tingle of recognition through me and I seriously hoped I was wrong.

Still, I vowed to hold back any further speculation until the identity was confirmed by the authorities—assuming I stayed around here long enough to find out, that is.

I tucked the video camera under my sweatshirt when the boat came up to the boulder I was sitting on. "Miss Holliday," the inspector said with a nod.

I pointed the beam of my flashlight across the moat. "The body's right there, Inspector. I think it's lodged against those tree roots."

The inspector half turned and pointed his own flashlight across the water. "Yes," he said without further comment on the floater. Turning back to me, he asked, "And how did you come to be here?"

I pulled the camera back out and held it up for him to see. "I was on a ghost hunt for our cable show."

"*Ghost Getters*, is that right?" he asked me. I saw that he'd done his homework. Mostly.

"*Ghoul Getters*," I corrected, "but you're close enough."

"Still," he said flashing his beam all around the small bit of land I was stuck on. "How did you get *here* specifically?"

I pointed up to the door ten feet above. "From there."

The inspector's eyes bulged. "From *there*?"

"Yes."

He flashed his beam around again. "But there's no ladder or rope. However did you get down?"

"I jumped."

"You jumped?"

I pulled up the legs of my jeans and shone the flashlight right at the bruises just forming along my legs. "Yes, Inspector, I jumped. And I promise, it hurt like hell."

"Why the devil would you jump from such a height only to be stuck here?" he asked me.

"Because I was running from the Grim Widow."

It was hard to tell in the dark, but I could've sworn the inspector's complexion paled a bit. "I see."

"Inspector," the constable said nervously. "Can we please help the miss into the boat and be off? I don't like being so close to this end of the castle."

"This end?" the inspector asked. Apparently, he liked to repeat stuff.

"We're at the south side," I told him. "The Grim Widow's territory."

"Ah," he replied before standing up carefully and offering me his hand. I moved gingerly to the top of the boulder and with his help I got in the boat. "You look quite cold," he told me.

"I still haven't warmed up all the way from yesterday."

He seemed to take that in before telling the constable, "Niles, let's get Miss Holliday across the moat and into your car. We'll turn the heat on for her and wait with the body for the coroner."

I smiled gratefully at the inspector. "Thank you, sir."

"You're most welcome, and while Constable Bancroft rows us to shore, why don't you tell me why the drawbridge is up?"

From the way he said that, I had the feeling the drawbridge was never up. "None of us are sure how that happened," I told him. "I came home from visiting Heath in the hospital—"

"That would be Heath Whitefeather? The young man who nearly drowned?"

"Yes. He's my boyfriend and a fellow member of our crew."

"How is he?"

"He's much better, thank you. They just wanted to keep him overnight to make sure his temperature came all the way back up and that his metabolism was functioning correctly again."

"That's good to hear," the inspector said. "I'm sorry, I interrupted you: What time did you arrive back from visiting with Mr. Whitefeather?"

"Close to midnight. When I got to the castle, I discovered that a few other crew members had gone on a ghost hunt without me and they hadn't been seen or heard from."

"They're missing?"

The inspector was back to repeating again. "Well, at the time I thought they were, but it turns out they were out on the moors trying to get some footage of the Desperate Duke and they got locked out of the castle."

At the mention of the Desperate Duke the inspector's face turned down in a frown. "It'd be best for them if they never saw the duke."

I cocked my head. I was fairly certain I'd had an encounter with Sir Mortimer on the rocky ground below the door, and he'd done me no harm. The inspector must have noticed my curious expression because he said, "Legend has it that the duke only appears to those marked for death. It's also said that he haunts the area near here and taunts his wife's ghost from the shore."

I suppressed a shudder. I'd witnessed several spooky apparitions that night—not including the Widow. I wondered if they'd all been the duke. Had he been rowing the boat in the moat? And was he also the figure making his way along the moors? I felt certain he'd been the ghost six feet away from me after I'd jumped out of the door, but did that mean that I was marked for death?

My thoughts spun nervously until the inspector called my attention back with his next question. "When you returned from your trip to the hospital, was the drawbridge up?"

"No, sir. But about fifteen minutes after I arrived back in the main hall, my best friend, Gilley—he's the technical adviser to the show—tried to leave with another man to go into town and have a drink, and that's when we all discovered that the drawbridge had been pulled up and the mechanism that controls it tampered with."

The inspector's brow furrowed. "Tampered with how exactly?"

I shrugged. "I'm no mechanic, but the box that houses the switch was broken open and all the wires were cut. Oh, and all the phones inside the castle are dead too."

By this time we were at the shore across from the

front of the castle, by the road where it stopped and turned onto the drawbridge—or where it would have turned onto the drawbridge had it been down. Constable Bancroft eased the wooden boat close to the short dock that jutted out from the shore and acted like a cradle for the drawbridge. The inspector stood up slightly and held out his hand so that he could assist me getting onto the dock. "After you," he said kindly.

I eyed the water nervously—I couldn't help it, the memory of swimming after Heath in those murky depths would probably haunt me the rest of my days—but I forced myself to reach across the bow to grip the railing. As I was pulling myself up, however, I saw something long and white glide under the dock.

I gasped and scrambled up, scuttling quickly to the center of the wood planks and trying to peer through the cracks. "What is it?" the inspector asked.

I shuddered, pointing toward the water. "I saw something."

Both the inspector and the constable leaned over the side of the boat and looked into the dark water. "What did you see?" the constable asked me after they'd had a good long stare.

"I . . . I don't know." I barely dared to peek over the side. What I *thought* I'd seen was the ghostly figure of a person swimming under the dock, but that's not something I was really willing to confess at that moment. The two men in the boat were probably nervous enough with all the strange goings-on of late. Still, I felt it appropriate to caution them. "When you retrieve the body, please be careful, okay?"

The constable eyed me with nervous curiosity, and I could see he didn't discount my words. "We'll take the most care," he promised. "Now go warm your bones in my motorcar. The keys are in the ignition."

I nodded and turned to his vehicle, but couldn't help looking back when I'd gotten off the dock and onto dry land again. The inspector was already speaking into his cell phone to alert the coroner, and his trusty constable had just turned their boat around and was rowing back toward the south side, when I caught another glimpse of something thin and white at the stern of the boat. Something that looked eerily like a bony white hand disappearing below the surface.

I put a hand to my mouth and nearly called out to the two men to stop and come back, but as I squinted toward the water, I saw nothing but darkness. There was no hint of anything near the surface.

I watched the men in the boat for a long time, even though I was freezing and the warm car was only a few feet away. I saw nothing out of the ordinary, but even that did little to settle my nerves.

After five minutes of watching the back of the boat, I turned away with weariness born of being frightened to the core over and over and moved up to the car.

The constable's car was unlocked and the keys were in fact left in the ignition. I turned the engine over and in no time was enjoying the warm air coming through the vent. I held my hands up to the heat and rubbed them vigorously, but my fingertips had long since gone numb.

Every once in a while I made sure to look around at the area outside the car. I wasn't quite sure how far the Widow could travel. I knew that she haunted the south wing and the moat, but did that mean she couldn't come out of the water to the shore?

I reasoned that if she did, I'd throw the car into gear and drive away fast, but as the minutes wore on and the heat from the car settled around me, I began to grow more and more sleepy.

My lids felt heavy and my mind was muddled. It grew harder and harder to stay awake, no matter how many times I tried to shake off the oppressive fatigue.

Finally I gave in. "I'll just close my eyes for a little while," I promised myself.

The next thing I knew, Inspector Lumley was knocking on my window. I jumped and flung my arms up, adding a frightened shriek to boot.

Outside the door he held up both his hands and apologized. "It's only me, Miss Holliday. Terribly sorry to give you a fright."

I used the hand crank to roll down the window. "It's fine, Inspector. I must have dozed off there." I then had the chance to look around and I could see that the sky in the east was just beginning to soften from the deep hue of night. The clock on the dashboard read four thirty a.m. I yawned and rubbed my face. It felt like I'd only just nodded off.

"The mechanic is here working on the drawbridge," the inspector was telling me.

I blinked a few times and tried to focus on his words.

"He should have it down within the hour. You may stay here if you'd like, or use the ladder to go up the wall and climb down the other side."

I clambered out of the car to get a better look and that's when I saw a long ladder propped up against the castle wall. I assumed that a twin had been positioned on the other side.

It was a no-brainer as to which one I'd opt for, even with the added danger of crossing that moat by boat again. "I'll take the ladder," I said to the inspector. I wanted a real bed and some real sleep so bad I could hardly stand it.

"The ladder's quite sturdy," the inspector said as he walked with me toward the boat.

I didn't much care if it was crazy rickety. I was going to get inside and head straight to my room and not come out until I'd had some decent sleep. As we walked, I noticed the coroner's van again, parked in a similar spot to where it'd been the morning before. "Did you pull the victim out of the moat?" I asked the inspector.

"Yes," he said, his mustache turning down. "Nasty sight that."

"Do you know who it is?" I don't know why I was so curious, but I was.

"The identification in his pocket indicates his name was André Lefebvre."

I stopped dead in my tracks even though that was exactly who I'd feared it was when I'd seen that silver hair. "The fashion designer?"

Inspector Lumley eyed me keenly. "We believe it's him," he said. "Did you know him?"

"I didn't know him personally, but he was a guest here at the castle. He brought a group of models with him for the shoot, but I was told that he'd gone into town with them earlier in the evening."

"Apparently he came back," said the inspector.

"Is there any sign of his wife?" I asked, remembering the elegant woman seething with fury when she caught her husband kissing one of the models.

"His wife?"

"I believe she may have been with him," I said, worried that a similar end had come to her. The Widow was definitely capable of drowning two people, as Heath and I could attest to.

The inspector waved to the constable, who was just getting off the boat after having come back across the water, and the man came right over. "Yes, Inspector?"

"Niles, it seems that Mrs. Lefebvre might be missing. Please see what you can do to locate her whereabouts immediately."

"Oh, but I've already found her," the constable said. I held my breath, waiting to hear that her dead body had also been discovered. "She's inside the castle, sir. Arthur let me into Mr. Lefebvre's room, and we found her there fast asleep, oblivious to our knocking because of her earplugs and the sleeping pill she took a few hours ago. Seems she never went out with the others due to a migraine or some such. And she didn't even realize her husband had gone missing until we woke her. She's in a terrible state at the moment, as you can imagine. As soon as we get the bridge down, she'll come out to see about identifying the body."

"Inspector!" a man called, and we all turned to see a portly-looking man with strikingly white hair and matching beard waddling over to us.

"Yes, Doctor?" Lumley said when he got close.

The doctor put a hand to his chest, as if he was having trouble catching his wind, and said, "There's something I've taken note of on the body that I believe you should be aware of."

"Which is?"

"There is a sizable lump on the man's head." I took it that the good doctor was likely the coroner.

"A lump, you say?" the inspector asked. The man certainly liked to repeat things.

"Yes. At the base of the skull."

"I see. Then he slipped and fell into the moat, striking his head, and that's perhaps why he drowned?"

The doctor shook his head and rocked on his heels. "Oh, I doubt it, Inspector."

"You doubt what? My theory?"

"Yes."

"Why?"

"Because there is also a sizable lump on the man's forehead."

My brow furrowed, and I wanted to ask the doctor why that mattered, but the inspector asked first. "What does that prove, Dr. Engels?"

"Well, the man certainly didn't strike both the front and the back of his head at the same time, Inspector!"

Lumley looked taken aback. "How do you know they happened at the same time?"

"The blow to the back of the man's head was severe enough to crack the skull, and by the swelling evident there, it's clear to me that it occurred antemortem. He would have died within minutes if he hadn't drowned first. The blow to the front of the head also shows signs of swelling, though not as severe. I believe Lefebvre was struck very hard from behind before he tipped forward into the moat, striking his head on a rock or the bridge as he went in."

"Are you suggesting what I think you're suggesting?" Lumley asked.

The doctor smiled wryly at him. "Yes, Inspector. You have another murder on your hands."

"*Another* murder?" I said, and the inspector turned to look at me, his expression suggesting he was quite surprised to see me still standing next to him. Without answering me, he said, "Thank you for alerting us to Mr. Lefebvre's body, Miss Holliday. I'm sure I'll be in touch with you very soon." With that, he motioned for the doctor to accompany him back down to the tarp that I guessed was covering Lefebvre.

"This way, Miss Holliday," the constable said, extending his arm out to me like a proper gentleman.

The constable was growing on me. "I never thanked you for saving my life yesterday," I told him.

"Least I could do after you went in after Mr. Whitefeather," he said humbly. "I give you a fair amount of credit too. That water was bloody cold."

"It really was," I agreed, my mind still on the mystery behind what the coroner had revealed. "Constable Bancroft?"

"Yes?"

"What was the doctor referring to when he suggested that Mr. Lefebvre's death was *another* murder?"

The constable lifted my elbow to steady me as I got into the rowboat. He didn't answer me until he was settled in too and had lifted the oars away from their resting place on the sides of the boat. "I believe he was referring to the suspicious nature of Mr. Brown's drowning," he said, leaning back to dip the oars into the water.

"What suspicious nature?"

The constable pushed on the oars, bringing his face closer to mine in the process. "Merrick's wrists appeared to have been bound before he went into the moat."

My eyes widened. "He was tied up?"

The constable managed to shrug in between rows. "Maybe. There's no sign of the rope, just the burns on his wrists. Could be that he got free of them but drowned anyway, or they popped off when his body became bloated. Either way, Dr. Engels thinks his hands were tied together before he went into the water."

I sat up a little straighter in my seat as a cold chill traveled down my spine and I shuddered. Had Merrick really been murdered by someone other than the Widow? Certainly her ghost wouldn't have tied him up before drowning him. And why would someone kill the kindly desk clerk? He'd seemed like such a nice young man, why would anyone want to hurt him?

And, for that matter, who had murdered Mr. Lefebvre? A likely suspect had to have been his wife. She'd had the most murderous expression on her face when she'd spied on him kissing the male model.

But then I reconsidered that. For good reason the spouse was always the most obvious suspect—why would she risk murdering him when she could simply divorce him and take half his wealth?

We were midway across the moat as I considered who else might have had a hand in the fashion designer's death. I had the sudden feeling I was being watched and looked to my left, and that's when I saw the faint outline of a man near the water's edge on the castle side of the moat. He was tall and slim, and tugging at something around his neck, and in an instant I felt I knew who it was. But a moment later, he was jerked violently forward, and pulled headfirst into the water. I could even hear the splash of water that accompanied it, and I put a hand to my mouth, knowing that I'd just seen Mr. Lefebvre's ghost being hauled into the water by the Grim Widow.

"Did you hear that?" the constable said, drawing my attention back to him.

"What?" I asked, unsure what specifically he'd heard.

The constable paused his rowing and looked in the same direction where the splash had come from. "It sounded like someone just fell into the water," he said. Then his eyes swiveled to me. "You didn't see anything over there, did you?"

I shook my head. I didn't want to alarm the kind man, and even if I'd told him what I'd seen, there wasn't anything he could do to help Mr. Lefebvre now.

After another search of the water with his eyes, the constable got back to rowing. "This castle has always given me the willies," he muttered.

When we made it to the shore, I barely waited for the constable to secure the boat before I was out of it and scrambling up the bank to the bridge, where a very tall ladder was angled against the stone. I eyed it a bit warily until Bancroft came up beside me and promised to hold it steady.

"How will I get down once I make it up there?" I asked him.

He pointed his flashlight up the stone. "There's a watchtower with a set of stairs leading down into the courtyard. Just climb through the open window and you'll be able to find your way from there."

I thanked him and got to the task at hand. I made it over to the other side within just a few minutes.

John greeted me as I was coming up the walkway to the front steps. After giving me a brotherly hug, he said, "There's a lot of yelling going on in there."

I eyed him quizzically until I picked up the faint sound of raised voices coming through the thick wooden front door. "Who's upset now?"

"One of the other guests. First, he was ticked off that someone was yelling loud enough at three in the morning to wake him—"

"Don't tell me, let me guess—Gilley?"

"Yep. Gil's been doing a lot of shrieking since you headed over to the south wing."

I sighed wearily. "Is Mr. Crunn kicking us out?"

John actually laughed. "Nope. The opposite. He's suggesting that the guy find other accommodations more to his liking. They're arguing about it right now actually."

I rubbed my eyes tiredly. Man, was I beat. "I have a feeling I know who the guy is."

"He's a total douche bag," John commented as we both turned to the door.

When John opened it, the full volume of the man in the main hall yelling at poor Mr. Crunn came to my ears and I winced. "Jesus," I said, nudging John in the side. The ghastly man had worked himself up into a frenzy, yelling so loud his complexion was crimson, and he was pointing his finger straight into Mr. Crunn's face. "I'll sue!" he bellowed. "I'll sue you lot for the full cost of our holiday and pain and suffering and I don't give a blast who owns this old pile of rubble, even if it's owned by the bloody queen!"

"Mr. Hollingsworth, please!" cried Mr. Crunn. "It is hardly conceivable that we would be responsible for such unfortunate happenings as these! And while I am quite sorry that your stay with us has been made unpleasant by recent events, I can hardly compensate you over and above the cost of your stay here, especially as you and your wife have suffered no other ill effect other than to have had your sleep interrupted this morning."

"No other ill effect?!" Hollingsworth bellowed. "What about the emotional toll? Here we are, on holiday in this musty old place, which you lot have overpriced, I might add, and we're not here but a day when there's not one but *two* deaths on your doorstep! Not to mention Mrs. Hollingsworth and I couldn't leave if we wanted to! Mechanical failure to the drawbridge, my aunt Petunia! The emotional toll on my wife alone has been enough to warrant a sizable contribution from this establishment!" In the corner I saw his poor wife cringe as her husband's beady eyes flashed to her.

"Mr. Hollings—"

"Plus room and board! Plus a bit extra for petrol to see us back home! Now loosen those purse strings, Mr. Crunn, or I'll sue, I will!"

"Hey, hey, hey!" I snapped, moving forward quickly to the two men. "That's enough!"

"Mind your own bloody business!" Hollingsworth yelled at me.

"When you yell loud enough to wake the dead, pal, it becomes my business!" I meant that quite literally too.

Hollingsworth stepped forward threateningly and John shot to my side like a rocket. "The lady said to chill out, buddy," John said, holding himself to his full height, and he was at least three inches taller than Hollingsworth. For good measure, John even poked the belligerent man in the chest. "Now get back upstairs and stop causing a scene, or you and I are gonna have a problem."

Hollingsworth's eyes appeared to welcome the challenge. He snarled menacingly and pushed up the cuffs of his bathrobe, and that's when Michel stepped forward and aligned himself with John. "Don't even think about it, bloke," he said levelly.

Next to me, Gilley also sidled up, crossing his arms over his puffed-up chest like he was Dwayne Johnson.

With the four of us squaring off against him, Hollingsworth didn't have much choice but to back off. He gave us all a really dirty look before stalking away with threats to ring up his solicitor and sue our pants off. We waited until he'd disappeared up the stairs to relax our stance. "I *hate* that guy," I muttered.

"Maybe we should feed him to the Grim Widow," John said.

I smiled wickedly at the thought, but then I remembered his wife and my eyes sought her out, hoping she hadn't heard. By the horrified expression on her face, she had. "Aw, crap," I muttered. "Ma'am," I said, moving over toward her, "I'm really sorry. That wasn't very nice of us."

She said nothing. Instead she ducked her chin and hurried off down an adjoining hallway. I noticed she didn't go up to her room to join her husband, which I thought was smart. In the state of rage he was in, she'd be a fool to be locked in the same room with him. Of course, I probably already thought her a little bit of a fool for staying with him in the first place.

"I'm dreadfully sorry to have dragged you into that," Mr. Crunn said, pulling my attention back.

"It's not your fault, Mr. Crunn," I assured him. The sweet old man looked as exhausted as I felt. "I think you should turn in, sir."

But the old man shook his head. "I can't, Miss Holliday. The police may need something from me, and I have poor Mrs. Lefebvre's tea to prepare."

"The police probably don't need you for a little while yet, Mr. Crunn. Why don't you see if you can catch at least a little bit of sleep until then, and we'll go prepare the tea for Mrs. Lefebvre, okay?"

Crunn looked ready to drop, and he sighed gratefully. "Thank you, Miss Holliday," he said. "The kettle is in the kitchen on the stove and the tea is on the shelf above it. There are several tea service trays already set out for breakfast. Mrs. Lefebvre is in room two twenty-seven. It's down the hall on the left from your room."

I waited for Crunn to move off before I motioned for the boys to follow me. I wanted to tell them about what I'd learned from the constable. They were full of questions that I couldn't answer, and now that the adrenaline from confronting Hollingsworth had worn off, I was finding my thoughts becoming muddled again. And when Gil demanded his sweatshirt back, I didn't have the energy to fight him, so I shrugged out of it and gave it over.

Once the tea service was prepared, I handed off the duty of taking it up to Mrs. Lefebvre to Gil. My *ever* supportive (insert sarcasm here) BFF almost said no until Michel said he'd be glad to go with him, and then Gil's sullen mood turned downright perky. I didn't think Michel would return Gil's obvious affection for him, but that was an issue best dealt with later, after I'd had some solid sleep. As Gil and Michel left to take the tea service upstairs, I put a hand on John's shoulder and said, "I'm going to bed. Wake me in six hours. Once Heath gets back, the crew has a lot to discuss." I then headed straight upstairs to bed, and was asleep almost before my head hit the pillow.

John didn't wake me in six hours. Or eight. Or even ten. He left me alone for nearly eleven solid hours, so when I woke on my own at four p.m., I was much better rested, but seriously out of sorts.

Emerging from my room, I was about to go in search of someone from the crew when I found John coming up the stairs. "I was about to come get you," he said.

"Is it really four o'clock?"

"Yep. Teatime. You hungry?"

My stomach growled loudly. "Apparently so."

"Come on. Heath's downstairs. He's been waiting for you to get up and I had to threaten bodily harm when he said he wanted to wake you."

I was a little miffed that I'd missed my sweetheart's return from the hospital. "I told you to wake me at eleven a.m."

John offered me a sideways smile. "One thing I know about you and Heath is that you are the two most sleep-deprived people on this crew. Whether you agree with me or not, you needed some rest, M. J."

After a moment I put a hand on his arm. "You're right, guy. Sorry I snapped at you."

"You didn't snap," he said, allowing me to go first down the stairs. "It's all good."

We reached the landing and began to make our way toward the left to a hallway that I had yet to explore. As we neared the entrance, however, a strong arm snaked around my middle and I was pulled backward into someone else. "Hey, babe," Heath whispered into my ear. "I missed you."

I turned and flung my arms around him. He was warm and strong, and his breath felt wonderful against the crook of my neck. "God, it's good to hug you!" I whispered.

He squeezed me tight, pulled back, and gave me a sweet kiss. "Me too."

"Oh, are they at it *again*?"

I turned my head to see Gilley standing behind us with his hands on his hips and an annoyed look on his face. I couldn't help but also take in the *enormous* sweatshirt draped over most of Gil's body. It was puffy and bumpy—no doubt filled with fresh magnets—and it made him look like the Michelin Man.

"Aw, cut 'em some slack, Gil," John said. I had to hand it to our sound tech. He was seriously turning out to be one good egg in my book.

Behind Gil I saw someone else wave and realized it was Michel. I waved back and then my stomach gave another loud rumble and Heath laughed. "We should get you something to eat," he said, taking my hand and leading me into the hallway. I glanced behind me and saw that Gilley, Michel, and John had fallen into step behind us.

We emerged into a large dining hall with a currant-colored carpet, round tables draped in crimson table-cloths, and burgundy curtains along the windows. At one of the larger tables sat the rest of the *Ghoul Getters* crew, in the middle of a heavy discussion by the look of it.

As the four of us approached, they all looked up and their happy expressions at the sight of me made me feel really good inside. "Hey, guys," I said as Heath pulled out a chair for me.

"How're you feeling?" Meg asked right away.

"I'm good." My eye fell on the basket of baked goods in the center of the table and I added, "Just hungry."

Kim pushed the basket toward me, while Heath waved to an elderly woman clearing a two-top. "Mary, can we please have another cup of tea?"

"And two more for us too, please?" Gil added, pointing to himself and Michel. "Oh, and maybe another basket of those yummy pastries while you're at it if you don't mind?"

The elderly woman seemed taken aback by so many requests, but recovered herself and with a nod hurried off to get us more tea and goodies for the table.

I lifted a buttery scone out of the basket and decided not to wait for the tea. I was too famished. "I assume the drawbridge is back down again?" I asked after I'd swallowed the first delicious bite.

"It is, but no one's owning up to dismantling it in the first place," Gilley said. "We think it was an inside job."

"Why do you say that?" I asked.

"He would've had to use a ladder to climb down from the watchtower on the other side, and then he'd have to get that ladder across the moat, haul it and a boat up out of the water, and disappear. Way too much work, if you ask me."

But I wasn't so sure. "He could have easily come in through the side door that Crunn led us through when we first accompanied him to Merrick's body."

Gil leaned in and narrowed his eyes suspiciously. "Crunn could have done it, you know."

I blinked. "Done what?"

"Dismantled the drawbridge."

I scowled at him. "No, he couldn't. He was in here with us, remember? I came across that drawbridge just a minute or two before entering the front hall last night and he was behind his counter while you guys were trying to figure out what to do about Gopher and the rest of the crew."

Gilley made a face. "Crap. I forgot about that. Okay, so it couldn't have been Crunn."

"Thank you, Sherlock Holmes," I deadpanned. "Plus, I don't think anybody with intimate knowledge of that side entrance would ever brave it in the dead of night right after Heath was nearly drowned."

"So how did an outsider do it?" John asked. "And why?"

Heath leaned forward to answer. "I took a good look at the rigging of the bridge on this side, and if someone dismantled the system, they'd still have three minutes to exit over the drawbridge before it was too high to get past. The thing takes forever to open and close."

"So you're saying that somebody could have tampered with the mechanism and either run across the bridge and jumped, or gotten across by boat?" I asked.

"Easily," Heath said.

John scratched his head. "But that still leaves the question of why. Why lock us in here?"

"Maybe they weren't locking us in," I said. "Maybe they were locking Lefebvre out." Several puzzled expressions eyed me across the table. "He was the only one killed last night, right?"

Gilley shivered into the silence that followed. "This place gives me the weirds."

I didn't pretend to look surprised, and instead turned to Heath. "I assume someone's filled you in on my run-in with the Widow last night?"

"I did," John said, raising his hand. "And now that you're here, we can finally vote."

Our beverages and pastries arrived just then and I thanked Mary, who looked very much like her brother, Mr. Crunn. I guessed her to be in her early seventies, but she was quite spry. "What are we voting on?" I asked when she'd left us again.

"To stay or go," Gil replied, glaring hard at Gopher. I

had the feeling that I'd come to the table in the middle of a pretty good argument. "Gopher wants us to stay and shoot more footage, and some of those fools"—Gil paused to point across the table at Kim and Meg—"also want to stay."

Kim scowled at Gilley before turning pleading eyes on me. "My mom just lost her job, M. J., and she can't make it on unemployment. I *need* this job!"

"So do I," Meg added quickly. "I've got student loans up the wazoo, and this gig was hard enough to find. If we quit, I'll have to go back to waitressing at the IHOP."

I held up my hand and focused on Gilley. "You sent Chris the footage I took from last night, right?"

"Yes," he said. "The footage of the Widow when she first jumped out at you *and* all the other stuff too!"

Exasperated, I turned next to Gopher. "How can Chris watch that and *not* think it's good enough?"

"Oh, he loved it," Gopher said, tracing small circles with his finger on the tablecloth.

"Which is the problem," Heath muttered.

I picked up another scone and broke it in half to spread on some homemade butter. "I don't know that I'm following what the heck the problem is. Any time one of you wants to make some sense, please clue me in."

"We knocked Chris out of the park with what you caught on film," Gopher explained. "He wants to do a full-length movie."

I dropped my knife and stared in shock at my producer. *"What?"*

Gopher opened his laptop and peered at his screen. "He says, and I quote, 'That is the scariest shit I have ever seen!'"

I offered him a level look. "He should try living through it."

Gopher smiled tightly. "Yeah, I know, and remind me to thank you for being such a trouper about trying to rescue us last night."

"I wouldn't have had to, Gopher, if you'd at least left us a note or something."

Gopher pointed to John. "I told him we were going out on the moors!"

"No, dude, you didn't," John said firmly. "You said you were going on a bust with or without me. You never said you were leaving the castle."

"Well, I'm not stupid enough to go into the south wing after what you guys went through when M. J. went back to retrieve her stuff, especially not after what happened to Heath! Seriously, do I look like an *idiot*?"

Absolutely everyone at the table dropped their eyes or looked away.

"Oh, thanks, you guys!" he growled. "The point is, we've got some really amazing footage, and Chris thinks it's a serious winner, but we need more if we're going to make a full-length feature out of it."

Heath leaned in over the table, his face hard with anger "Are you *crazy*?" Gopher just frowned at him. "Seriously, sending any of us back there would be suicide! I mean . . . Jesus, Gopher! She almost *killed* me! And then she almost *killed* M. J.! And then she *did* kill Merrick Brown and André Lefebvre!"

But Gopher was unfazed. In fact, Heath's last statement actually seemed to animate him. "But that's the hook, don't you get it? All those other fake ghost movies that've come out in recent years—they've made hundreds of *millions*! Our movie would be *real*, backed up by actual verifiable events!"

I crossed my arms and stared hard at him. Our producer liked to play a little too fast and loose with our lives for my taste.

Gopher turned pleading eyes on me. "M. J.," he said, knowing full well that if he had a chance in hell, he'd have to convince me, "if you agree to get more footage, and we sell this as a movie, you and every person at this table would stand to make a *lot* of money."

I cocked a skeptical eyebrow.

Gopher seemed to take that as a sign to continue the argument. "I've crunched the numbers with Chris, and told him that for this kind of dangerous work you guys would need a couple of points on the back end of the deal."

I wasn't going to agree to stay, but he had piqued my curiosity a little. "In English, how much is that, Goph?"

"*If* we get enough for a full-length film, and *if* the studio takes it to the big screen, we're talking a couple of million for you and Heath, and about a half million apiece for the rest of the crew." My eyes bugged. Was he serious?

"Or," Heath said testily, "the two of us might die."

Meg scowled at him and nudged Gopher with her elbow. "Tell her about the bonus."

"The bonus is really more of an incentive for you and the crew to stick with this no matter what, but basically Chris is offering a thirty percent bonus for this shoot if everybody agrees to stay on to the end."

"No matter what?" I repeated. That was the part of his speech that worried me.

Gopher shifted in his seat and dropped his eyes.

"He means, no matter if someone from the crew gets hurt or dies during filming, Em," Heath said softly.

Around the table both Meg and Kim looked at me with hopeful eyes, while Heath's position was perfectly clear, and Gilley of course was shaking his head adamantly, but John kind of looked undecided and Michel seemed to be taking in everything that was said with rapt curiosity. I had a feeling John would grudgingly vote whichever way I was leaning. The guy had seen too much in that hallway to not have a personal appreciation for the level of danger we could face.

And I'll have to admit that my mind was racing with the offer. Gil and I had lived close to the edge of poverty since college, and I suddenly realized what kind of lasting financial freedom making that kind of money could buy us. "How much more footage?" I asked, and everyone looked at me with no small measure of surprise.

"Maybe three or four hours' worth," Gopher said. "But not all of that would need to be usable. If we edit what we've got now, I figure we'll only need about thirty to forty more minutes of solid scary stuff, and not all of that has to be taken in the danger zone. I mean, if you fill some of that with a few knocks, bumps, disembodied footsteps, or whatever, then that should get us by."

I felt the weight of the decision settle onto my shoulders, so I decided to play devil's advocate. "We have enough for an amazing episode of *Ghoul Getters*, Gopher—why are you asking us to risk to get more? I mean, is a movie *really* a big enough reason?"

"No, but think what the money could do for you and the crew, M. J.," Gopher countered.

"That and the thirty percent bonus," Kim said. "Me and my mom could *really* use that cash right now."

"There is one more incentive," Gopher said, in that way that clearly indicated he hadn't told us everything yet.

Heath rolled his eyes. "Here we go."

Gopher took a deep breath before continuing, as if weighing whether to even let us in on it. "Chris believes in this movie idea so much that he's laid it all on the line. He said that this would be an all-or-nothing offer."

I blinked and looked around the table. It seemed that everyone was just as confused as I was. "Come again?" John said.

Gopher leveled his gaze at me. "Either we proceed with getting more footage for the movie or he's pulling the plug on our show."

Several loud gasps echoed around the table, but I wasn't surprised. I'd met Chris only once and even then it'd been brief. Still, it'd been long enough to label him a total douche bag.

"I'm assuming the clock is ticking on our final decision?" I asked.

Gopher nodded. "We have until midnight to give him an answer."

Looking around the table, I knew exactly how the vote would go. Meg, Kim, and Gopher—yea. Gilley and Heath—nay. John was the swing vote, but even if he voted yea, my voting no would effectively veto it. Gopher couldn't proceed without at least one of his mediums.

So the decision rested on my shoulders. Again.

I sighed heavily. At that moment I was so damn tired of the show, I knew that I could easily walk away and not look back. I'd head back to Boston and carve out a living doing readings for clients and the occasional ghostbust, but what tugged at me—besides the pleading eyes of Meg and Kim, who I knew really needed the cash—was the nagging thought of the souls of those victims the Widow had claimed. I suspected there might be at least a dozen or more names to her macabre roster—Mr. Lefebvre and Merrick were only the two most recent. The look on the ghost of Merrick Brown's face really bothered me. He'd seemed so scared and confused. I hated the thought of him spending an eternity with the likes of the Widow, and I knew that if we worked this bust right, we'd have to look more in depth at that, and at least try to find a solution to freeing those poor souls.

But could I do that without getting myself, or one of the crew members, killed? That was the central dilemma tugging away at me, and one I couldn't answer with confidence. So were the financial gain for me and the rest of the crew and the freeing of several imprisoned souls worth taking such a big risk?

I reminded myself that there were other things that had to be considered as well, namely, the dismantled drawbridge, the blow to the back of Mr. Lefebvre's head, and the rope burns on Merrick Brown's hands. Along with a dreadfully deadly poltergeist, was there also a living murderer loose among us?

"In light of the two deaths here in the past two days I'm kind of surprised the castle is still open to guests," I said, stalling for time while I tried to make up my mind.

"The police told us not to go anywhere," Gilley grumbled. "Even that cranky Mr. Hollingsworth has to stay put until they're done with the investigation. They're interviewing everybody who was here at the castle last night, which, it turns out, wasn't very many people."

I had no idea how many guests were currently staying at Kidwellah, but by the size of the castle and the dining hall we were sitting in, I felt it could easily be anywhere between fifty and a hundred people. "How many people were here inside the castle last night?" I asked, simply out of curiosity.

Gil said, "You, me, Michel, Mr. Crunn, his sister Mary, Mrs. Lefebvre, the Hollingsworths, and that's about it."

"For real?"

"André Lefebvre and the models weren't here, and neither was Gopher and his troupe," Gil reminded me.

"No," I said, "I meant, this is a pretty big castle. I just thought there'd be more guests staying here."

Gil shrugged. "It's the off-season. And from what I understand, business has been way down since oh-seven. Mr. Crunn as much as admitted to me that he was really relieved that our crew and the fashion-shoot people booked this week."

Michel grimaced. "If I hadn't insisted to André that we use Kidwellah for its dramatic setting, then he might still be alive."

"Not if he was murdered by someone he knew," I said, and Gilley laid a hand on Michel's arm in sympathy.

Michel nodded reluctantly, but his expression was still clearly guilt-ridden.

"But who could have killed him?" Gil asked, turning back to me. "I mean, come on! His wife was upstairs sleeping, the Hollingsworths were in their room, and Crunn said that Mary turned in right after cleaning up from dinner. The models all went into town and have each other as witnesses. Michel, me, John, and Mr. Crunn were together until you got back from the hospital. Gopher and his crew were somewhere out on the downs, and they all have each other for witnesses. Everybody's accounted for, so who could it have been?"

"Not everyone's accounted for," Meg said, her eyes darting sideways to Kim and then Gopher.

"What do you mean?" I asked.

"Well, Franco left our little party just after we set out for the downs. He said he was cold and had changed his mind about going on the ghost hunt with us."

Gil and I exchanged a surprised look. "Where is he?" Gil asked immediately. "That guy still has my phone."

Michel also looked surprised. "I haven't seen him since he left with you three," he said, pointing to Gopher, Meg, and Kim. "Did he make it back to the castle?"

Meg shrugged. "I don't know."

"M. J.," Gil said, waving impatiently at me, "call my cell and see if he picks up."

I pulled out my phone and called Gil's phone. "Hello?" a male voice answered.

"Franco?" I asked.

"Yes?"

"Where are you?"

"Who is this?"

Gilley reached out and grabbed my phone. "Hey, sugar," he said in his most sweet voice. "This is Gilley. Any chance I can get my phone back?" There was a pause and then Gil's brow furrowed. "Gilley Gillespie," he said. Then, "You borrowed my phone from me last night before you went on the ghost hunt. Remember?"

There was another longer pause, during which Gil's brow lowered to the danger zone. "What do you mean, you lost it?" he demanded. Another pause, then, "Franco, you stupid queen! I'm currently calling *my phone*! And, as you've answered it, it appears that you have *my phone*!"

There was another pause and then Gil said, "Hello? Hello? Ohmigod! He actually hung up on me!"

Michel made a motion for Gil to give him the phone and he redialed the number. "Hello, beautiful, it's Mickey. I need a head shot of you in the main hall. Meet me there in an hour, okay? *Ciao, bello.*" He then handed me my phone back and said, "I'll get the phone, Gilley, don't worry. Franco is a pretty boy but bloody stupid."

Gil settled back into his chair and for a moment he truly didn't look like he knew whether to be grateful or still irritated with Franco.

"Well," I said, "at least we know Franco is accounted for."

"Can we get back to the vote about the movie, please?" Gopher asked with impatience.

Gilley and Heath both said, "No. We vote no."

Meg pointed to herself, then to Kim and said, "We vote yes."

"You know I'm a yes," Gopher said.

All eyes swiveled to John. He sighed like he didn't really know what to say and just shook his head.

"I vote yes," I said, taking all the pressure off him.

"I knew it," Gilley grumbled. Looking at Heath, he added, "I told you she was a nut."

"Em," Heath began, but I laid a hand on his shoulder.

"Honey, my mind is made up. We're stuck here anyway, right?"

"*How* can that be a good enough reason to put your life on the line?" Heath asked me.

"It's not. But there are a few reasons why I'm saying yes."

"And they are?"

"Well, for openers, I keep thinking about Merrick. You saw him, Heath. His ghost was so scared and so confused.

The Widow had him chained to her, and I think she might be collecting the souls of the people she's murdered. I saw Lefebvre's ghost chained to her as well, and I don't know that I can walk away from here knowing those two and who knows how many others will spend the next several centuries tied to that murderous witch if we don't intervene. She's torturing them, Heath," I said pleadingly, and although he was staring hard at me like I had to be crazy, I could see that I'd moved him with my reasoning.

"Also," I said, knowing I might have some momentum, "I hate to sound materialistic, but if we go through with this full-length feature idea, the money is seriously hard to turn down. The crew benefits too, honey. I mean, if we quit now, what're they going to do?"

Heath's eyes swung across the table to Meg and Kim, who were both wearing anxious hopeful expressions. "With a million or so bucks in the bank, I could retire," I went on. "*We* could retire, sweetie, and we could live anywhere. We could afford to spend half the year in Boston and half the year in Santa Fe. Think about it."

But Heath was still resisting the idea. "I have thought about it. In fact, I had a lot of time to think about it while I was in the hospital. Em, you don't know how strong she is! She pulled me over that half wall and underwater like I was a rag doll. I'm a damn good swimmer and she still overpowered me like it was nothing!"

"So we'll stay away from the half wall," I told him. "And the moat."

"But what about that thing in the south wing?" John asked me.

I knew he was talking about the shadow demon that'd chased us down the hallway. I was a little worried about that too, but then again, I hadn't seen any signs of it the night before. "I'm not saying we won't have to be careful. We'll have to be damn careful, and we'll definitely need more of Gilley's sweatshirts. One for every member of the crew."

"John hasn't voted yet," Gil said, eyeing the sound tech with an intense look. "He's the tiebreaker."

I held back from telling Gilley that it didn't much matter how John voted—if I was in, Gopher would have his medium and he could hire a new technical person and a sound guy anywhere. Instead, I turned to John and said, "Gil's right. Now that I'm in, what do you want to do?"

John spent a few seconds looking everyone at the table in the eye. "I vote yes," he said at last.

Gilley pounded the table and Heath swore under his breath. "You guys don't have to participate," I said.

"If they don't, they're fired," Gopher snapped angrily.

I turned to him and glared hard. "If they're fired, then I'm changing my vote, Gopher."

"Aw, come on, M. J.! If they're out, then they shouldn't get paid!"

"Heath has *more* than earned his fair share on this bust," I said icily. "And for that matter, so has Gilley. Who do you think set up the camera to stream to the computer and capture that footage of the Widow in the first place? And for that matter, who do you think sent Chris the footage? No, they're getting paid either way." Gopher opened his mouth to protest and I leaned way in over the table and growled, "Do *not* test me on this, Peter."

I felt Heath's hand on my back. "That's okay, Em. If you're really going to do this, then I'm in too."

That shocked me. "You mean it?"

"I can't let you face her alone, can I?" he said with a sheepish grin.

"You're all crazy!" Gilley yelled.

"We can find another tech," I told him.

"Good luck finding someone as good as me," Gil scoffed.

"They don't have to be as smart as you, honey. They just have to set up the monitors, computer, and cameras and make sure it's all running smoothly."

Gil made a face and slouched in his seat. "No one's touching my equipment but me."

"What does that mean?" I asked him. I knew that if we went ahead and agreed to do the movie, Chris wouldn't have any problem widening the budget for more monitoring equipment and a new tech to run it, but that would take time to arrange.

Gilley's answer surprised me. "If you fools are all in, then I guess so am I. But I'm going to monitor the screens from a safety zone."

"If you're too far away, the feed won't connect," I reminded him.

"I won't be that far away, M. J. I've been playing with the electrostatic meters all afternoon. There's a safety zone right in the center of the main hall. Not a peep on the meters registers when I stand there."

"Suit yourself," I said. "I'm just happy you're in."

Michel raised his hand and I motioned for him to speak. "Would you by any chance need an extra set of hands for your shoot? I'm as good with a video camera as I am with a still camera, Mr. Gophner. And I don't scare easily."

"You need some extra cash now that your boss is dead and your photo shoot went to hell?" asked our ever-tactful producer.

"A bit like that, yes," Michel replied.

I couldn't help but notice Gilley's scowl completely disappear and in its place was the most hopeful face I'd ever seen him wear.

Gopher must have noticed Gil's change in demeanor, because he squashed a grin and nodded seriously. "Sure, Michel. I guess we could use you. Consider yourself hired." Turning to Kim, who began to pull out several stapled sheets of paper, he added, "Get his paperwork prepared right after the others sign."

I squinted at the sheets of paper. They looked like contracts, and sure enough, Kim began passing them out around the table according to name. "You came ready to do this, didn't you?" Heath asked, with a hint of irritation.

Gopher ignored him. Instead he focused on all of us and said, "Read these over, initial at the bottom of each page, and pass them back to Kim when you're through."

I sighed as I skimmed my own contract, which was basically one paragraph detailing how we would be paid, plus twelve pages of all the many, many ways Chris and the network could sue us if we backed out or quit before the shoot was finished. Heath looked at me sideways as if to ask if I really intended to go through with it, and as I read the contract, I came very close to backing away from the table to go pack my things, but Merrick Brown's terrified face kept flashing through my mind, and with a heavy sigh I initialed where indicated, signed the last page with a scribble, and shot the contract over to Kim, who accepted it with a grateful smile.

Once everyone else had signed, Gopher took up the contracts, nodded to us, and stood to leave, already dialing his phone—probably to call Chris and let him know we were a go.

Once he'd left, I turned to the remaining crew members and said, "All right, gang, what we need most before we set out to gather more footage is a plan."

"Let's pick one that doesn't get us all killed," Gilley said smartly.

"Gil?"

"Yes, M. J.?"

"Shut it."

Chapter 8

We spent a long time at that table working to come up with a plan, so long that Gopher returned and took up a seat to join in the discussion. The problem was that several of us were working at cross-purposes, which made it difficult for all of us to agree on how to proceed. I just wanted to find some way to help Merrick and the other prisoners of the Widow, but Gopher just wanted footage, footage, footage.

Gil and Heath just wanted to stay alive, alive, alive, and Meg, Kim, and John pretty much just wanted to get paid, paid, paid. Only Michel stayed out of the argument, but I had a feeling he was on my side, because every time I brought the discussion back to helping the imprisoned ghosts, he would nod as if he agreed wholeheartedly.

I kept pushing for time to do our homework, but Gopher now had the fear of Chris in him, and he wanted us to get some footage of anything spooky within the next twenty-four hours and he wasn't backing down. Finally I had an idea and offered the following suggestion: "Last night I think I saw the Desperate Duke."

"Yeah!" Gil said, pointing to me. "That ghost out on the moors that just disappeared when you aimed the camera through the window."

I started to nod, but then shook my head. "Maybe," I said.

"I'm confused," Gil said.

"What I mean is that the ghost out on the moors that you guys saw through the camera may have been the same guy I saw up close, but I'm not sure."

"You saw the duke up close?" Heath asked, concern evident in his eyes.

"Yep. It was after I jumped out of the door to get away from the Widow. He was standing about ten or fifteen feet away from me, and if not for him, I think the Widow would have come out that door after me. She took one look at him, though, and slammed the door. Then he disappeared. It was all pretty weird."

Gilley's hand was covering his mouth in shock. "M. J.," he said in a breathy whisper, "before you came down, we were talking about the local legend that says that seeing the duke up close means you're going to die!"

I rolled my eyes and forced myself to laugh. "A bit dramatic, don't you think?" When no one laughed with me, I added, "Oh, come on, guys! I'm still alive, and the duke certainly didn't attack me. If anything, he protected me last night, although why he'd do that I can't really figure out."

"It might be that those people who get close enough to see the duke in person end up at the south end of the castle, and if you're on the south end of the castle, then you're more likely to become a victim of the Widow," Heath said wisely.

I gestured to him. "Exactly!" But I couldn't help taking note of the doubtful expressions of my crew around the table. "*Any*way, I think we should investigate the duke's ghost out on the moors for our first shoot, and in the meantime we can come up with a game plan for the Widow."

"We already wasted a whole night hunting for him, M. J.," Gopher said in a way that suggested he was about to nix my idea.

Michel jumped up. "That reminds me," he said. "I'm supposed to meet Franco and get your phone back, Gilley. Back soon!" he said, and hurried off.

Gil began to get up too, but I laid a hand on his shoulder to keep him at the table. "You stay here," I told him firmly. I needed him to help me convince Gopher to investigate the moors until we had a solid plan for tackling the Widow.

"I say we stick to the Widow and forget about the duke," Gopher said.

"I say we don't," Heath countered, his jaw set firmly. "Last night you guys didn't have a medium with you to guide you to the duke's ghost. If you want to find a spook, Gopher, you need either M. J. or me to feel out the area and tell you where to aim the camera."

"That's a good point," John said, and Meg and Kim began to nod too.

"It makes sense to add the duke to the story," Gil added. "It'll help round out the bigger story of why the Widow is so crazy."

Gopher sighed and grumbled a little, but at least he didn't protest much about the plan. What he did protest a lot about was the timeline. I wanted to take at least the next couple of days to gather some intel and work through a plan so that no one else got hurt. We'd also have to be careful to avoid stepping on the toes of Inspector Lumley as he investigated the murders of the two men who'd died there in as many days.

"And let's not forget that there's a possible living killer on the loose, people," I told the crew. "A killer who hasn't been caught yet. We don't know if it could be someone here at the castle, or if he or she is long gone by now. So even when we're not filming, we'll need to be careful. I think we should buddy up at all times and not let your partner out of your sight during off-hours."

Around the table the crew silently began to pair up. Heath took my hand and squeezed it, Meg and Kim looped arms, and Gopher and John nodded at each other . . . which left Gil.

"Oh, come on!" he yelled. "Why am *I* always the odd man out?"

"Maybe because you're such a delight to be around," I mumbled.

"I heard that, M. J.!"

I sighed and that's when Michel appeared at the table with Gil's cell phone in hand. "Here's your mobile, mate."

Gilley giggled like a schoolgirl and patted Michel's seat. "We're buddying up, Michel," he informed the photographer. "Just to be safe and all, because there's a killer on the loose. Even in the off-hours we should be together. Like share a room . . . you know, for safety."

Michel took his seat. "Works for me," he said with a sweet grin and a wink.

Gilley blushed and smiled so hugely I thought he might dislocate his jaw.

I ducked my chin to hide a smile, and Gopher rolled his eyes. "Fine. Everybody's got a buddy. What else?"

I turned to Gil. "I need you to do some research."

"Maybe I can just tell you what you need to know," Gil said smartly while he played with his phone, probably to make sure Franco hadn't broken it.

"Oh, you know all, do you?" I asked him, crossing my arms over my chest.

"More than you give me credit for," he replied. "I read a lot, you know."

I raised a skeptical eyebrow. I'd never seen a book

that could hold Gil's attention for more than a few pages. "You read," I mocked.

"Yes."

"Really?"

"Yes."

"Like what, Gil? Name one periodical, book, news article, or other source material that you've read recently that has made you so knowledgeable."

Gilley's face flushed, and he paused, tapping at his phone to look up and see that everyone at the table was staring at him. Like Sarah Palin squaring off against Katie Couric, Gil had been caught off guard. But then his face lit with an idea. "The Internet."

"Excuse me?"

"I've read the Internet."

Several of our crew giggled, and I glared at them. "Don't encourage him." I then refocused on Gilley. "As knowledgeable as reading the *entire* Internet would make you, I'd appreciate it if you'd indulge me by scouting around for anyone who may have firsthand knowledge or experience with a spook that is powerful enough to hold other ghosts prisoners. The Widow has some kind of hold over Merrick and Mr. Lefebvre. I want to know what that is, and how to break it."

Gil jotted a note to himself, then went back to playing with his iPhone, but then he said, "Huh. That's weird."

"What's weird?" I asked.

Gil showed the display of his recent calls list, and there were at least half a dozen calls made to another phone number I didn't recognize, and then Michel, leaning in to look at the display, said with mild surprise, "That's André's number."

I put my hand on Gil's wrist to bring the phone closer. "They were made last night," I said. My eyes met Michel's and I knew instantly that he knew about Franco's affair with Lefebvre.

I turned my attention to Kim. "What time did Franco leave your group?"

Kim and Meg looked at each other as if silently debating the time. "Some time around midnight," Kim said, and Meg nodded.

"None of us looked at our watches, but it wasn't long after we set off on the moors."

I'd gotten back to the castle right around midnight and argued with Gil over the sweatshirt for at least fifteen to twenty minutes, which meant that the drawbridge had been tampered with some time between twelve and twelve twenty and Lefebvre could have been murdered anytime after that. Franco should definitely be looked at as a suspect.

"You need to show this to the inspector," I told Gilley, which caused Michel to grimace.

"Why?" he asked, and I could see he didn't really want to get involved.

Given the fact that Michel seemed to like Franco, I was careful with my answer. "Because all these calls were made after midnight, Gil. If Franco talked to Lefebvre, it might help narrow down a time frame for the murder."

"It also may point the finger at Franco," Gilley said, and Michel grimaced again.

I nodded reluctantly. "I still think it's important for you to bring that to the inspector's attention."

Gil didn't say anything—he just glanced at Michel, then pocketed his phone, and I could tell he and Michel would probably talk about it later and decide what to do. My mind was already made up that if Gil didn't show it to Lumley, then I'd make sure to mention it to the inspector. If Franco was guilty of murder, I certainly didn't want him anywhere near me.

We talked for a while longer about logistics and the layout of the castle. Gil was also assigned to get some background on the history of Kidwellah, and after he did a little more bellyaching about being the only one tasked with so much, Michel offered to do much of that for him.

Like Gilley, I was kinda digging the photographer more and more. Around seven I suggested we break for dinner. Interestingly, all the paired groups immediately headed off in different directions, which left Heath and me at the table. "I'm sorry," I said once we were alone.

"For what?"

"For saying yes to this gig."

Heath reached out and took my hand. Kissing the top of it, he said, "You're right, you know."

"About what?"

"About why your motivations are justified. If we left here knowing that Merrick and Lefebvre were chained to the Widow, it'd bother us until we worked our way back here to see if we could help."

I smiled knowingly. "And the extra cash helped convince me too."

"I know, but I wanted to give you some altruistic credit first."

"Good of you."

Heath leaned in and kissed me sweetly. "If we do end up surviving this thing, the money would solve a lot of problems. I mean, I could set my mom up in a nice house of her own instead of that cramped little condo, and I could get her some better medical care. You and I could hang out together without ever having to do another ghostbust again. We could do a few readings here and there just so we wouldn't get rusty, and have a real life together, Em."

My mind drifted to that wonderful prospect, but was quickly overshadowed by doubt. "Truthfully, though, sweetie, is this too dangerous?"

Heath sighed. "I don't know. The Widow caught us both by surprise the first time, but the second time you got away from her, so she's not infallible. We just have to be smarter than she is and make sure that we know as much as we can about where she can go and what she's capable of."

I shuddered. "She's the most powerful spook I've ever seen."

"But she's not a demon," Heath countered.

"True, but she *is* keeping one for a pet," I said, referring to that incredibly creepy black shadow that had terrorized John and me.

"Yeah, but I think that, given John's description, her pet demon is under her control. We shut her down, more than likely we shut it down."

I shook my head and stared at the tablecloth. "How the hell do you shut something like *her* down?"

"Hey," Heath said, getting my attention so that I would look him in the eyes. "Don't go to that space that makes her more than she is, babe. Once upon a time she was a living, breathing person, which means, as a ghost, she's vulnerable."

"Her portal," I said, knowing where he was going with that.

"Yep. We find her portal, we might be able to shut her in on the other side."

I shook my head again and added a sigh.

"What?"

"We can't lock down her portal without making sure we free Merrick and the other spirits tied to her, or they'll be trapped too."

Heath rubbed his chin. "That does complicate things, doesn't it?"

"And let's not forget we've got a murderer on the loose," I added.

"See, that's another thing I don't understand: If Merrick and Lefebvre were both murdered, how did the Widow end up taking their spirits prisoner?"

"I have no idea. But then, we don't know if Merrick

was truly murdered by someone other than the Widow. We only know that his hands may have been bound before he drowned."

Heath rubbed the back of his neck and rolled his head back and forth. I figured he was still sore from his bout with the Widow. "The one question we also need to find an answer to is why Merrick set us up in the south wing of the castle in the first place. I mean, he separated us from our crew and sent us to a seriously dangerous place. It's like he wanted us to have an encounter there. Why'd he do that?"

"I don't know," I admitted. I hadn't the foggiest clue, and it really bothered me that someone so seemingly pleasant as Merrick Brown would put Heath and me in danger.

Heath eyed me ruefully. "And yet you still want to help his ghost."

I shrugged. "We don't know for certain he had any kind of unscrupulous intentions by sending us to the south wing."

"What other intentions could he have had?"

"I'm not sure. And until I know for certain, I'm gonna give him the benefit of the doubt."

Heath chucked me playfully under the chin. "You're a good person, Holliday."

"Thanks, Whitefeather."

Heath chuckled again, but then he sobered and leaned forward to cup my face and stare hard at me. "Are you sure about this?"

"Nope."

His eyes softened. "As long as you're confident."

I grabbed his wrists. I was so tired of worrying, and thought we both needed a distraction. "I have an idea."

"I'm all ears."

"How about we blow this Popsicle stand and go out on a date?"

His brow rose. "You mean a date-date? As in, just you

and me, some food, some wine, a little nooky under the table?"

I grinned. "Something like that."

Heath didn't even reply—he just stood and pulled me up with him. I laughed until I realized I really had to use the restroom. Promising to meet him out in the court-yard, I was dashing up the stairs heading for my room when I happened to spot Mrs. Hollingsworth and Mrs. Lefebvre in the hallway. The two were quite close to each other, and what was odd was that Mrs. Lefebvre didn't look happy, and I don't mean she didn't look happy in that my-husband-just-died kind of way; she looked seriously pissed off.

I couldn't see Mrs. Hollingsworth's face, but I did see her reach out to the other woman, only to have her hand slapped away. "Don't you dare!" Lefebvre spat before she pushed the other woman rudely aside with her shoulder and marched down the hall toward me.

Seeing me, she paused, but then she squared her shoulders, averted her gaze and passed by me as if she hadn't noticed my existence.

My eyes returned to Mrs. Hollingsworth, who was still turned away from me, and apparently on her cell phone. "You lied to me!" she said, but not very loudly, and truth be told, I wasn't really sure that's what she said. "I tell you, the situation is most desperate! I implore you to keep your word!"

I stopped walking toward my room, uncomfortable with what I'd seen and was now overhearing. I wondered if maybe I should skip the bathroom break and move off without alerting Mrs. Hollingsworth that I was there. I still had a little bit of a soft spot for the poor battered woman, and even hearing her on the phone, I could tell that she was crying.

I'm ashamed to say that I didn't move off. I stood there listening, and hoping that if she turned around, I could fake the fact that I was eavesdropping.

"*How* long?" she asked, her shoulders hunched and her weeping intensifying. "No, no! That simply won't do!"

I bit my lip, still undecided about making my presence known, and a second later it no longer mattered because Mrs. Hollingsworth hung up abruptly and moved quickly to her room without a backward glance.

I stood there for another second or two, and then I made a decision. I moved to her door and pressed my ear against it. Faintly I could still hear the poor woman crying, but whether she was on the phone again I had no idea.

I raised my fist and knocked gently and the sobs from inside the door abruptly stopped. I waited, but she didn't come to the door or answer my knock. "Ma'am?" I called softly. "Are you all right?"

Mrs. Hollingsworth didn't reply and my chest felt tight for the poor woman. I imagined her stifling her tears while she waited for me to leave. Not wanting to cause her another moment of distress, I simply said, "I'm leaving now. I hope you're all right." I then went to my room, took care of my personal business in the bathroom, and called down to the front desk. Mr. Crunn answered the call and I asked if I could possibly order up some tea for Mrs. Hollingsworth. "Please put it on my tab, Mr. Crunn. And if you have any of those delicious scones still on hand to add to the order, would you do that for me?"

"Of course, Miss Holliday," he said. I could tell he thought the request to order some tea and scones for my neighbor a bit odd, but he was too polite to ask about it.

I then left my room, determined to find Mrs. Hollingsworth in the morning and give her a reading whether she wanted one or not. Maybe there'd be someone on the other side who would have some advice for her that she'd actually listen to. Maybe a deceased loved one could help see a clear path for her to get away from that awful man she was married to. One way or another I vowed to help her.

Having made that decision, I went off to meet my date.

Heath and I got back to the castle fairly early for a date out with each other. This had less to do with hormones and more to do with the fact that the Welsh are a rather proper lot, with a relatively low tolerance for those foreigners playing a little nooky under the table.

After being kicked out of not one but two restaurants, we decided to bring the nooky out from under the table and move it to the bedroom.

It was quite dark as the taxi pulled to a stop and let us out at the drawbridge, and it could have been my imagination, but I had the feeling the cabbie didn't exactly like being asked to drive out to Kidwellah. Maybe he'd heard the rumors or maybe he was just familiar with the local ghost stories, but the minute Heath paid him, he sped off with a squeal of the tires and nary a backward glance.

Still, it wasn't enough to dampen our mood. In spite of the embarrassment of being asked to leave, Heath and I had enjoyed ourselves (and not entirely in the way you're thinking . . .) and we were giggly and flirtatious with each other for a change.

It had been ages and ages since we'd had a chance to go out as a couple, and I'd really missed my sweetheart's playful side.

We held hands as we made our way onto the drawbridge, and I noticed that Heath subconsciously stuck close to the middle. We'd gone only a few steps onto the planks when we heard it. A sound that was so odd and out of the ordinary that it stopped both of us in our tracks.

"*What* was that?" I whispered.

"It sounded like something pounded on the underside of the drawbridge," Heath replied.

"I think we need to get across," I said, hurrying forward again.

Heath came right with me, but the moment we were

in motion, the pounding on the underside of the bridge picked up; only this time it felt like it was right underneath my feet. I could even feel the vibrations of the blows as I trotted forward, and after the shock to my shins from the night before, these bursts of pressure to the planks under my feet did not feel good.

Abruptly, I stopped and held Heath back too while I hoped the pounding would carry on away from me down the planks. Instead, the moment I came to a stop—so did the pounding. "It's *right* underneath my feet!" I whispered to Heath.

He looked about nervously. The drawbridge was well lit, which should have bolstered our courage, but I will be honest here—the pounding, which was thump for thump in step with my footfalls, was incredibly unnerving.

"Come on," Heath mouthed, lifting his feet slowly and carefully so as not to make any noise on the planks.

He took two steps away from me, and there was no sound from below. Encouraged, I took a step on tiptoe, but the moment the pad of my foot landed, there was a thump so hard and so loud that I felt the vibration up through my knee.

I gave a loud shriek and bolted. I ran as fast as I could, but with each step a loud whack bumped the planks from the underside of the drawbridge. Even when I tried darting to the side, the corresponding pounding found the underside of my footfall every time. Soon it felt like the whole bridge was vibrating and I couldn't move fast enough to get across and away from the sensation. Heath was right next to me, and he even reached out, grabbed my arm, and pulled me with him. Stride for stride we tore down the drawbridge before we both leaped the last few feet toward the stone of the courtyard.

With Heath's grip on my arm, I was pulled a little too far to the right and I landed oddly and tripped, stumbled, then fell to the ground, tearing my jeans and skinning both my knees, but I didn't even pause to consider the pain. Instead I jumped to my feet and whirled around to face the bridge ... but the pounding had ceased the moment we'd leaped to safety.

Heath moved to my side and placed a hand on my leg. "Damn, Em! Your knees! Are you okay?"

My chest was heaving with fear and exertion. "I'm fine," I said before pointing at the bridge. "What the *hell*, Heath?"

"I don't know," he replied. "And I don't know that I want to find out. Come on. Let's get inside and get you cleaned up."

Heath turned away first, but my eyes lingered on the bridge. And that's when I saw him—Inspector Lumley, soaking wet and standing on the drawbridge with his arms stretched out to me pleadingly. At first I was too stunned by his sudden appearance to move. Where had he come from? But then I realized that he was also wearing a metal collar with a long chain extending from a ring at the side all the way down to the ground and over the edge of the drawbridge.

My eyes darted from Lumley's pleading face to the chain and back again until a grim understanding took hold. "Inspector!" I cried in the same moment that the loose chain was pulled violently and Lumley was cruelly jerked to the side. He staggered, attempted to straighten up and fight against the chain, but he lost the battle and went into the water with a loud splash.

I stood frozen in shock for several seconds until I heard Heath call my name. "Em?" When I didn't answer, Heath hurried back to my side. "Hey, babe, what is it?"

I opened my mouth to try to explain it to him, but it was as if my vocal cords wouldn't cooperate. No sound came out and all I could do was raise my hand and point at the spot where the inspector had just been standing.

Heath looked from me to the side of the drawbridge and said, "You saw something?"

I nodded.

"Okay," he said, beginning to take a wary step in that direction. I realized he was going back out onto the bridge to take a look and I latched hard on to his arm, finally finding my voice. "Don't!"

Heath turned back to me and placed his hand over mine. "What did you see?"

"The . . . the . . . inspector. He . . . he . . . he . . ."

"He what, babe?"

"He was dead. The Widow got him."

Heath rocked back on his heels, his eyes wide. "You're sure?"

"Yes," I whispered, stunned, frightened, and surprisingly affected by the realization that the inspector had perished. "He was wet and . . . and . . . he was wearing a chain around his neck! Just like Merrick and Lefebvre!"

Heath's lips compressed and it was as if we both had the same thought at once. We'd seen no sign of police or ambulance, and as we'd only been away from the castle for a couple of hours, we knew the poor inspector hadn't been reported missing or discovered drowned at the castle . . . which could only mean that he'd somehow fallen victim to the Widow and his body was likely floating in moat as yet unnoticed.

Heath took my hand and steered me around to face the castle. "Come on," he said. "If there's another body floating in that moat, I don't think we want to be the ones to find it."

We ran to the door of the castle and pushed it open, finding a very weary-looking Mr. Crunn behind the desk, just putting away his registration book. "Mr. Crunn!" I yelled from the doorway. "Please call the police immediately!"

The poor gentleman flinched at both my raised voice and likely my request. "Oh, no," he said. "Please . . . don't tell me . . ."

I hurried over to him. "It's the inspector. I believe he's fallen victim now too."

Crunn's face turned so pale it became ashen. "Not Jasper!"

I nodded grimly. "I'm afraid so."

Arthur's hand shook as he took up the telephone and dialed. After requesting the police and an ambulance, he set the phone aside, moved over to a nearby chair, and sat down heavily.

Heath and I exchanged a look and went over to comfort him. "Did you see it happen?" he asked us.

"No," I told him.

"But you discovered his body?" he asked weakly.

"Not exactly," I admitted. "I saw his ghost on the side of the drawbridge. The Widow got him."

Crunn put a hand to his mouth and stared at the floor. He seemed quite distraught and I wondered if he and the inspector were more than just acquaintances. Perhaps they'd been friends?

We waited with the elderly gentleman for about ten minutes until we heard the sirens. I worried that by calling the police we might be putting one of them in danger, but there was nothing for it—a man had died and the matter needed to be dealt with. I just hoped they brought enough people so that the Widow wouldn't try anything wicked.

While we waited, Mr. Hollingsworth came into the hall from the parlor and inquired about the whereabouts of his wife. He seemed completely oblivious to the fact that poor Mr. Crunn was pale and shaking—obviously distraught—and after receiving the answer that the castle manager did not know where Mrs. Hollingsworth was, he set off in an irritated huff.

Once the overbearing man had left, I took Crunn's hand and studied his face, which continued to show signs of great distress. "Can I get you anything, Mr. Crunn?" I asked.

He lifted his sad eyes to mine. "No. Thank you. It's just a shock, you know. I keep thinking of the poor man's mother. She's not a well woman and it was only a few years ago that she—"

Arthur was cut off by the abrupt entrance of a ghost. Or I thought it was a ghost. At least at first.

"I say, Crunn, if these reports of drownings continue, I will well insist Kidwellah close its doors!"

We all stood up and stared with wide eyes at Inspector Lumley, who appeared very much alive. In fact, at that moment, he looked quite robust and healthy. Not at all like the pale-faced spirit I'd seen out on the drawbridge.

"What the devil are you staring at?" he asked us when we continued to ogle him, dumbfounded.

"You're . . . alive," I managed.

His brow furrowed. "And you had expected otherwise?"

I shook my head, as much to clear it as to answer his question. "I saw the ghost of a person out on the drawbridge about ten minutes ago who could have been your twin. I was sure it was you and that the Widow had claimed another victim, but now that I see you, I know I must've been wrong."

As I spoke, it was the inspector's face that drained of color, and it was as if I'd just said something most upsetting. In fact, behind me, Mr. Crunn actually gasped.

"What'd I say?" I asked, looking from one to the other, more confused than ever.

Neither man seemed able to answer me. At last the inspector came forward, and when he stood in front of me, he said, "You say you saw my twin out on the drawbridge. Did he . . . did he speak to you?"

That question wasn't at all what I was expecting. "No," I said after a moment. "He just stood there, soaking wet with his arms outstretched, before the chain attached to the collar around his neck was yanked hard and he went into the moat."

Lumley cringed and then he and Crunn exchanged

looks. It was the castle manager who was the first to turn away in what appeared to be shame.

Heath must have been as frustrated with their lack of information as I was, because he said, "Will either of you please tell us what's going on?"

The inspector pulled a silver lighter from his pocket and rubbed his thumb against it as if for some comfort. "I believe you saw my brother, Miss Holliday. Oliver. He was indeed my twin, and he drowned in Kidwellah's moat some three years past."

My jaw fell open. I reached out and touched the inspector's arm. "Oh, sir, I'm so sorry. I didn't know."

A forced smile appeared on Lumley's face. "Of course you didn't," he said. "How could you? You've only come here recently."

A million questions entered my mind, but at that moment a terrible scream echoed through the corridors and we all turned in alarm as Mrs. Lefebvre came running out from the hall leading to the dining room. "She's dead!" she cried. *"She's dead!"*

The inspector flew to her side and took her by the arms. "Who, ma'am? Who?"

But Mrs. Lefebvre was inconsolable. "It's horrible! Horrible!" she cried, pointing toward the dinning hall. Heath and I took off ahead of the inspector, which probably wasn't the smart thing to do, but we were acting on instinct. Heath reached the big room ahead of me, and came to an abrupt halt about a third of the way into the room, looking around frantically, searching for the injured party. The inspector pushed past me as I entered, and moved up next to Heath. "Where?" he asked.

But there didn't appear to be anyone in the room. It was still and quiet and quite normal looking. I moved to the far end, looking under tables, and both the inspector and Heath followed suit, but search as we might, no one could find anything amiss.

"There's no one here," the inspector said at last. "The bloody woman's having a hallucination."

"She did just lose her husband," I said tersely.

The inspector inhaled deeply and rubbed his face. "Yes. Of course. You're quite right. Forgive me."

"Inspector?" Heath said.

I turned to see him over by the window, looking out at the water of the lake.

"Yes?"

"I found your dead body."

The inspector dashed over to Heath and it took me only a moment longer to reach his side as well. And then I followed Heath's finger as he pointed to the figure of Mrs. Hollingsworth, her body only partially submerged just beyond the window.

Chapter 9

I turned away from the sight the moment my brain registered who it was, and locked eyes with Mr. Crunn, who came into the room along with Mr. Hollingsworth. "What's happened?" Hollingsworth demanded. "Mrs. Lefebvre is in quite a state!"

I went immediately to him. "Sir, perhaps we should leave the scene to the inspector." I then looked meaningfully at Mr. Crunn.

He seemed to understand and said in a shaky voice, "Yes, Mr. Hollingsworth, I believe we should allow the inspector to handle this."

Behind me I heard Lumley talking loudly on his cell phone, calling for the constable and the coroner to come back to Kidwellah immediately. "There's been another death, Niles," he said. "Call Dr. Engels straightaway and bring the crime tech lads with you."

"Who is it?" Mr. Hollingsworth asked, and for the first time I saw a crack in that bombastic demeanor. It was as if he knew that the victim was someone close to him. "I say, Inspector, who is it?"

Lumley turned to Heath and asked him to go wait for the constable at the front door, while he went out the side door to inspect the scene. He then focused his attention on Mr. Hollingsworth. "Please go to your room, Mr. Hollingsworth. I'll be along to speak with you shortly."

Hollingsworth simply stared at the inspector, his eyes wide and beginning to glisten with tears. "Not Fiona," he said feebly. "It's not Fiona, is it?"

The inspector didn't answer him; he simply turned away and headed for the side door.

"Fiona!" Hollingsworth shouted, and made to run after the inspector, but Heath stepped in front of him and physically restrained the man.

"Come with us," he said, holding firmly to Hollingsworth's shoulders. The older man was in such a state, however, that he seemed to have difficulty understanding Heath.

"It's all right, Mr. Hollingsworth," I said gently, trying to move his attention away from the open door where the inspector had gone outside. "Come with us and we'll wait for the inspector together, all right?"

"Fiona!" Hollingsworth cried weakly, his voice cracking with emotion.

At last he allowed us to lead him out of the dining hall, but he steadfastly refused to go to his room. Instead he insisted on waiting on the first floor for the inspector, so we set him up in the parlor, where we could keep an eye on him.

He did little more than sit in a chair and whimper, and when Meg and Kim came into the room to find me and see what I knew, I pulled them aside and asked them to stay with Hollingsworth. "I think the inspector will be in soon to talk to him," I said. "In the meantime, I'm going to try and find out what happened."

After getting them (reluctantly) to stay with Hollingsworth, I went in search of Heath. I found him with Gilley, Michel, Gopher, John, and Crunn. Gil was devouring a package of potato chips like it was his last meal, sprinkling crumbs on his bulbous sweatshirt. "What's the word?" I asked them.

Heath spoke first. "She was strangled and her neck was broken."

"What? Not drowned?"

Gilley pointed to John, who said, "I overheard the inspector talking on his cell. I don't know who he was calling, but he said that the coroner confirmed that Mrs. Hollingsworth was strangled and as a result her neck was broken."

I grimaced. "God, that's awful!"

Heath nudged me. "We should go out and see if her ghost is around."

I sighed heavily. Man, I wanted to quit this castle. If poor Mrs. Hollingsworth was another of the Widow's victims, she'd be one more soul I'd have to worry about freeing. And I had that thought even as the guilt of not having tried to help her sooner hit me hard in the solar plexus. "Okay," I said, and followed after Heath as we headed toward the garden to the right of the dining hall.

We got no farther than the door when we were blocked by Constable Bancroft. "No one's allowed out on the terrace," he said when we opened the door to peer out. I realized that the terrace overlooked the crime scene, and while I understood why the police wanted us to remain well away from there, Heath and I might be able to help. "Constable," I said, adopting a smile, "I know this might be an unusual request, but you see, Mr. Whitefeather and I are professional spirit mediums, and if we can find the spirit of Mrs. Hollingsworth, we might be able to help identify her killer."

This was a stretch, as most newly grounded spirits are so panic-stricken that getting them to focus on the events leading up to their crossing is often a lost cause. But I had to know if Mrs. Hollingsworth's spirit was now a prisoner of the Widow, and neither Heath nor I could tell that from inside the castle.

"Spirit what?" the constable asked.

"Mediums," I replied patiently. "Heath and I talk to the dead."

The constable looked like he wanted to laugh, but couldn't quite figure out whether we were joking.

"We're not kidding," Heath told him. "We really do make our living talking to the deceased."

"Right," the constable said skeptically.

"Who's Fran?" Heath asked suddenly.

The constable's brow shot up. "Who?"

"Fran. Franny. She says she used to live with you. And I feel she was very short," he added, putting his hand low to indicate someone about three feet tall.

Even I looked at him oddly, but the constable's mouth was agape and all he could do was stare.

"Hold on," Heath said, "Fran was a dog, wasn't she?"

Ah. That would explain the "very short" comment. And I had to smile because we don't always know we're connecting to the spirit of a pet. Sometimes the bond is so strong between pets and their humans that it can feel more like child and parent.

The constable gulped audibly. "How do you know 'bout Franny?"

"Did she have a favorite squeaky toy?" Heath asked next, and he closed his eyes to concentrate. In my mind I saw a carrot the moment Heath opened his eyes again and said, "It was in the shape of a carrot, right?"

The constable nodded and his eyes never blinked. He stared at Heath as if he was afraid blinking would cause the connection to his beloved dog to sever. "You wear something metal of hers," Heath said, pointing to the constable's neck.

The constable reached into the collar of his shirt and

pulled out a long silver chain, on the end of which was a dog tag engraved with the name Fran. "She was the best dog ever whelped," he said, his voice a bit liquid with emotion. "Better than any human friend I ever had."

"Was she black and white?" I asked, sharing a bit of the energy that Heath had opened up. "Sort of a dapple color?"

The constable nodded and wiped at his eyes. "She was an English setter, and so beautiful she'd make you weep at the sight of her. I had to put the poor love to sleep last year, and I miss her more than I care to admit."

"She's very honored that you carry her with you," Heath said, pointing to the tag. "And you buried her with your dog tags, didn't you? The ones from your military service, right?"

Bancroft put a hand to his mouth. "How'd you know that?" he asked. "No one on this earth knows that!"

"Franny told him," I said easily.

Bancroft wiped again at his eyes and seemed to suddenly become aware that there were people around. Leaning in close, he said to Heath, "Will you tell Franny that I love her, and I miss her?"

He smiled. "She can hear you, Constable. And she knows, and feels the same for you."

The kindly man nodded and cleared his throat, but it was a moment before he spoke. "Let me try to get the inspector's blessing," he said. "After that demonstration, if it were up to me, I'd let you in, but Lumley would have me head if I let you out here without asking his permission first."

We waited at the door and watched the constable give a pretty long-winded explanation of what we could do and, more to the point, wanted to do out on the terrace. It seemed that he managed to wear the inspector down, because Lumley finally waved impatiently at us to come along and Heath and I stepped outside into the cool night air.

The wind and cold spray off the lake went right into me, and it was difficult to focus on my sixth sense while being assaulted by the elements. Heath moved forward to the railing and looked out over the water, but I stood back and hoped that maybe he'd be the first to discover something.

I hoped wrong.

I felt a tingling to my left and turned around with my back to the water. I didn't see anything on the terrace, but I certainly felt it, and I knew immediately that I had Mrs. Hollingsworth within the perimeter of my sixth sense. I squinted into the darkness, but didn't see her as much as felt her frantic energy. *What's happening?* she asked me desperately.

I sent her calming thoughts, and told her I was there to help. She seemed to settle down a bit once she knew that I could communicate with her. *No one else will talk to me!*

I'm so sorry. I know this must be very upsetting to you. What's happened to me? she asked again.

"You found her?" Heath whispered next to me.

I nodded to the far right-hand side of the railing and I felt his energy expand as he attempted to communicate with her as well. I couldn't hear his thoughts, but I felt that Mrs. Hollingsworth began to communicate with him too. "We're here to help you," he said out loud.

Just tell me what's happened to me! she pleaded.

Heath and I exchanged a look. The woman clearly didn't remember her own murder, and at the moment, it was doubtful that she even knew she was dead.

"Come over here with us," I said, knowing how important it was for her own sake to accept that she was no longer part of the living.

I walked over to the opposite rail and Heath came too. I could also feel Mrs. Hollingsworth follow us. Once we were at the rail, we had a very good view of the authorities as they worked the crime scene, and at that moment, Mrs. Hollingsworth's body had yet to be covered. She was laid out on a tarp identical to the one that Merrick Brown and Mr. Lefebvre had been set on.

I braced for Mrs. Hollingsworth's reaction—it was bound to be emotional—but she actually surprised me. For the longest time her ghostly energy just vibrated next to me and Heath, and then I felt her sort of accept what she was seeing.

"Do you know who did this to you, Mrs. Hollingsworth?" I asked her.

What do I do now? she asked, avoiding my question. *Where do I go? If you can see and hear me, then you must know.*

"Is she talking to you?" Heath asked me.

"She is," I said, then turned a little in the direction of her energy. "Mrs. Hollingsworth, this is very important: We need to know who did this to you. Can you remember anything of the past few hours?"

At that moment I felt a shift in her energy—something to the effect of being startled.

"She's found the light," Heath said, tilting his chin up.

I knew he didn't see anything physically; it was more an awareness of where the light was coming from. I closed my eyes and rode the wave of energy to see it in my mind's eye, and sure enough, I had the mental image of a bright white light coming down to envelop Mrs. Hollingsworth. In the next two or three seconds, she was gone and once again I was completely aware of the bitter wind and sea spray whipping against my body.

"She's crossed," Heath said.

I sighed and opened my eyes. "Yeah, but at least we know for certain that she didn't end up like the others." Heath looked at me quizzically and I explained. "She's not a prisoner of the Widow."

"Ah," he said, looking at the scene below. "That kind of fits, though, don't you think? I mean, she didn't end up in the moat. She's in the lake."

"Which means the Widow didn't kill her," I said.

Heath wrapped a protective arm around me, and at that moment the constable looked up and noticed us standing there. "Did you find her?" he asked after he walked up the rock to us.

"Yeah, but she couldn't tell us anything."

"Can you try a bit later?" he asked.

"She's gone, Niles," I said. "She's crossed over to the other side, and it will take her some time to adjust, which means in all likelihood we won't be able to communicate with her for several weeks."

He frowned and pointed to the body. "She really told you nothing about who did that to her?"

"She was confused and then in some shock about her circumstance, and before we could really get her to focus, she found her way to the other side," I explained.

At that moment the inspector called to the constable and he left us to head back inside. Once we were alone together again, Heath said, "I don't like this, Em."

"I'm with you. This is bad."

"I think we should quit," Heath said bluntly. "There's a murderer on the loose, and who knows who he's gonna come after next?"

"How do you know it's a he?"

"You ever see a girl break someone's neck while they strangle them? That takes a lot of force, babe."

He had a solid point, and I will admit that my resolve to help Merrick's ghost was starting to waver. I began to entertain the idea of coming back someday after the murderer was caught and trying to free the imprisoned ghosts then. But something still nagged at me, and that was the possibility of more victims for the Widow to ensnare.

Also, I was reminded that if Heath and I quit, the network had the ability to sue our pants into poverty, and I had no doubt that Chris would do just that.

As I was wavering, the door behind us opened and

Heath and I both turned to see the inspector moving toward us. "Mr. Whitefeather, Miss Holliday," he said with a nod. "A word, if I may?"

"Of course, Inspector," I said.

I figured he'd want to grill us about insisting on going out to the terrace, but instead he surprised me by saying, "When you encountered the ghost of my brother earlier, are you quite positive he did not say anything to you?"

"Uh . . . yes, sir. I'm positive he didn't say anything."

That seemed to trouble the inspector. Still, he didn't explain; instead, he eyed his watch and said, "I wonder if later on this evening I might have a discussion with the two of you in private—somewhere outside the walls of Kidwellah?"

I was a bit surprised at the request and it took me a moment to respond. After looking to Heath, who nodded, I finally said, "Of course, sir."

"Excellent," the inspector replied, handing us his card and noting the mobile phone number on the back. "I will be finished here within the next two hours or so. Will you both meet me at the front entrance at eleven o'clock?"

Heath agreed before I had a chance to question the inspector about what he wanted to talk to us about, and once he heard we'd meet with him, he saluted us with two fingers and told us he was heading off to find Mr. Hollingsworth and interview the other guests of the castle.

"That was . . . odd," I said once Lumley was gone.

"Yeah," Heath agreed. "But so far, nothing about this place has been normal."

For the next two hours we hung out in our room. At one point another constable knocked on our door, and it was clear he was helping the inspector gather statements from all the guests. He took our names, and documented where we said we'd been that evening, and I was grateful that there would be at least two restaurant managers who weren't likely to forget Heath and me.

"That should take us out of the suspect pool at least," Heath said once the constable was gone.

At five to eleven Heath and I went downstairs only to find Mrs. Lefebvre with her suitcase packed standing at the front entrance. She ignored us and stood resolutely staring at the front door.

At eleven on the dot the inspector arrived in the hall and approached us, but he paused long enough to take note of Mrs. Lefebvre's luggage. "You're departing the castle?" he asked her.

The older woman squared her shoulders, as if she expected a challenge. "I'll not stay in this dreadful place one moment longer."

"I'd prefer it if you didn't leave the area, Mrs. Lefebvre," the inspector said, in a way that clearly suggested he wasn't pleased she was abandoning Kidwellah.

"You may take it up with my solicitor, Inspector. My husband is dead, and even though I had agreed to stay long enough for you to finish with your investigation, in light of that poor woman's murder, I see no other choice but to leave this death trap at once, if only to preserve my own safety."

The inspector grunted, but didn't protest further, and at that moment a taxi driver poked his head in the front door and said, "Someone 'ere call for a car?"

The inspector told Mrs. Lefebvre that he'd be in touch soon to inform her when her husband's body would be released for burial, and motioned for us to follow behind him.

We went along with him to his car, and climbed in.

"How is Mr. Hollingsworth?" I asked once we were under way.

"He appears to be quite distressed," Lumley replied.

"Appears to be?" Heath said, noting the emphasis the inspector had placed on the word.

"I'm afraid I'm a bit suspicious of Mr. Hollingsworth," Lumley told us. "Several people have informed me that he's got a bit of a temper and he'd been seen berating his wife at dinner this evening. There were also quite a few old bruises on Mrs. Hollingsworth's person. I'm convinced he was abusive to her."

"I overheard him yelling at her yesterday," I confessed. "And earlier today I heard her talking on the phone to someone and she sounded close to panic."

The inspector eyed me sharply. "Why in heavens's name didn't you tell me this earlier?"

I felt my cheeks flush. "I'm sorry, sir. I think that I was still in some shock over her death."

The inspector grunted and focused back on the road. "Speaking of her death," he said, "Constable Bancroft informs me that you made contact with her spirit but were unable to glean any details as to who might have murdered her?"

I shifted in my seat. "That's correct. Mrs. Hollingsworth crossed over very quickly after we found her spirit."

"Odd business you two are in," he said, and was silent for the rest of the drive, which it turned out wasn't very far at all.

The car turned down a narrow lane and stopped shortly thereafter in front of a tidy-looking two-story home with a thatch roof and an arched front door. We got out of the car and moved up to the picket gate, which the inspector held open for us. "Where are we?" I asked. I'd expected the inspector to take us to his office at the police station or someplace similar. To come to a residence was quite a surprise.

"We are at my home," Lumley told me.

Heath took my hand, and when I looked up at him, I could read his expression. He didn't quite trust the inspector. We moved to the door and Lumley opened it for us. As we stepped through into the front hall, a woman appeared from the other end. "Jasper?" she called, looking quite surprised to see us first.

"Good evening, Penny, I'm so sorry to have kept you so late. How is she?"

The woman glanced toward a set of stairs to her left and wrung her hands. "I tried calling you on your mobile, but it went straight to voice mail."

The inspector's posture stiffened. "What's happened?"

Penny eyed us nervously and Lumley seemed to remember that we were there. "Excuse me one moment, please," he said and he moved with Penny to the kitchen, leaving Heath and me to wonder what the heck was going on.

At last Penny and the inspector appeared again, and she was wearing her coat. He walked her to the door and she apologized for not keeping a better eye out, to which Lumley replied that it was hardly her fault and he'd see her the next day.

He then closed the door behind her and turned back to us without explaining a thing, although the strain in his eyes spoke volumes. "Shall we?" he asked, motioning to the sitting room, which was off to our left.

We preceded him there and took our seats next to each other on a rich chocolate leather sofa with an aubergine throw and striped green and purple pillows. Instead of sitting across from us on a matching sofa, the inspector shrugged out of his suit coat and moved to the fireplace, where he began busying himself with a fire.

Heath and I exchanged another look, and I could tell he was about out of patience with this whole mysterious meeting business. "Earlier this evening, Miss Holliday, you saw the ghost of my brother. What can you tell me about him?" the inspector asked abruptly.

For a moment I was so taken aback by the question that I found it hard to gather my thoughts and answer him. "Well . . . I don't know that I can tell you much more than that I thought I was looking at you, and that his spirit has unfortunately become chained to the Widow."

The inspector paused almost imperceptibly as he was

loading the fireplace with logs, but he kept his tone conversational when he asked his next question. "You've said that he didn't speak, but did he gesture to you, or signal in any way that might lead you to believe he was trying to communicate some message?"

"Not really, sir. But that may have been because he didn't really have a chance. I only saw him for a few moments . . . seconds even, and in that time he only held his arms out to me, as if he was pleading with me to help him."

The inspector stiffened again, and it was a moment before he relaxed the set of his shoulders and stuffed some newspaper under the logs before reaching for a match. Lighting it, he said, "Did you see the Widow along with my brother?"

"No, but I think she was under the drawbridge at that moment." I was recalling how Heath and I had been tortured across the planks by something pounding from the underside of the bridge.

The fire caught and Lumley stood. For several long moments he did nothing more than stare at the flames with his back to us.

"Inspector?" Heath said. "Will you please tell us why you brought us here?"

Lumley lifted his chin and reached for a photo on the mantel. Bringing it over to us, he handed it to Heath and said, "My brother, Oliver."

I peered at the image and was struck again by how similar Oliver was to the inspector. What also struck me was that Oliver was wearing a policeman's uniform. "He was a cop?" Heath asked.

Lumley took his seat across from us, his eyes betraying the pain he felt over the loss of his brother. "Yes. At the time of his death three years ago, Ollie was an inspector here in Penbigh."

"Whoa," I said. "That must have been awful for you and for the community."

"Yes," said Lumley as if the admission left a particularly bad taste in his mouth. "Of course, I wasn't here at the time."

"Were you away on holiday?" I asked.

A sardonic smile played briefly across the inspector's lips. "No. Not quite. I was at Met Pol."

"Met Pol?" Heath and I asked together.

"The Metropolitan Police Service," he explained. "At their headquarters in London. You Yanks might know it best by its nickname, Scotland Yard."

"You were with Scotland Yard?" Heath asked, and I could tell he was impressed.

"I was," said Lumley with a note of pride. "I'd tried at one time to convince my brother to apply to a post in London, but he preferred the country. My mother's family is from this region, you see, and we used to visit Wales quite a lot when we were young. I suppose Ollie preferred the tranquillity of a small village over the hustle and bustle of London. He settled here, and I settled there to pursue a prestigious career and look after Mother, but we remained close, as twins usually are."

I looked back at the photo of Lumley's brother. "Were you two identical?"

"Not quite," Lumley said. "Oliver was an inch shorter and his eyes were green rather than the brown of my eyes. Other than that, however, most people were hard pressed to tell us apart."

"Is that why you ended up here?" I asked. "You wanted to be closer to your brother's spirit?"

"No," the inspector admitted. "Not really. What I mean is that the driving force behind my leaving Met Pol and taking up the position here of inspector—vacated by my brother—was to investigate his death. I never believed for a moment that he drowned accidentally. Oliver was a very good swimmer, but the even bigger mystery was to ask, what the devil would he be doing swimming in a moat in the dead of night? He was a smart chap, my brother. He'd never do something so ridiculously reckless."

"I take it there were no prominent signs of foul play like you discovered on the two men found dead in the past few days, and like you discovered on Mrs. Hollingsworth?"

"None. But then, my brother's body was in the moat for three days before it was discovered. By then the elements had done their worst, I'm afraid."

"Three days?" Heath repeated. "How come nobody noticed?"

"According to the official police report, filed by a man that I later fired for incompetence, Oliver's body must have become submerged, and only surfaced when a heavy rainfall came through to stir up the currents."

I made a face. I get squeamish around stuff like that.

The inspector must have noticed because he apologized. "I'm so sorry to elaborate on the grim details," he said. "I forget how upsetting these things can be for you laypersons."

"It's fine," I assured him. "But I'm still not quite sure why you wanted to speak to Heath and me privately."

The inspector picked at a loose thread on his shirt cuff. "As you no doubt know, Kidwellah has a rather unscrupulous past. I've always believed in the ghost stories originating from the castle. Ollie and I would play near the moat as children, and the both of us would see things in some of the castle's windows that we couldn't readily explain.

"And while I was put off by such things, Ollie became fascinated. He would comb the library shelves for information about the castle and its most famous residents, and he knew all about the Grim Widow and her murderous past. I believe it was those summer holidays spent here that he fell in love with Penbigh and wanted to serve it in some way.

"After university he did the most unexpected thing; he applied to the Penbigh police department and was accepted. Mother of course was most upset—"

"She was afraid for his safety?" Heath asked.

Lumley shook his head and chuckled softly. "Oh, no. Not that. She expected Ollie to be an accountant, engineer, or perhaps even a solicitor. Something respectable, but he felt a calling to law enforcement, and to my mother's great dismay, after hearing my brother speak so enthusiastically about his new post, I applied to Met Pol and was accepted."

"What'd your dad say?" I asked.

Lumley looked at me oddly. "Nothing."

"He's the silent type, huh?"

"If my father has anything to say, Miss Holliday, it would likely be to you, not to me."

Heath said, "Your father passed away?"

"Yes. At least that's what we believe. You see, he left my mother when we were very small, barely three, and no one in his family ever saw him again. Mother finally won a decree declaring him dead when Ollie and I were ten. Mother claims that my father became involved with some unscrupulous characters, and they were the cause of his disappearance."

"Oh, that's awful," I said, and the inspector merely shrugged as if he'd had all these years to deal with it and it no longer bothered him. "Do you remember him?"

"No. But from what my mother told us, he was a wretched husband and father. His one contribution to the family was a sizable trust established for me and my brother when we were born, which allowed us all to live in relative comfort and attend some of the best schools."

I studied the ether around Inspector Lumley. Normally, when someone mentions a deceased relative, I'll feel a slight knocking sensation, almost like the spirit has been waiting to be asked to join the conversation and, immediately upon hearing his or her name, is all over my energy, but I didn't get any sense of the inspector's father.

I snuck a look at Heath to see if maybe he felt the man, but Heath looked at me and shook his head. "He's not around," he mouthed.

I thought that Lumley must be right; his dad really was a jerk not to want to make contact through one of us to talk to his son.

"We still don't understand why you asked us here," Heath said next.

Lumley loosened his tie. "Yes, quite right. You see, my brother's death was just one of several that have taken place at the castle in the past forty years."

"One of several?" I repeated. "How many are we talking about, Inspector?"

"Not including the three most recent victims, a total of nine, Miss Holliday. All of them ruled accidental, and all of them found drowned in the moat."

Nine deaths over forty years? That was quite a lot for one remote castle in the north of Wales. And now there were three more to add.

"You're suspicious of the number and manner of deaths," I guessed.

"Most suspicious," he said. "Especially of my brother's drowning. And my brother was suspicious too. As I said, he always found Kidwellah fascinating. He was drawn to it in a way I couldn't always understand, and I believe he discovered the great coincidence between these victims, namely, that they were all on holiday at the castle, all male, and all drowned at night. I believe it was the discovery of this similarity among the victims that caused him to open an investigation, and that is what led to his death."

"In other words, you may have a sixty-year-old serial killer on your hands," I said.

"Perhaps," he replied with a shrug. "Or it may be a

father-and-son team. I can't rule any theory out, no matter how implausible."

"So you don't believe the Grim Widow is solely responsible," Heath said. "Even though she attacked and nearly drowned me."

The inspector stared at Heath for a long time without answering, and when he finally did, he was careful to be as tactful as possible. "I do believe you when you say the Widow attacked you, Mr. Whitefeather. Miss Holliday and my own constable verify your account, but I cannot believe that all nine of these victims died as a result of some ghost. And certainly Merrick Brown and André Lefebvre were helped along in their demise. No, something else is at the root of these deaths, and I mean to discover what that is."

"How do we play into this?" I asked, and when the inspector's eyes swiveled to me, I added, "I'm assuming this is why you asked us here, Inspector, to discuss how we may be able to help you in your investigations?"

The inspector's mouth quirked at the edges. "You're a most insightful woman, Miss Holliday. And you are correct. I do need your help. As you've personally had several spiritual encounters with the most recent victims, I'm hoping that you might encourage one of them to tell you who is the person responsible for their deaths. The Widow aside of course."

"That's a bit of a tall order, sir," Heath said, and explained several of the issues involved, including the fact that ghosts didn't always remember their own deaths, and the fact that the Widow seemed to be controlling their appearances to us.

"Still," the inspector pressed, "I would appreciate any assistance I might prevail upon you and your special abilities to offer."

"I have a question," I said, thinking suddenly of something that should have been obvious.

"Yes?" Lumley asked.

"How is it that the castle is still open? I mean, you'd think that at least one of the victims' families would have sued the owner of the castle into ruin by now."

The inspector actually laughed.

"You Americans," he said. "So ready to take up the legal battle! We Brits are far less litigious. Our courts aren't nearly so inviting of such things. But I do in part agree with you; it is curious that not one of the families has sought a claim against the dowager."

"The dowager?" I asked. "Who's that?"

"Lady Lydia Hathaway," the inspector said. "Kidwellah has belonged to her family for the past several centuries. Her father, Sir Robert Mortimer, fell into some financial difficulty after the war and nearly lost the place to creditors. He was the one who turned it into a hotel and left it for his daughter as part of her dowry."

"They still have that?" Heath asked.

"Indeed," the inspector told him. "Lady Lydia has ruled over Kidwellah and most of Penbigh ever since her husband's fatal hunting accident some fifty years ago."

"How old is she?" I asked.

"Well into her seventies by now," the inspector said.

"It seems like Kidwellah is a hazard," I said next. "Why not shut it down?"

The inspector sighed. "I've spoken to the dowager several times about draining the moat or closing Kidwellah's doors in light of these 'accidents,'" he said, using air quotes, "but she steadfastly refuses, claiming that would be far too costly for her, as she depends on the income from Kidwellah to pay her taxes. And, as long as she wields the power in Penbigh, I'm afraid Kidwellah will continue to host the unsuspecting tourist."

"But in light of these most recent deaths, how can she ignore the obvious?" I pressed.

"You would be quite surprised what the landed gentry can ignore, Miss Holliday," he replied with a frown. "Especially when it comes to money."

From upstairs there was a thump, like a chair toppling over and hitting the floor, and we all jumped. Lumley was on his feet in an instant.

"Jasper!" came a croaky female voice. *"Jasper!"*

"Excuse me," Lumley said, darting off toward the stairs.

He made it up about five steps when we saw something small come hurtling down the stairs and Lumley had to duck to the side. "Where is my cocktail!" that croaky voice demanded.

"Mother," Lumley said firmly. "You've had quite enough and it's time for bed."

"I want my cocktail!" she yelled at him. Heath and I were both leaning way out in our seats looking toward the stairs, but all we could see was Lumley from the waist down. "You had no right to take it from me!"

"Mother," Lumley said, climbing to the top of the staircase, where it sounded like a slight struggle took place.

"Get your hands off me, young man!" she cried. "And give me back my gin! It was mine! Bought with my own money and you've no right to it!"

Her words were slurred and her voice ragged, as if she'd been yelling quite a bit recently. "Come along, Mother," Lumley coaxed, his own voice strained.

"You're just like your father!" she spat. "He took my things too! And look where it got him!"

She said that last part with an evil laugh and I turned my head to Heath and mouthed, "Wow!"

He nodded. For the record, we both have screwed-up family histories, but not *that* screwed-up.

The struggle at the top of the stairs continued and finally moved off to another part of the second story, where more things sounded like they were being thrown about. I wanted to be anywhere but there, and judging by the look on Heath's face, he did too.

"Should we go?" I asked him.

"Lumley drove," he reminded me.

"Yeah, but the castle's not far from here. If we stick to the road it'd only take us an hour at most to get back to the castle."

He didn't have time to reply because in the next moment a door slammed and Lumley came hurrying back down the stairs. "I'm terribly sorry," he said, his face red with embarrassment.

"It's fine," I assured him, hoping I sounded sincere.

"Mother has been doing so well lately, but tonight somehow she laid her hands on a bottle of gin."

"It's really okay," I repeated, and now I felt bad for wanting to run out on him. "Lots of families struggle with addiction."

"I've called you a taxi," Lumley said next, avoiding looking directly at us. "I must apologize for not being able to take you back to the castle myself, but I think I should stay here with Mother."

"Of course," I said, and next to me Heath nodded. And then we all fell into an uncomfortable silence until the cab came.

"We'll let you know if we get anything from any of the ghosts we encounter," Heath promised on our way out. He was probably also feeling bad about being there to witness the poor inspector deal with his alcoholic mother.

Chapter 10

The next morning Heath and I were up early. We had breakfast in the dining hall, which was practically empty except for Franco, the model I'd seen kissing Mr. Lefebvre. I wondered if Gilley had taken my advice and showed Inspector Lumley the calls to Lefebvre that Franco made on Gil's cell phone. That would explain why he was still here, as all the other models had long since departed once they learned of the fashion designer's demise. As I was wondering about all of this, Inspector Lumley walked in with Constable Bancroft, and they motioned for Franco to follow them.

"Wonder what that was about?" Heath said.

We learned just a short time later when both Gilley and Michel came hurrying into the dining room to tell us that Franco had been arrested for Mr. Lefebvre's murder.

Heath and I both sat forward with interest.

"I showed Lumley the calls Franco made from my phone," Gil said, clearly a little guilt-ridden about that. "It didn't help that he had absolutely no alibi beyond midnight," Gil added. "And he admitted to Lumley that he called André, asking to meet, but he claims that André never showed. and Franco fell asleep waiting for him."

"How do you know all that?" I asked.

Gil lightly tapped the floor with his toe. "We overheard him talking to Lumley in the parlor."

"Where did Franco say he was supposed to meet Lefebvre?" Heath asked.

"Their secret place," Gil said. "Whatever that means. Franco insists it was on the castle's grounds."

"I know where it is," I said, and everyone eyed me with surprise. "I saw Franco and Lefebvre making out in a corner of the courtyard partially hidden by foliage, but I don't know if I believe that he was asleep and missed the drawbridge being pulled up."

Gil shrugged. "Franco claims he didn't wake up until the police began to swarm into the courtyard from the watchtower."

I pursed my lips skeptically. "Convenient," I said.

"Too convenient," Heath added.

Still, I wasn't sure that I was willing to accept Franco as the killer. For one thing, the model didn't look smart enough to dismantle a drawbridge and plot a fairly sophisticated murder.

But Gil had more to share. "Lumley also showed Franco a statement from Mrs. Lefebvre swearing that Franco was trying to extort money from her husband. She gave him an e-mail from Franco to André where Franco supposedly tried to blackmail André, and Mrs. Lefebvre thinks that Franco killed André because André wouldn't pay up."

"It can't be true," Michel said, obviously distressed. "Franco would never kill André. He doesn't have the backbone or the stomach for something like that. And really the lad is quite daft. I can't see him killing André, and then coming up with such a bloody awful alibi."

"He had the stomach and brains to try and blackmail Lefebvre," Heath pointed out.

Michel's frown deepened. "Perhaps. But I know he didn't do it," he insisted.

"Everything points to him, though," Gilley said gently. He was sweet with Michel, a sure sign that my best friend was developing a serious crush on him. "The last person who saw Franco was Gopher and the girls at between twelve and twelve fifteen, and according to the inspector, André was murdered close to that time."

"It could have been Mrs. Lefebvre," I said. I agreed with Michel. Something didn't fit.

But Gil was already shaking his head. "That's what Franco said when Lumley and the constable were questioning him, but Lumley wasn't buying it for two reasons: One, the coroner said that whoever cracked André on the back of the head had to be pretty strong—the skull fracture extended almost the entire length of his head— so they're thinking the wound had to be inflicted by a male. And the second reason is that Mrs. Lefebvre has rheumatoid arthritis, and she can't lift anything heavier than a pencil above her head."

"But what about the other two murders here?" I asked. "Does Lumley also suspect Franco of committing them?"

"As it happens, he does," Gil replied. "He's got no proof linking Franco to those murders yet, but Franco doesn't have an alibi for the time they were committed either. Lumley thinks that it can't be a coincidence that three people were murdered here at Kidwellah in quick succession and in a similar fashion."

I turned to Heath. "You buying this?"

"After what Lumley told us last night of similar murders over the past forty years? No."

"Similar murders?" Michel asked.

"There have been several other suspicious drownings here at Kidwellah over the past four decades," I explained.

"Last night Lumley told us he suspected he may have a serial killer or killers on the loose here at Kidwellah. He even theorized that there could be a father-son team involved because of the span of time."

"Oh, *that's* what he meant when he asked Franco if his father had been released from prison yet," Gilley said.

Michel blanched and I knew he had details to share. "What?" I asked him.

"Franco and I were together briefly, until we arrived here and I realized he really had a thing for André and he was just using me to make him jealous. But during the time we were together, Franco confessed that his father was doing time for murder. He's been in prison ever since Franco was fourteen."

"The plot thickens," Heath muttered.

"He didn't do it," Michel insisted.

I felt bad for Michel. I knew that even though Franco had used Michel, it was obvious the photographer still carried a soft spot for the model. "You know, Michel," I said to him, "Heath and I have talked at length with Inspector Lumley, and I like him. I think he's smart and capable of uncovering the whole truth. If Franco is innocent, I think his best chance is to have Lumley try and find enough evidence to prove it, and in doing that, I think the inspector will uncover what actually happened to Mr. Lefebvre."

"You two could ask his spirit, couldn't you?" Michel asked, pointing to Heath and me.

I shifted in my seat uncomfortably. "We tried asking Mrs. Hollingsworth's ghost what happened to her right before she died, and she wasn't very cooperative. It's tricky, Michel, because the Grim Widow is also involved. Right now Lefebvre is being held prisoner by the Widow, and Heath and I don't know how that's even possible, let alone how to go about freeing him from her clutches long enough to ask him about who might've struck him on the head."

"I know how it's possible," Gil said smugly.

I cut him a look. "And you were gong to share this, when?"

"Right now," he said, and smiled at Michel.

"We're waiting," I told him when he didn't get right to it.

Gil turned back to me. "I called Ray Fairfield in Newark."

"Really?" I said, surprised to hear the name. Ray was a legend in the field of paranormal investigation. The guy had seen things and encountered stuff that made all the hairs on my neck stand on end. I think he's the only guy, in fact, who's had more scary encounters than me. "What'd he say?"

"He says that it's super rare, but he has heard of one ghost capturing the spirit of another. Basically, he thinks that your Grim Widow has signed a deal with the devil, so to speak."

"Not literally, though, right?" I asked. Even I'm afraid of stuff like that.

"Well, maybe not *the* head honcho of Hades, but Ray thinks that your spook has agreed to keep her portal open as a gate for a powerful demon."

"The shadow," I whispered, remembering that horrible black shadow that chased John through the halls.

"Yeah," Gil said with a shudder. "John told me about that thing. I'm glad I wasn't with you when it came out of hiding."

"Okay, so what does making a deal with a demon get the Widow?" Heath asked.

"Power," Gil replied. "Ray thinks that the demon is providing all the extra wattage for the Widow to throttle anyone willing to get close to her . . . like you two fools . . . and capture the souls of anyone she kills."

"But we don't think she killed Merrick or André Lefebvre, so how did she capture their souls?" I asked.

"Oh, she still could've killed them," Gil said. "If both

of them were incapacitated before they were thrown into the moat, then all she'd have to do is grab an arm or a leg and pull them under until they drowned."

"But I thought Lefebvre died of the blow to the back of the head?" Heath pressed.

"Nope," Gilley said, and I could tell he was enjoying knowing so much more than us at the moment. "According to the conversation Lumley had with Franco, Lefebvre was hit hard enough for the blow to be mortal, but not instantly fatal. The actual cause of death was drowning, and Lumley wants to make sure that when the case goes to trial, the jury knows that even though Lefebvre was cracked on the skull, he still could have been conscious enough to suffer while he drowned."

Heath made a small noise and I glanced his way. His hand was rubbing his chest and I knew he was remembering his own painful near-death experience.

Still, there was something about how the Widow's prisoners were chained to her that bothered me. "Did Ray have any theories on why the Widow's captives were all wearing a collar and chain?"

"Ray says he's seen something similar. He once saw a spook being dragged by the neck by another, more powerful spook with a length of rope. He thinks the collar and the chain are simply manifestations of the Widow's power. It's like, you know how on the lower planes everything is driven by thought, right?"

"Yeah," said Heath.

"Well, if the Widow convinces a newly made ghost that she's taking them prisoner, then all she has to do is *think* up a chain and a collar to put around their necks and they actually become a physical part of that newly grounded ghost's world."

"It's like she's an evil genie," I said. "She just snaps her fingers and she's got you in chains."

"Exactly," Gilley agreed. "To Lefebvre and Brown that collar and chain are very real. They could no more break free of them than if I put a real one on you. It's all about dominance. If she's really sucking energy from a demon, then she's got the power to keep them in chains for eternity."

We were all silent for several moments while we digested the horrors of *that*. Finally I asked, "Did Ray have any ideas about how to free the Widow's prisoners?"

He shook his head. "You know Ray. He told me to tell you to block up her portal if you can, and say a prayer for the poor bastards locked in with her. They'll be stuck in hell with the Widow forever, but it beats having her run loose among other possibly innocent victims." I stared hard at Gil and he simply shrugged. "His words, M. J., not mine."

"We're not shutting them in her portal without at least trying to set them free."

"It might help to know who she's got trapped in there," Heath said. "Maybe if we can surround her portal and call out personally to as many of her victims as we can, we'll be able to get them to make a run for it. If we can get enough of them to bolt, she'll have a hard time holding on to all those chains, and maybe we can get them to just this side of the portal right before we jam a few dozen spikes into it."

"Suicide," Gil said to him with a shake of his head. "Seriously, honey, that plan will get you killed."

I sighed. "We have to find the Widow's portal first, which may be just as difficult as shutting it down. Still, I think Heath's right and that we should do a little digging into who the victims were. Gil, there has to be a list of the poor souls found floating in the moat somewhere, and if there is or was a serial killer offering up sacrifices to the Grim Widow, then knowing who the victims are may be of some use to us. Lumley told us that besides Lefebvre, Merrick, and Mrs. Hollingsworth, there were nine other suspicious drownings here at the castle over the past forty years."

"More research," Gil grumbled.

"I only ask because you're so good at it."

Gil made a face, but I could see he was secretly pleased that I'd complimented him in front of Michel.

At that moment Meg, Kim, and John all came into the dining hall and took up seats at our table. Once Mary had taken their breakfast orders, we got down to the business of discussing that evening's shoot.

"Where's our illustrious producer?" I asked.

"On the phone with Chris," John said. "By the sound of their conversation, it's probably gonna be a long one. Chris wasn't happy that our shoot last night got postponed."

My jaw dropped. "A woman was murdered and the police were here most of the night investigating!"

John shrugged. "Chris doesn't think that's a good enough reason."

I scowled. I was really starting to hate that guy. "Well, I'd rather not wait for Gopher. Besides, we all know he's not great with prep work assignments. The seven of us can handle it." I pulled out my iPhone and lit up the notes screen where I'd typed out all the details we'd have to cover. "First," I said, "we're going to need to get the entire crew outfitted with Gilley sweatshirts. I don't want anyone walking around the castle or the moors without being fully protected."

"Even you two?" Kim asked, pointing to me and Heath.

"Yes. Even the two of us. This Grim Widow is crazy powerful. She appears in full form to us every time she's around. That takes amazing energy. She's also physically powerful enough to have nearly drowned Heath."

"She's at least twice as strong as me," Heath confirmed, and I watched everyone at the table stare at Heath for a good few seconds, taking that in. He's no wimp, that's for sure, and it had to be astonishing to believe he'd been overpowered by a ghost.

"This spook is beyond dangerous, guys," I said. "I know we all really need the money, but I have to warn you, whatever is going on in this castle, the Widow's ghost has been stirred up and she's definitely on the prowl for more victims. If she pulls any of you into the water, there won't be much we can do. And those magnets won't be a lot of help to you if you end up in the moat. She can just let the cold water and the weight of your clothing make your limbs too weak to function."

I let that sit a minute with the crew before I continued. "The important thing on this shoot is going to be to protect ourselves first, get the footage second. I don't want anyone taking unnecessary risks. Even if Gopher pushes you for it, you're to stick to the game plan and follow my or Heath's instructions. Got it?"

To a person everyone nodded.

"Good. Now, Kim and Meg, you'll need to go into town and find the right-size sweatshirts for the crew. You'll need two sweatshirts per person—I want backups just in case someone's gets torn or lost."

Meg raised her hand. "M. J.?"

"Yes?"

"I had a thought," she said hesitantly as she eyed the sagging mass of fabric around Gilley.

"Which is?" I really wanted the girl to just spit it out.

"Well, I know we've always glued the magnets to sweatshirts, but what if there was a better garment that might let everybody move a little easier?"

"What did you have in mind?"

"A bubble vest."

"What's a bubble vest?" Gil asked.

"You know what a bubble coat is, don't you, Gil?" she replied. "It's a puffy down-filled coat."

"Oh, I know what you're talking about," Gil said. "I have one of those at home in Boston, but I don't wear it 'cause it makes me look fat."

Everyone at the table seemed to press their lips together, because Gil's current choice of protective ghost-gear made him look like something out of a tire commercial. "Anyway," Meg continued, "I was at this store in town yesterday, and they have a whole section of bubble vests on sale—probably because summer's coming. I was thinking that we could take out some of the stitching in the quilting that holds the down, and shove in some magnets, then sew the seams back up again. That way the material wouldn't sag, the vest would still keep you nice and warm, and you'd have the full use of your arms without being weighed down by the magnets."

Shy little Meg surprised me with her ingenuity. "Girl, that's a fantastic idea!" I said. "How long do you think it'll take you to convert a vest into a magnetized version?"

"Maybe an hour and a half?"

I grimaced. We'd need a total of eight vests plus maybe one or two extra for security and it was already well after ten. Meg would also need to buy the vests after our meeting.

"I could help," Kim said. "I'm pretty good with a needle and thread."

"You're hired," I told her. "And I want you guys to head to town right away to purchase the coats. Get Gopher's credit card before you go, and if he gives you any flak about it, call me and I'll set him straight. John, can you take notes for the rest of the meeting and fill Kim and Meg in when they get back?"

"No sweat."

"Great. Kim. Meg. Go get 'em."

The two assistants pushed back their chairs and practically ran to do my bidding. I was rather liking my little power trip. Too bad I couldn't get Gil to react like that.

"I hope you don't expect me to jump to your command," Gil muttered, as if he'd read my mind.

I ignored him and focused on Michel. "When they get back, I'd like the first vest to go to you."

"Me?"

"Yes. I think we should get some stills of the castle, both inside and out, to use in the movie. I know Gopher's directing this thing, and he may toss out the idea of using stills, but if we have photos on hand, we can better formulate a plan about where to shoot first. All of the shots should be taken in the daytime, and the minute dusk hits, you hightail it back here so that we can have dinner and catch a little sleep before we set out tonight."

"Of course," Michel said. "I like the idea of using stills in the movie too."

"No getting too close to the south wing, though," I warned. "Even with a magnetized vest it's not a good idea."

"Got it."

Next I turned to John. "I need a blueprint of the castle, John. If there isn't one on hand, then please find Mr. Crunn and have him help you draw a map. Let him know I need to be able to see every secret passage and hidden stairwell he knows about. I don't want any of us to get caught like you did the other day when you fell against that sconce."

John nodded. "I'm on it."

Finally I turned to Gilley. "Yes?" he said with half-closed lids.

"I need some additional research."

"Don't you always?"

"Are you really going to be difficult on this bust too?"

"Why change now?"

"Because, smart guy, if you don't get us what we need, the Widow could strike in a way or in an area we don't expect, and Heath is the only one I'd go back in the water for."

Gil rolled his eyes. "What do you need to know?"

"I'm curious about this Desperate Duke character. I'm convinced it was his ghost I saw after I fell onto that strip of land outside the door I jumped from the other night, and the Widow was clearly wary of him. I think he's someone we may want to make contact with and maybe even enlist to help us fight his widow. I'm still not sure if he was also the ghost I saw out on the moors from inside the castle, so I'd like it if you could confirm that the duke also haunts the moors. And I want to stick to the original plan we had to go in search of him first, before we tackle the Widow. Also, see if you can find any good deeds done by this man when he was alive. Maybe he wasn't a total bastard and something you dig up will help us remind him of his humanity."

But Gil was already shaking his head. "M. J., you've already seen him once and that means you're marked for death! How many times are you gonna tempt fate on this bust?"

"I'm still alive, Gil, which means the legend is probably flawed. Besides, he helped me, which means in life he might have been a misogynist bastard, but in death he did a girl a great favor, and that has to count for something." Gil continued to glare at me contemptuously, so I repeated firmly, "Just get me the research, will you?"

He muttered something that I'm sure was unflattering to me, but he also tapped a few notes into his phone, so I didn't make a big deal out of it. "Anything else?" he asked.

"No. That should do it."

"What're you and Heath going to do?" John asked.

"We're going to pay a house call," I said.

Heath looked at me curiously. "Who're we going to see?"

"The Dowager Countess Lydia Hathaway."

Several mouths fell open.

"I don't believe the dowager would be willing to meet with you without an appointment," Michel said.

"Maybe not. But we have to try. I don't have a lot of confidence about our ability to shut the Widow down, and if we fail in that goal, then I think we'll need a backup plan. Ideally, I'd like to see the castle closed and locked up tight, but I think I'd settle for having the moat drained. Either way, Kidwellah Castle shouldn't be a vacation destination for anybody. And with three recent deaths on castle grounds, I can't see how the dowager could reason otherwise."

"Good luck with that," Gilley said, and not like he actually meant it.

I gathered up my messenger bag and stood to end the meeting. "We'll regroup back here at six for dinner, get some shut-eye for a few hours, then start filming around one a.m. If you run into any issues with your assignments, please call me on my cell." And that's when I remembered something else and I turned to Gil again, dreading that I had to ask him one more favor.

"Oh come on!" he yelled, clearly reading my expression. "Pick on somebody else, would you?!"

"Heath needs a new phone," I said, ignoring the drama queen fit he was throwing, but conscious that the rest of the crew had paused to listen.

Gilley glared at me. "Let him get it himself," he snapped, clearly irritated that he'd been assigned so many tasks.

"You have the crew's cellular account info, Gil," I reminded him. "It's a lot easier if you handle it."

"I'll go with you," Michel said, and I could've hugged him, because Gilley immediately softened.

"Yeah?"

"Of course," Michel said. "It'll be our little date. You can convince me to get a mobile and I can keep you company."

I thought Gilley might float right out of his chair—he was so pleased—but then he remembered me and cut me another dark look. "You owe me."

I sighed. "Don't I always?"

Gil muttered again, but I could tell it was all an act. I turned my attention one last time to the crew. "Okay, everybody, you have your assignments. Let's get to it!" With that, everyone scattered.

Once we were back in the main hall, I asked Mr. Crunn to order me a taxi, and Heath and I waited out on the road, well away from the drawbridge. While we stood there, Heath turned back to stare at the castle. "What?" I asked him, wondering what he was looking at.

"You'd never know it was such a terrible place in the light of day."

I looked back too. But I wasn't fooled. I'd seen way too much in the past few days to ever think of it as anything but an awful place. I turned away without comment and stared instead out at the moors. To my eye, the rolling hills and lush green grasses were far more picturesque. The taxi didn't take long to reach us, and I couldn't help but notice how the driver looked a bit relieved that we met him out in front of the castle so that he didn't have to drive across the bridge. Once we were seated, I said, "Do you happen to know where the Dowager Countess Hathaway lives?"

In the rearview mirror, his eyes grew wide. "I do, ma'am, yes."

"Can you please take us to her home?"

The driver shifted in his seat. "Pardon my asking, ma'am, but do you happen to have an appointment to see the countess? And I'm only asking because without one, you're not gettin' an audience with the likes of 'er."

"Well then," I said, unperturbed, "we'll ring her bell, make our inquiries, and ask you to wait for us should we get turned away, if that's all right by you?"

The driver mumbled something that sounded an awful lot like "It's your funeral," but he didn't try to talk me out of going.

We drove in silence the fairly short distance to a large redbrick home that sat atop a hill overlooking Lake Byrn y Bach. When I realized how close the house was, I felt a blush touch my cheeks. If we'd only asked Arthur for directions, Heath and I could easily have walked.

We got out and I paid the driver, thanking him and letting him know that we would find our own way back to the castle. He smiled and winked at me, knowing he'd just taken another American for a few pound notes she could easily have kept.

Heath and I approached the front drive a bit warily. I had no idea what the dowager was going to be like, or if she would even see me, but I had a compelling urge to talk to her, and I don't usually ignore my own intuition.

At the front door I let Heath press the bell. It gonged with a somber tone. A few moments later the door was opened by an elegantly dressed gentleman, tall and imposing, with silver hair, a long hooked nose, very erect posture, and a clear disdain for the appearance of strangers on the dowager's doorstep. "Yes?" he said, in that way that suggested his next comment would be "No thank you, good day."

For a second, I had no idea what to say, but then I just blurted out a partial truth. "Hello, sir, my name is M. J. Holliday and this is my associate Heath Whitefeather. As you can probably tell from our accents, we're from America, and we're currently staying at Kidwellah Castle filming for a television show we're featured in, and I was wondering if the Lady Hathaway might perhaps be able to give us some history on Kidwellah—if it's not too much of an imposition, that is."

The man at the door stared down his hooked nose at me as if he could barely fathom the audacity of such a bold request, and just as he opened his mouth to speak, from somewhere inside we heard, "Fredrick? Who is it?"

Into view came a woman perhaps in her early to mid-seventies, smartly dressed in fine silk and cashmere and with perfect ash-blond hair cut to just under her chin. "Hello," she said cordially.

"These are two Americans, my lady," the butler said with a slight bow.

"Oh?" she replied, her eyes alight with interest. "Are you here on holiday?"

"No, ma'am," I said, wondering if it was correct to address the countess as "ma'am." "We're here on business. We're filming a television show at Kidwellah Castle."

The countess stepped forward. "Oh, yes! I had heard you were coming to investigate my beloved Kidwellah. How are you enjoying your stay?"

Her question took me by surprise. Surely she'd heard about the tragic happenings of the last few days. "It's been . . . eventful, ma'am."

The half smile she'd worn since making her appearance never wavered, and I didn't quite know what to make of that, but I really wanted to have a chat with this woman, so while the opportunity presented itself, I took it. "I hope you'll forgive our unannounced intrusion, ma'am, but our producer told us this morning to call on you and beg an audience. You see, we have very little background on Kidwellah, and he thought it might be a good idea to ask you about it. I mean, no one could be a better resource for the castle's history than its owner, right?"

Out of the corner of my eye I saw the butler subtly roll his eyes. He didn't care for my informalities one little bit, but either the countess forgave me my ignorance or she had nothing better to do that morning. "Would you and your gentleman friend like to join me for a spot of tea?" she asked.

"Yes, please!" I said with great relief as the butler stepped to the side and opened the door wide to allow us entrance.

Both Heath and I formally introduced ourselves and followed Lady Hathaway a little deeper into the beautiful home. I knew that her house had been described by the taxi driver as a "cottage," but it was by no means modest. However, it was quite cozy.

By the look of it, the dowager's home was at least five thousand square feet, with large airy rooms adorned in the most beautiful fabrics and rich array of colors. A lovely collection of artwork graced nearly every wall, and fine antique furnishings completed the setting.

There was also none of that musty old smell that comes with homes filled with the furnishings of centuries past. Instead the air smelled clean and lemony, and each wood surface gleamed with a polished sheen. I immediately loved the home. It was one of those places that just welcomed you at every turn.

The dowager led us into a beautiful robin's-egg-blue parlor with gold accents and teal blue furnishings, and the moment I sat down on the sofa, I wanted to marry it. I'd never sat on something so plush and comfortable.

Large windows allowed a good bit of the late-morning sun to warm the room, and as we initially made small talk with the dowager—informing her of our backgrounds and how we met and came to be in the cable TV business—I also warmed to the lovely woman and wondered why I'd allowed the inspector's words to shape my opinion of her before meeting her.

After tea was served by a young woman in a traditional maid's uniform, the countess turned the conversation to Kidwellah Castle. "Now, you had asked about the history of Kidwellah. The castle was built in the late thirteenth century and has a very rich past—too much to go into for one sitting, so please tell me what era you'd most enjoy hearing about and I'll do my best to keep the history brief."

Heath spoke up before I could. "We'd like to hear about the Grim Widow, ma'am. That is, if you don't mind sharing?"

That amused smile the dowager had worn since we first met widened and she actually laughed. "Oh, of course you want to know about the Widow and her duke! It's a sordid tale, I assure you."

The countess then recounted the story of the Grim Widow in much the same way as Arthur had when we'd first asked him. Of course, the dowager's account held a bit back in that she didn't mention the fact that the former Countess of Kidwellah had also murdered a number of her husband's friends and a house servant or two, but she did suggest that the Widow had driven her husband mad and no one knew what had become of him. It was speculated that he died somewhere out on the moors, or perhaps even drowned himself in Lake Byrn y Bach.

When she'd finished, I took a deep breath and asked, "Ma'am, do you believe there's any truth to the rumors that the Widow is still murdering people?"

The dowager waved a dismissive hand. "Oh, pish!" she said. "Of course there's no truth to that. But if it will help bring the tourists to Kidwellah, then who am I to argue?"

I felt Heath sit back in surprise. I was pretty shocked too. "You don't mind that Kidwellah's resident ghost has a murderous reputation?"

"Of course not!" she said with a light laugh. "It's been very good for business, actually. I cannot imagine why anyone would spend their holiday at a frightfully haunted castle, but there are plenty of common folk in the world who seem more than willing to come to my spooky little corner of Wales, and I for one am grateful."

I looked again at the lavish surroundings. I couldn't imagine the dowager was hard up for money, so why would she encourage such rumors about her family's heritage?

"You must think me rather vulgar," she said when both Heath and I sat there a little stunned by her admission.

"No," I said quickly. "It's just . . . surprising."

"That I'd want to encourage a story like the Grim Widow's ghost to entice tourists to come stay at

Kidwellah? My dear young lady, the high times of yes-teryear's aristocracy have long gone by! Most of the landed gentry in this country have had to resort to such measures as charging the general public admission for a guided tour of the family home in order to save those estates from ruin. The farmers who once tilled our soils and paid us rent have moved to the cities, and grand es-tates such as Kidwellah have suffered greatly for it. I would do anything to save my family's castle, and I am not above turning Kidwellah into a tourist trap in order to keep it from being gobbled up by the tax man and ultimately sold off piece by piece."

"So sorry," I said. "I hadn't considered that. Still, ma'am, if you'll pardon my intrusion into your personal affairs, people are dying at Kidwellah Castle. It's a very dangerous place. Just in the last few days two men and one woman have been mur—"

"And their killer has been caught!" the dowager in-terrupted, and it was clear I'd finally struck a chord.

"I don't mean to argue with you," I replied very gently. "But I have my doubts about the man they've arrested."

"Inspector Lumley told me he feels quite confident he's arrested the right person," she countered. "He also believes this male model is responsible for the other two deaths in recent days. A most unsettling thing to have hosted that murderer at Kidwellah, but how was I to know he had such nefarious intentions?"

"Even if Franco did murder those people, ma'am, I still feel the moat is exceptionally dangerous, and per-haps you might consider draining it?" I asked.

"Drain the moat?" she repeated, as if she couldn't be-lieve I'd suggested it. "What is a grand castle like Kidwellah without its moat?! Just another castle in the countryside, I say. No, no, no, Miss Holliday. I will never rob my castle of its most appealing aspect."

"Forgive me, ma'am," Heath said, "but I very nearly drowned in that appealing aspect two days ago."

The dowager looked at him in surprise. "You were the young man that fell into the water?"

"I didn't exactly fall, ma'am. I was pulled in by the Grim Widow."

Lady Hathaway put a hand to her mouth. "Where were you when this happened?" she asked.

"We were in a little tunnel leading from the main courtyard to the other side of the moat," Heath told her.

"Who the devil let you in there?" she demanded. "That area is restricted. Absolutely no one outside of castle staff is allowed in there."

I gulped, afraid we were about to get Mr. Crunn in trouble. "We found it ourselves, ma'am, when we heard that the police had discovered Merrick Brown's body."

"The door was unlocked?" she pressed.

Heath and I exchanged an uncomfortable look. Either way we sliced it, we were about to rat out Crunn. "It was locked, but then I tried the handle a second time and it gave way. I believe the Widow unlocked it, as ghosts are known for tricks like that," I said.

Lady Hathaway narrowed her eyes at me, and I thought she could sniff out the lie, but she didn't press the point and shifted her gaze to Heath. "Well, you were in a restricted area, Mr. Whitefeather. The castle is perfectly safe if you keep to those areas designated for guests. I should think you would be mindful of that the next time you two attempt to access locked doors."

Heath nudged me with his knee. It was clear that the countess was in a state of total denial about the dangers lurking in her family's estate, and convincing her to shut the doors of the castle, or even to drain the moat, was out of the question.

Somewhere in the background the dowager's phone rang and after a moment her butler appeared and said, "Ma'am, the telephone is for you."

Heath and I stood up, knowing that was our cue to leave. "Thank you so much for your time," I said, feeling no real appreciation whatsoever. Still, I managed to tamp down my anger and frustration with our host and move with Heath to the door.

"Do let me know when your little show will be airing!" the dowager called after us. "I should hope it brings a good crowd of eager ghost-hunting tourists to Kidwell-ah's doors!"

I felt my stomach muscles clench and I had to clamp my jaws together to bite back the remark threatening to bubble up and insult the Countess Lady Hathaway. I desperately wanted to tell her off, but Heath's gentle hand on my arm kept me on course, and we made our way quickly out of the cottage.

After we'd gotten to the road, Heath wrapped his arm around my shoulder and pulled me into his side for a hug. "I know you're mad...."

"That woman is so...so...stupid!" I snapped. "And all for the sake of the almighty pound note! Keeping the doors of Kidwellah open so that even *more* people can drown in her moat? *Who* does that?"

"You know what this means, don't you?"

I looked up at him, my rant temporarily sidetracked. "Means? No. What does it mean?"

"It means that we have no choice, Em. We've got to find a way to shut down the Widow."

That sobered me, and all the anger I'd felt only a moment earlier evaporated at the prospect of directly taking on a spook as powerful and deadly as the Widow. "Do you have any ideas?" I asked him.

Heath scratched at the scruff on his chin. I noticed he hadn't had a chance to shave that morning. "Well, we'll have to find her portal, free the prisoners, pack the opening with magnets, and avoid getting killed in the process."

I sighed. I knew he was just trying to lighten the mood with a little mocking humor. "So you have no ideas—is that what you're saying?"

"Not a one," he admitted.

I sighed a second time. "I need to talk to your grand-father."

Heath grinned. "He hasn't been around much on this bust, has he?"

"Actually, he has. He helped me out the other night when I went looking for Gopher, Meg, and Kim in the south wing. He kept me safe from the Widow for as long as he could, in fact. I think he expended a ton of energy and he's been recharging since then, but I've really been feeling his absence. Maybe before I catch a few z's to-night I'll call out to him and ask him to visit me in my dreams."

"Man, I hope he can help us with some ideas about how to tackle this bust. What's your game plan for to-night's hunt, by the way?"

"Well, assuming the girls manage to make us all vests, I thought we could set out for the moors and possibly get some footage of the duke...." My voice trailed off as I realized something.

"What?" Heath asked.

"You know what's funny? We've heard that the Widow drove her husband mad, then he wandered off and likely drowned, but he's the only one of her victims we've encountered so far that's not chained to her. I wonder why that is."

"Because he died before her," Heath said simply. "If the duke became a ghost before the Widow, he would have had time to adjust to his new state of existence, and would have not been influenced by her ghost after she died."

"Of course," I said. "That's why he was able to stare her down when he stood next to me on that little strip outside the south wing. He's got her number, which is why I really want to find him and talk to him. He might be able to help us."

The castle came into view just then and we both

paused along the road to stare at it. "Run all that by Gramps, though," Heath cautioned after a moment of silence. "Also, tell him thanks for the other day. Now that I'm back hanging out with you, I remember why I like this plane so much."

I took up his hand and said, "Count on it, sweetie, and, from my heart, thanks for coming back to me."

Chapter 11

Heath and I scouted the moors for an hour, trying to map out where we wanted to shoot and what physical objects to watch out for in the dark. Once we'd settled on a section of the moors close to the south end of the castle, we headed back to the bus stop, caught a ride into town, ate a quick lunch, then got back to check in with Gopher and the rest of the crew.

Our illustrious producer started yelling the moment he heard where we'd been earlier that morning. *"What do you mean, you sat down with the dowager of Penbigh and didn't get it on film?! How could you let an opportunity like that go by without even thinking about capturing it?!"*

I stared at him through half-lowered lids. "It's not like we carry a camera with us everywhere we go, Gopher."

Gopher reached out and grabbed my wrist. As he lifted it up dramatically, I realized I was holding my iPhone . . . the one with the built-in video recorder. I yanked my wrist out of his grasp. "I didn't think about documenting it," I admitted.

"The dowager probably wasn't gonna let us record her comments anyway, Gopher," Heath said.

"You could've at least asked," he growled. Then he motioned for us to follow him and we did, walking the now familiar path into the dining hall. Immediately I realized that most of the section in the back had been converted to Gopher's new command post. On the large round table he'd piled up all our ghost-hunting equipment—save for Gilley's monitoring computer and additional view screen—and on the wall he'd posted a whole series of notes that listed things we had, things we needed, shots to consider, and a rough outline of the storyboard for the movie.

As we walked to the table, I noticed the stiff set to Gopher's shoulders. It'd been a long time since he'd done a movie, I knew, and maybe all this pressure from Chris at the network was starting to weigh heavily on him.

"Here," he said when we reached the table. I took what he'd picked up and was now handing to me. It was a small digital camera—brand-new, I noticed, a rarity on our shoots.

"Thanks," I said, eyeing the object moodily. "But why don't I just use my iPhone?"

Gopher answered me while fiddling with several other gadgets. "Because the quality on the one I just gave you is much better and it's equipped with night vision."

"Really?" Heath said, taking one for himself. "But it's so little."

"It's cutting-edge," Gopher explained. "We've got the budget for it now, so I figured it was okay to splurge a little."

"How'd you get it here so fast?"

"The manufacturer is in Britain. I ordered these late yesterday express delivery. They came in about an hour ago. The whole crew should have one, and from here on out I want *everything* on film." I couldn't ignore the stink-eye accompanying that last remark.

"Noted," I said drily. I had no intention of walking around stupidly with my camera on, but when Gopher was in one of his moods, I'd learned it was best not to argue.

Next, Gopher handed me a small object that looked very much like a Nano iPod. "That's your new electro-static meter," he said before picking up a third object, which looked a bit clunky. "That's a full-spectrum HD video recorder. It's got an infrared sensor on both sides of it, which should allow you to see any spook even if they aren't in full form."

Heath reached out and took the camera from Go-pher. "No way," he said with obvious admiration. "I read about these. The theory goes that spooks kick out a lot of infrared light even when they're powered down."

"That'll be good out on the moors," I said, thinking the duke wasn't likely to be as powerful as the Widow, and therefore less likely to hold a full form as he wandered the moors. Maybe we could find him more readily by using this newest gizmo. "And speaking of gadgets, has anyone seen Gil?"

"He and Michel went into town a while ago," Gopher told me.

I remembered that I'd asked Gil to get Heath a new cell phone, but I didn't think it would take this long. I glanced at my watch and asked, "How long ago, Go-pher? Do you remember?"

He shrugged. "Right after the meeting, I think."

I felt my jaw clench. That was several hours before. "He should've been back by now. I assigned him a ton of research I need by tonight."

Gopher looked at me critically. "And you thought he'd listen?"

I growled low in my throat and marched away from the table, intent on finding Gilley and knocking some sense into him. Preferably with a large heavy object.

Heath came to my side, still carrying the full-spectrum camera. "This thing is too cool."

"You'll keep saying that until the Widow fills the screen."

"Good point," he said. "You heading out to have a talk with our little buddy?"

"No."

"No?"

"I'm going to kill Gil."

Heath chuckled. "Well, Uma, it's a good thing I'm coming along, then."

We spent the next two hours looking for Gilley and Michel. Heath and I rode the bus back into town, and searched all the cellular stores (okay, so there were only two, but they were at opposite ends of town). We checked the restaurants, library, park. No sign of them. All the while I repeatedly texted and called Gilley, with no reply, and as the time went by without a hint of either of them, I could feel a tightening in my chest and my worst fears about Gilley's well-being began filling my mind. At last, Heath and I went back to the castle, and as we got off the bus, I saw a taxi pull up, and Gil and Michel got out, giggling and nudging each other playfully.

After closing the car door, Gilley tapped at his phone dramatically, placed it to his ear, and waved at Michel, when the shiny new phone he was carrying began to ring.

I balled my hands into fists as I began to make my way to the pair. Meanwhile Michel put the phone to his ear and said, "Hello?"

In an awful upper-crust English accent, Gil said, "Collect call from London, Michel. Will you accept the charges?"

Michel laughed and said, "No!"

To which Gilley replied, "Very well! The queen will call back!"

Both of them dissolved into a fit of giggles and were I not so furious, I might have found them funny too.

"Gilley!" I yelled, and both he and Michel jumped, their giggling coming to an abrupt end.

"Uh-oh," Gil muttered as he spun around to see me. "Hey, M. J.! I got Heath his cell phone." He dug into his pocket and pulled out another phone, which he meekly offered up to me.

By now I was so mad I couldn't even form a sentence. "You . . . I . . . told . . . *research*!"

Gilley sighed. Knowing he was in trouble, he adopted a completely different attitude. Disdain. "Shrieking like that isn't a good look for you, honey."

For a second I saw red and I flew at Gilley, ready to thump him but good. Heath caught me around the waist and turned with me in a half circle until I stopped clawing the air and threatening to cause Gil great bodily harm.

When I'd regained my composure (translation: when I'd stopped frothing at the mouth), Heath turned me back to face the two truants and this time I noticed that Gil appeared a little less confident about being in my presence.

"It took forever to get the phones," he said lamely.

I didn't even bother to answer. I just glared at him. For all I was worth.

"Okay, okay!" Gil finally said. "I'll head in and get you your precious research!"

"I want it by tonight!" I yelled as he and Michel hurried to get away from me.

After they'd gone on ahead, Heath's soft laughter filled my ears. Finally feeling the relief of discovering that Gilley was okay and letting go of some of my anger, I couldn't help but smile too. "Not too loud or you'll encourage him," I said to Heath.

"Oh, I think he's way past needing encouragement, Em."

"The little bugger," I grumbled. "He has some nerve giving me that attitude. Not a good look for me . . . can you believe he said that?"

"Well, you did kind of embarrass him in front of Michel," Heath said gently. "And Gilley definitely has a thing for the photographer."

"Damn," I said.

"What?"

"You're making me feel bad about yelling at him."

"Oh, you had every right to yell, babe. I mean—he had it coming."

"Yeah," I said, feeling considerably less guilty now that Heath reminded me of that.

Just then we saw Michel spin around and hurry back up the path to us. "I almost forgot to ask. Did you want me to e-mail you the photos I took? Or should I just send them to Gopher?"

That came as a surprise. "You already took the photos of the castle?"

Michel nodded. "Before we went into town. It didn't take long."

"Did you wear a vest?" I asked, seeing that he had nothing more protective on than a light coat.

"Gilley wore his sweatshirt and stuck close to me. We never came into danger."

"Ah . . . ," I said, at a loss for words. "I guess you can e-mail the photos to both me and Gopher. Gilley's got the addresses."

Michel nodded and was off again to Gilley's side. As I stared at them and the way they so easily fell into step together, I wondered if Gil had at last met someone special. I hoped so. He'd been having a hell of a dry spell for nearly a year and a half now. And as long as I'd known him, Gil had never before had a dry spell longer than a month or two.

"They make a good pair," Heath said.

I bumped him playfully with my shoulder. "You softy."

He looped his arm around me. "It'd be nice to see Gil have someone special in his life. I think it's been hard on him being our third wheel all this time."

"Yeah. You're right. It would be good for Gil. Just as long as he doesn't get too distracted from his job."

Heath chuckled. "You say that like you actually believe he won't."

I grinned. "Wishful thinking. Come on, let's check in with the girls and see how the vests are coming along."

Once we were back at the castle, I went up to Meg and Kim's room to check on their progress, while Heath went in search of Gilley to retrieve the cell phone we'd both forgotten to take from him. To my surprise and relief Meg and Kim had completed five of the eight vests we'd need. "That one's yours," Kim said. "But there's a problem."

"What's that?" I asked, picking up the heavy garment and trying it on. Once I had it zipped, it really wasn't uncomfortable or overly heavy.

"We're running out of magnets. I figure we'll only have enough for six vests."

"Gil's got some reserves," I suggested, remembering the packs of magnets he'd stuffed his pockets with on the night he'd given me his sweatshirt. I knew he'd added many of those to the sweatshirt once he'd gotten it back, but still, he had to have a lot left over.

"He already gave us all his extras," Kim said.

My brow furrowed. "When?" I knew Kim and Meg had left the meeting early, and Gopher had said that Gil and Michel had gone into town right after the meeting.

"We bumped into him when he and Michel were coming in from taking some photos of the castle. He told us he had a few packets we could use upstairs, which was good, because we really underestimated the number of magnets we'd need per vest. We've already used all of Gilley's extra packs up, and the ones we bought this morning."

I looked at my watch. It was already quarter to five and we'd never have time to make a third trip to town and try to hunt for more magnets before the night's shoot. "Crap. Okay, so Gil can just wear his sweatshirt until we get more magnets tomorrow."

"But that still leaves one person without protection."

"I know," I said, trying to think through the issue. The problem was that anyone out in the field tonight would absolutely need a vest.

"We could undo some of the ones we've finished and take out a few magnets here and there," Kim suggested.

"How many magnets have you put in each vest?" I asked. My own vest felt packed with a small stack of magnets in each quilt.

"Fifty. We doubled up in a few places because we wanted to make sure we're all protected."

I tapped my lip, still calculating in my head. "Gilley's sweatshirt had at least that many and the Widow still hit me pretty hard when I encountered her. No . . . don't take out any from the ones that are done. Someone's going to have to stay behind tonight."

"Who?" they asked in unison.

"Someone who's not going to like it," I muttered. I didn't want to tell them before I'd had a chance to talk with my chosen person. "Listen, you two keep up the great work. We're all heading to dinner in about an hour. Do you think you can finish the last vest before then?"

Kim held up the garment she was working on. "It's almost there, M. J."

"Awesome. You guys rock. I'll send John up to help you carry these down and we'll hand them out at dinner, but I'll take mine and Heath's for now." With that, I bid them adieu and headed back downstairs to the dining hall.

I found Gopher on the phone, pacing back and forth. He wasn't talking much, but he was absently nodding his head. I had a feeling Chris was on the other end of the line. "Yeah, buddy, I know," Gopher said while I waited patiently for him to end the call. "We'll work on getting more of her on film. I think we're going back into that wing tonight or tomorrow." There was a pause, then, "Okay, you got it. We'll definitely go there tonight."

My left eyebrow arched. There was *no way* we were going back into the Widow's wing tonight. I didn't feel prepared and I knew the crew would be on edge until we'd at least done some preliminary shooting as a group.

Once Gopher hung up, I first confronted him about what he'd just agreed to. "We're not going hunting for the Widow tonight, Gopher."

My producer set his phone down and pinched the bridge of his nose. "M. J., please . . . not now. I've got a killer headache."

I stood there silently for a beat. I didn't want to let the subject drop, because he'd interpret that as backing down.

Gopher let go of the bridge of his nose and sighed. "What?"

I held up Heath's vest. "We're about out of magnets."

"So?"

"So, we're one vest shy of making our quota for the group."

"Can't someone just carry some spikes?"

"No. We'll need the spikes in case we encounter the Widow or her black phantom."

Gopher's brow rose with interest. "What black phantom?"

At first I was frustrated with his question, because I was fairly certain we'd talked about it in his presence, but Gopher's listening skills weren't great, and with the added stress he was under lately, I had to concede he wasn't exactly taking a lot in. So I patiently explained that when John and I had been trapped in the south wing, a black phantomlike creature had chased us down the hall. "Was this thing human?" Gopher asked. "I mean, not human, but the ghost of a human?"

"Definitely not," I said. "It moved more like a panther, but I doubt it ever walked this plane alive. I think it's a demon from the lower realms, and I think that it's made a deal with the Widow—swapping her the access of her portal for some of its power."

"Do you think you can get it on film?"

I laughed but not with mirth. "Dude, if you get close enough to this thing to get it on film, you probably won't survive the encounter."

Gopher frowned like he didn't believe me. "Okay, so back to this vest thing, what do we do?"

"Someone's got to stay behind with Gilley while the rest of us go out on the hunt."

"Well, it can't be you or Heath. We need both of you guys in the field."

"True."

"And it can't be John—he's our sound tech and if we don't catch anything on film, we might still get something on his microphone. And Michel should definitely go on the hunt. I had a chance to look at his photos—the guy is really good with a handheld."

"Also true."

"What about Meg or Kim?"

"They've already made the two smallest vests. The one missing the magnets would be a size large."

Gopher blinked at me and then it registered. "You did that on purpose."

"I had nothing to do with the order the girls made the vests in, buddy. It just happened that the last vest they were going to work on was a size large, and since you, John, and Heath all share that size, one of you has to stay behind."

"But I *can't* stay behind, M. J.!"

"Why not?"

"Because I'm your *director*, or have you already taken over this whole operation?"

I bit back the retort on the tip of my tongue, and instead I laid the size-large vest on the table in front of Gopher. "You want the vest? It's yours. But you'll have to decide between Heath and John, which one of them stays behind. Oh, and if you choose Heath, I won't be going on the hunt, and if you choose John, you're going to have to hold the microphone, and we all know you've got a bad shoulder."

"Dammit!" Gopher swore. "What am I supposed to do while you guys are out on the hunt?"

"We'll all be connected by the headphones; there's no reason you can't watch the footage in real time from Gilley's monitors and call the shots from here. In fact, I think doing it that way should make you happy."

Gopher glared at me. "How could I possibly be happy?"

"It's warm and dry in here, and the forecast calls for rain tonight. You'll be downright cozy with access to food and drink all night long. And with the live stream you won't miss a minute of the hunt."

I could see Gopher's mental wheels turning while he considered that, and at last he let go of his moody glare. Handing me the vest, he said, "Fine. I'll stay here. But tomorrow, there had better be a vest for me to wear."

I saluted him smartly and headed off in search of Heath.

We all met for dinner at six o'clock. Mary served us a lovely meal of lamb stew with fresh biscuits and plenty of hot tea to wash it down with. I ate heartily and felt like I was relaxing for the first time in days. "So you'll be ghost hunting tonight, then?" she asked.

I nodded. "Yes, ma'am. We'll be heading out just after one a.m."

Mary shivered. "Lady Mortimer's ghost is a frightful thing, she is. I don't envy you."

"Have you ever seen her?" Heath asked.

"Aye. Only once, and it was enough to scare me socks off. It's a terrible thing, working here and fearing that she'll break out of her end of the castle or grab one of us from the drawbridge and pull us under."

I noticed that her complexion had paled a bit since she'd brought up the topic of the Grim Widow. "If she frightens you so much, why work here?" I asked her.

A blush replaced the paleness of Mary's cheeks. "Oh, I couldn't leave Arthur to face her alone," she said. "Me brother's not quite so fearful of her as I am." I thought Mr. Crunn was plenty frightened of the Widow, but I didn't say that to Mary. "He says as long as we stick to our end of the castle and the middle of the drawbridge, there's nothing to fret about." She then topped all our cups off with more tea and coffee before hurrying away to fetch our desserts.

I looked around the table and saw the trepidation in the eyes of my crew—especially John. Which reminded me about the assignment I'd given him. "Did you have a chance to talk to Crunn and draw us a map of the castle?"

John nodded and reached under his seat for his backpack. Pulling out his iPad, he tapped at it for a minute before handing it over to me.

"Wow," I said, gazing at the screen. "I'm impressed. This is really good."

John's blueprint had the whole castle neatly mapped out for both the first and second stories, and it even included the secret passageway we'd stumbled upon. I focused on that detail and asked, "Does this lead anywhere?"

John got up and came around to look over my shoulder. "Arthur didn't know," he said. "I put that in because we found it, but Crunn said he had no idea there was a secret passage there."

I compared John's first-story drawing with his second-story blueprint. I remembered the spiral stairs when the trapdoor had opened, and how he'd nearly fallen down them. I shuddered a bit at the memory of trying to pull him out of there and get away from the Widow and whatever that black demon thing had been. But I felt I was remembering only things that were superficial. There had been more to that moment that I felt I needed to recall. I closed my eyes and thought back. John had fallen into the opening and onto the first few steps of the staircase, I had looked at him sprawled out on the stone steps, it'd been cold . . . *really* cold, and there had been a sound that had come up from the depths below. A chorus of wails, but there had been something more. What was it?

"Em?" I heard Heath say, jolting me out of the memory. My eyes snapped open and I found him looking at me with concern.

"Water," I said. Heath moved his water glass over to me. "No," I said with a shake of my head. "I heard water."

"You heard water?" John asked over my right shoulder.

I turned in my chair to look at him. "You might have heard it too. When you fell through the passageway and onto the steps, do you remember what you heard?"

He frowned. "It was pretty dark, M. J."

I shook my head. "Not what you saw, buddy, what you *heard*."

His frown deepened and I happened to catch the rise of goose bumps along his arms. "I don't know. I heard moaning, and . . ."

"And what?" I pressed.

"Like . . . the sound of waves. It was pretty damp and smelly in there too."

I sat back in my chair and turned my eyes to Heath. "I think I know where the Widow's portal is and how she gets out of the south wing."

Heath tipped the iPad toward him to look at the blueprint and I tapped at the secret passageway. "I think that's how she gets into the moat."

Heath's lips compressed. "Her portal can't be the

whole stairwell, Em. It'd have to be someplace along the wall."

"I know."

Heath and I were both silent for a minute while we considered how impossible it was going to be to make it to the stairwell again and find the Widow's portal while holding off both her and that big-ass demon long enough to drive a few magnetic stakes into solid stone. Oh, yeah, *and* free the Widow's prisoners to boot.

"There's no way you'll be able to get to it," Gilley said, leaning way over in his seat to look at the iPad. "If her portal's in that passageway, you'll never live long enough to make it there and shut it down."

"Thanks for the vote of confidence," I told him.

He made a face and went back to his dinner.

"Maybe Gramps will have an idea," Heath said, squeezing my hand under the table.

I nodded, but I wasn't feeling so confident now that I thought I knew where the Widow was hiding her portal. I knew it also had to be the place she was hiding her prisoners. It made sense as the only places we'd seen the souls that she'd captured had been around the moat. She could've dragged them out of the stairwell, through the water, then put them on or near the drawbridge just to taunt us.

The thought of those prisoners made me remember that I needed their names handy to call out to them when the moment of truth arrived. Turning back to Gil, I asked, "How's that research coming?"

Gil bent low and picked up his own iPad. I waited while he powered it up and scrolled through his notes. "I only had two hours to do the research," he said, "and already I can tell you there's not much online. I'll have to go to the library tomorrow and leaf through the newspapers and public records."

"Did you find out anything useful?" I pressed.

"Not so much useful as weirdly coincidental," he replied.

"How do you mean?"

"I was able to find a few articles on some of the more recent victims, and I now know why Lumley thinks they were the work of a serial killer."

I leaned in closer to Gil. "I'm listening."

"The six cases of documented drownings at Kidwellah since nineteen eighty-five were all white males and all but one were between the ages of forty and sixty-seven wealthy, married, and visiting here on holiday with their wives."

"None of the victims were women?" I asked.

"Nope."

"But you said all but one—what was the one?"

"Lumley's brother, Oliver Lumley," Gil explained. "He was only thirty-two and unmarried at the time of his death, and he wasn't so much here on holiday as he was investigating the suspiciousness of the deaths."

I nodded. I knew that, but something else struck me as odd about Gil's description of the men. "What about kids?" I asked. "Did any of the victims have children?"

"Four of the five married men had kids, ranging in age from six to forty, but I think you hit on the other really odd coincidence—none of the kiddos were here at the time of their father's deaths."

"That is weird," I said. "It's as if the killer was just waiting for a specific type of man to show up. Married, with no children on vacation with him."

"Lefebvre and his wife had a daughter," Gil said, glancing at Michel, who was listening in.

He nodded. "Zeta. She's a model in Paris. Hates both her parents. I've photographed her on a number of occasions, and she's not exactly the most congenial personality."

But I wasn't concerned with Zeta; I was concerned about the fact that I'd doubted the theory of a serial killer since Lumley had first proposed it, but now I was faced with a number of victims who seemed to fit a very specific type of profile—save Merrick Brown, Oliver Lumley, and Fiona Hollingsworth. How did they fit into this crazy puzzle?

"Thanks for looking into it," I told Gil. "Anything more you can get for us tomorrow would be great. Oh, and I'll need a list of the names of the victims."

Gil reached again into his backpack and retrieved a pad of paper. Tearing off the top page, he slid it to me. "That's who I have so far. I'll get the full list tomorrow."

I tucked the list away and asked, "Did you get me anything on the duke?"

Gil nodded and tapped at his iPad. "That's an interesting character, M. J. But let me just say this, I really want you to rethink going out on the moors tonight to look for him."

"He can't be as dangerous as the Widow," I countered.

"He may be worse," Gil told me. "The duke has a reputation for marking people for death. Everyone he's supposedly appeared to has died. If you find him, you're a goner."

"Like I said, I'm already in trouble, then."

Gil shook his head. "Yeah, but you didn't have the crew with you. If you expose them, then they're all marked for death too."

I laughed but looking around the table, I could see Gilley had struck a nerve. Kim, Meg, and even John had gone pale. "You'll be fine," I told them, but they hardly looked reassured. Turning back to Gilley, I said, "Tell me about the duke so I have some background to work with."

Gil eyed me doubtfully, but he did consult his notes once more. "It's pretty much the way you've already heard from Crunn. The duke was married to and supposedly murdered the Grim Widow's sister, Catherine. Then he married Lady Jane, she goes nuts, and he locks her up in the south wing. She then figures out how to get out of that section, probably through the secret passage John found, and just for kicks, she kills off a few of his friends. He beats her, puts her back in the south wing, cutting her off from all human contact, and somehow she's able to still get out and continue to kill even more people. Finally, when his illegitimate son from another woman comes to stay at the castle, Lady Mortimer drowns him too, which sends the duke into a deep depression and he heads off onto the moors one night never to be seen again."

"She killed his son?" I gasped. God, this woman was nasty!

"Yep. It's never been proven, of course, but the story goes that one night after the young man got a little rough with one of the lady servants who'd been nice to Lady Mortimer, he was found facedown in the moat the next morning."

"Got a little rough with the servant? How old was this kid?" Heath asked.

"Nineteen. He was born in between the time the duke was married to the sisters, and I think I read that the duke really wanted to marry the woman he had the kid with, but Lady Mortimer's father insisted that the duke marry Jane."

My mind was skipping over certain details of Gil's research and focusing on other clues too consistent to be mere coincidence. A theory began to form in my mind. It was sketchy at best, but I wondered . . .

"What?" Gil asked, and I realized he'd stopped talking and was waiting for me to say something.

"Nothing," I said. I didn't want to share my theory yet. I wanted to think on it and maybe find something else to help connect the dots, but what I was thinking wasn't good, because it meant we'd all been looking in the wrong direction.

Shortly after dinner, Heath and I went up to bed. I was dopey eyed by the time my head hit the pillow, and just before giving in to sleep, I remembered to call out to

Sam Whitefeather, asking him to come visit me in my dreams.

"Hello, M. J.," I heard from somewhere close.

I opened my eyes. "Sam?" I was standing on a dock at the edge of a beautiful moonlit lake and there was someone just to my side. Turning, I saw him — my spirit guide and Heath's grandfather — looking effervescent in a white cotton shirt and linen pants, and with a beautiful glow about him.

"You rang?" he said, bending over to pull at something behind us. I noticed it was a stool, and he placed it just behind me. I sat down and he snapped his fingers and another stool appeared. He took his seat by my side, crossing his legs leisurely.

"Thanks for coming," I said.

He winked at me. "Least I could do. You had some questions for me?"

"Almost too many to count, my friend. But let me first ask you what you might know about the Grim Widow."

Sam shook his head distastefully. "She's an evil, evil spirit, M. J. One of the worst you've ever taken on, I'm afraid. She's completely given herself over to forces of evil and she's hungry to add more victims to her collection."

"She's added at least one more since the other day, Sam," I said. "André Lefebvre. I saw him chained to her, just like Merrick. The one small bit of grace we've had lately is that it doesn't look like Fiona Hollingsworth was killed by the Widow, and she managed to get across to your side without trouble."

Sam nodded. "Yes, Fiona is here, but she's not in very good shape. She's having trouble with the adjustment and several angels are working with her as we speak."

I cocked my head. "Angels? As in pretty people with white wings?"

Sam laughed. "Not exactly. Although I've never seen

an ugly angel, most take on a human-looking form minus the wings."

"How can you tell them apart from regular people?"

Sam grinned. "Trust me, the minute you see one, you know."

"Huh," I said, then got back to the point of the conversation. "I'm glad Fiona's all right, but I'm still concerned over Merrick and André."

"For good reason," Sam said in agreement. "I've managed to connect with Merrick's grandmother. She's beside herself because she can't locate him anywhere in the ether. And André's father is also quite upset that his son may be lost to him forever."

"See, now, that's what I really don't understand, Sam. How is it possible for one spirit to keep another spirit prisoner? If Merrick knows he's dead, why can't he just cross?"

Sam sighed heavily. "You, more than most, should know the answer to that, M. J. Merrick can't cross because he *believes* he's a prisoner of the Widow. He's blind to the possibility that he can escape from her clutches by merely believing that he can. For him, the prison is real, and while it remains so in his mind, he won't be able to cross. His mother can't reach out to him because he spends most of his time stuck behind the barrier of the Widow's portal. No spirit from the higher realms can cross into the lower, but we can sometimes meet in the middle in your realm."

"It's still hard for me to believe one soul could have that effect on another," I said. "I mean, he's bound by a *chain*, Sam. And I know the chain isn't real—it's a manifestation of the Widow's thoughts, so how come Merrick can't figure this out?"

My spirit guide smiled wisely before pointing to my hands. The moment I looked down I felt a cold heavy weight on both my wrists. I gasped as I held them up—they were bound by shackles. I tugged on them and the shackles tightened. They were very, very real. "Whoa," I said. "How the heck did you do that?"

Sam tapped his temple. "I have control here," he explained. "The stool you're sitting on, this dock, and that lake were all created by me. You see it, feel it, *experience* it, because you've allowed me to have control of the world you currently find yourself in. When Merrick and the other victims enter into their grounded state, they're very confused. If the Widow gets to them before they can cross over, she sets the structure of what they see and experience. The chains that bind them are very real to them."

I eyed the shackles again. I felt there was a lesson Sam was trying to teach me more than what he'd just shown me, so I closed my eyes and focused. Feeling a little dizzy, I concentrated on the shackles around my wrists, making myself believe that I had control over them and my surroundings, and that I could make them disappear simply by willing them gone. In an instant I felt them disappear. I then fell right on my ass. "Ow!" I said, rubbing my bum and looking up at Sam, who was laughing heartily. I realized belatedly that the stool I'd been sitting on had also disappeared.

"You focused a little too hard there, M. J.," he said, snapping his fingers again so that another stool appeared.

I got up and sat down again, grinning myself. "Thanks for the lesson," I said to him. "So really, what we have to do is convince the Widow's ghosts that the chains binding them to her aren't real, right?"

"That would be ideal, but I'm not sure she'll allow you the opportunity, M. J.," Sam said, losing all traces of his former humor.

"Do you have any other ideas for freeing the Widow's victims?"

Sam turned to look out at the lake for a while, and I could see his easy countenance become troubled. "I do have one," Sam confessed. "But it's complicated."

"Complicated? In what way?"

Sam turned back to me. "You're my spirit daughter, M. J. I promised your mother that I'd look after you, and I know she'd want me to talk you out of even the thought of something so dangerous as freeing the Widow's victims. Heck, she'd want me to tell you to pack your bags and hightail it right out of Wales, but I don't know that I can do that. I took on the role of your spirit guide to be just that. To guide you, not to tell you what to do. Also, I know that if I tried to tell you what to do, you'd ignore me and do what you wanted anyway."

I felt a small smile tug at the corners of my mouth. Sam was the best in so many ways, but mostly in the way he really understood me. "What's the idea, Sam?"

"I'm thinking of a prison break," he said. "Obviously the Widow is keeping these souls locked up in her portal, but if you can somehow damage the portal to the point where it weakens, then you might be able to have them all break out at once. The tricky part is getting around the Widow and that demon she's attached to."

"Yeah," I said with a chuckle, "*that's* the tricky part."

"You'll need to find a way to weaken the demon," Sam continued, as if I hadn't just made fun of him. "The best way to do that is to engage the Widow. She's drawing all her energy from the demon, so if you can suck her dry by having her try to go after you, you'll effectively rob it of its energy too."

"Is that why it didn't show up when she and I were going at it in the south wing the other night?"

Sam nodded. "I think it is."

My mind was once again awhirl with thoughts. Heath had suggested almost the exact same idea, and I really thought the two men might be onto something. "Thanks, Sam. I'll talk to Heath and the others and see if we can't come up with a plan. The other hard part is finding her portal. My theory is that she's hiding it in a secret passage on the second floor of the south wing."

Sam eyed me quizzically for a moment before leaning out to wave his hand over the water. Its black calm surface swirled a bit before becoming a little smoky; then as if by magic an overview of the castle appeared—as if we were looking straight through the roof into the second story. I could see details like the burgundy carpet, the peeling paint, a lopsided portrait, and then, when Sam pointed, I could see a dark swirling blob of energy obscuring the secret passageway and the stairwell within it.

"You're correct," Sam said. "Somewhere in there is her portal."

"It's getting to it without getting killed that'll be the tricky part," I muttered.

"Isn't it always?" Sam said with a nudge to my arm. "I'll help you in any way I can," he vowed. "The vests were a good idea."

"Wasn't mine, but I'll pass along your compliments to the help." And then I focused back on my other questions for Sam. "We're also going to try and find the duke on our ghost hunt tonight. I know I saw him after I jumped out the door of the south wing, but I may have also gotten a glimpse of him out on the moors too, and I can feel it in my gut that I need to find and engage him, but the local folklore suggests that those who encounter the Desperate Duke are marked for death. Should we be worried about that?"

Sam laid a gentle hand on my arm. "I think you should be worried about everything, M. J. But maybe not that in particular. Ghosts who appear to those who die soon after get a bum rap. The ghosts don't bring on death; they're there to warn that particular soul to be careful, do something other than what they were planning to do, like evacuate in the face of a hurricane instead of riding it out. They act as a warning, not as a curse. I also don't think you should go against your gut. Your own spirit is attempting to lead you in the right direction, and that's something you should never ignore."

"Yeah, that was my feeling too, Sam. Thanks for the affirmation."

"Anything else?" he asked me.

I was grateful for all the advice that Sam had given me, but one of the things that still troubled me greatly was this demon the Widow was involved with. I didn't really know what it was or what it could do, and that was something to be worried about. "Do you have any suggestions for how to fight the Widow and her pet demon if we happen to encounter both of them at once?"

Sam actually shuddered. I'd never seen a spirit do that before. "My advice to you is this: If you see both of them coming for you at the same time, run like hell, M. J. Run like hell."

Chapter 12

The alarm went off at twelve thirty a.m., but I'd been up for at least half an hour, considering all that Sam had told me. Next to me Heath stirred and slapped his arm across the nightstand to shut off the alarm . . . which was on my side. I quickly silenced it and propped my head up on one elbow to look at the hot guy in bed next to me. "Hey, there," I said.

Heath opened one lid. "I know that tone."

"What tone?"

"That's your how-you-doin'? tone."

"Well," I said, "how you doin', baby?"

Heath chuckled. "You realize this is gonna make us late."

I leaned over to wrap my arms around him. "So we'll be late."

Thirty minutes later as Heath and I shuffled quickly down the staircase, I could hear Gilley saying, "They're probably bonking. Those two can't keep their hands off each other. You should have seen them in Santa Fe."

This of course was an exaggeration ... well, at least for the first part of our trip to New Mexico. Still, Gil shouldn't have been wagging his tongue about my personal business, so when we reached the group and everyone looked up at us, I made sure to give him the old death-ray stare.

"You look freshly tousled," he said to me.

Damn my nonexistent superpowers! "Shut it, Gil."

Gil turned to Michel and mouthed, "Told you so."

"Now that we're all here," Gopher said to us, "let's go over our strategy for tonight. We should have at least four hours of good film time before the spooks quiet down, and I'd like to start in the south wing—"

I'd been afraid Gopher would change his mind about letting us work our way up to that, and luckily, I had my speech already prepared. Truthfully, it had been part of my plan to take advantage of Heath and make us late. "Actually, Goph, while Heath and I were getting ready, I swear I saw the duke out on the grounds. I think we should head out there right away and get him on tape. That way we'll have some good variety to show Chris in the morning. I mean, if we can get him on film, it's bound to make our movie even more compelling."

Gopher's brow shot up. "You saw him?"

I nodded, and prayed that Gil—who always knew when I was fibbing—kept his big yap shut.

"How long ago?"

"Just a minute or two!" I said, trying to appear anxious. "Come on, Goph, we've got to get a move on if we're going to get him on film!"

All around me the crew began to hoist backpacks and equipment onto their shoulders, and Michel, John, Meg, and Kim were already following Heath (who was in on my ruse) to the door. "Yeah," Gopher said. "Okay. But let's regroup here in the main hall around three so we'll have lots of time to—"

No one waited for Gopher to finish his sentence; we all hurried out the door and left him to gab at Gilley. I almost felt bad for sticking our producer with Gil, but then, Gilley was getting on my last nerve these days, so I stopped short of actually feeling sorry for him.

As we walked, John quickened his stride to come up next to me. "What's your game plan?" he asked, making sure to put his palm over his microphone. I didn't think that Gil and Gopher were listening in yet, but I was glad that John wasn't taking any chances.

"I really do want to try and find the duke," I told him, covering my own mic too. "When I was inside the south wing, I spotted him along the far right side of the castle, near the lake."

"Okay," he said. "I'll tell the girls and we'll all keep an eye out for him."

John dropped back to whisper to Michel and the girls and Heath took his place next to me. Holding up the new expensive infrared camera, he flipped the switch to the attached lights on the top of the camera and nothing happened. "Great," I groaned. "The infrared is already broken. Didn't Gilley test all this stuff before sending us out in the field with it?"

"For your information," I heard Gilley say tersely in my ear, "I did test it. It works perfectly well. Have Heath turn on the viewfinder and look into it."

Heath did that with me watching over his shoulder, and as if by magic the world was illuminated in a purple blue haze. "Cool!" we both said.

"I read about these," Heath told me. "This has better results than the night-vision cameras, because even spooks who aren't visible on the night-vision cameras can be seen on an infrared."

Heath and I were leading the others toward the draw-bridge, and I was about to give them instructions on where to point their equipment when I heard a loud thump right underfoot that stopped me in my tracks.

Looking down, I noticed that I'd taken the very first step onto the drawbridge.

"Not this again," Heath whispered, pointing the camera down at the planks, and as he did so, he sucked in a breath. "Em! Look at this!"

I gulped and leaned over to look. Below us, seeping through the cracks in the planks I could see a purple glow. I lifted one foot and took a tentative step, and the blob moved to that exact spot, and just as I set my toe on the dock, a tremendous whump vibrated through the planks.

"No . . . freaking . . . way!" I heard Gilley whisper in my ear.

"What's happening?" Gopher asked, replacing Gil's voice with his.

"M. J.'s got a friend," Heath said quietly. I could feel the crew gather at the edge of the drawbridge, watching the screen over Heath's shoulder.

Meanwhile I held perfectly still. I didn't quite know what to do. I'd been through this before and wasn't in any hurry to repeat it.

"Why is she just standing there?" Gopher complained. "M. J., *move!*"

I looked back at the group, uncertain, and caught Michel's eye. He was filming with a night-vision camera, and he lowered it to move around the group and approach me. "We'll go across together," he said, but the moment he stepped onto the planks, two tremendous thumps echoed up from the wood. "There's a second one!" Heath whispered.

Michel had stopped dead in his tracks too, and I saw that he now looked properly frightened.

"Maybe we should all go together," John suggested. "I mean, it can't follow all of us, can it?"

Bravely he and Heath stepped out onto the planks, and each of their footfalls was followed by the same kind of pounding I'd been subjected to. "Damn," I swore, looking to the far side of the drawbridge, which felt a million miles away. "We'll need to run for it."

"I don't want to!" Kim cried.

"Me either!" said Meg.

Meg and Kim were along as backup should one of our cameras fail, and I figured that as long as the three guys and I had working cameras, then we should have plenty to spare.

"Go back inside, then, ladies. We'll take it from here," I told them while eyeing the boys meaningfully. "On three?"

They all nodded, but just then in the center of the drawbridge we heard three loud raps—as if whatever evil under the planks was daring us to go for it.

At the end of the last rap, John took off running, and his sudden bolt for the other side of the bridge got the rest of us moving.

The planks underneath were a thunderstorm of noise from our footfalls and the matching pounding from the underside. My feet and knees felt every jarring blow and my teeth seemed to be rattling in my head. The traverse was painful, and as much as I tried to pour on the speed, my body couldn't help but brace a little at each footfall, which hampered my pace.

All of us were in the same boat, because no one seemed able to keep a steady stride. Through the noise I could hear Gopher yelling something, but what he said I hadn't a clue, nor did I much care. I just wanted to get across to solid ground.

At last John reached the cobblestones, leaping onto them in a move that Baryshnikov would've envied. Heath was next, followed by me and finally Michel.

Upon reaching the safety zone, we all fell to the ground and lay there panting. I rubbed my shins and knees and cursed the thing below the bridge that had made the run so painful.

"I have no picture!" Gopher shouted. "What's happening! Gilley, make them tell me what's happening!"

"It's not like they listen to me," Gil snapped. "M. J.? Heath? Are you okay? Over."

I pulled the microphone closer to my mouth. "We're okay for the most part, buddy."

"If you're all okay, why aren't you filming?!" Gopher shouted.

I pulled the headset off my head and rolled onto my side to get to my cell phone. Lifting it out of my back pocket, I dialed Gil's number and he took the call right away. "He's driving you crazy, right?" he asked in a muffled whisper.

"You've got to do something," I told him.

"Who're you talking to?" I heard Gopher demand in the background.

"My mom," Gil said without hesitation. "Her bursitis is acting up again."

"Gil," I said softly. "Seriously. His headset needs to have a major malfunction or I'm going to kill him when I get back."

"Gilley!" Gopher demanded. "No one's responding to me!"

I looked around. The guys had all removed their headsets—John had even tossed his a few feet away.

"Leave it to me," Gil whispered. "And tell everyone to switch to channel nine."

I sat up and told the boys to switch to the new channel, and reluctantly they all donned their headsets again. At first all I heard on the new channel was static, but then Gil's voice came through loud and clear. "I don't know, Gopher," he said. "Your headset was working fine just a minute ago."

"Well, now it's full of static!" I heard Gopher shout. The pressure of pleasing Chris was really starting to take its toll on our producer. I mean, Gopher is almost always a pain in the ass, but even he's not usually this much of a tyrant.

"I can either stop the shoot and try to fix your headset or I can let them continue and relay your instructions to them. You'll still be able to hear everything they say through the feed," Gil told him. "Once I turn it on, that is."

"Don't we have any spare headphones?" Gopher asked.

"No," Gilley lied.

"God bless you, Gil," I said.

There was more grumbling in the background, and while Gilley and Gopher worked it out, I gathered the shaken remnants of my crew and motioned them well away from the drawbridge. "Is anybody hurt?" I asked first.

Michel pulled up one pant leg and I sucked in a breath when I saw his knees were both swollen and blue. "I fell," he said. "While I was down, they pounded against my knees."

My own feet were seriously sore, so I gingerly took off one boot and the accompanying sock. I flashed a light onto the sole and hissed. My entire heel and the pad of my foot were a light purple, and I knew they'd get much darker as time wore on.

The other crew members also took off their shoes, and all of us had some bruising, but mine was by far the worst.

"Those boots have no padding," Heath said.

"And it's the second time I've been through that pummeling," I reminded him. "Not to mention that ten-foot leap out of the south wing the other night."

Heath reached out and pulled me into him. "Maybe this was a bad idea."

"I'm okay, honey," I told him. And for the most part, I was. The drawbridge was bad, but going after the Widow in her part of the castle would be far, far worse. Plus, now we were on the other side of the bridge, and away from the Widow's reach. Or at least I hoped we were.

"What's it going to be like when we have to go back?" John asked, staring with dread at the drawbridge.

I shuddered. "Probably just as bad."

John only shook his head, and I was beginning to think he wished he'd voted another way when we were deciding to stay on or go home.

Once we had all put our socks and shoes back on, we set out for the hills on the far side of the castle. There were two ways to get there: take the road, which Heath and I had done earlier in the day and found it to be long and winding, or take a walking path, which appeared to be more direct. So, we chose the path and before too long we realized we should've stuck with the road. The route we were on was muddy and rough going, and there were more steep inclines than we'd anticipated.

At last we crested a particularly big hill and found ourselves exactly where I thought I'd seen the ghost wandering the moors from two nights before. Heath came to stand next to me. "Should we look around here?" he asked.

I nodded and pointed over to a flat area leading to the edge of the moat. "Can I look through your view screen at that section there?"

Heath handed his camera to me and I raised it to shoulder level. I scanned the area to the right, middle, and left, but nothing unusual came into view. "Gopher wants to know what's happening," Gilley said.

My jaw clenched. Gopher could be such a pain in the keister and I needed to shut his annoying pestering down or I'd be walking off this shoot in a hurry. "Tell him that every time he asks that question from now on, we're going to stop filming for ten minutes."

I heard Gilley repeat what I'd said and then Gil said, "Gopher says it was just a simple question."

"He can see what's happening, Gil. All he has to do is look at your monitor." I was still using the camera to survey the area, but I'd stopped paying attention to the screen because I was too busy trying to quell my irritation with our producer.

"He says he can see the monitors, but he'd like to know what your plan of action is."

I looked at Heath, who could hear everything in his ear too, and he grinned when I rolled my eyes. "My plan of action is to find the duke. Gopher doesn't need to know anything more than that for now."

A rumble of thunder sounded in the distance behind us, and we all turned as a gust of wind blew across the moors and brought with it the damp smell of rain.

"Gopher wants to know if that was thunder he heard?"

"It was," I said, still eyeing the horizon when a bright flash of lightning lit the sky. It was followed about ten seconds later by another rumble of thunder.

"Gopher wants to know how far away you think that storm is."

"It's about ten miles away, Gil," Heath answered, knowing I was getting close to the boiling point. "We're gonna have to wrap this up and get back to the castle soon."

"Gopher wants to know if you think that's really necessary."

I let Heath handle that one. Of course it was necessary, unless our producer thought we'd be overjoyed to turn ourselves into lightning rods out here on the moors. I aimed the camera back toward the castle, but I was still listening to the conversation and I could feel my blood pressure ticking up as Gopher argued through Gilley to get us to stay on the hunt, no matter what the weather. But finally, I couldn't take it anymore.

"Gopher wants to know—"

"You tell Gopher that if he asks *one* more stupid, unnecessary, or annoying question, we will all walk off this job!" I snapped.

Heath eyed me with surprise, but I didn't care. He had

more patience for stupid than I did. And for several long seconds we heard nothing through our earpieces. But then . . .

"Gopher wants to know what that is. And he swears it's not a stupid, unnecessary, or annoying question. He really wants to know what that is."

The question took me by surprise. "What what is?" I asked, looking around.

"That purple thing on the monitor. It's coming from Heath's camera."

Belatedly I realized I was still holding Heath's infrared in my hand. I looked at the screen, and so did Heath and behind me I felt John take a step forward to look as well. And that's when we all saw a purple blob moving near the water. "The duke!" I gasped, and had to resist the urge to dash forward.

"Come on," Heath said. Taking me by the elbow, he led me toward the blob. As we neared, the frenetic pacing of the purple bubble of energy stopped, and I had the distinct feeling that the ghostly spirit had suddenly become aware of us. But as we moved closer, the purple blob moved sharply away.

It was an odd movement, because I'd had the strange feeling that the moment the duke had seen us, he'd been glad . . . almost relieved that we were there.

"Gopher wants to know where the duke is going."

I pulled my earpiece out of my ear. Heath could handle Gopher right now—he was one distraction too many, especially since I tried to figure out why I was feeling like the duke wanted us to come forward, but when we did, he flinched away . . . and then I suddenly realized why. We were all wearing enough magnets to freak out even the most stalwart spirit.

I handed Heath the camera and quickly unzipped my vest. Heath grabbed my arm. "What're you doing?"

"It's the magnets," I told him, pulling a little to get out

of his grip and continue shrugging out of the vest. "We can't get close if we're wearing these."

"Em," Heath said, his voice firm. "We're wearing these for our own protection. We know nothing about this spook, and you saw Lady Catherine on our first night here—you said she'd been beaten bloody. What if he's as violent now as he was when he was living? What if he's as deadly as his widow?"

I hesitated. Heath had a solid point. Still, I could feel the energy of that spirit at the edge of the lake calling out to me, and another rumble of thunder—this one much closer—reminded me that we'd have only one chance at this tonight. I turned to John and motioned to the big microphone on a pole he was carrying to capture any unusual sounds. "That thing's a lightning rod, buddy," I told him, waving at him to lower it. "We all have microphones on—we should be able to record enough sound just fine." I then handed him my vest. "Here. Watch me and if I look like I'm getting into trouble, run to me and throw the vest over my head, okay?"

John nodded and set the sound boom on the ground to take up my vest and hold it like a bullfighter.

Heath, however, was doing his protective-boyfriend bit. "You're not going over there alone, Em."

I stared hard at him. "We can't risk both of us, Heath. I need you to watch for any other spooks that might be lurking out here. Who knows who or what else may be haunting these moors?"

"It's too dangerous," Heath insisted.

"Everything about this shoot is dangerous." The sound of my voice was nearly drowned out by another rumble of thunder just as the first big raindrops started to fall. We were in for a douser, that was for sure.

Through the earpiece around my neck I heard Gopher's voice yell, *"Cover the cameras!"*

I took the opportunity created by Heath's being too

distracted by the need to cover the expensive new equipment and bolted for the area where I'd last seen the purple blob of energy. I couldn't see the duke, but by opening my sixth sense wide, I could certainly feel him. Behind me I heard Heath call out to me, but I ignored him and kept on truckin'.

When I approached the water's edge, I stopped short, certain that the ghost I was searching for had just stepped up right next to me. For a moment, I dared not to even breathe. I didn't know what to expect, and he'd come up so fast and so close that it'd taken me by surprise, so I held perfectly still until I could figure out if this guy was friend or foe.

For several seconds, nothing happened, and I took that as a good sign. "Hello?" I said tentatively.

I had this feeling of warmth in my mind—it's hard to describe, but I had this sense that this ghost was welcoming me, and again there was that added element of relief.

"My name is M. J." I said, hoping the duke would understand me. I mean, the guy was Welsh and he died several centuries ago—what if he spoke only Gaelic?

Clarence, came a name into my head so clear and so crisply enunciated that there was no mistaking it.

"Your name, sir, . . . it's *Clarence*?" I repeated.

I had this sense of affirmation, which I took to be a yes.

"Clarence" wasn't at all what name I'd been expecting; in fact, if memory served me, Lord Mortimer's first name had been John. Wanting to make sure I hadn't misheard the spook, I tried a different tact. "Sir, are you the Duke of March? Lord Mortimer?"

I felt a sense of mirth fill my head, and this other feeling of a proper British gentleman saying something like, *Why, heavens no!*

"Sir," I said, feeling the ripple of electrostatic energy tickle the atmosphere—the storm was getting closer— "could you please tell me who you are?"

"Clarence," came the soft whisper in my ear. I hoped my mic had picked it up.

"Clarence who?" I asked.

But the spook didn't elaborate; instead, clear as day, he said, "I know her secret."

"You know whose secret?"

No answer came to my ear or my mind; instead, I had the urge to look across the water, which shimmered as a lightning bolt flashed behind me again. I saw nothing out of the ordinary, but I still felt the urge to continue looking, and then for the briefest moment I saw what looked like a small rowboat and realized that Clarence—who'd been standing next to me until then—had suddenly moved to the center of the lake and was guiding the rowboat toward the castle. Another series of lightning flashes lit up the water again, and it was then that I clearly saw a man in a small wooden boat, rowing hard straight for the castle wall, and a second later when yet another flash lit up the area, the boat had vanished, and Clarence was gone.

"M. J.!" I heard Heath yell from some distance behind me. "Come on! We've got to head in! The storm is getting too close!"

I knew I'd have to heed the warning, but I felt as though I'd just missed something huge. Something Clarence had shown me had tremendous significance, but I couldn't quite put it together.

"*Em!*"

I turned reluctantly away and trudged up to the group, shivering with cold. The rain was really starting to come down now and I was getting soaked. As I approached the guys, I put my headset back on and heard Gilley in the middle of an argument. "I don't know why she's not answering, Gopher!" Gil snapped. "If I knew, I'd tell you!"

"Gil!" I said loudly so he could hear me above the storm. "We're coming in."

"M. J.? Oh, thank the baby Jesus! I was beginning to worry."

"Did my mic pick up any of that?"

"You mean what your friend Clarence had to say?"

I felt a little bubble of hope in my chest. Maybe there'd be even more captured on film once we took a good look at it. "Can you analyze the tape for me while we work our way back to you? I want to listen to it after I dry off."

"You think there may have been some EVPs?" he asked, using the acronym we ghostbusters have for the recorded sounds and whispers of spirits too soft for the human ear to hear.

"I do think there may be one or two," I said. "All I audibly heard was Clarence say his name and something about knowing a secret." By this time I'd reached the boys and John handed me my vest, which I gladly took and shrugged into.

"I'll get on it," Gil promised. "Gopher wants to know, how soon before you'll be back?"

I sighed, really sick of Gopher and his wants-to-knows. "Ten minutes or so. But then I'm heading straight for a warm shower, so if he wants to talk, it'll have to wait until I'm warm again."

There was a pause while Gilley relayed what I'd said; then he came back with, "Gopher wants you guys to get right to the south wing before we run into daylight."

"Tell Gopher to—"

"We're not filming any more tonight," Heath interrupted, his voice hard. "And, Gil, tell Gopher that if he has a problem with that, he can meet us on the drawbridge." Heath winked at me; then he clicked off his headset, and I did the same. I noticed that John and Michel quickly followed suit, and in spite of the miserable weather and the fast-approaching lightning, we all had ourselves a good laugh.

We hurried at a swift jog through the rain, which got

worse the longer we were out there, and to add to the misery a blowing wind began sending the rain in sheets against us. We also had to be mindful of our equipment, and luckily John had brought along a waterproof wrapper for the fuzzy microphone he carried on his boom, but none of the rest of us had thought ahead to hazardous weather, so we each had to tuck our cameras inside our coats—well, except for Michel. He kept his out and at the ready, covered by his own vest, and I gave him high marks for dedication.

We reached the drawbridge just as the lightning was starting to get scary close, and I prayed that with the storm and the wind we'd be able to sneak across it without encountering that horrible pounding from the underside.

When we stood at the edge of it, however, we got another most unwelcome surprise. Our idiot producer, dressed in a blue rain slicker, stood with his arms crossed over his chest just on the other side of the bridge. He looked ready to give us a piece of his mind. "Damn," I swore. Why was he being *such* a pill?

"I should give him a few points for having the balls to meet me out here in this," Heath said, squaring his shoulders and preparing to have it out with Gopher.

Gopher must have taken the movement for a challenge because he began striding purposefully toward Heath. It was then that I noticed Meg and Kim huddled under an umbrella with a camera, and I *tsk*ed in disgust at the way Gopher was clearly attempting to fill a few minutes of film with the created drama of our crew squabbling when the pressure of the bust was getting to be too much. It was gratuitous, exploitive, and so unnecessary when we had plenty of scary footage to offer the audience.

"Here," Heath said, carefully handing over his camera to John. "Take this while I go talk to him."

"Shouldn't we go in?" John asked.

"Yes," I said. "We're definitely going in. He can't stop all of us, right?"

"I'll distract him," Heath said, shrugging next out of his backpack.

At that exact moment a bolt of lightning struck so close to us that I was physically thrown off my feet. I felt a slight buzzing go through my whole body and it took me a moment to get my wits about me. When I could lift my head, I saw that the boys were in exactly the same position, lying on the ground trying to shake off the effect of a jolt of electricity surging through the atmosphere. Heath appeared a little dazed next to me, because he was lying on his back staring blankly up. "Heath! You okay?" I crawled over next to him.

"Yeah," he said with a groan. "Just got the wind knocked out of me. Check the others, would you?"

I pushed myself to my knees and saw that John and Michel were rolling onto their sides. They looked sore and stunned but otherwise okay. Then I looked for Gopher and the breath caught in my throat.

By the looks of it he'd received the worst of the jolt from the lightning, because he'd been thrown nearly six feet and was now perilously close to the side of the bridge. I saw him raise a hand slowly to his head, and I knew he'd likely gotten the wind knocked out of him too.

I staggered to my feet, intent on helping him, when I saw a bone-white hand rise up out of the water and swiftly move toward Gopher's shoulder—like a cobra striking its prey.

I cried out, but I was too far away to help him, and in the blink of an eye, the hand had grabbed hold of Gopher's slicker and was pulling on him hard. For his part, Gopher tried to sit up, but the power of that hand kept him from doing anything other than flail about. *"NO!"* I screamed as Gopher's head and torso were heaved violently over the side toward the water.

A shape flew past me at incredible speed and that's

when I realized Michel had gotten to his feet and was racing toward Gopher. Six feet from him the photographer launched himself into the air like a baseball player diving for home, and he managed to land on Gopher's shins a nanosecond before our producer would have gone completely over the side.

I wasn't far behind Michel and I too dived toward the two men, landing with a terrible thud on the planks. I grabbed for the backs of Michel's legs to steady him while he attempted to anchor Gopher.

Heath was next to me in an instant, and so was John, and the two of them grabbed hold of Gopher's waist and pulled hard to get him above water.

I watched in horror as Gopher's top half was shaken back and forth like a rag doll underwater. The Widow had hold of him, and she wasn't about to let go. *"Get him up!"* I screamed, even though Heath and John were doing their level best to free Gopher from the Widow's grasp. I knew our producer could easily drown in the panic of being hauled under by the Widow.

"Pull!" Heath shouted. *"Pull!"*

While keeping my weight on the backs of Michel's legs to hold him steady, I wriggled around and got my hands on Gopher's jeans, then inched up until I had hold of his belt. I pulled as hard as I could and heard the groans of Heath, Michel, and John as they heaved up too, and suddenly, Gopher's torso flew up out of the water as if the Widow had simply let go.

We all fell back in a tangle of bodies and I had the unfortunate position of being close to the bottom, so I was mashed into the planks right before a fury of pounding began right under my own chest. Over my shoulder I could just make out Gopher's frightened face, gasping for air. "Get up!" we heard Meg and Kim cry. "Get off the bridge!"

I felt a heavy weight move off me, but I was still trapped in the tangle of limbs, and the pounding intensified, striking my sternum so hard I worried that one bad blow might stop my heart. I struggled to get up, but both of my arms were pinned, and then in a blink I was free and being lifted to my feet. Heath had hold of me and he was panting hard as he shoved me toward the center of the drawbridge. "Run!" he commanded. "Run for your life!"

Chapter 13

Kim and Meg helped me to the door of the castle. I took about five steps through it before I sank to the hard stone floor, where I lay down and rolled onto my back, shivering with exertion, cold, and fear. "Get her a blanket or something!" Meg yelled to Kim. Kim's footsteps could be heard dashing up the steps.

"Oh, my, God!" Gilley cried, and I realized he'd just come out of the dining room. "M. J.!"

Gil rushed to me and squatted down and as he gazed at me, I saw him hiss in a breath. "What the hell happened to you?"

I stared up at him. Was he kidding?

"Didn't you see the feed?" Meg asked, trying to get me to sit up against her. "We recorded the whole thing!"

"My entire monitoring system shut down about five minutes ago," Gilley said. "I was gonna wait for these guys to get back and check the cameras, but they were taking so long that I thought I'd try to see what was happening." Gil then bent a little closer to me and put a hand on my collarbone. "You're black and blue, honey," he said.

I didn't really have time to take that in because in the next instant Michel burst in through the door, followed by Heath and John, who had a gasping Gopher slung between them.

Gilley's jaw dropped. "Somebody tell me what the hell happened!"

Everyone ignored him in favor of tending to the wounded, which was pretty much everybody in attendance save Meg and Gil.

Kim came back downstairs with an armload of blankets and quilts. She distributed these to the whole crew and we took them gladly. I was so miserably cold that I couldn't really speak until Gil came to my rescue with a hot cup of tea. "Here," he said gently. "I put some sugar in it, which I know you hate, but you need the calories right now, so don't fight it. Drink it down, okay?"

I nodded and sipped the brew. I wasn't usually a fan of sugar in either my tea or my coffee, but this hit the spot. Once he'd made sure Gopher was okay, Heath came over to sit next to me. I offered him a sip of the tea and he took it gratefully. And then he must have had a good hard look at me, because his eyes squinched up and he fiddled with the opening of my hoodie. "What the hell . . . ?" he asked.

"I was lying flat on the planks when the pounding started," I explained.

Heath laid his cool hand on my tender skin. "Jesus, Em!"

"Is it bruised bad?"

"It's not good," he replied. He then sighed and wrapped his arm around my shoulders to draw me in for a kiss on the forehead. "I'm sorry you were on the bottom of the tackle, babe."

"Me too. How's Gopher?" I asked, nodding toward our producer, who was being wrapped in blankets, plied with tea, and treated like a wounded soldier back from the war. Meg and Kim were really sucking up to the boss after nearly getting fired for not having gone across the drawbridge.

"He'll be okay," Heath said. His face clouded with worry, though, which troubled me.

"You sure he'll be okay?"

"Hmm?" Heath said. He seemed a little distracted and then he must have realized what I'd just asked him, because he said, "Yeah. He'll be fine. It's us that I'm worried about. A million bucks is great when you live long enough to enjoy it, but I'm not sure even that's worth all this."

"Maybe Gopher will call a halt to filming now that he's had his own up-close and personal encounter with the Widow."

"Even if he hasn't, we can still walk off the job, you know."

"Not without getting our butts sued right into the poorhouse." Still, something was really troubling me about what'd happened tonight and I was having a hard time letting it go. "You know what's weird?"

Heath smirked. "Besides everything here at Kidwellah?"

I gave him half a smile and a nudge with my shoulder. "I'm serious."

"Okay, so tell me."

"Clarence."

"The ghost out on the moors?"

"Yes."

Heath scratched his chin. "He's not the duke, is he?" he said, more statement than question.

"No. He's someone else."

"Another of the Widow's victims?"

I took another sip of tea before answering. "See, that's what's weird, Heath. He didn't seem to have died at the Widow's hands, and yet he makes a point to show me that he's connected to the moat and the castle. And not just any part of the castle—he wanted to show me that he's connected to the south wing."

"Okay, that is pretty weird, but I get the feeling you think it's even more significant than that."

"I do," I admitted. "When I first began communicating with him, I had the strangest feeling that we'd met before."

"You've met Clarence before?"

"Well, maybe not met him formally, but he really felt familiar. It's weird, but I swear I know him from somewhere. I also had the strangest sensation that he'd been waiting for me to come to him. And the more I think about it, the more convinced I am that the night I went looking for Gopher and the others, it was Clarence I saw out on the moors, not the duke."

Heath shrugged. "Well, sure, it could have been him, Em. But why is that sticking with you?"

I frowned. "It's less about seeing Clarence out on the moors and more about figuring out why he's haunting that area. Obviously he died there or somewhere close by, and yet he's not chained to the Widow. So how did he die, when did he die, and why did I feel so strongly that he had some message that he was trying to impart to me?"

"Maybe he's not connected to the Widow at all."

I shook my head. "No, there's a connection. I can feel it. I'm just not sure what it is, and that's the mystery I think we need to figure out." The moment I said it out loud, I knew it to be true.

Heath ducked his chin and rubbed the back of his head. I knew he was thinking hard about what I'd said, and wishing that I'd simply gone along with his idea to ditch this bust and head for home. "You want to stay, don't you?"

"I do. But only because I think we're close to figuring all of this out, sweetie. And we have to figure out a way to help Merrick, Lefebvre, and the inspector's brother.

We can't damn them to an eternity with the likes of the Widow."

Heath grinned sideways at me. "Life with you would be so much easier if you weren't such a good person, you know."

I rolled my eyes. "Yeah, yeah, come on, let's get a shower in and then let's play back our footage."

Heath bounced his eyebrows. "Are we conserving water by doubling up in the shower?"

"I'd love nothing more than to see you sudsy and naked, but I don't know that I have the energy for any more of *that* tonight."

"How about if we just soap each other up, no hanky-panky."

I cocked a skeptical eyebrow. "You promise?"

He held up three fingers. "Scout's honor."

I'm not quite sure which scout troop Heath belonged to, but it certainly wasn't the "I will totally honor my previous promise of no hanky-panky in the shower" troop. Of course, I should've known better. I see that man naked and I lose any shred of willpower.

Needless to say we were a little late getting back downstairs, and by that time it was almost four a.m. Surprisingly, we weren't the only ones missing. John, Meg, Kim, and Gopher were nowhere in sight, but Gilley and Michel were in the war room huddled very close to the monitors. And to each other. "Hey, guys," I said, and both of them jumped. Well, Gilley jumped *and* squealed, but what would you expect from him anyway?

"You scared me half to death!" he cried.

"And yet, you're still able to draw breath." I pulled up a chair behind him and Michel. Heath carried another over for himself and sat down next to me. "So, what're we looking at?"

Gil glared at me, but it didn't last. Whatever he'd discovered on the footage was too exciting to keep under wraps. "Take a look at this!" he said, swiveling back around to tap at his computer screen.

"All I see is snow," I said.

"Just wait a second!" Gil replied impatiently.

I peered at the screen, but the snow was starting to make me a little dizzy. I was just about to complain again to Gil when something really weird happened—from the right side of the screen something like a dark shadow appeared, and if I had to describe it, I would say it looked like a man walking through the fuzz until he got to the center of the screen; then he stopped and seemed to turn toward the viewer. It was as remarkable as it was incredibly creepy.

"Whose camera caught this?" Heath asked.

Gilley paused the image and turned to us, excitement in his eyes. "That's just the thing—none of the cameras were feeding anything at this moment. It was captured *after* we all came inside and had gathered in the main hall. At that time, no one's camera was even on."

"Are you sure?" I asked.

Gilley pointed to every camera, including mine and Heath's, laid out on the table next to us. "I've checked them all," Gil said. "The last camera to film anything was Meg's. She captured the footage of Gopher being pulled over the side and you guys wrestling to keep him from drowning, but she turned it off the minute you five were safe."

"That's crazy," I whispered, stunned by the image. And the even weirder thing was, I thought I knew who the image was.

"You know," Heath said, squinting hard at the screen, "that sort of looks like the shape Clarence took through my lens when you were talking to him, M. J."

I nodded. "I was thinking that it was Clarence too."

Michel said, "Whoever this Clarence guy is, he seriously wants to get our attention."

I sat back in my chair and thought about my encounter with the unusually lucid ghost. Most grounded spirits I meet tend to be somewhat confused about their world. Many of them don't accept or even know that they're dead, and the plane that exists between our physical world and their grounded reality seems to be an awfully confusing place.

But Clarence had shown none of the confusion or distress or irritation that almost all the ghosts I'd met over the years had shared ... and that in itself was quite remarkable. If I had to guess as to why, I would have to say that Clarence had not died suddenly. He'd known he was dying, accepted it, and after his body ceased to function, he'd denied himself the light that could have swept him home. But why he'd decided to stick around was a mystery. "I had the strongest feeling that Clarence had been waiting for me," I said, almost more to myself than to the others.

"What for?" Gil asked.

I shrugged and added a sigh. "I really wish I knew, Gil. I think it was to tell me something important, but he's limited in his ability to communicate. So he showed me instead."

"What did he show you?" Gil asked next.

"Not much. Just him getting into a rowboat and rowing over to the side of the castle." Something kept bugging me about the image I'd seen of Clarence rowing across the moat—it was as if I'd seen that exact same thing before and there was something significant about that sense of déjà vu, but what it could be I had no idea. "Did you analyze the recordings from our mics for any EVPs?" I asked.

Gil nodded. "We've listened to them a couple of times, and there's one part where I think I hear him, but it's pretty garbled. I'll have to work on it to try and enhance it."

I yawned and leaned back in my chair. "Sounds good." Then I turned to Heath and said, "I'm bushed. You ready for bed?"

"I am, but one thing you haven't told me yet, did you get a visit from Gramps?"

I sat up straight again. "Oh, yeah! Sorry, I forgot to tell you." I then shared with them all that Sam had told me.

"A prison break, huh?" Gil said thoughtfully, referring to Sam's idea on freeing the Widow's imprisoned souls.

"We'll need to make sure the Widow is weakened when we call out to the prisoners," I said. "And that the demon is too."

"How're you gonna manage that?" Michel asked.

Heath shook his head. "I have no idea."

"The other night when the Widow had me cornered in the south wing, she used up a ton of energy trying to tackle me through the magnets. If we goad her long enough, Heath, she'll weaken. And when she's weak, the demon is also weakened and less likely to attack us."

"She could also kill us in the process," he replied.

"I think that you and me together could do it," I insisted.

Heath rubbed his face and blinked tiredly at me. "Okay," he said. "Let's get some shut-eye and work on this idea of yours after we've had some sleep."

I got up and took his hand before turning to Gil and Michel. "You guys should go to bed too. It's been a long night."

Gil blushed, and to my surprise, so did Michel. "I'm not that tired," Gil said, and very subtly he looked at Michel.

"Me either," Michel said, which made Gilley smile wide. "We should stay up a little longer and listen to that tape a few more times."

Gilley turned big gooey eyes to Michel. "We should."

I pulled on Heath's hand. "Come on, honey, let's leave them to their . . . uh . . . work."

Heath and I slept in until noon, and when I woke up, I had the rough outline of a plan forming in my head. We headed downstairs only to find Gilley and Michel still up and hovering over a table full of wires and electronic parts. "M. J.!" Gil said excitedly when he saw us. "Ohmigod! You totally have to come here and check this out!"

Now, Gil does well on very little sleep. He's one of those rare birds that can get by on four hours or less with very little effect, but as I looked at Michel, it was clear he was a lot more like the rest of us, and needed to nap . . . soon. "You look beat," I said to him as Gilley pulled me over to the monitors.

"I'm okay," he said, barely stifling a yawn.

I knew then that Michel had a thing for Gil. Only someone so romantically intrigued would stay up so long just to be near the object of his affection. And, by Gilley's decidedly chipper mood, I could see the feeling was definitely mutual. "Have a seat," Gil said.

I sat in front of the largest monitor and Gil tapped at his keyboard. He then turned the volume up and we listened to the sound of snow again, but it was somewhat muted; then a garbled voice said, "Tell the twins I love them."

I sat back and stared in stunned disbelief at Gilley. "Did he just say what I thought he said?"

"Yeah, it's weird, right? I mean, that's the only EVP that came through, and I even ran it through the voice spectrum. It's definitely Clarence's voice."

I jumped to my feet. "Gil, I know you've been up since last night, but I need some additional research from you and it's super important. Can you give me another couple of hours?"

Gil nodded, for once not fighting me over the request.

"I need you to find out if anyone named Clarence Lumley was ever connected to this castle."

Gil squinted at me. "Clarence Lumley? You mean, like, someone related to Inspector Lumley?"

"Possibly. Just do some digging and see what you come up with, okay?"

"Okay, but I'll need to go into the city and search through the library."

"If that's what it takes, please go do it. I need whatever information you can find, fast."

Michel stood and stretched. "Come on, Gilley, we'll go together."

I wanted to hug the man! Instead, I turned to Heath and said, "We have a call to make."

An hour later Heath and I were helping Inspector Lumley push his rowboat into the moat. All three of us wore magnetic vests, and I'd taken the liberty of adding Meg's and Kim's vests to the bottom of the boat just to ensure we didn't get tipped over from below.

The inspector had fought me on the need to wear the garment, but I'd insisted that I had something very important to show him, and I wasn't taking him along without it.

Heath pushed us off from the shore and he took up the oars while I studied the water for any signs of the Widow.

I was very nervous about embarking on this hunch, but my gut told me that I absolutely had to investigate my suspicions, and as Gilley wasn't back yet from town, I had no choice but to act while the sun was high and the Widow would be at her weakest.

Heath rowed steadily across the length of the moat, keeping to the middle, and no one spoke while we glided over the smooth waters. The inspector tapped his finger on the side of the boat, a sign that he was a bit impatient about this venture, and I could only hope that my hunch panned out. Otherwise, he'd be pretty ticked off.

At last we rounded the curve of the moat to the south end of the castle, which appeared as foreboding as ever. I signaled to Heath at the point where I thought Clarence had stood next to me, and he pulled hard on the left oar, turning us right and directly toward the castle.

I then got up and moved to the very front of the boat,

holding on tightly to the bow and shifting my eyes from the water to the wall of the castle, then back again.

At first as we came closer to the wall, I thought my hunch was completely wrong, but then, about ten yards away I felt my breath catch. "There!" I said, pointing to a crevice in the wall of the castle.

Heath stopped rowing and twisted in his seat. "Whoa," he said. "Would you look at that?"

"It's a false facade," I said as the boat continued to glide forward and I was getting a better look. "The left side of the wall curves out and stops, creating a blind corner for another section set farther back to continue. If you didn't know it was here, you'd never guess it existed."

"I've heard of these," the inspector said, also eyeing the gap in the wall that was visible only when you were up close to it. "It would allow the castle's lord and his family to escape should an invader breach the main gate. He could slip out in a small boat and make his way to the lake or to land if need be."

Heath took up rowing again and navigated around the curve of the false wall, bringing us into a large dark circular space at the opposite end of which was a set of stairs. "No way!" I heard Heath say softly.

"Can you get us to the stairs?" I asked him.

"No sweat." Heath rowed us right to the center of the steps and I hopped out. Grabbing hold of the lead line, I searched for a place to tie it off. "Em!" Heath barked, and I looked up to see an angry look on his face. "Get back in the boat and let me go first!"

I leveled a look at him; who did he think he was, ordering me around?

Heath took a deep breath and tried again. "Please, Em?" he said, reaching out his hand to me.

I hesitated. I'm the independent stubborn sort. Meanwhile Inspector Lumley also jumped out of the boat, took the lead line from me, and wound it around a rock jutting up out of the water. "Crisis averted," he said smartly.

Heath didn't look pleased, but I ducked my chin to hide a smile. Soon enough the three of us were all safely on the stairs and staring up at the enormous crevice that seemed to go all the way up to the top of the castle. "Shall we go in?" the inspector asked, already beginning up the rest of the stairs.

I reached out and grabbed hold of his arm. "Hang on," I said. Then I reached into my messenger bag and pulled out several magnetic spikes, handing them off to the inspector and Heath while keeping a few for myself. I then motioned for the inspector to get behind us. He leveled a look at me similar to the one I'd given Heath, but complied, and we all moved up the steps slowly and carefully.

As we inched our way to the top of the stairs—which totaled roughly twelve to fifteen—I could feel my heart-beat quicken. I was super nervous because I suspected this was the hidden section of the castle that the Widow used when she was alive to access the moat and kill her husband's friends. I also believed this was the general location of the Widow's portal, but where specifically it was I didn't know, and that's what made me incredibly wary about proceeding up those steps.

None of us spoke as we climbed. Heath had his infra-red camera out and recording, and I kept glancing his way, waiting for him to announce the appearance of something spectral on the viewfinder, but he didn't and so we moved steadily on.

At last we crested the top of the stairs and found ourselves in a very large cavernous space with what appeared to be a metal door at the far end. Heath motioned to it, but my eyes were moving all around and they settled on what my own intuition had suggested I'd find here. "There!" I whispered, pointing to what at first appeared to be a pile of old clothes.

Heath pointed the viewfinder to it, his eyes squinting at the screen. "Is that . . . ?"

"Is that what?" the inspector asked close to our ears. "What the devil is it?"

I pulled a flashlight out of my pocket and clicked it on. Pointing it at the pile, I noticed something out of place; something that was a sort of creamy brown color was illuminated within the glow of my flashlight, and for a moment my brain struggled to make sense of what I was seeing.

I heard the inspector's breath catch. "It's human remains!" he said, and started for them, but again I caught his arm.

"We all go together, sir," I said. "And we move slowly and quietly in here, understood?"

The inspector nodded, albeit a bit stiffly, and I turned to Heath. "Keep the camera on that door, and if you see anything start coming out of it, let us know."

"Got it," he said.

I guided the men to the skeleton propped ghoulishly against the stone wall. Even given the damp environment, it and the clothes it was wearing were in remarkably good shape.

The inspector bent down and lifted a bit of the dead man's lapel. Clear as day there were three perfectly circular holes in the material. "Appears to have been shot," the inspector said.

That answered one question, but it also opened up several more. I had a theory going but still needed a few more clues to be able to resolve it. "No signs of identification," the inspector continued as he probed the skeleton with his pen. "But the clothing appears to be quite old. At least a few decades."

I thought it was probably closer to thirty-five years by my guess. "I wonder who this poor chap was," Lumley said, getting to his feet to wipe his hands.

"His name was Clarence," I said, watching the inspector closely. As expected, his head snapped up and he eyed me keenly.

"Clarence?" he said, and I saw the light of recognition in his eyes, and also how he was quick to cover it. "How do you know what his name was?"

"I met his ghost last night out on the moors. I watched him get into a rowboat much like the one we brought and come this way. I suspected there was something like a secret passageway leading into the castle here, and I also suspected that Clarence had been murdered near the spot where he disappeared from my view."

Lumley turned back to the skeleton and he stared at it for a long time without comment. I could only imagine what he was thinking.

Just then Heath's chin lifted and he turned to the large metal door at the far end of the castle. "Uh . . . oh," he said softly.

I felt it too. A bit of a ripple in the ether that gathered into a wave of negative energy, and it was coming right for us. "Guys!" I hissed. "We've gotta go!" The inspector was still focused intently on the skeleton, and I reached out to grab him by the shoulder and pull him backward. "Now!" I commanded. Heath had the viewfinder trained on the metal door and I could see the screen over his shoulder.

One quick look showed me purple ooze starting to drip out of the seams around the doorframe and from the crack underneath the door. The rest happened a bit in slow motion. I let go of the inspector's arm and put spikes in both my hands while I ran toward the stairs leading to the boat. Behind me I could feel a rush of cold air come into the cavern and surround us. My breath fogged in front of me as I panted and tried to run faster.

I could tell just from the feel of the awful energy behind us that it wasn't the Widow's energy oozing into the area—it was the demon. *"Get to the boat!"* Heath shouted, and the three of us ran for our lives. The inspector was a bit slower than us, and as Heath and I reached the stairs and began to leap down them, I could hear Lumley's footfalls several feet behind me.

I was too focused on getting down the stairs to stop and see how far back he was, and inwardly I simply had to hope that he made it, because I didn't think I'd survive a head-on encounter with that demon, not even with all the magnets I was packing.

Heath reached the boat first and grabbed for the lead line. He was so shaken that the rope slipped out of his fingers and into the water, and he simply left it and turned to grab my arm and practically hurl me into the boat before leaping aboard. Dashing to the oars, he took them up and I cried out to stop him, "The inspector!"

Heath hesitated a few seconds, and only long enough for the inspector to also leap from the stairs toward the boat, which was starting to drift out away from the steps. I heard a terrible thud when the inspector's leg hit the bow. I lunged for him, grabbing on to his shoulders to prevent him from going over the side. With effort I managed to drag him into the boat and then I shouted for Heath to row hard. The inspector and I were jostled a bit when Heath set the oars in the water and gave a tremendous pull.

Lumley and I were half lying on our sides in the bottom of the boat and I couldn't see above the rim of the boat to the stairs, and honestly I didn't really want to. Heath's face pretty much said it all as he pulled and pulled for all he was worth. I felt around next to me for one of the spare vests and shoved it closer to Heath, hoping that'd be enough to protect him. Just when I thought we were home free, the boat came to an abrupt stop so jolting that Heath lost his balance and fell forward nearly on top of me.

Somehow he managed to clamber back into position and he dug his oars into the water and pulled hard, but the boat wouldn't budge. In fact, it seemed to be moving backward. "What the . . . ?" I said, crawling my way to the seat and looking around. The bow felt like it was dipping lower into the water than the stern, and when I looked, I could see why. Our lead line was pulled taut by something holding on to it from underwater. I jumped to the front of the boat and tried to pull up on the line, but whatever had hold of it felt heavy enough to sink us and it wasn't letting go. "I need a knife!" I said, looking desperately back at Heath, who was straining so hard against the oars the veins in his neck were bulging.

"Back . . . pocket!" he grunted through gritted teeth.

I pushed past the dazed and frightened inspector and ducked low so as not to interfere with Heath's attempt to row. I then reached around to his back pocket and wormed my hand inside. Immediately I found his pocketknife, but it caught on the inside seam and for a moment, I couldn't pull it free.

"We're moving back to the stairs!" the inspector shouted, as if he was only just now realizing what was happening.

I clenched my jaw and turned my shoulder a bit to get a better angle, and finally freed Heath's knife. As I was moving toward the bow with it, however, a tremendous thump banged against the underside of the boat. "Damn you!" I shouted at whatever was currently wreaking havoc upon the boat.

I grabbed the other vest from the bottom of the boat and shoved past Lumley to the bow, where I laid the vest over the top section of the rope and began slicing away at it.

Heath's knife didn't have a serrated edge, so cutting through the thick rope wasn't easy or fast. While I worked, I heard Heath call out for Lumley to help him, and the shuffling behind me told me he was moving to do that. "I'm cutting as fast as I can!" I shouted to let them know that it was hard going. Slowly the rope fibers were giving way, and my arm hurt with the effort to slice through it as fast as I could. Underneath the boat came another very hard pounding and I was knocked slightly sideways, hitting my head against the side so hard I saw stars.

"Em!" I heard Heath shout.

I shook my head and got back up; moving quickly to the rope again, I sliced and pulled faster than ever. "Cut, you bastard! Cut!"

"We're getting close!" Lumley shouted.

"Al-most . . . there!" I yelled back as I pressed hard on the knife to cut the last few strands. With a jolt the rope came free and I went sailing backward, landing on my back and striking my head again. "Dammit!" I swore. I'd get a concussion out of this for sure. Rolling to my side, I got to all fours and looked back at Heath and Lumley. Each of them had an oar and they were heaving as fast as they could while trying to keep in rhythm with each other. We sped backward through the water and away from the cavern and the stairs, but we still had to get across the moat.

Taking a risk, I shrugged out of my vest and moved up close to Heath's and Lumley's feet, where I gathered the other two vests and made a magnetic quilt right underneath us. I huddled low and hoped all that magnetic interference would dissuade the Widow from using her energy to make us miserable by pounding on the underside.

The trick seemed to work because we made it back across the moat without further incident and both Heath and Lumley were soaked through with sweat from the exertion. When Lumley paused because he was having a hard time catching his breath, Heath grabbed the oar and used both to propel us up onto the rocky ground. I jumped out first and held the boat steady while the boys wearily got to their feet and stumbled out. Once they were back on dry land again, both of them sank to the ground and lay there panting.

At last Lumley sat up and eyed me curiously. "How did you know?" he asked.

"About your father, Clarence?" I guessed.

He nodded.

"Some things you just know, Inspector. The question is, who killed him, and what the hell was he doing snooping around a secret entrance to the south wing thirty-five years ago?"

Chapter 14

The answer to my question came shortly after we returned from our harrowing experience. Bypassing our producer—whose first question to us was "Did you get anything good on film?"—I made a beeline for the war room and hoped that Gilley and Michel would be back. Luck was with me, as immediately after entering the dining hall (being trailed by Gopher, Heath, and Lumley), I discovered Gil and Michel there. Just as I got their attention, Gopher's cell phone went off. "It's Chris," he said, retreating back out the door to give the update of our progress to Chris in private.

"Thank God," I muttered as I watched him walk away.

Heath laughed softly next to me. "In my next contract I want a clause that says that I can punch Gopher in the arm every time he annoys us."

"He'd never be able to lift his arm again," I said, focusing on Gil, whose expression told me that he had a whole lot of good intel to share. However, the minute he saw that the inspector was with us, he seemed to lose his enthusiasm. "It's okay," I told him, already knowing what he might've discovered. "The inspector knows."

"He does?" Gil asked.

"Knows what?" Michel said.

"That the ghost we ran into out on the moors last night was the spirit of Inspector Lumley's father," I replied. I eyed Lumley, who appeared dazed—likely as much by our narrow escape from the Widow as by the discovery of his father's remains within the hidden section of the castle.

"So it's okay to tell you what I found out in front of him?" Gil asked.

I looked again at the inspector, and he nodded. "What've you got, Gil?" I said.

"Well!" Gil began, motioning for us to take a seat at the table while he went through his notes. "When you said to look up Clarence Lumley, I thought I wasn't gonna come up with much, but as it turns out, there's a bunch of local news stories related to his disappearance thirty-four years ago."

"I never knew he disappeared here in Penbigh," the inspector said. "Mother has been light on the details of his departure. She would only say that he came home late one night drunk, after having spent the evening in a pub, and they had a terrible row, after which he stormed out and was never seen again."

Gilley was nodding his head like he knew all that. "There's an article in the newspaper archives that quotes her as saying almost exactly that. The odd thing, according to the reporter, was that no one remembers seeing your dad in a pub that night. In fact, no one remembers seeing him past five o'clock when he left his office."

I turned to Lumley, wondering what had led his father to the castle in the first place. "What was your father's job, Inspector?"

"He was an accountant," Lumley said. "He worked for Inland Revenue."

"Inland Revenue?" Heath repeated. "Is that like the IRS?"

"Yes," Lumley replied. "It's now called Her Majesty's Revenue and Customs, but back then, Inland Revenue was responsible for collecting the national income tax for all British citizens."

Gil was bouncing on the balls of his feet and I knew he had more to share. "What else did you find?" I asked him.

He grinned. "Your dad wasn't just an accountant, Inspector—he was a special investigator with the IR, and at the time of his disappearance, he was assigned to investigate the current dowager countess. Apparently, there were some discrepancies in the amount of income Lady Lydia claimed to be making off Kidwellah."

I sat back in my chair as all the pieces began sliding into place, my theory taking real shape now. "Inspector?"

"Yes?"

"I have a personal question to ask you, and I'm sorry to invade your privacy, but you said that after your mother had your father declared dead, you were able to live comfortably off the proceeds of a trust fund he set up for you and Ollie, is that right?"

"It is," he said.

"How did your father come by his money?"

The inspector seemed taken aback by my question, but he answered me anyway. "My father's family was quite wealthy. He inherited it."

"I see, and if you'll indulge me a few more personal questions?" I paused to see if he would and he nodded. "When did your mother's drinking become an issue?"

The inspector's spine stiffened and his face flushed and it took him a moment to answer me, but he said, "I suppose it was shortly after Ollie died. Mother fell into a terrible depression, and because of my own grief, I didn't notice her drinking until it had become a problem.

She told me once that she blamed herself for Ollie's death, and I don't know that she'll ever recover from the pain of his loss."

"And who had control over your inheritance? Was that her or someone else?"

"It was Mother until Ollie and I reached the age of twenty-five; then we took control."

"I see, and who inherited Ollie's portion when he died?"

I could see that my questions were making the inspector more and more uncomfortable, and I braced myself for an outburst from him, but he surprised me by keeping his cool and saying, "Mother inherited it, and when she dies, it will go to me. But I'll have you know that when the solicitor informed her that she would receive his portion of the trust, she protested and claimed to want no part of it. I've been managing her accounts since Ollie's death."

I had an even more probing question to ask the inspector, and I hoped he wouldn't get too angry with me. "Sir, I'm very sorry to have to ask you this, but did you ever notice that, when you turned twenty-five and took over your own finances, that there was less there than expected?"

The inspector shifted in his seat, but I could see that I'd touched on the truth. "There may have been slightly less than expected," he said grudgingly. "However, Mother was never really very good at managing money. She spoiled us a bit, I'm afraid."

"I see." I knew he wasn't being totally honest with me.

Lumley's face darkened. "What exactly are you getting at, Miss Holliday?"

"I believe I know who your serial killer is, Inspector. And I also believe I know who her accomplices were."

The inspector stood up and balled his hands into fists. "Are you implying that my mother is somehow responsible for these murders?" he demanded.

I was careful to keep my tone cool and even. "No, sir," I said. "At least, not directly responsible. But I do believe she was involved."

"What's your theory, Em?" Heath said, moving protectively to my side to show Lumley he'd better think twice about yelling at me.

Before I told them, I wanted to be absolutely sure, so I turned first to Michel. "You said the other day that you had suggested Kidwellah to André for the location shoot. How did you come across this castle, Michel?"

He cocked his head quizzically at me and said, "Jaqui sent me an email with a link to the castle. But she also sent me several other choices."

I thought on that for a minute before I followed up with another question. "And these other choices that Mrs. Lefebvre sent to you, how did they compare to Kidwellah?"

"Well, they didn't," he said with a slight smile. "Kidwellah's hall was exceptional by comparison. I knew it was the perfect location for the shoot the moment I laid eyes on it."

I nodded knowingly. Then I turned to Gil and said, "The other nine victims that ended up in the moat, Gil. Did you happen to find out anything about them?"

Michel raised his hand to get my attention back to him. "While Gilley was looking up Clarence, I was able to come up with some information on them, and just like the others they fit the profile. Two of the three remaining victims were middle-aged wealthy men, here on holiday with their wives, and those who had children did not have them in attendance when they were here."

"And who was the third victim?" I asked.

"He was a groundskeeper here at the castle. His name was Richard Farnsworth. I doubt he was a wealthy man."

"But I'd wager he was a mean one," I replied, recognizing the last name immediately.

Michel cocked his head as if I'd just said something

odd. "You know, you might be right, M. J. I did come across a small article about Richard which said that he spent a night in the Penbigh jail on suspicion of battery to his wife."

"Farnsworth," Heath said, eyeing me curiously. "Where have I heard that name before?"

And as if on cue, Mary Farnsworth, the hotel waitress and cook, came into the dining hall and asked us if we'd care for something to eat or drink.

Wanting to send her out of ear range, I told her that we'd all love some tea and pastries, and off she went to see to preparing it for us.

"Oh, my Lord," Lumley said, as if a lightbulb had just gone on above his head. He turned wide eyes to me and I nodded.

"Yes, Inspector. I believe she was, and perhaps still is, an accomplice too."

"Would someone please tell me what's going on?" Gil complained.

I kept my eyes on the door that Mary had walked through into the kitchen while I answered Gilley. "I believe that the person murdering all the men at the keep was none other than the dowager, Lady Lydia Hathaway."

Heath's jaw fell open. "Lady Hathaway?" he said. "But, Em, she's got to be in her seventies if she's a day. How would she have done it?"

I shrugged. "She had help. You saw her butler. He's not quite as old as she is, but he's certainly capable of striking someone on the head from behind, and if it's not him, then it could've been some other hired hand to do the dowager's dirty work."

"But *why* would she want to murder all those men?" Gil pressed.

"For the money, honey," I said. "I doubt that Kidwellah Castle has generated enough income to keep the dowager so finely furnished all these years. Her house is like a museum of priceless antiques, artwork, and expensive furnishings. If, according to her, she had the castle converted years ago into a hotel, I doubt it's been able to pull in enough money to keep her in that kind of lavish lifestyle."

"But how does she make money off of murdering the men?" Michel asked.

"By having their widows be in on the scheme. You know how tight-lipped these European aristocrats are, Michel. Entrance into their little club of wealthy elite comes only with a title or a great deal of money. And I'd wager that there's likely a rumor out there amongst the women of this aristocratic circle that if you have a difficult, abusive, or irritable husband whom you can't afford to divorce, the dowager Lady Hathaway may just be someone who can help you."

I allowed my eyes to settle on the inspector and his jaw clenched.

"Do you know what you're suggesting?" he asked me so softly it was barely audible.

"I do, sir. I'm suggesting that your mother may have been involved in the murder of your father, and when her own son was drawn to Kidwellah Castle for inexplicable reasons, she tried to redirect him. But he wouldn't let it go, and when he became the inspector here, she must have been deeply worried that he'd discover something about his father's disappearance that would lead him back to her. What's worse, when Ollie was murdered by one of the dowager's helpers because he might have been getting too close for comfort, your mother must have known that she was indirectly responsible for his death, and the guilt got the better of her, and she began drinking, trying to numb herself from the pain." The inspector looked visibly stricken by my speech. "Inspector Lumley, I'm so sorry, I know this hits very close to home for you, but the theory is at least worth checking into."

"How the devil would you propose I prove something like that?" he snapped. Clearly I'd touched a nerve.

"I think you should have a talk with your mother. And if that's too difficult a task, then find the widows of the men who were drowned in the moat over the past four decades, and begin questioning them. Better yet, go over their finances. My guess is that right after their husbands were found floating in the moat, there was a sizable withdrawal from their accounts. In fact, I'd start with Mrs. Lefebvre and work your way backward. Question the widows, because I have a feeling that the farther back you go, the more willing these women will be to cooperate. Especially if I'm right in thinking that Lady Hathaway had blackmailed them."

"I think M. J.'s right," Heath said. "But I still don't understand why Merrick Brown was murdered, or Mrs. Hollingsworth."

"Well, I actually have a theory about both of them too," I said. "I think that Mrs. Hollingsworth was a victim of circumstance. I believe she lured her husband here to have him taken care of, only Mrs. Lefebvre jumped ahead of her in line, probably by paying more money. That's when Mr. Hollingsworth lost his temper and probably took the opportunity to murder Fiona, thinking she'd just end up as another of the castle's mysterious victims. He has the perfect case for reasonable doubt, even if he is fingered for the crime.

"And as for Merrick, I don't think my first impression of him as a kindly young man was off. I believe he might have figured out what was happening here at the castle, but, given the dowager's sizable influence in Penbigh, was probably too afraid to go to the police. I think that when he learned our film crew was coming here to investigate the ghosts of Kidwellah, he did something a bit drastic, and he put us in the south wing on purpose. He might have felt confident about our abilities to deal with the Widow, and also to expose the truth." Turning to Heath, I said, "Do you remember what he said to us? That he'd looked us up online and thought we were amazing investigators?" Heath nodded. "At the time I thought he was talking about our ghost-hunting abilities, but have you seen what's been written about us? There're more than a few articles out there giving us credit for solving a couple of murders. We've got a reputation for being not just ghostbusters, but amateur murder investigators too.

"And I bet that's what Merrick was referring to, and I also bet that's why he put us in that room in the south wing, to ferret out the truth about what's going on here, but unfortunately, someone must have discovered what Merrick was up to, or worried that he was getting too suspicious and they murdered him."

"But who?" Heath asked. "Who murdered Merrick?"

"Me," said a voice behind us. We all jumped and turned in our seats to find Arthur Crunn standing in the doorway holding a pistol. The inspector reached for his own weapon and Crunn cocked his gun and said, "Ah, ah, Inspector. I'd hate to shoot you and ruin this carpet. It'd make such a mess for Mary to clean up."

At that moment Mary came into the dining hall and dropped the tray she was carrying. Dishes clattered and broke and she reeled backward a few steps. "Arthur!" she gasped. "What do you think you're doing?"

"They know, Mary," he said, his eyes full of meaning.

Mary's hand flew to her mouth and it took her a moment to reply. "But . . . but . . . you can't kill them all!"

Crunn tugged at his collar with his free hand, clearly nervous. "Of course I can," he said. "They'll find them all floating in the moat, their boat capsized. Just another dreadful accident."

My eyes slid to the inspector, who was watching Crunn like a tiger considering its prey.

"I'm too young to die!" Gil cried as big wet tears filled his eyes. I wanted to comfort him, but I was afraid to move.

Crunn glared hard at him, as if Gilley's pleading face was an irritation. "Stop blubbering," he snapped. "Now all of you, get up and move against the wall. Mary, go get a good length of rope. You'll need to tie their hands and feet, but not too tight. Just tight enough for them to struggle for a bit before the Widow gets them. Not to worry, I'll show you. I've had some practice with Merrick."

Mary stood frozen in place, and while she didn't move, neither did we. "Now!" Crunn yelled, and we all jumped.

Mary hurried off to get the length of rope and I wanted to call out to her to stand up to her brother, but I realized that Mary wasn't the type to stand up for herself. Not with her brother, her late husband, or the dowager, who'd likely enslaved her here at the castle as repayment for killing Mary's husband.

In the silence that followed, the inspector softly said, "He can't shoot all of us."

"Stop talking!" Arthur yelled. "And move over to the wall or I'll shoot you first, Jasper."

The inspector took a subtle step to the side, close to a table stacked with clean dishes. I chanced a look at him, and he glanced meaningfully at the dishes. I understood immediately, and my heart quickened.

"I said move!" Crunn yelled again. Gilley sniffled loudly and said, "Is he really going to kill us?"

I ignored him and focused subtly on the inspector. I saw his right hand—hidden from Crunn—count down, three . . . two . . .

"Hey, guys, sorry about that. Sometimes it's hard to shut Chris up," Gopher said as he came hurrying into the room wiggling his cell phone.

Arthur turned and began to raise his gun toward Gopher, and that's when Heath, the inspector, and I all reached out and grabbed for a plate, hurtling them toward Crunn. Two of the three found their mark, striking him in the forehead. Crunn's gun went off, Gilley screamed, Gopher fell to the ground clutching at his chest, and Heath took off like a rocket. He covered the floor in six paces and launched himself into the air, tackling Crunn and taking him down. The pair hit the carpet and there was a loud crunching sound, and Arthur screamed in pain.

Meanwhile I raced forward to get to Gopher, who was lying on his side, his face away from me. "Gopher!" I cried, falling to my knees in front of him. "Are you hit? *Are you hit?*"

The inspector was at my side in a moment and together we gently rolled Gopher over. To my immediate relief I could see that Gopher's eyes were open and he was conscious, but he was quite pale. "Owwwwwww!" he moaned. "What the hell?"

"Are you hit?" I asked him again, gently probing his bubble vest for any signs of a wound.

Gopher lifted his hand, which was bloody and badly cut. "He shot my phone!"

I gave a huge sigh of relief. "Oh, thank God," I whispered, bending forward to hug Gopher.

"We've got Mary!" Gilley called, and I looked behind me to see that Gil and Michel were busy using all of Mary's rope to bind her to a chair. That woman wasn't going anywhere.

Meanwhile Crunn was still squirming under Heath, his face contorted in pain. Clearly he'd broken something—probably a hip. Heath didn't seem to have an ounce of pity for him, and he held him in a headlock until the inspector could come over and handcuff him.

Several hours later the inspector had made half a dozen arrests: Crunn and his sister, Mary; Lady Hathaway; her butler (who'd been the primary hit man and the one to actually pull the trigger and murder Lumley's father so many years before, we later learned); Mrs. Lefebvre; and, sadly, the inspector's mother.

I couldn't imagine how difficult it must have been for him to arrest his own mother, but Lumley seemed to see her with a different set of eyes now. I could tell from the news broadcast that evening that he had emotionally, and perhaps permanently, divorced her.

Mr. Hollingsworth was brought in for questioning on the murder of his wife, which Crunn and the others flatly denied having a hand in. But Hollingsworth had already had many years' practice denying the abuse of his wife, and he wasn't about to confess to her murder. Still, his DNA was collected, as the inspector had noticed some scratches on the top of Hollingsworth's hand when he'd interviewed him on the night of Fiona's murder, and the coroner had discovered some foreign skin particles under her fingernails after she'd been pulled from the lake. I figured it was only a matter of time before it came back from the lab pointing to him as a match. I had no doubt the trail would lead back to the bastard husband, and he'd spend the rest of his life rotting in some cold prison.

As for us, well, at first we didn't know if we were even allowed to stay on the premises. Lady Hathaway's solicitor had her out on bail within a few hours and I was sure she'd kick us out. But the inspector intervened, declaring the entire castle a crime scene, and with his permission we were allowed to stay in a small section that didn't fall under the area of investigation—namely, our rooms, the front hall, the kitchen, and a small section at the back of the dining hall next to the kitchen.

I told my crew that the minute the Widow was taken care of, we'd be out of there, never to set foot on those moors again. At least that was the hope.

We met the next day to come up with an actual plan, and to my surprise, it was Gilley who proved just how valuable a team member he was. "I was thinking about Sam's idea to stage a prison break," he said, hoisting up a box the size of a large radio onto the table. "And I think I have an idea."

"Is that what I think it is?" Heath asked warily.

I knew it was. Several months earlier we'd been involved in a particularly nasty ghostbust in Scotland, and on that shoot we'd come across a gadget that could enhance the electromagnetic energy within a given area. The effect was to thin the veil between our realm and the realm that spooks walked in. With the veil weakened, a powerful spook would become even more so, and any living creature within the vicinity would be vulnerable. In other words, it could turn a dicey situation downright dangerous, and a dangerous situation downright deadly.

"It's the Super Spooker," Gilley said with a big ol' grin. "Like it?"

"No!" we all said at once.

Gil made a face. "I've tweaked it a little," he told us, like that was supposed to make us feel better. "It has directional controls now."

"Meaning?" I asked, afraid of the answer.

"Meaning that if you want to give your spooks a boost of energy, you can actually control in what direction you aim the electrostatic ray." Gilley demonstrated by turning the dial to the right. "This will give you about a three-foot-wide by six-foot-long ray to the right, and moving the knob to the middle shoots it in the middle, et cetera. In other words, if you find yourself at an odd angle to the portal where the prisoners are, then just turn the dial and point the electrostatic ray."

"But, Gil," I said, already seeing a dozen problems with that. "How're we supposed to boost their energy to escape the portal without making the Widow crazy strong?"

Gil nodded to Michel, who pulled out from underneath the table a tennis racket strung with what looked like piano wires. "Tennis, anyone?" he said merrily.

I leveled a dark look at Gilley. "Are you kidding me?"

Gil waved his hand with a flourish and said, "Show 'em what it can do, Michel!"

Michel pulled a handful of paper clips from his pocket and tossed them up into the air. He then swung the racket and we all ducked, covering our heads. I heard several small thwacks and waited another half second to lift my head, preparing to yell at both of them. To my surprise, Michel was holding the racket like a trophy and immediately I could see why. All the paper clips were stuck to the metal wires. "It's magnetized?" I said.

"Yep," Gil said proudly.

Next to me Heath began to chuckle, and he held out his hand for the racket, which Michel gave to him. "Nice work, Gil," he said.

Gilley eyed Michel adoringly. "It was Michel's idea."

"Is there only one?" John asked.

Gil nodded. "We didn't have time to make any more than that."

Heath turned to me. "Should we wait until we can make more of these?"

"That'll take time," Gil said. "Those things aren't as easy to string as you might think."

"How'd you come up with this?" I asked. We'd stuck to our spikes for so long that I'd stopped thinking there was anything better.

"Well, at first we thought maybe a bat or a club would work," Gil said, "but when John described how the Widow's demon could break itself up into small parts, I thought a racket might be better. You could have yourself a nice Whac-a-Mole party with it! Every time the Widow or her demon comes at you, just whack 'em, and whack 'em hard. They'll begin to weaken soon enough. I figure the demon will tire out first and he should go back through the portal, leaving the Widow without her power source. You'll need to keep after her until she's so weak that she goes back through the portal too, and once you accomplish that, just start yelling to the prisoners—you have their names, right?"

Gil had given me the list of known names of the nine

men drowned in Kidwellah's moat. The reason the list was only nine names long was that we didn't think that the men the Widow had drowned when she was alive were in the portal with her, because she wouldn't have had the ability to capture their souls while she was alive. "Got it right here," I said, pulling the list from my own pocket.

"Good," he said. "Call them one by one and tell them to come to the top of the portal. Then point the Super Spooker at them and hope it gives them enough energy to break free."

Heath sat back in his chair and ran a hand through his long black hair. "This is seriously dangerous," he said. "Are you sure about this, Em?"

"No," I said with a halfhearted laugh. "But what choice do we have? I mean, we can't just leave them to spend eternity with the Widow. And what about Clarence? Doesn't the inspector deserve to have his father's remains back? As long as the Widow remains on the loose, he'll never be able to retrieve those remains and get closure."

Across the table Gopher had been sitting silent— unusual for him—while he played with the thick bandages covering his hand. "You don't have to do it," he said, and we all turned to look at him.

"What did you say?" I wanted to be sure I'd heard him correctly.

Gopher cleared his throat and lifted his chin. "We have enough footage. If it's too dangerous, we can just walk away, and tell the audience that the Widow still haunts this castle."

"Not!" I said, and Gopher looked back at me in surprise. "Dude, the minute we say something like that, you *know* some dumb amateur ghost hunter is gonna come across the Atlantic and go on a hunt for the Widow and they'll not likely live through the encounter. And you know what? That guy will be followed by a dozen more after him."

"Then we could lie," Heath suggested. "We could say something like the Widow was imprisoned in her portal and will never haunt the castle again."

I shook my head. "You'll still get the same group of amateur ghostbusters checking out Kidwellah to see if that's true. Naw, I'm afraid we've opened up this can of worms, and we've either gotta put the lid on or scrap the film altogether."

All eyes turned to Gopher, who squirmed in his seat. "Chris would never go for scrapping the film."

"That's what I thought," I said. "So it's settled. We're definitely taking on the Widow. Tonight. But we're not taking a full crew with us. That's too many people for Heath and me to worry about, so we'll take volunteers, but before I open it up to that option, let me just say right up front, Meg and Kim, you're out. You stay here, wear your vests, and keep Gil safe. Understood?"

The girls looked immensely relieved and they both pumped their heads up and down like a couple of bobbleheads.

I motioned to the boys. "You may volunteer at will."

Michel immediately raised his hand and Gilley tried to get him to lower it, but the photographer was insistent. I winked knowingly at Heath. Gil was so cute when he was enamored. "Michel volunteers," I said, just to irk Gil. It worked. He glared hard at me.

"I'm in," John said, and I couldn't help but notice the way that Kim bit her lip and barely held back from reaching out to touch John. I had a feeling their little romance wasn't quite as over as they both pretended.

"Thanks, John," I said. "Anyone else?"

Gopher sighed. "Yeah, I'll go," he said.

I grinned. "Sorry, pal. You're going to have to sit this one out."

"Why?" he asked, clearly insulted.

I pointed to his hand. "No way am I taking someone

with an injury like that along. You can stay behind, but you're not allowed to pester me on the headset, got it?"

"Yeah, yeah," he said, but I could tell he was relieved.

"I'm in," said a voice from behind me, and I turned to see Inspector Lumley standing in the doorway of the dining hall.

"We didn't expect to see you here," I told him as he came forward and took a seat. He looked like he'd been up all night.

"I just came from my office," he admitted. "I knew you'd be taking on the Widow tonight and I wanted to help in any way I can."

I eyed Heath and he nodded. "Okay," I said. "You're in. If anyone can get your brother to come out of that portal, it'll be you. But you're going to need to get some sleep before we set out—at least a couple of hours. I'm not taking some sleep-deprived, punch-drunk man along on a hunt this dangerous."

"No problem at all," he assured me. "What time are we setting off?"

"Midnight," I told him. "If you leave after the meeting and go right to bed, you should have at least seven hours to recuperate."

"Which access point are we going to take?" Heath asked, reaching for Gilley's iPad to pull up the blueprints of the castle.

That was the hardest decision we were going to have to make. If we picked the wrong location to strike an attack on the Widow, then we could pay for it with our lives. I studied the map of the castle and finally made up my mind. "There," I said, pointing to the entrance from the kitchen. "We'll go in there and take the Widow and her demon on in the large main hall of the south wing."

"But that's not near her portal," John said. "I mean, if we're guessing that her portal is in that secret passageway I opened on the second floor."

"Oh, I'm positive it's there," I assured him. "But if we can make it to the main hall, we'll have a lot of room to fight her and wear her out. We'll be covered in magnets, and there won't be any water or narrow hallways around. If we get into trouble, we can always jump out the door to that little patch of rock I landed on."

"Isn't that a ten-foot drop?" Heath said, like he really didn't like that idea.

"Beats getting tackled by the Widow," I replied.

"Good point."

"Hopefully, we'll be able to draw the Widow and her demon out into the open one at a time, and the four of us," I said, pointing to myself, John, Michel, and the inspector in turn, "can all box her in while Heath pounds on her with the racket and weakens her to the point that she retreats."

"Then what?" Gil asked when I'd stopped to think through the plan.

"Well, then we'll have to head upstairs and try to push her into the portal, while getting the others out."

No one at the table looked like they thought that was a very good plan, but I'd thought it through for hours and hours, and any way you sliced it, it was a very dangerous mission that would call for a lot of improvisation and could go horribly wrong in a dozen different ways.

"Okay," Heath said at last while he stood up to effectively end the meeting. "We meet back here at eleven thirty to go over the plan one last time and gear up. Until then, let's all try to get some shut-eye."

Chapter 15

I woke up at ten o'clock, anxious and fidgety. Heath was still asleep, so I spent the next hour lying awake, staring at the ceiling. At last I heard him say, "How long you been up?"

"A little while."

He pushed himself onto his elbows and considered me blearily. "I know what'll take your mind off things."

I pushed him playfully and said, "No way, buddy. No time for hanky-panky. We need to be downstairs in twenty minutes."

"I could work with that," he said, wrapping his arms around me to pull me underneath him for a kiss.

I indulged him for only that, then wriggled out from underneath. "Come on. We've gotta get moving."

We were the first ones into the war room, or at least I thought until I heard someone giggle from the kitchen. I poked my head through the doorway only to pull it back immediately. Heath looked at me curiously as I walked quickly away. "Gil and Michel," I whispered.

"So?"

"They're having . . . er . . . a *moment*."

"Ahh," Heath said with a light laugh. "Good for Gil.
Have you noticed how much more cooperative he's been
lately?"

"Yes. And I'm praying that it continues. Gil tends to
run through the boys, so we'll see how long this lasts."

About eleven twenty the others began to make their
way into the dining hall. The inspector showed up first,
and he looked very handsome out of his dress shirt and
blazer. Tonight he wore a white long-sleeved polo and
dark jeans, and I could tell the few hours' rest had done
him some good, although there was still a hard edge to
his eyes, something that he'd developed the minute I'd
suggested his mother may have had a hand in his father's
murder.

Meg arrived and got to work making us some hot tea,
and Kim and John came in together. Something the rest
of us pretended not to notice. Gil and Michel came out
of the kitchen when Meg went in, and I noticed that Gilley's shirt was on inside out. No one said anything, but
we all noticed and snuck secret smirks at one another,
which I thought was funniest of all.

At last Gopher arrived, and he took up a seat next to
Gil. "Dude, did you get dressed in the dark?" he asked,
pulling on Gil's shirt.

Gilley looked down at himself and turned bright red.
Both he and Michel blushed down to their toes. "Oops,"
Gil said, after clearing his throat. He quickly turned his
back to us and turned his shirt the right way out.

The attack team then geared up, donned headsets,
and made our way over to the entrance to the south wing
via the kitchen. It took us only moments to move the
shelving aside again and we all squatted down in front of
the door. "I'll lead the way," I told the boys, but Heath
shook his head and held up the racket.

"*I'm* on point, Em. You navigate me from behind, okay?"

"Do I have a choice?"

"Nope."

I rolled my eyes. "Fine. After you, pal."

Heath crawled forward to the front of the line and I tucked in right behind him. We moved through the door and I whispered, "Do your best to hold on to your nerves until we get to the main hall, fellas. Spooks are attracted to fear, so stay calm."

My words were much easier said than done, I knew, but nobody complained and we all moved forward through the door and stood up again. Then we continued down the hallway, creeping along on tiptoe as we slowly inched our way forward. We instinctively paused at every creak, moan, and groan coming from the old castle.

Faintly I could hear the sound of a door slamming intermittently. I thought it might be the very door I jumped through the last time the Widow had me cornered. Heath stopped to listen every time it slammed, and finally I leaned in and said, "That's normal. There's a door leading to the outside that slams with the wind."

He nodded and we moved a bit faster after that. At last we came to the end of the corridor, and I motioned to the right in the direction of the central hall. I had a hand on Heath's shoulder, and I could feel the tension radiating through him. He'd never admit that he was scared, but I knew that his near drowning by the Widow had to be setting him on edge.

The hallway we were in was short and it emptied out into the large central hall. Heath paused and held up his camera, turning the viewfinder so that we could all see the area illuminated. When I looked through it, my breath caught. I hadn't realized when I'd been in here the first time that the walls were practically oozing with spectral energy. They were slimed with ectoplasm—a sort of oozy substance that some spooks leave behind when they walk through something solid, like a wall.

But this was ectoplasm on a scale I'd never seen before. Great dark swaths of it coated every wall both up and down, and I shivered because I had a feeling that this particular ectoplasmic mess wasn't created by the Widow, but by her demon.

"You *actually* spent time in here?" Heath whispered to me.

"I didn't know it looked like this," I told him, still in frightful awe of the scope and size of the slime.

"What *is* that?" the inspector asked from behind me.

"It's ectoplasm," I said. "And I think we should be careful to stay away from the walls, guys."

I wanted to move forward again, but Heath wasn't budging. He just kept sweeping the camera up and down the walls. I could feel the tension running through him kick up a notch, and I knew that he had to be struggling internally. I gave him a minute and then I saw him square his shoulders and step forward into the main hall.

As we entered, we fanned out to walk side by side, everyone's eyes roving the walls and hallways to the left and right to make sure nothing was sneaking up on us. "Should we head upstairs?" John asked.

I looked over at him and saw that he was looking a little pale and clammy. "You okay?" I asked. I hoped he wasn't going to freak out again and take off running. That would spell disaster for both him and us.

"Yeah," he said, but he hardly sounded confident.

"Do you want me to carry that?" I asked, pointing to Gilley's Super Spooker.

He shook his head and I put a reassuring hand on his arm. "Hang in there, buddy. We'll get through this."

Michel was also trembling and looking scared, while the inspector was faring only slightly better, or at least he hid his fear better. I had a feeling the vibe in this place was doing its number on everybody. I motioned to Heath to head to the stairs. We needed to get on with this or get the hell out of here.

As we were making our way over to the stairs, the door I'd leaped out of suddenly blew open with a loud bang.

We all jumped, but John actually shrieked. I clamped my hand over his mouth, but I had a sinking feeling that his outburst had given us away.

"Em!" Heath whispered.

I looked at him and saw that his chin was lifted in the direction of the upstairs landing. There, at the railing, was the Widow, levitating two feet off the ground as she smiled evilly down at us.

In my ear I heard Gilley shriek. It was the first I'd heard from him since entering the south wing, and I knew he was reacting to the appearance of the Widow.

Immediately Heath handed off the camera to me and stepped in front of me, holding up the magnetized racket threateningly. Michel and John also edged closer to me, which blocked my view of the Widow.

I tried to peer around Heath's shoulders, but I was boxed in, and for several seconds I didn't know what was happening. Then Gilley gave another shriek and shouted, "Michel! Look out!" And I knew Michel's camera had picked up something.

An instant later Michel vanished from my side as he flew across the room to land in a heap on the floor. I realized belatedly that the demon had come up from the rear, and struck us from behind.

Heath whirled around as the demon—a big black mass of shadow with red glowing eyes—came around for the second attack.

"Hit it!" I shouted just as Heath swung hard with his racket. The demon and Heath's racket connected, and Heath was knocked off his feet from the force of the blow, but oddly there was no sound. It simply connected, sent the demon tumbling backward, and in the explosion of energy, Heath fell back to the floor.

I tried to get to Heath to help him get up, but John was in my way again, and with the inspector behind me, John got to him first.

As Heath was being helped to his feet, I was slammed hard from behind and sent tumbling headfirst into the banister, cracking my head hard on the wood. For a few seconds I lost my wits, and just as I was attempting to stand, I felt another blow from behind, which once again sent me headfirst into the banister.

Stars danced behind my lids and I rolled to the ground and tried to cover my head. "You bitch!" I shouted when I managed to open one eye and saw the Widow there flashing me her sick smile.

Behind her I could see the inspector, John, and Heath all struggling to fend off the demon, who kept going for Michel—himself dazed and moaning on the floor. Heath managed to get between the demon and Michel and every time Heath would strike at the big black blob with the racket, the demon would spin and whirl away, but come charging right back again.

Behind Heath, Lumley and John used their hands to prop Heath up so that the blows wouldn't knock him off his feet again, but I was separated from them with no chance of giving or getting help.

The Widow glanced over her shoulder at the scene, and turned back to me to laugh wickedly. In a flash, however, her laugh vanished and she hissed in my direction. I got to my feet and reached down to my tool belt for a spike in one of the canisters I was carrying, but my fingers were too slow and the Widow came at me again.

She slammed into me hard, but this time my back took the blow from the banister and I managed to keep on my feet. Realizing that she had the advantage, I allowed my eyes to rove over to the door—the same one I'd run out of when last she had me cornered here. The door was slightly ajar and I pretended to start for it. The Widow moved quickly to intercept me and that's when I cut back and dashed up the stairs, turning just in time to find her hurtling toward me. She hissed again and came at me with hands outstretched for my throat. I got a spike up in the nick of time and she screamed from the impact.

I darted up a few more steps as she spun away. I needed the advantage of high ground. What I forgot was that the Widow could levitate. When she recovered, she rose up a few feet, nearly level with me and tried to strike at me again. I slashed out at her with my spike and she pulled back.

I made it up another stair and again fended off her advances. The third time she came at me, however, she feinted to the right before striking me from the left. I fell against the stairs, barely holding on to my spike.

I kept my entire focus on the Widow, but I could hear shouting all around me. I heard it from the boys down the stairs, and from Gilley in my ear. It was hard to ignore, but I was determined to keep my wits and when the Widow came at me a fourth, fifth, and sixth time, I managed to get in a few good jabs with my spike.

By now she was tiring, and she was holding her hands out to the sides, as if they physically hurt her, and I had no doubt they did. She kept striking at my torso, which was covered in magnets from the vest, and it had to be wearing on her.

Her attacks then came a little further apart, and she no longer levitated. Instead, she stalked me on the stairs, darting up two or three steps at a time, then tumbling down again as I fought her off.

It was obvious she was losing energy, and when she appeared to have weakened enough, it was I who went on the attack. I chased her down three steps and struck with my spike. She shrieked and darted to the side of the wide stairs, and somehow she managed to get up the steps above me.

Two minutes earlier this would have greatly concerned me, but I knew that I had her on the ropes now, and I went after her with a vengeance.

I darted up the stairs, my spike straight out in front of me, and hit at her again and again. In my ear I heard Gil cry, "It's weakening!" and knew that Heath and the others must be winning the battle against the demon.

I also knew that by draining the Widow, I would be draining the demon too, so I increased the speed and ferocity of my attacks on her, driving her up the stairs. At last, as she reached the landing, she hissed one final time and whirled around to run down the hallway. I gave chase, but as I crested the landing, the Widow suddenly vanished.

I was panting hard by now, and it took me a few seconds to catch my breath. Before I was really ready, I forced myself to move forward at a trot. I figured she'd go for her portal, which I hoped I could find in the maze of hallways and corridors. Behind me I heard Heath yell at me to wait, but I wanted to close in on the Widow and drive her into her portal in as weak a condition as possible. "What's happening?" I heard Gilley shout. "M. J.? Are you there?"

"I'm . . . here . . . Gil," I panted. "Closing in . . . on . . . the Widow."

"Wait for Heath!" Gilley yelled.

"No," I said. I wasn't waiting for anyone. If I lost the Widow in one of these rooms or hallways, then we'd never free her prisoners, because I certainly wasn't coming back for round two of this.

I saw movement at the end of the hallway, and I had a feeling it was the Widow. Pouring on the speed, I dashed down the hallway and turned left, only to come to a stop when I saw a woman huddled in the middle of the hallway, weeping uncontrollably. I realized that she was the same woman I'd seen the first night we'd stayed at the castle, and I also realized that she was once again directly opposite my old room.

I began to run again, but I was very quiet in my approach and she didn't even realize I was there until I stood right behind her. "Catherine," I said, and she started and looked up at me with a mixture of bewilderment and fear. "It's time for you to go home." I then lifted my chin and yelled out, "Sam Whitefeather! I need help! Show Lady Catherine Mortimer the light! Help her!"

I looked down again at the poor battered sister of the Widow, and she was staring at me with a mixture of fear, horror, and bewilderment. And then all that changed and she gasped, eyeing something I couldn't see right above her.

"That's it," I said. "That's your ticket home, sweetie."

There was a sudden shriek at the end of the hallway and I looked up to see the Widow reaching out with one hand toward her sister, who graced her with a sad look before winking out of ghostly existence as the light took her and carried her home.

In that instant both the Widow and I understood that the sisters would never see each other again, because over the centuries of haunting the castle, the Widow's soul had turned as black as coal, and the doors of heaven are closed against such vileness, especially when that vileness courts the likes of a demon in exchange for power.

As if to prove me right, the Widow smiled wickedly and next to her a chain appeared. She gave a tug on it and poor Merrick Brown appeared. He was shaking in fear and when he saw me, he cried out pitifully, "Help me!"

The Widow yanked hard on the chain and Merrick was pulled roughly to the side.

"Merrick!" I shouted, but the Widow was once again in motion, and she was pulling the young man with her.

I raced down the hallway after them, but they were several yards in front of me. Just as I was closing in on the Widow, Merrick, and the secret passageway, I was struck from behind again, but this time the blow wasn't nearly as bad as anything I'd sustained earlier. When I looked around, I could see small bits of black shadow— maybe a dozen or so—moving along the walls and the floor, dispersing toward the hidden passageway. A moment later they'd faded into the wall next to the sconce along with all signs of the Widow and Merrick.

I stopped at the sconce, panting hard and attempting to catch my breath. At the end of the hallway while I was taking in lungfuls of air, Heath and Lumley appeared.

"Em!" Heath shouted.

"I'm fine!" I called back.

The two raced to me and Heath wrapped me in his arms. "Don't you ever take off on me again like that!"

I pushed at him a little. "No time for that right now, sweetie. We've got the Widow to deal with." And then I looked around for Michel and John. "Where are the other two?"

"John's helping Michel back to the safe zone," Heath replied.

"And I've got this gadget," Lumley said, holding up the Super Spooker.

"I think the Widow and her demon are in the portal," I said. "It's now or never, guys."

Heath handed me his spikes and took up Gilley's gadget. He aimed the speaker right at the place on the wall that I pointed to and I moved to the sconce. Before I pulled it, I handed Lumley the list of the eleven victims drowned in the moat, including his brother, Merrick, and Lefebvre, and said, "The minute I open this door, Inspector, we're going to move down a set of stairs while you call out to every name on that list. Command them to come to you. Tell them they must come if they want to be free."

"Understood," he said.

I then opened up my messenger bag and pulled out two dozen spikes, and laid them on the floor well to the side of the passageway door. I then got back into position and gripped the sconce. "On the count of three," I whispered, looking at Heath to make sure he was ready. Once he nodded, I said, "One . . . two . . . three!"

I pulled hard on the sconce and the passageway door opened. Lumley's flashlight flicked on and we headed into the stairwell, which was dank and smelling horribly of sulfur and mold. I went first and Heath came up right behind me with Lumley at the rear. "Now, Inspector!" I shouted.

He began calling out the names on the list, demanding that they all come to him, and as we made our way down the stairs, I could hear Heath fiddling with Gilley's gadget. The atmosphere of the stairwell altered, and I could feel the electromagnetic energy ratchet up several notches. The first to appear was a balding man in a long overcoat, looking terribly confused and scared. There was a collar around his neck and a length of chain, but the Widow wasn't with him and he seemed to be moving of his own free will. "Get out of the stairwell!" I shouted at him. The minute I yelled at him, he took off running up the steps. Then, another man appeared, and another and another, and at each of them I shouted instructions to go up into the hallway above.

They all complied. I counted the number of prisoners, eight so far, and no sign of Oliver Lumley, Merrick, or André Lefebvre, even though Lumley had called out their names. The minute we turned a corner on our way down, I came up short. A skeleton in amazingly good shape lay on the stairs, a silver knife still clutched in the hand. We all paused to look at it and immediately I felt the presence of the duke enter my mind. For a moment he took over all my thoughts and showed me the image of himself in his final moments, brokenhearted at the loss of his son, stumbling onto the secret passageway, intending to kill his wife. But here he'd paused to consider that every ill thing that had befallen him had been the result not of her, but of his own evil deeds. Had he not beaten his first wife and killed her, none of the rest of the terrible events that had happened to his friends and loved ones would have come about, and knowing that all of it was a result of his own actions was his undoing. Depressed and forlorn, he'd pulled out his dagger and slit his wrists, and he'd died here by his own hand, as much to send a message to his wife that she'd finally beaten him as to also show her he took responsibility for his own role in the death of her sister.

I felt a hand on my shoulder then and Heath said, "Em?"

I shook my head to clear it. "Let's keep going," I said, stepping carefully around the duke. In my mind I called out to him to come help us, but I didn't feel him move with us. His spirit seemed to hang back, still angry. Still heartbroken. Still lost.

When at last we got to the bottom of the stairwell, I knew why we'd seen no sign of Merrick, André, or Oliver Lumley.

At the base of the stairs was an enclave carved into the stone wall, and it was oozing with ectoplasm. It was near the steel door on the other side of which was the hidden cavern where we'd found Clarence Lumley's remains. Within this enclave was a pulsing orb of energy, which was blacker than the surrounding stone, and from the depths of it I could hear cries for help. I knew that the Widow would hold tight to the people most important to us, and she wasn't about to give up without a fight.

"There's her portal!" I shouted, reaching inside my bag for another spike and a hammer.

Heath pointed the Super Spooker directly at the pulsing black orb and I held up my spike and the hammer, getting ready to pound a spike into the wall. Turning to Lumley, I yelled, "Call your brother!"

The inspector did over and over, but he didn't appear. I knew we were close to the point of giving the Widow enough energy to reappear and attack us again, and was just about to give up and drive the spike home when Ollie's face appeared directly within the portal window. "Help me!" he begged.

"Come out!" Heath and I shouted together.

"Ollie!" the inspector cried. "Ollie! Come out of there! Just climb through!"

Ollie attempted to climb out of the portal, but the chain around his neck was taut, and he couldn't seem to move forward.

I had no idea what to do and looked around for something, anything, to use to help him break free. If I stuck a magnet in the hole, he'd be stuck there forever, and if I moved forward without my vest on and tried to pull him out, I risked getting my ass kicked by the Widow.

Just as I was looking around wondering what I could use, a shape appeared from the steel door. A very handsome man who very much resembled the inspector and Ollie came forward and held his hand out to his deceased son. "Come on, lad," he said. "Daddy will help you."

Ollie took his father's hand and together the two managed to get Ollie out of the portal, although the chain around Ollie's neck never relaxed. And then Merrick appeared and André right behind too. Clarence helped them out of the hole as well, but try as they all might, they couldn't break free of the chain about their necks. It kept yanking them backward and to our horror, one by one they were pulled back into the portal.

"No!" I cried. "Ollie! André! Merrick! You only *believe* you're chained! You're not! I promise you! You *can* break free!"

But it was no use, and Clarence refused to let go of his son's hand and was in danger of being pulled into the portal too. I looked desperately at Heath, and I knew we were both thinking the same thing; if we jammed our spikes into the portal, we'd lock all three of them in, and possibly cause terrible injury to the spirit of Clarence.

"Help them!" the inspector cried, beside himself with grief.

And just when I thought all hope was lost, I felt myself roughly pushed to the side and in front of me stepped the duke!

He looked exactly the same as he had when I'd seen him outside on the thin strip of land, but there was even more anger and determination to the set of his jaw. Without pause he shoved Clarence aside, breaking the hold he'd had with his son, and climbed into the portal. For a moment all we could do was stare, but then quite suddenly out of the hole flew Merrick, then André, and at last Oliver. All three were free of their chains and they all scrambled quickly away from the portal. In another instant the Widow appeared and I'd never seen such vile anger in a face! She spat and she swore and she attempted to lunge at us, but a firm hand grabbed her by the back of the neck, placed a collar and chain on her exactly like she'd placed on her prisoners and yanked her firmly backward. The duke then appeared to us again and nodded to the spikes in my hand, his face clearly pleading with me to use them.

I hesitated; I didn't want to lock him in with the Widow, but then a large, black, clawlike hand latched onto his shoulder, and as he struggled against the demon's grip he barked angrily at me and again motioned to the spikes. I took a step back, shocked and terribly afraid for him. Heath was in motion before I could fully collect myself. Grabbing hold of my spike and hammer, he lunged forward and drove the spike into the center of the alcove, pounding on the spike so hard that he cracked the stone. I pulled out several more spikes and handed them to him one by one and he continued to pound away long after the portal had vanished.

Meanwhile I happened to glance behind me to see the inspector standing in awe as his father and his brother both embraced, then turned to wave sweetly at him before looking up at something that couldn't be seen with the eyes of the living. A moment later Merrick and André were also off on their journey home. The scene was so amazing that it made me cry.

"I forgot to turn the gadget off," Heath said, panting as he came up next to me. I looked to where he was pointing at the Super Spooker on the ground. It was keeping the electromagnetic energy of the area strong enough for Lumley to witness his brother and father crossing over.

"Everyone down here got across," I said.

Heath's eyes drifted to the alcove. "Except for the duke."

I felt a pang for the man who'd sacrificed his own soul for the sake of others. And I hoped that somehow, someway, even though he was now locked in a lower realm, there'd be a path for him to the other side too.

"Come on," I said to Heath. "Let's make sure the others find their way to the light too."

About an hour later we all gathered once again in the dining hall. Meg and Kim fussed over us like two triage nurses, finding blankets to wrap us in, tea to warm our bones, and some day-old scones to munch on. While Gilley alternated between setting up the film we'd shot for Gopher and making sure Michel was okay after his clash with the demon, Inspector Lumley gave us a little more insight into what his investigation had uncovered.

"You were right, you know," he told me. "A few of the widows of the men found drowned in the lake are stepping forward one by one to confess their sins. Lady Lydia has been blackmailing them for years. We estimate she's extorted several million pounds, in fact."

Heath reached under the table and squeezed my hand. When I looked at him he was eyeing me with pride. I smiled and blushed. Much of my hypothesis about the murders had been just that—a theory—but it sure felt good to be proven right.

"The dowager's butler, Fredrick Carlisle, was in on it from the start. We ran a background check on him, and it seems that in his youth he was anything but a good citizen. He did a short stint in prison for beating another bloke senseless, and it appears he was recruited by Lady Hathaway specifically for those credentials. She had him trained as a butler and gave him a small portion of the take from the women who came to her for help in disposing of their husbands."

"What about Mary?" John asked. "She didn't look like she had any money. How did she and her brother get wrapped up in all this?"

"Mary's husband was a brute," the inspector replied. "She confessed everything to me, and she claims that her husband beat her regularly. She says that there were rumors when she and her husband came here to work that wealthy troublesome men were drowning in the moat, but she held off asking the dowager for help until her brother, Arthur, came to manage the hotel. It was Arthur in fact who approached the Lady Hathaway about Mary's husband, Richard Farnsworth, and Lady Hathaway agreed to take care of the groundskeeper in exchange for paying Mary and her brother a mere pittance of what they were worth to work here the rest of their lives. That's the real reason why neither she nor her brother carried mobile telephones, Miss Holliday. She told me you'd asked about them on the night the drawbridge was tampered with. Neither Mary nor her brother could afford a mobile. They couldn't afford much of anything, in fact, which is also why they took up residence here. They were allowed free room and board, but barely any salary.

"And for twenty-five years they looked the other way as husband after husband was found facedown in that moat. Mary swears that she never took part in anything else, but she was less forthcoming about whether or not her brother had assisted Fredrick with the killings. I suspect that Arthur was not involved in André Lefebvre's murder; however, I do suspect he knew when and how it would be carried out by the butler."

"Which is why he made sure to stay up late with Gilley and John the night I went to visit Heath in the hospital," I said. "I did think it was a bit weird that he would've been up so late after such a harrowing day. I chalked it up to the fact that he was shorthanded without Merrick. But that brings me to another question, Inspector: Why did Arthur kill Merrick?" I'd been such a fool to believe the old man's act. His shock and grief over the clerk's death had rung so true for me that I'd never suspected he might be a killer too.

"Mary and Arthur were very nervous that Merrick was becoming a little too suspicious of the events taking place here at Kidwellah," he explained. "Mary caught the young clerk eavesdropping on a phone conversation Mrs. Lefebvre had with Lady Hathaway—ostensibly to plan the murder of her husband and arrange payment—and Mary knew that Merrick might be perilously close to alerting me.

"She began to spy on him, and on a trip upstairs to bring Mrs. Hollingsworth her tea service, Mary happened to see you two unlock and enter the south wing. Knowing there was only one way you could have obtained a key, she confronted Merrick, who confessed that he suspected there were murders taking place here at the castle. He told her that he believed someone was using the Grim Widow to kill unsuspecting guests, and he hoped the two of you would help to expose the scheme and the murderer. He had no idea that Mary was a part of the evil plot, and after she told her brother . . . well, young Merrick had to be dealt with. Quickly."

I sighed sadly. Poor Merrick. "I'm really glad we stayed and freed him from the Widow's clutches," I said after a lull in the conversation.

The inspector looked at me with a sad smile. "I'm very glad you stayed as well, Miss Holliday. For me, my brother, and my father. We owe you and your friends here a sincere debt."

"What'll happen to your mother?" I asked as gently as I could.

Lumley sighed heavily. "She'll have to face the charges and stand trial. It's the least I owe my father."

I reached out my free hand and squeezed his. "I'm really sorry, Inspector."

His sad smile remained. "Don't be. Yes, I may have lost Mother to this mess, but in another sense I've gained back the honorable name of my father. I know now that he was a good and decent man, and bloody courageous to boot. Someone to be proud of, and someone I hope can be proud of me."

"Oh, he's proud of you," Heath told him and I was suddenly aware of Clarance's energy hovering right behind my sweetie. "He wants to thank you for helping him and your brother, and he also wants to let you know that they'll be just fine, so don't worry about them. Also, after this case is all cleared up he wants you to get your butt back to London. He says you belong at Met Pol."

The inspector's jaw fell open, and all he could do was stare at Heath.

Right about then I felt Clarance withdraw, and I knew he'd probably used up all the energy he could've mustered after being on the other side such a short while. "He's gone," Heath said, and the inspector nodded, attempting once again to smile, but it was still very sad. Heath must have noticed, because he added, "Inspector, I'll make you a deal. Any time you need to hear from your dad or your brother, you call me, and I'll give you a reading."

I felt my eyes mist at Heath's sweet offering, and across the table from us, the inspector's smile lost all of its sadness, and I knew he'd be okay.

Two days later the whole crew was up early and everyone was packed and ready to move on to our next location shoot. We were all anxious to be away from this castle and its memories, even though we'd had the most successful shoot we'd ever recorded and Chris was thrilled with our footage.

Heath and I had made sure that all of the dowager's victims had made it safely to the other side, and for kicks we'd also rooted out three other spooks haunting the main side of the castle and had gotten them over as well.

The crew had been doing a lot of high-fiving since Gopher told us that our bonus checks would be cut by the end of the week, and in general everyone was once again in very fine spirits. All except for Gilley, who was in the foulest of moods. I couldn't understand it until I saw him having an almost tearful farewell to Michel.

As I watched the pair, I really felt for poor Gilley. It was a rare thing for him to put his heart out there. When we lived in Boston, he had a new guy on his arm every week, but none of them lasted more than a few days. He just didn't let himself get too close to someone. But Michel was different. The photographer was sweet and gentle and a great conversationalist. He laughed at all of Gilley's jokes and snarky comments, and Michel could keep up with him quip for quip.

I knew that they'd promise to keep in touch, but it wasn't the same, and both of them traveled so much for their jobs that it wasn't likely they'd ever be in the same place together.

But then I noticed that Gopher was eyeing the two of them with a sort of half smile, and my curiosity was piqued. At last I watched him walk over to the boys and say, "Michel, I was wondering. Would you be open to a permanent job? I mean, I know you're mostly freelance, but we really benefited from having you on this shoot, and I could use someone like you for the rest of the season."

"Ohmigod yes!" Gilley cried, and then he realized that he'd spoken for Michel.

I laughed softly and ducked my chin, pretending I

hadn't noticed. But I heard Michel say, "I'd like that, Gopher. I've nothing else lined up at the moment, and I had a grand time on this adventure."

I lifted my eyes to see Gilley so happy and excited that he was practically dancing.

Next to me I heard, "About time Gopher made him an offer. I thought I was gonna have to step in there for a minute."

I eyed Heath keenly. His look was a little too smug. "Wait . . . you did that?"

He grinned. "Gil deserves to be as happy as you and me, so I merely suggested to Gopher that now that Chris has opened up the purse strings, we have room in our budget for a professional cameraman, and Michel's footage was the best out of anyone's. I also may have hinted that with Michel in the field, Gopher could hang back with Gilley and direct from a safe zone."

I couldn't help it, I laughed. Then I wrapped my arms around him and said, "You are *so* getting lucky tonight, do you know that?"

Heath bounced his brows and replied, "We've got twenty minutes until the shuttle arrives to take us to the airport, you know."

I grabbed his hand and took off for the stairs. "We forgot something!" I called to the crew. "Be back down in a few!"

We ended up being just a *little* late for the shuttle too.

Read ahead for a sneak peek at the next

GHOST HUNTER MYSTERY

Coming in January 2014 from Obsidian.

Being a psychic medium definitely has its downers. As a group, we're a pretty haunted lot. (Yes, I went there. . . .) Many, if not most, of us had troubled childhoods that caused us to develop a sixth sense in order to cope. And I'm no exception. My mother died on an autumn morning when I was eleven, and in his subsequent grief, my father turned to the bottle and his work. In many ways I lost both parents that day.

It took years, but Daddy finally let go of the grip he had on his daily half gallon of vodka and sought help. He's been sober for about sixteen years now, but the residual damage to our relationship has remained. During my teenage years we fought constantly. In fact, I spent most of my junior and senior years of high school at my best friend Gilley Gillespie's house, being looked after by Gil's wonderful mother, who'd been treating me like one of her own from the moment my own mama passed away.

Things didn't improve even after high school when Gil and I moved from Georgia to Boston. Daddy and I just couldn't seem to make peace even with those twelve hundred miles between us. And every visit home thereafter was torture for me—usually ending with an early flight back to Boston. Recently, however, that's changed, and I can safely say that these days we've never gotten along better. Although that could be because we haven't spoken to each other since I started showcasing my talents on TV.

Daddy was willing to tolerate my rather, as he put it, "disturbing" ability to talk to the dead as long as I didn't make a public spectacle of myself. Nearly two years ago I'd done a cable special on haunted objects, and since then I've landed a nice contract working on my own ghostbusting cable TV series, called *Ghoul Getters*. News of my success on the airwaves spread like wildfire in Valdosta, fueled no doubt by Mrs. Gillespie, who's crazy proud of both Gilley and me. The consequences, however, are that now the only acknowledgments I get from Daddy are a Christmas present (picked out by his secretary) and a birthday card (also picked out by his secretary) with a check inside (probably forged by his secretary).

And as I brought the mail inside my office in Boston, so happy to be home again after a grueling four-month filming schedule, my mood dampened the moment I saw the return address on a small package mixed in with the mail.

"Well, I guess my birthday *is* next week," I said with a sigh, passing through the inner lobby of the little office space I rent out on Mass Avenue, about three blocks away from my condo. After setting the other mail aside, I searched my desk for a pair of scissors.

"Come 'ere!" I heard a squeaky voice cry.

"In a sec, baby," I replied.

"Come 'ere!" the voice insisted.

I ignored the command and fished around the drawer, finally coming up with the scissors, and began to carefully cut through the package.

"Come 'ere! Come 'ere! *Come 'ere!*"

I share my office (and my condo and my life) with a

feathered red-tailed African gray parrot named Doc—whom I've had since fifth grade. He's adorably sweet, funny, and maybe a teensy bit demanding. "I'm busy, honey," I told him.

Doc climbed along the bars to exit the little door of his cage and hike his way up to the roof—which houses a nice play stand, and where he could perch and have a better view of what I was fiddling with. "What you do?" he asked. Doc speaks better English than most toddlers.

"Opening a package." At this point I got the thing opened and managed to pull out a square black box with gold lettering on top that indicated it'd come from one of the finer jewelry stores in Valdosta—my hometown. Lifting the lid, I sucked in a breath when I took notice of an absolutely beautiful gold charm bracelet with three charms—a golden parrot, a small happy ghost, and a heart. For a moment I just stared at the gift, completely taken by surprise. "What're you up to?" Doc called, trying to get my attention again.

I realized I had my back to him, so I turned and lifted the beautiful bracelet up for him to see. He cocked his head curiously.

"What do you think?" I asked him.

Doc blew me a really good raspberry.

"Everyone's a critic," I laughed. But I went back to staring at the charm with a mixture of bewilderment and delight, while Doc added to the raspberry a long litany of clucks, whistles, and happy chirps.

Doc's been with me since right after Mama died. My paternal grandmother had given him to me after my mother's passing to help bring me out of the terrible grief I was silently suffering.

The baby parrot was like a beacon of light in a world filled only with heartbreak. My mother had been the kindest, most wonderful and loving person I'd ever known, and her loss devastated me right into muteness. I spoke not one word for many months after her funeral.

Even when I fell and broke a finger, I cried silently, unable to free my vocal cords from the crushing weight of my grief. Doc changed all that. Like a phoenix he pulled me from the ashes, and slowly, with his help and love of mimicry, I healed and started talking again. But the chatty, charming bird seemed to have no effect on Daddy. And I'll never understand why, but right from the start Daddy had seemed to resent my delightful pet. In fact, he'd tolerated Doc a lot like he'd tolerated my ability to talk to dead people . . . as in, he'd barely tolerated him at all.

So, opening Daddy's gift to reveal something so lovely and thoughtful as a parrot charm and a ghost charm was a real surprise. And the heart was also an out-of-character choice from Daddy. He just wasn't sentimental or outwardly emotive. He was more like a closed door that I'd long since given up knocking on.

For a second I thought that it simply must have been his secretary's choice, but she'd never shown one shred of sensitivity for me. Previous gifts were simplistic items, like a pair of candlesticks or a paperweight or a picture frame. I'd long thought of Daddy's secretary of twenty years, Willamina, as a harsh, cold woman who preferred dressing all in black except for the bloodred lipstick she coated her thin lips with.

Her style made her look as if she were perpetually in mourning, and given how my mother's death had turned Daddy into such a terribly cold and bitter person, I found some irony in that.

At last I tore my eyes away from the charm and fished around inside the envelope it'd come in, finding a card inside too. I opened it to read a lovely handwritten note in beautiful cursive, wishing me the happiest of birthdays and hoping to catch up soon. The handwriting wasn't anyone's I recognized, but the signature was clearly Daddy's. And not the forged signature of his secretary, but Daddy's real scraggly scrawl, which added even more mystery to the gift.

I moved to my desk and sat down, because I needed to sit down. Slipping the bracelet on, I stared at it and wondered first, what was going on with Daddy, and second, how should I respond to such a lovely, thoughtful gift?

The average person would have immediately picked up the phone to call and thank her father for the kindness, but as you may have guessed, I'm not exactly the average person, and our relationship was complicated. There were too many years of missed opportunities, broken promises, harsh words, and judgmental attitudes to be swept aside by a bit of precious metal.

Still, after taking off the bracelet to set it gently back inside the box, I did reach for the phone. "Sweet baby Jesus, gurl! Why are you calling me so early?" Gilley answered by way of greeting.

"I just got a package from Daddy," I said, getting right to the point.

Gilley yawned, and I could imagine him bleary-eyed and mop-headed, tangled in his bedcovers. "Let me guess: This year's check is for two hundred, right?"

"No. It's not a check."

"His secretary just sent a card? Jeez, M. J., why does that man even bother anymore? I'll call Ma, she'll make sure you get a nice present on your birthday."

I smiled. Mrs. Gillespie had been making sure I received lovely gifts on my birthday for twenty-two years now, and she never needed prompting from her son, either. "No, Gil, you don't understand. Daddy sent me a really nice gift."

That won me another yawn. "Black leather gloves?"

"A solid gold charm bracelet with three charms: a parrot, a heart, and a little Casper ghost."

Gilley was silent for about five seconds. "Is your dad sick?"

I leaned back in my chair and threw an arm over my eyes. "I have no idea. We haven't spoken in almost a year and a half."

"Leave it to me," Gil said. "I'll call Ma and get the scoop." Mrs. Gillespie was tied to all the gossip in our hometown.

I hung up with Gilley but kept my arm over my eyes. What if Daddy *was* sick? What if he was *really* sick? I knew that with my abilities I could probably find out the answer, but I was too chicken. There was a part of me that didn't want to know, because I'd already lived through one parent's terminal illness, and it'd nearly been my undoing.

Doc began singing a Village People song and I knew he was trying to coax me out of the distressed state I was in, but my mind was going in circles and I couldn't pay attention to him at the moment. Instead I turned my chair around, propped my feet up on the windowsill, and went back to laying my arm over my eyes. After working four straight months in the middle of the night, I find that I think better in the dark.

"M. J.? Are you all right?" a voice asked several minutes later.

With Doc's singing and my whirling mind I hadn't heard the front door open. What's more, as I stiffened and sat up in the chair, I realized I recognized that voice. The day suddenly went from disconcerting to crazy weird. Turning slowly to the front, I took in the tall, dark, and incredibly handsome man standing in my doorway and had to work hard to appear calm and nonchalant. "Hello, Steven," I said. "What brings you by?"

My ex-boyfriend smiled in that way that'd always made my heart quicken ... okay ... still made my heart quicken. Also, the bastard had the gall to smell really good too. "How've you been?" he asked, his voice deep and rich, like a great cup of coffee.

I felt my head bobbing. "Good ... good. You?"

"Good."

"Good."

There was a bit of an awkward pause and then the

door opened again and in walked my current boyfriend, Heath—who also happens to be rather tall, dark, and seriously hunky.

Things went from awkward and weird to, *Are you kidding me, Universe?*

Heath said nothing; he simply came in wearing a smile, took one look at Steven, darted his eyes to me, back to Steven, then back to me as if to say, *"Seriously?"*

I pretended not to notice. Oh, and I also held in the urge to run out of there as fast as my feet could carry me. "Steven, you remember Heath. Heath—Steven. Steven—Heath."

The two surveyed each other with narrowed eyes and forced smiles. I had a moment to compare the two of them side by side and it occurred to me that as similar as they are in the basics of black hair, dark eyes, and tall stature, they're still strikingly different. Steven's shoulders are broad and his chest is very defined, while his legs are very long. His face is also distinctly European in structure with a wide brow and square features, while Heath's face is very angled with high cheekbones and deep-set eyes. His frame is also more proportional and corded with lean muscle. In other words, neither was the kind of guy you'd kick out of bed for eating crackers ... at least not until after you'd had your way with him.

While the men stared each other down, I cleared my throat and shuffled a few things around on my desk, and that's when Heath must've noticed the charm bracelet I'd set back in the box. "What's that?" he demanded, pointing to the box on my desk. "You giving her presents now, Sable?"

Steven's brow furrowed. "Pardon?"

Hastily I put the top of the box back on to cover the gift. "It's from my father, Heath," I explained quickly.

"For your birthday," Steven said with a knowing nod. "That was nice of him."

I noticed Heath paled a little. "Today's your birthday?" he blurted out; then his face flushed red. "I mean, yeah, totally. Happy birthday, honey! I came to take you to a birthday breakfast!" Glancing back at Steven, he said, "My gift's in the car."

Steven smiled (a bit evilly, I thought). "Her birthday is next week, Whitefeather. The eleventh. Might want to mark that down on your calendar."

"What brings you by, Steven?" I nearly screeched, desperate to change the topic before this came to blows, and judging by the furious expression on Heath's face, we weren't far from that.

Steven and Heath glared at each other for a few more seconds before my ex turned back to me and said, "I need your help."

"My help? With what?"

"A haunting."

That took me by surprise . . . much like the entire morning. I waved at a chair and he came forward and took the seat directly across from me. Heath grabbed the other chair and brought it around the desk to park it right next to mine. I held in a sigh and sat down, hoping there'd be no suggestion from either of them of lowered zippers and measuring tape before the conversation was at an end. "Where?" I asked, pulling a pad forward to write on.

"It's not a where," Steven said, and for the first time I could see that his eyes were lined with worry. "It's a who."

I blinked. "Who what?" (I may have been a little off my game from all the testosterone fumes.)

Steven shifted in his seat, and I suddenly noticed how nervous he was. Coming to me hadn't been something he'd done on a whim. He'd had to talk himself into it. "It's not a place that's haunted. It's a person. My fiancée's brother. We think he's possessed."

"Your *fiancée*?" I gasped at the same time that Heath said, "He's possessed?"

Heath turned narrowed eyes on me while the corners of Steven's mouth quirked, and that rather big ego that'd been a part of the reason I'd left him came shining to life again. "Yes. To both of you," he said. (But I thought he looked a bit smugly at me.)

"Well . . . er . . . ," I sputtered, doodling large circles on the notepad while I tried to collect myself. (He was getting married? We'd only been broken up for a few months! What the hell?) "Congratulations!" I said. Perhaps a bit too enthusiastically.

"Why do you think this guy's possessed?" Heath asked.

Steven sighed and rubbed the stubble on his chin. "You have to see it to believe it," he said. "But I'm telling you, there is a ghost haunting this young man. My fiancée, Courtney, can tell you about it better than me. I'd like to introduce you if you're interested in taking on the case."

"Possession isn't exactly our area of expertise," I said. No *way* was I getting involved in this. (Okay, so really, no *way* was I meeting his fiancée!)

"It wouldn't hurt to meet her and talk about it," Heath said, never once turning his face away from Steven. "Is Courtney nearby?"

I felt my posture stiffen. Again the corners of Steven's mouth quirked. "She's at work at the hospital."

Now my smile was forced. "Oh? Is she a candy striper or something?" (Please, oh, please let her job be unimpressive!)

"Surgeon," Steven said.

(Dammit!)

"General surgeon?" I asked. Before a devastating injury to his hand, Steven had once been one of the best heart surgeons in the world. Maybe he'd met another heart surgeon he was attracted to but secretly competitive with. Maybe their competitive nature would eventually escalate to the point that they'd hate each other. . . .

"Neurosurgeon," he said.

(Double dammit!)

"Ah," Heath said smugly. "A brain surgeon. That's cool."

I was sincerely regretting not having dashed out of the room ten minutes earlier. "Well, I'm sure she's lovely," I said. No one in the room believed me. "And while I'd *really* like to meet her, we're just coming off a crazy intense shooting schedule and I'm not sure we'll have time on this hiatus to take on any new cases."

Steven cocked his head. "That's not what your Facebook page says. Forgive me for keeping tabs on you," he said with a sheepish grin, "but I needed your help and looked online to see where in the world you were. I was surprised to find you back here in Boston, and your status this morning said that you couldn't wait to get back to work on some regular cases."

(A dammit three-peat!)

"We can at least meet her, Em," Heath said agreeably. I wanted to choke him. "How about dinner tonight?"

"That'd be great," Steven said, already standing up. "Say around seven?"

"Seven thirty would be better," Heath said, just to be a pain in the butt, I thought.

Steven smiled tightly. "Of course. Courtney will be coming off a twenty-four-hour shift, but if it's better for you . . ."

Heath wavered and I was still looking for a way out of this. "We can probably make seven," he said.

"Good," Steven said, and with that, he turned and headed to the door. Before exiting, he paused and turned back to look at me. "We can meet at the place I took you to on our first date. Do you remember?"

I felt my posture stiffen again. At this rate I'd need the Jaws of Life to ever get myself to relax again. "I do."

"Excellent," Steven said. "See you." And with that, he was gone.